THE FOLKS

Books by Ruth Suckow

COUNTRY PEOPLE

THE ODYSSEY OF A NICE GIRL

IOWA INTERIORS

THE BONNEY FAMILY

CORA

CHILDREN AND OLDER PEOPLE

THE FOLKS

THE FOLKS

BY RUTH SUCKOW

VOLUME TWO

Drawings by Robert Ward Johnson

FARRAR & RINEHART, Inc.

PUBLISHERS · NEW YORK

Part Four
The Other Girl

I. THE HIDDEN TIME

MARGARET had locked her door again. At least she had a door that would lock. That was her one consolation in this house. It gave her a savage pleasure to shut herself in with her own misery and to keep the folks outside. She lay on the floor—the bed was too soft for her wretchedness—and her head rolled from side to side. This was the culmination of all her unhappiness at home. Let mother plead now. Let dad break the door if he wanted to. He had shaken it once until the whole upstairs seemed to shake. She would never forgive them again. She felt her heart as hard as a stone inside her—imagined hands tearing apart that frozen stone . . . The folks had not believed her. They had believed that old—Margaret couldn't think of anything bad enough to call her—of a Dean of Women. She had never really belonged to her own family, and now she wasn't going to pretend at all any more.

Lying there on the floor, on the harshness of the rug, feeling the stealthy drafts that managed to get through the storm windows, Margaret went back through the whole story. She felt as if she were looking back into the seductive shine of Sybil's eyes—but remote, with a sense of hopeless estrangement, almost as if Sybil were dead. She couldn't exactly wish for the old—it wasn't exactly friendship; more fascination—back. The folks had spoiled it for her. They had believed just what the Dean of Women had told them. Well, it was true, Sybil *was* deceiving her father and the faculty, and she *was* in love with a man who was getting a divorce, and meeting him "outside." Yes, and Margaret *was* helping her to deceive. But none of it in the way that the folks thought. She felt again the futile, struggling pain of not being able to make them understand her side.

But then, she had never been able to explain anything to them. Her real life had always been lived inside herself, in secret. The others were the kind of children that mother and dad really wanted. She had always been the off one.

"Where does she get it?" Margaret could hear Aunt Ella saying that, in her flat, naïvely wondering voice. Sometimes mother said it too, in despair.

Margaret remembered how she used to brood over being adopted. She had always felt like an aristocrat in disguise. "Margaret always thinks she must have the best of everything." That had long been an accusation against her. She used to imagine the kind of parents it seemed to her she must really have had instead of just the folks. She wanted her father to have distinguished gray hair and black-rimmed eyeglasses with a very broad black ribbon. And she wanted a father who adored her, like those artist fathers in books—the mother had conveniently died at the birth of the child, who was so exactly like her that the father would turn pale. Virginia Brattle's father was a little like that, so that Virginia had always seemed to Margaret something like a girl in a story—except that Mrs. Brattle was very much alive, and she and Mr. Brattle spoiled the story by squabbling over Virginia. The things that dad had said to her when he came to the Normal after her were cut deep into Margaret's memory in a bleeding pain. She felt that she could never have a father again. But she was frightened of being in the world without one. She imagined herself leaning her head against a big strong chest, smelling of harsh expensive wool like Frank's, a deep voice telling her indulgently that he would look after her . . . Frank Gesell was more her father, in her heart, than dad was.

Margaret began to cry again, but drearily, rolling her head on the harsh nap of the rug. How could she stand never to see Sybil again, to lose all the luxury and loveliness and brightness, Sybil's white arms in sleeveless dresses, the square-cut bottles with ribbons from which Sybil dabbed little dampnesses of perfume on Margaret's hair, so that she went stepping down to dinner in a dreamy, scented luxury. . . .

She moved with restless impatience, away from the soothing

heat of the radiator, and in the chill from the north window the wretchedness of the whole winter enveloped her. She could never get back to that day in Geneva. The folks believed that she had disgraced herself forever by going there. Margaret didn't care. It was always the "bad" things that she did that gave her any happiness—like skipping school, or playing with the wrong crowd, or slipping up to dance in the Odd Fellows Hall with that red-haired kid on the basketball team from Hanging Rock. If she were to die right now, she would choose that day with Sybil and Frank as her one day to remember. That was Margaret's chief fear: that she might die without having had one perfect day. Even the day in Geneva wasn't enough her own for that. But if it hadn't been for Sybil and Frank, she would have thought it was just in books that people were ever really happy. She never thought of any other people she had known as being actually *lovers*. They just went together, or were silly over each other, or something like that. Regular marriage meant being like the folks, presenting a united front to the world, neither one doing as he or she wanted to do. Or like Aunt Ella and Uncle Ben, stuck together and forever bickering. Or like Grandma and Grandpa, who had always seemed to think that young people when they reached a certain age must just naturally get married unless there was "something the matter with them," and then the next step was to begin raising a family. "What's the matter with him?" Grandma would always demand, when she heard of any single young man past twenty-five. Marriage, Margaret had always thought of as just the end.

She didn't regret a single thing about that whole day. She was glad she had lied to the Dean of Women—the Dean deserved it. Dad had tried to make her apologize. He couldn't see that it was because she scorned to lie that she wouldn't say she was sorry; and he hadn't known what awful, shaken, painful courage it had taken to hold out against both of them. Margaret felt as if she could have stood it if the Dean had asked her straightforwardly, when she got back from Geneva that night, if she had been with Sybil. But not a word! Margaret remembered how sweetly the Dean had greeted her going

in to dinner, walking beside her and asking her if she had had
a nice day and had found her sister—while all the time she
knew everything about it, knew that Sybil had gone with
Margaret to Geneva, and was writing the folks.

And the folks thought it was all right for the Dean to deceive *her* like that. It was the Dean's "business," they thought
—they actually thought that!—to sneak and spy. It was papa,
her own father, who had taken the Dean's part against her. He
had told her that he and mother were both ashamed of her.
She had given them more trouble than their other children
put together. They would rather have their boys at war, he
said, fighting for their country, than to have a daughter acting
as she had done when they made sacrifices to let her go away
to school. And then he threw it up to her that she hadn't stuck
it out at Wilson, either—she was just restless, didn't know her
own mind. . . . Her own family, her own folks. That was
the worst of all. She wouldn't have cared about being suspended if they had felt some sympathy. Oh, mother did, in
a way—but they both acted as if she had done all this on
purpose to make more trouble for them just at this time! *She*
couldn't help it if the country had gone to war, and if even
Carl might have to go. They just didn't understand that she
had felt that she was doing the real, hard, underneath kind
of right in helping the lovers.

Mother laid it all on Sybil. Sybil had corrupted her. Margaret had planned it just as much as Sybil! She had asked the
Dean for a day's leave of absence in Geneva to meet her sister
—of course she hadn't any intention of seeing Dorothy. Margaret had put some of Sybil's things in her own bag; and Sybil
had pretended to be going over to the campus, but had stopped
in at the little drug store and telephoned for one of the two
town taxis—Sybil was the only one of the girls who dealt
boldly with things like taxis. She had stayed hidden in the
ladies' toilet, because people from the Normal might be on the
train; and then at the Junction, she and Margaret had got off,
and Frank had met them with the car. . . . That long, smooth,
purring ride through the misty rain that clouded the windows
and shut them all three in together in the luxurious warmth

of the richly upholstered car—now it was a dream. And a still brighter dream was the dining room of the hotel—their secluded corner table, with the rosy light casting a circle of shade on the glittering tablecloth, the spiciness of the roses intermingled with the good smell of food, and the dark little waiter bowing and running. It didn't seem as if it could have been just Geneva. It had seemed like a city somewhere else. Margaret, in spite of her last year's coat which she hated, had felt that she and Sybil were fêted beauties. Sybil and Frank had made her almost more the heroine of the occasion than Sybil herself! Now she could get a sad exultance remembering the things Frank had said to her. "We don't need any lights with those eyes at the table." "Some lucky man's going to get a big kick out of that hair some day." They were compliments about the very things she had always wanted praised. They seemed to make her over into the kind of person she ought to be. And all the time they were eating, the rain was making splintered streaks of brightness on the dark windowpane. . . .

Sybil and Frank hadn't dared take her to the courthouse. The wedding was to be absolutely secret. That was part of their loving protection of her. "If they ask you if we were married, you weren't there, see—you don't know anything about it." Frank had got a taxi for her, and a magnificent violet-colored box of candy sheathed in glittery tissue paper—Sybil wouldn't let him get flowers, because the girls in the dorm would be sure to ask about them . . . and then they had both kissed her—she was pressed to the glowing softness of Sybil's face in the midst of the wet gray fur of her big coat collar, and she felt the exciting male pressure of Frank's big lips and smelled the wet wool of his expensive coat with shining mist caught in the harsh weave . . . and she was in the taxi, back in the familiar, overheated train. . . .

And now she was just at home. That was over. She was going to visit Frank and Sybil in Chicago, and they were going to take her to dine at the Drake, and Frank was going to let her and Sybil—"both my girls"—go to Marshall Field's and each pick out an evening dress. A new life had been opening before her in a dazzle of radiance. And here she was back at home, with only the folks and Bunny. How awful home had looked to her when she had come back to it! The wind struck icy along the brick platform where Margaret stood dumbly waiting and staring at the red-and-black water tank on black cinders flooded with ice. They rode home in the town taxi, where she was squeezed in between her father and a traveling man, on the broken-down seat of black leather worn to the weave on the folds. The cold got in around the flapping side curtains. The traveling man coughed, and she thought they were all going to get the flu. They had to keep silent because they couldn't let Bob Wessel know that she had been sent home. Bob Wessel, who had got his foot cut off in an accident when he was drunk, and wasn't fit to do anything but drive this old taxi! Margaret couldn't see much of the streets through the dirty panes in the side curtains; but she knew how they were, icy and lonely, the trees looking scrubby and bare, old vines frozen against the streaked side walls of houses. Dad fumbled around to get just the right change out of his purse. Margaret thought of Frank Gesell's opulent roll of bills in a smooth brown leather folder that he carelessly shoved down into his pocket after he had paid for everything. She saw the house standing in its winter ugliness, dark streaks down the light-painted walls from the bent-over pipe at the eaves, patches of ice on the withered brown grass, that horrible old urn with a few brown stems sticking up brittle and thin from the caked, frozen, flower-pot earth.

And of course by this time everybody in Belmond knew that she had been suspended from the Normal! Margaret thrashed about, beating the rug softly with her fist. Still, in a hard way she was glad. It put her really apart from the rest. The Dean in her letter, trying to smooth things over, had pretended that Sybil was "a bad influence" and "not the sort of girl"—that was the worst of all, that suave implication that Margaret really was "the sort"! Her eyes sparkled with fury. But the folks didn't even know it was an insult.

Sybil and Frank had seen. They had treated her as the only girl in the Normal worth their attention. They took it for granted that she was a person to whom wonderful, out-of-the-

ordinary things would naturally happen as soon as she got out
of the wrong pew. Mother and dad, at best, thought her someone to be pitied, because she wasn't popular like Dorothy and
Carl. Margaret wanted to do something desperate to show them!

No, they were on the other side. She classed them in with
the Dean of Women. Dad had written that terrible letter—but
mother had let him write it, and instead of taking it back, just
cried. Mother wanted to be on all sides at once. That was like
all married women! Nothing—no worry over her being thin, no
shamefaced suggestion from dad that it might be nice to visit
Aunt Louie next summer—could ever make her forget. She
remembered the horrible pain of that trip home when the
coldness of the November cornfields outside the window had
seemed to cast her out, because she was suspended from the
Normal, and her own folks were against her.

The hideous winter seemed to have lasted for years. The
town was worse than it had ever been. The dark cloud of the
war and the epidemic hung over it. Now even the movies
were closed. And, thank heaven, so was church! How could
the folks still pretend to believe the Bible and then think a
whole nation ought to be killed! Now they would never get
her to church again. She wouldn't go through the misery, if
that was all the good it did. Fighting with the folks, and then
rushing up to lock herself into her room! But in a way, Margaret reveled in these quarrels. They gave her a chance, when
she got thoroughly wrought up and off her guard, to tell the
folks things she had hidden and brooded over since she was
a child. She had accused them of not caring for her. That hurt
them. They tried to deny it.

"But you never would open up to us the way the others did."

"Because you never understand or believe me. You don't
believe me this time."

"Yes, darling, I do believe you didn't mean—"

"I did mean. Oh, you just don't see!"

They might talk about loving her!—loving *all* their children.
But Margaret had heard mama, years ago, saying how she
was so dark and Dorothy was so fair—she had heard that
and never forgotten it. That had given her some reason for

311

thinking she might be adopted. But anyway, Shakespeare had fallen in love with a "dark lady"! The discovery of the "dark lady" was the one thing she had got out of that dreadful old Shakespeare class where all they ever did was read the different speeches and then "tell the meaning in their own words."

The folks had tried to make friends with her. Mother had even suggested that she have some of the girls over and play cards. Once, what wouldn't she have given to be allowed to play cards like other people! But then the folks had been too religious. Now even Bunny played.

Lately they had been trying another tack. They were letting her stay in her room, "not noticing" and not trying to force her to open the door. Nothing more was said about her returning to the Normal. Dad had gone back to the bank. The warm, steam-heated house was flooded with its silent afternoon leisure.

But Margaret would not sink back into that leisure. She was hard against her childish desire to break and cry in mama's arms, away from this awry aloofness, folded warmly into harmony. At night she thought wildly of running away and breaking with the folks. But her inexperience terrified her. Darkness and danger and sickness were everywhere. Now she couldn't even teach. She had only gone to the Normal because it wasn't Wilson—and then teaching had seemed a sure way of getting away from home, buying her own clothes, not going to church, saving enough money to go off on her own.

Anyway, she wouldn't stay in this house!

She got up, stealthily tiptoeing as she dressed, expecting every minute that her mother would come to the door.

The sense of loneliness rose bitterly in her throat as she walked down the street.

All the same, if the inside of her life hadn't been so empty and miserable—if she had been having some romantic affair, with a married man, like Sybil and the heroines in modern books—she could have got a dark kind of pleasure out of this lonely walk down the long street past frame houses with ice crusting the roots of the pine trees in the yards.

Margaret thought about Dr. Redmond. He was the only

possible person for such a rôle in Belmond—he had prematurely white hair and wore Palm Beach suits; and he belonged to that fast young married set—still called "young married set" although they were all middle-aged—that the folks thought were so dreadful. Richard Spencer was cute-looking and a good dresser. But he was in the bank with dad. Sometimes Margaret's dreams reached through darkness into bright future, and then the man with whom she was having the great love affair was a stranger, in New York, or even Europe—an artist, so that she would be known to history. But sometimes, even in a dream, she couldn't wait that long. She had to imagine something that could happen right the next minute and make living possible— make her have a great tragic experience behind her when she left—and then it was Dr. Redmond. But he always loved her more than she did him, and she always left him. She couldn't contemplate staying in Belmond. That was why she had never really been interested in any of the boys in high school, although she had wanted them to admire *her*—they seemed to bind her to Belmond. How could she make all this begin to happen? She had to *know*. Her innocence was a humiliation. Then she could be equal to Sybil, not just hungrily admiring. She could deal with men like Frank Gesell with no more timid fear. Then she could read poetry with a satisfied feeling that it had all happened to her, instead of with that baffled, shamed, hungry wonder. She could write poetry. It was a love affair, of course, that she wanted, not to settle down and get married, like Lillian and Carl.

One of those side streets, a block or so long, led off from this street. Margaret felt again its shoddy, unnamed quality that seemed in some queer minor way native to her. It was here where she used to sneak off after school and play with Irene.

Irene Jackson! What had become of her? And that mean little Gowan kid whom they used to call "Squirrel-Eyes"! Margaret suffered still from the way her clandestine friendship with Irene had been broken off. She had never forgiven Carl. What was that dark, different wisdom that girls like Irene possessed, that made them mockingly superior to the people who talked about them? Just as, in a way, Lucifer was superior to God. He *knew* more. Afterwards, though, Margaret had been so ashamed of not being able to ask Irene to her house that she had gone through agonized maneuvers to avoid Irene at school. Even now it hurt her to remember her cowardly perfidy. Lucille and Edna Mae had never been interesting again—and of course she detested Mildred!

When she looked back into her life, there were just two people in this town with whom she had not been friendly from force of circumstances, or from her own frozen fear of coming out before disapproving eyes in her own colors. Irene was one. And the other was that woman from New York who had visited Mrs. Richard Spencer.

"Grimmie," Mrs. Spencer called her. She and Ethel Spencer had been schoolmates. Miss Grimm was the first woman Margaret had ever seen who was really what she thought of as "different," "distinguished," who had a style of her own. Of course, mother and the other ladies called that queer-looking. "But isn't she *queer*-looking?" She wasn't pretty like Ethel Spencer. Margaret had not yet fully decided whether she liked odd, distinguished looks the best, or whether she wanted the most completely impeccable Parisian elegance. At any rate, Miss Grimm didn't look like anybody in Belmond. Ethel was beginning to pay more social attention to the Fergusons now that dad had become more important in the bank. She had invited mother to the reception she gave for Miss Grimm; and Margaret and Dorothy had very graciously been asked, with Virginia Brattle, to pass the refreshments. Margaret, bringing in the handsome silver cake basket that Ethel had resurrected from the old Spencer house, had walked softly with her lashes drooped in awe, but lifting them once for a look of adoration at the eagle profile and the fuzzy black hair drawn in straight bands down each side of the face to a knot at the back. Miss Grimm had worn a big rope of beads and queer earrings, and there was a sort of Russian embroidery on her flowing sleeves. Afterwards, when the girls had gone to get their wraps, Ethel Spencer, flitting gracefully to thank them, had taken Margaret's hands in her soft little fingers and murmured, with that luminously flattering look she could give—"Grimmie asked me, Who was that child with the marvelous eyes?" She had seen. People who were different did see.

Now if she could get to New York, where people like Ethel Spencer's friend might like the queer things about her looks, then she, too, might have a chance to become a person with a style of her own! But it was too tragically distant. On a day like this, with a bleak watery feeling in the air, the trees motionless against the gray sky, she seemed to have no power of getting anywhere. She dreamed of writing to Miss Grimm and asking if she couldn't get a position in a bookstore.

But she was afraid. Margaret thought of New York as filled entirely by "different" people, all sophisticated in a glittering way, and knowing strange secrets of art and life. She would be a coward if some time she didn't try to find out those things.

The walk ended here. Margaret's final dream, no matter how she started out, was of herself in marvelous clothes and long earrings coming back to Belmond—not to stay, of course!—but interesting and a little weary, after a life of passionate, tragic and glorious experience, such as no one could have here at home. Now she had finished her new variation of that. To go on into the country would be a kind of lonely triumph. But then she could never stop thinking until her mind was screwed up into a painful whirl.

She turned, and walked hurriedly to her old haunt the library, although a feeling of dreary stuffiness came over her the instant she went up those whitish stone steps, traced now with wintry footprints, and on into the hushed, overheated stack room. She ranged forlornly among the rows of books. There were only those rebound copies of *Lazarre* and the Red Pepper Burns novels in the little cart. The librarian came tiptoeing into the stacks and whispered, "Finding what you want?" She had always been interested in Margaret, she had once told the folks, Margaret was such a reader! But the favor of Miss Vanchie Darlington hurt almost more than it pleased Margaret's vanity, for Vanchie approved only nice quiet children and sent the kids who came for dates out of the library. Margaret writhed under the ignominy of being thought "quiet."

She sat down in the rocker near the magazine rack. The

unbecomingness of her old coat and brown hat that looked so
shabby at the tail-end of winter would not let her have the
superiority that her pride demanded over Vanchie Darlington's
thin, sallow, sweetly smiling face and two pathetic loops of
fading brown hair. Margaret reveled in dark satisfaction at
having been suspended from the Normal.

"Oh, here you are!"

Her mother had come into the library. She was smiling
brightly and ignoring the last quarrel in that way she and dad
must have agreed to try now. Her gray velvet hat was a little
crooked, and Margaret disapproved severely of the way her
skirt hung.

"What are you reading, dear?"

They never liked the things she read, so why pretend to
answer?

"Let's go downtown now. I want you to help me choose
things for supper. What would you like?" her mother asked
cheerily.

"Nothing."

It was all the worse to have mother so sprightly and pretending they were such good companions—she had acted that way
ever since Margaret had told her she was always more friendly
with Dorothy.

Just outside the library, they met Mrs. Viele.

"Well! Doesn't this look nice? These two pretty young ladies
in their nice warm furs going about together!"

Margaret saw her mother beam at that. How could she? But
the folks didn't seem to care anything for the truth. While the
two ladies talked, Margaret stood aside. The things Mrs. Viele
said were always worse, because she saw everything in a rosy
light and never knew the facts of the case. Margaret dug with
her oxford toe into the hard crust of snow while she had to listen
to, "And how is Carl? And Lillian and the little ones? But it's
so lovely that you can have Margaret this winter!"

"She's so nice!" Mrs. Ferguson said gratefully, as they
went on.

"I can't bear her."

"Oh, Margaret!"

"Well, she just gushes. She knows I got sent home from the Normal and that you and dad don't want to have me here."

She was savagely pleased to have brought tears to her mother's eyes. They went on down the street silently.

2

Margaret had put two big kettles of soft water on the oil stove for her bath. She lay full-length across her bed while the water was heating, with her blue crêpe kimono open across her chest which she contemplated with frowning absorption. Her skin tinted with brunette was smooth. But she was so skinny. Her collar bones showed. Her breasts looked small and unripe. She thought of Mildred's breasts, how softly white they were in the glimpses she had caught of them when they undressed for gym, and of how they swelled, adequate and womanly, beneath her silk blouse. Mildred Summers had been more popular with the boys than any other girl in high school. Nasty little snip!—pretending to be so sweet, and just working her schemes all the time, wanting nothing else in the world but to get married. Dorothy, even when the two girls had started to college, was what their mother called "developed"; and that had always made Margaret, with her little long thin arms, and her scrawnily unfledged neck with its brunette darkness, feel herself at a resentful disadvantage. She had always felt that Dorothy, with her easy-going good times, was really the daughter of the household.

Their bedroom was almost all Dorothy's. She was the one who had the photographs of smiling college girls with marcelled hair and youths with hair combed wavily or slickly back from their open foreheads. Sybil's picture was lovelier than that of any of these girly-girly regulation friends of Dot's. But of course Margaret couldn't put that up!

There was just one thing in this room that was really hers. That was her desk.

She got up and padded over to it, barefooted. It had been promised to her once when she was getting well from pleurisy, and she had been allowed to pick it out for herself at the furniture store. The cheap little varnished affair with curlicue ornaments and rickety legs was still precious to her. Every few weeks, Margaret went over her books, to rearrange them according to some strictly personal plan. At one side, she kept only "new" books, the newest and most dangerous, that she thought no one else in Belmond would read. Between brass book-ends she had set her own personal, intimate favorites—Marie Bashkirtseff, and *Wuthering Heights,* and Mrs. Gaskell's *Charlotte Brontë,* because in the seclusion and stormy emotions of the Yorkshire sisters she felt some of her own loneliness and rebellion. And then, most preciously kept of all, the small notebook with shiny red covers in which she copied with exquisite care, in the blackest India ink, all the poems that seemed to fit into her own existence. She had just copied, when she found time at the library, some of the *Sonnets from the Portuguese.* She hated those that talked about God and the angels. But she got a dark joy out of reading to herself—

"I lift my heavy heart up solemnly . . ."

Standing there now in her bare feet, curling the toes of one narrow foot over the other, Margaret whispered it to herself.

"Behold and see
What a great heap of grief lay hid in me,
And how the red wild sparkles—"

Her cheeks burned, and she felt a sweet, fiery thrill . . .
"Margaret! Your water *must* be hot!"
Oh, dear, she couldn't even take a bath without the whole family getting excited! In angry haste, Margaret rushed into the bathroom, and got some of the black off the bottoms of the kettles onto the white rim of the tub when she dumped in the water. Why didn't the folks put in a water heater, like other people? Dad always had to be so careful. He would do it some day, when the children were all gone, and he and mother were too old to enjoy it. "Two?" her mother always said. "Do you have to have *two* kettles every time? You know what dad said about the cistern." But Margaret had decided not to care if the family did run out of soft water before the next rain, be-

318

cause of the importance to her of indulging in these wonderful steamy baths in which she had a mysterious hope that the delicious amber softness of the water would make the dark places around her collar bones white and perfect in preparation for going somewhere and beginning her real life.

But she avoided the sight of the mirror because of the scrawny, sallow look she feared she would have until the bath had flushed and freshened her skin. When she finished, however —in spite of her dissatisfaction with the family's plain white soap, which they always bought from that crippled man—she rubbed away the silvery mist from the glass. She looked at the thin little naked image, shrinking with sensitive consciousness of its defects, beseeching it to know if she dared take hope from elusive intimations of a different kind of attraction from Dorothy's blooming prettiness, and Mildred's blond softness— even from Sybil's charm, with the warm ripe body, and those shining, seductive, greenish eyes under the fluff of sandy hair. Her eyes glowed darkly with the memory of Frank Gesell's praise. She was sensitive and unsure about them even yet, thinking of how Carl and Harry Santley used to tease her and call her "Pop-Eyes." "Where did that child get those great black eyes?" How often she had heard that! There always seemed to be a kind of reproach in it. Margaret had the trick of letting the lashes droop, partly because of the boys' teasing, but even more to veil the ardor that she felt would give her away if people really looked into her eyes. But Frank Gesell was a real man, who had a business of his own, and had been married and divorced, and could order taxis and flowers and send waiters on the run. What did innocent, goody-goody boys like Carl and Harry matter beside him—boys who felt important ushering in church?

Margaret had always known that there was something romantic in store for her. Frank—an admitted connoisseur of women—had recognized it. Her own confidence in it made a burning core of pride in the empty blackness of her heart.

She spread out her long black hair all around her, and turned, with a dancing motion, until she had the very best light on the image in the mirror. The dark eyes flashed back at her

319

from between black draperies of hair, and for a single moment she was as she wanted to be. Passionately she yearned to overcome all her awkward and scrawny defects so that she could be worthy of that strange delight of which poetry was full, and for which she felt that fate had marked her out. She saw the secret triangle of black hair curling softly below the white belly with its subtle brunette tints. She felt rare and precious.

But she heard steps outside the bathroom door, and halted, poised in her secret dance, startled and wildly shy. Hastily she put on the detested blue kimono and twisted her hair up into a top-knot—perversely glad to look just as plain and hideous as she could. Now if mama saw her, she ought to be satisfied!

"Wait a few minutes, dear, and I'll go with you."

Margaret heard that as she was putting on her hat.

"I have to hurry. Vanchie wants to leave."

She didn't intend the folks to think that because she was working in the library now, and Vanchie liked her, she was going to be satisfied to stay in Belmond! "How lovely for Margaret to be in the library!" She made a face. It helped her pride to be able to walk down the street in lofty solitude and not to have succumbed to the weak craving for having her mother with her—to keep on the bad terms that her pride and integrity demanded, instead of slipping down into false, easy good terms. She couldn't help cringing a little when she had to meet and speak to people, because she knew how they regarded her having been suspended from school. Vanchie thought she had been a victim! The library was tedious, when hour after hour passed and no interesting stranger came in to discover her reading good books. But it was a refuge.

Vanchie was alone.

"What pink cheeks our lady has!"

"My cheeks are never pink."

"Oh! Just look in that glass!"

Vanchie put on her coat and rubbers—the drab-brown coat that Margaret knew as well as her own—and the wide black hat trimmed with the ribbon bows of a past era. "Where does she *get* those hats?" people always marveled.

"Listen, Vanchie!" Margaret suddenly cried. "Tell my folks

that I'm such a good librarian I ought to go away and take a course."

Vanchie took it very seriously, although Margaret didn't know whether she'd thought of saying it until just this minute.

"Where have you thought of going, dear?"

"I don't know. I just want to go somewhere."

Margaret looked up at Vanchie with eyes fiercely tearless. She drew into herself, hard and untouchable, because she didn't want Vanchie to get too near her. There was something too pathetic and personal about Vanchie's affection, although it helped Margaret's vanity. Vanchie had fallen under Margaret's domination with meek gladness. It was almost the way that Ada Rist used to be. Vanchie had a wistful, older woman's faith in the radiance of Margaret's future. She was nervous now about Margaret's judgment on books. Margaret liked to come out with wild, bold statements. They flustered and pleased Vanchie—Vanchie who, to so many people in town, seemed patrician and aloof!

Vanchie was reluctant and afraid to lose her, but too dreadfully and sweetly unselfish to give in to that.

"Oh, I do wish you could go to Boston!"

There was a faded shine in Vanchie's colorless eyes. Her big hat was crooked and fine short hairs strayed from the two loops.

"Did I ever tell you about my trip East? It was the most wonderful . . . Wait. I think I have the pictures."

Vanchie went into the sacred inner room about which—Margaret remembered guiltily—the girls used to have jokes, pretending that Vanchie retired there to pen love letters to Lawrence Brattle who was supposed to be the most cultured man in town. How mean they all used to be! The little room was neat and intimate, with a framed photograph of Vanchie's parents, and a couch with faded college cushions where Vanchie made Margaret lie when she had a cold.

"Here they are!"

Vanchie came out looking eager but a little embarrassed.

"It was one summer—oh, I'd hate to say how long ago! You wouldn't even remember. There were three of us, Amy

Sanderson, and Julia Viele, and I. Can you find me?" Vanchie gave a little trill of embarrassed laughter. "Look at the hats!"

The picture was taken with one of those old-fashioned cameras and mounted on gray cardboard. Of course she could find Vanchie. She wore her hair in just the same loops, and her wide sailor hat—which Vanchie thought so funny!—wasn't very different from those awful hats she wore now. What did surprise Margaret was that Vanchie looked young! There was an evanescent softness, a rounding of her prim slenderness, a radiance in the too-sweet smile that lingered only in that wistfulness now.

"Where were you?"

"Where was it taken, you mean? In front of Longfellow's home in Cambridge. There, you can just see the house. I *loved* New England. It's so full of interesting, quaint old places. Just look at us! Don't we look like three gypsies? What a time we had to make our parents consent to let us go gallivanting off that way—three young girls by their lonesomes! It was the most wonderful time I ever had."

Margaret gave the photograph back to Vanchie. While Vanchie put it reverently away, Margaret sat staring at the bust of Longfellow once presented by old Mrs. Spencer. She supposed in Vanchie's day it *had* been adventurous for those three girls to make a trip East and visit historical places. But did Vanchie think anything like that would satisfy *her*?

"This bean jar came from Boston. We got it in the funniest little place down in a basement—I remember Amy wouldn't go down, and she thought Julia and I were terribly bold!" Vanchie touched the bean jar with loving remembrance. There were some pussy willows in it now. "Well," she said, "good-bye, dear. I'm so glad you spoke to me. If you really do want me to have a talk with your mother and father . . . I know you're wasted working here in this little library. But I shall hate . . . oh, I have that new book of poems you wanted, dear. I slipped it into the list."

She left. Margaret sat wrapped in the heated, silent air. Her hands were clasped lightly on the shiny desk. The new volume of poems was by a woman. Margaret had seen the title in the catalogue which she always searched hungrily. Maybe the book would yield her—if it was any good—more of those tantalizing hints of the way love seemed and the way it had turned out in another person's life. That was why Margaret had to devour books of poetry and memoirs by women, even those titled British women who only wrote gossip about other "important" people and tried to make themselves sound ravishing and smart.

She couldn't actually make herself intend to be a librarian. But after the things that Sybil had said about the girls who wanted to be teachers, she couldn't bear to think of teaching. Besides, being a teacher always made Margaret afraid that she would get to be like Fannie Allison, who had taught the third grade ever since anyone in Belmond could remember, who stuck little net yokes into her collarless dresses, and who lived with her brother and his wife and took care of the children when they went to card parties. There was a cloistered but more æsthetic atmosphere about Vanchie, with her love for "the best in literature," and the nice old chairs and dishes from the Darlington home in her room at Mrs. Keppler's . . . Yes, but if she was going to get away, there was the long, awful time of forcing her own way against the folks—who didn't believe in her, didn't think she was capable of getting on by herself, or of keeping on with what she had started. "You know the other times," they would say.

3

They had to call Margaret two or three times to get her to the supper table. Mr. Ferguson wanted to be angry, but Mrs. Ferguson gave him a warning look.

"Come, dear, now. Put on your kimono. Don't dress until after supper. We want to get through in time to all go to the concert."

They were taking it for granted that she would go with them.

Margaret tried not to give in the least bit to the homelike pleasantness of the dining room at this hour. She tried not to see the evening light across the table and the bright red jelly in the cut-glass dish—or to see the funny little sawed-off bouquet that was the kind her mother always picked, cosmos and nasturtiums mixed up together, with some little scraps of sweet alyssum.

"I wanted you to arrange the flowers. But I couldn't find you. You can make so much prettier bouquets than I can."

Margaret wouldn't answer that, nor be diverted by praise of her taste in arranging flowers from the issue that must be settled if there was to be any real friendliness between them. It was like a hard transparent wall between her and the folks. Mother tried brightly to ignore it, when it wasn't just absolutely visible. But she needn't try to make out that they were a loving family party sitting here at the pleasant supper table ready to go to the concert together, as Mrs. Viele would picture them.

"Why, no, Fred!" mother was saying. "You mustn't go over to the church now, there isn't time."

"Why not?"

"Why, the concert!"

"Oh!"

Dad looked ashamed, and naïvely uncertain. He followed mother into the kitchen. Margaret was left sitting alone at the supper table finishing her raspberries, with thick cream from the farm that turned a faded pink as she stirred it. It made her almost ashamed herself that dad failed with such awkward honesty to play up to mother's little schemes. Mother was trying to show how, when none of the others were here, she and dad and Margaret could have such good times together! But now that the wedding was over and all the company gone—everyone away that could get away, even Bunny escaped on a camping party—all that mother had to fall back upon was an ancient, resurrected band concert! Margaret put down the souvenir spoon—mother was using the pretty silver, and the best china, trying to make her contented . . . oh, it was all such an entanglement!

"We won't stop to do the dishes, dear. We want to get nice seats. What are you going to put on?"

Margaret wanted to say, "Nothing. I'm not going." But that

bright little hopefulness of mother's overcame her. She could only be sullen and unresponsive. They were pretending that now that Dorothy was married, and she was "the only girl they had left," they could all be sweet and happy here at home. They were counting upon Margaret to stay at home and "comfort" them when Bun went away to college.

"I've ironed your yellow dress. You can wear that."

What a tremendous concession! It was the dress that mother hated, because she said it made Margaret look "so dark"; and that made Margaret think again, just as when she was a little girl, that the family really thought her dark and hideous.

Margaret sat down on her bed and took off her old slippers. But then she couldn't seem to get any farther. The house was awful again. For a little while it had been filled with the excitement and éclat of the wedding. But now the household seemed to have slipped back into the dreariness of an earlier day. Margaret was the only one left. Carl and Lillian were grown-up married people. Dorothy was married and gone. Even Bunny, before long, would be a college boy. And Margaret could see herself, getting older and older, a spinster daughter and a fixture in the house—as bad as Essie Bartlett! That seemed to be what the folks wanted. They were afraid to let her go. For a little while, they had kept her contented, by letting her furnish her own room and go to Geneva to do her shopping. Vanchie had told them that "Margaret was doing so well in the library, it would be lovely if she could take up the work"; and they had gone so far as to talk about "some time." This summer, after her brief bridesmaid's radiance, she was getting thin and sallow. Everyone noticed it. Aunt Ella had said cheerfully, "Maybe she's getting consumption." Dad's brother John had died of consumption, and *he* had been thin and dark. She would get thinner, take revenge on them, die if they didn't send her away —get rid of all scruples, all compunctions. But they were afraid to let her go!—for mother knew that if she went, it would be forever.

"Here's your dress, Margaret." Mother had come to the door. "Oh, haven't you even begun to get ready? Never mind—" she went on hurriedly—"there's time if you start right away. We'll be out on the porch."

Anything was better than staying in this room. Now that it had lost the fragrant luxury of Aunt Louie's things, it seemed bleak and ordinary; and Margaret couldn't be consoled any longer by having her own furniture in her own colors. The pleasant light was in the bathroom, too, and the clean-smelling towels and the cool tingle of the water wouldn't let her hold to her hardness. Her big eyes looked back at her from the mirror dark with remembrance of Frank's praise. She couldn't be hideous. Not if Frank and Sybil didn't think so. There must still be hope for her in this world.

But when she started to put on the yellow dress, perversity made her take it off again. What was the use of trying to look decent when everything else was wrong! She would wear as unbecoming things as she could, to please the folks, and then when she got away she would dress exactly as she wanted to.

"Oh, here she is!" Then mother noticed. "But why didn't you—"

Margaret answered proudly, "I didn't want to."

They had to ignore it. They were afraid of a storm from her, knowing that now their vague promises would have to be fulfilled. Mother had wanted to drive, but dad didn't want to use the car until the brake-bands were fixed. "All right, let's walk!" mother said brightly. But at least she didn't take hold of their arms, an arm of each, to show how friendly they all were, when they weren't.

"How lovely Mrs. Viele's flowers are!"

Margaret wouldn't be interested in anything in Belmond. Dad looked vaguely over at the Viele lawn, but he never even pretended interest in such feminine things as flowers.

"How do you do? Yes, isn't it?"

Mother nodded and spoke brightly to people.

They reached the little town park where the band concert was to be held. Not many people were there. They needn't have hurried. "Do you want to sit close, or at a distance?" "Oh, this'll be all right," dad said. They took one of the straight, green-painted benches with the seats sawed off slant-wise at the ends.

Mother sat down, smiling, nodding to an acquaintance here and there. How silly to pretend that this was fun, when almost nobody cared that they were trying to revive the old band concerts again. Cars stopped now and then for a little while, and then drove away. Margaret sat disdainfully silent.

Mr. Ferguson said, "I don't call this much of a crowd."

"Well, they haven't begun yet. You know everything is always late." But Margaret saw that even mother realized the entertainment wasn't turning out very well. "There's Mrs. Dunn! Shall we go over and sit with her?"

"What's that? What do we have to move for?"

"Why, dad, I thought it would be nice to sit near Mrs. Dunn. But if you don't want to—"

"Oh, that's it. No, I don't mind."

Margaret silently followed the folks. As if she cared about sitting with Mrs. Dunn! If the folks thought *that* was any entertainment—! Now they would have to hear all about the sorrow of having Lloyd so far away, and Mrs. Dunn's pride in having her son a soldier. It *would* be someone like Lloyd Dunn, Margaret thought disdainfully, who didn't have brains enough to do anything for himself, who would stay and get into the regular army! Mrs. Dunn laid it on thick about Lloyd, giving Margaret sharp little glances of mingled resentment and satisfaction, meaning that she had now forfeited forever the glorious chance of Lloyd's attentions. Margaret looked coldly at Mrs. Dunn's fat, creased neck, with the gray and brown hairs straggling below the brownish coil, and the thick fat of the shoulders above the corset and under the cottony texture of the figured voile.

"Yes, isn't it nice they're starting again. I think every town ought to have a band. It brings people together."

Rains had made the grass in the park thick and dark green, and the leaves thicker and even darker, so that in the sultry heat of the middlewestern summer night the trees overhung the little frame band stand with an ominous heaviness. Margaret moved her feet uneasily as she felt the mosquitoes at her ankles. She intended to stick it through grimly, though—show mother,

327

when it was over, how much there was for her here in this town.

"Do you think we want to hear all of this?" dad asked at last. "These mosquitoes seem to be after me."

"Some folks they bother," Mrs. Dunn said.

"Well, unless Margaret——"

"I don't care," Margaret answered with disdain.

Mrs. Dunn accepted complacently the offer to go with them. Finally they were back on the sidewalk. Margaret could see that her mother's face was troubled, and wondered, with a mixture of scorn and compunction, if mother was thinking of her own young days when the band concerts had been great occasions. She tried to picture dad bringing mother into town and buying her a sack of popcorn. But she could only see the folks at the age they were now.

"I thought perhaps some of the girls might be here," mother said.

"What girls?" Margaret coldly demanded.

On their way out of the park, through the blare of band music, she could see that mother was nudging and making signs to dad. When they reached the walk, he said, in that shamefaced tone in which he followed mother's lead:

"Well, shall we stop and have some *ice*-cream?"

Margaret went upstairs ahead of the folks, when she got home, and into the refuge of her bedroom. It was a refuge, even in the breathless thickness of the heat. She got into bed quickly, so that she wouldn't have to talk any more to the folks.

After a while she could hear them getting ready for bed in their room. So fixed—so dumpish—such a united front to the world, and then mother was always lying inside and acting as if she agreed with dad when she didn't. It made her disgusted and impatient—that flat, bare sound of heavy, middle-aged feet on the floor.

"I'm never going to get like that!"

But she simply couldn't endure it to stay at home any longer. She couldn't stand it any longer when mother and Aunt Ella and the rest got started on marriage. Somehow she had to escape from that humiliating superiority of married women, the wise "You'll know some day!"—the humiliating admonitions at the wedding, "Margaret, you oughtn't to let your little sister get ahead of you this way!" Mildred Summers had married Gardner Allen right out of high school. Not that Margaret considered *that* much of a triumph any more! Still, it had been a triumph at the time—"the first of the girls to be married." And Mildred greeted her with smiling patronage, saying, "Hello, Margaret —what are *you* doing these days?" Now even little Dorothy was admitted to the wise, whispering company of the matrons, who could look down upon the uninitiated, and put them slightingly aside. To marry anybody in this town would be to forfeit the real story of her life. What she wanted was to look *down* upon this town—to know something wild, rapturous, free. . . .

But it was different since Dorothy was married. The memory of the bridal kiss on the lawn seemed to open up a new world with a presage of piercing delight. As once, the male touch of Frank's big lips had given her just a fleeting, hungry suggestion of joys more hotly actual than those of the pure passion between the characters in *Wuthering Heights*—until then, her ideal. That, she didn't have to experience to understand. But what was bodily must be experienced. Imagination only brought a frustrated, aching pain. It used to be her dream—to find the perfect complement, the other self, who thought and felt exactly as she did. She had thrilled with passionate sympathy when Catherine said, "I *am* Heathcliffe." But now, seeing Jesse's face with the dark line of the brows bent toward Dorothy's tenderly feminine face, Margaret felt instead the portending excitement of difference. That was the thing she craved to break the narrow, intense, self-bound world in which she was imprisoned, and to make her complete. Not marriage, though—the kiss of marriage was consecrated and made docile and pure before it was even experienced!

> "And for one hour of ecstasy
> Give all you have been and could be—"

one of the things she had copied in her red notebook. What did it matter if you dragged through a whole lifetime without

329

that—without the very most rapturous thing there was to know?

Margaret kicked off the sheet impatiently. She looked down the length of her body in hard disdain. She knew all her deficiencies better than anyone else could—with a searing knowledge, after the hours, secret and agonized and lit with hope, that she had spent in front of the glass! But she had never felt that *this* was really herself. There was something pent up and concealed within this hard little body, if only it could have the chance to get free. There had been just a sparkling glimpse of it at times—with her powdered hair, in her Martha Washington costume, in the rose-and-green sheerness of her bridesmaid dress. She would have to endure and go through anything for the sake of that—and soon, for she couldn't stand the humiliation of her innocence any more.

That made her afraid. Here at least, hidden and dreaming, she had herself—her little hard, untouched self. She exulted in that knowledge. The life of last winter, now that it had passed, seemed to have a lonely romance about it. That was always the way when she looked back upon things! Margaret could see that aloof little self, guarding its secrets, writing in the red notebook, crouching hungrily on the outskirts of passion. The glamour of her books had seemed to make a kind of starlight inside the room. The folks couldn't stop her. It was because she had feared, inside herself, to break away from that dim, cold, starlit security, bounded by frosty darkness, in which she had her secret being untouched.

Yes, but if she was ever to know what the splendid, reckless kind of people in books and history know—Cathy and Heathcliffe, and the mistresses of kings—and that was the only kind of life she cared about having!—then she couldn't keep herself hidden and intact any more. No matter what it did to her, she would have to break through her self-distrust and fastidiousness and pride. It was a kind of consecration to ecstasy.

In the hot secret darkness—a dog barking outside, a car going past with the grinding of the clutch—her thin body uncovered on the bed was quivering into a dream of blossoming . . . not just her body, her whole self. Sybil's choice of her, and Frank's

330

praises, the devotion she had always drawn from people like Vanchie, and like Ada Rist, her old satellite in high school days —she had these things to go on, besides the queer absolute certainty that she had always felt, like a tiny glowing core of fire, under the blighting coldness of fear and disapproval and misunderstanding. Out at the farm, she used to run into the grove, feeling that the dark fir trees standing there were on her side.

That was what she wanted more than anything else—to come to herself. But until a man whom she could love had recognized and confirmed its special kind of beauty, her body would have to stay thin and cold in its alien sheath of self-distrust—and her whole self stay, tight and unripened, within her body.

II. BASEMENT APARTMENT

MARGARET sat in the train, in the green velvet seclusion of her Pullman section. She looked out at the stations between the wide stretches of country. But somewhere in her mind, beneath these actual sights, was the memory of the car drawn up beside the station platform; and she could still see the folks as they stood there together, looking up at her, while the train was pulling out.

All her life she had meant to get away from them. And now, finally, she had got her way. There was a dreadful wrench of loneliness in the onward-rushing noise of the train, in the rattle of the couplings, when at noon she went unsteadily through the Pullman coaches to the dining car. The coffee joggled in her cup, and not even the silver shine of the cover that the colored waiter lifted with a cherishing flourish from her platter of sweetbreads could take away the solemn finality of the backward rush of country she was leaving. All the little towns they were passing made her think of home. She kept seeing people who looked like the folks, and cars that were just like their own car. The train stopped, and she stared out at another brown-

and-yellow depot, another town that—with its vacant lots across the track, and its asphalted street under shady trees leading to the business section past a dingy old frame house with a shingled tower—might just as well have been Belmond. The innocent sameness of these towns made her queerly guilty and remorseful, and harassed her with a sense of failure.

But she wanted to get away from these places that kept the the sense of failure alive in her—that made her as she had always been, and yet knew she *wasn't*. The country itself was shadowed over with the feeling that she could find no acceptance in it. It belonged to the folks and the folks' ideas . . . the great rolling country, where the rough stubble was getting brown in the fields, and autumn was drying the rich pastures. She had always felt more at home in the landscapes in books than anywhere here . . . in the picture of some old palace garden in the bound magazine copies in the library . . . in the fairytale house with the green door that stood in the midst of the forest. . . .

All the distasteful phases of her meager little history in Belmond were smarting in her. If only she had something romantic behind her!—if she were leaving someone like Dr. Redmond a sad and broken man. No boys had ever kissed her, except Harry and Carl for meanness—and she had scratched and fought back and given them as good as they gave her. She had had her little triumphs, but they had all been the wrong ones. It was Mildred who had won the Gardner Allens!—while Margaret, by some dreadful fatality, had attracted only the Lloyd Dunns. Oh, yes, her horrid little triumphs—but always on the wrong grounds—always with a fatal flaw. Worse than anything else— far worse—was the smarting sense of her own unsatisfactoriness. But she had never *been* herself. Only at moments—when she had jumped off the highest pile of shingles in the lumber yard, and won the admiration of even Carl and Harry for her daring. As long as she stayed with the folks in Belmond, she could be nothing but a kind of shadow, creeping resentfully about the edges of things, or staying apart in frozen agony—never able to get into the open.

Oh, the folks had their grievances, too. They told her she thought more of anybody else than of her own father and mother. She had forced them to take in that tramp dog one night last winter—the dog that was around town everywhere, and that dad said ought to be shot for his own good. And look what had happened! Right on the best rug. And then after they had chased the dog out of the house in righteous wrath, Margaret had gone out to the alley and petted the poor old uncouth, homeless creature to make up for their cruelty. She could always make excuses for cats and dogs, they told her. But she didn't care how she hurt *them*.

But Margaret knew with secret shame and torture that she did care. She had to go about the house wrapped in her air of scornful dissatisfaction, or she might have given in to her mother's hurt, uncomprehending eyes, and piteous, sprightly little efforts at cajolery. Only she couldn't, mustn't care about hurting the folks—they were too close, she had to keep her purpose secure against them. Just because dad had worked hard when he was a little boy, and because mother's arms had a pleading touch, she couldn't let herself forget that they had never acknowledged, never even perceived, a single one of their wrongs against her. Her way of doing things was always queer, and they cared more for their other children than they did for her . . . oh, that conviction was at the very center of her count against them, so that she couldn't give in to them no matter how she ached with loneliness. "What makes you do that? We don't understand you. You're the queerest child we ever saw." So she couldn't admit *them*, either. No matter how good everyone thought them, how everyone trusted dad in the bank, how Mrs. Morgan and Essie Bartlett and everyone said that mother and dad were the salt of the earth. Her life wouldn't fit in with theirs.

The strange, long, broken night passed, in the swaying darkness of the Pullman berth.

Now, at last, the landscape was beginning to get different! A station of an unknown, unexpected town—an old brick station, of a between-stage in architecture, with an arcade and fancy posts stained dingily by the weather. But at least it was not just like the station at home. The ground was getting thicker, more turfy, older, darker. There were great brown

333

rocks with ancient water streaks painted blackly down their sides, and houses of discolored red brick with shutters that made Margaret think of the Revolution.

Oblivion came over her as she stared through the window—but the oblivion of restless expectation. The country was visibly different now, and that, while it frightened her, seemed to set her free. When something had happened to her—when she *knew* —Margaret had always thought she would write great poetry. A series of love sonnets, maybe. She could almost see their vast, shining outlines in her mind.

Margaret took her bag, and trying to look haughtily traveled and impersonal and experienced, she went to the dressing room. No one else was there. The mirrors shone with intimate secrecy. The thin, dark, secretive face looked back at her from carefully veiled eyes. Was that herself? The complexion wore the sallow tinge it always had when she was a little upset. She could see now, against her will, that she really *did* look a little like Grandma Ferguson—and the thought made her furious. She didn't want to look like anyone in the family. She cherished the thought of being just herself. Grandma's hair, when she was a girl, had been long and black. But Margaret's large dark eyes with the full eyelids were not like Grandma's sharp black eyes, or Aunt Ella's dull ones. They were her own. No one knew where they "came from."

She went back to her section, around the smooth turn from the dressing room. The trip was almost over, and there had been no exciting and gratifying adventure. None of the men were distinguished-looking; and Margaret had frozen out those two fussy women who were always calling the porter. She settled back into the almost unendurable brightness of her visions—because she didn't have much time for them, soon she would be put to the perilous test of making them come true.

They were going through miles and miles of dingy suburbs that seemed to be left out of any real scheme of architecture—to be on the desolate, nameless outskirts of any recognizable way of existence. But any place that was strange held romantic possibilities for Margaret. She scorned to be too eager to put on her wraps, like those two elderly women, who were calling to the porter again to know how soon they would be in New York. Margaret's hands were trembling. But her inner excitement held her tense and darkly scornful in the midst of a stirring, large excitement that threatened to dissolve the boundaries of all she knew of life.

The darkness and sudden static feeling of a great railway terminal had come over the train. Now Margaret was glad to have the ladies ask and the porter confirm it. They were there. It gave a sense of queer let-down and of trembling, vast expectancy. Through this darkness, people were moving toward the door—halting—step by step they were getting out of the train. Margaret felt the strangeness of firm ground.

People and people and people poured into the open doors of the great station. And she was here in the midst of them, one separate little person arriving in the multitude—not looking, in her tan coat and small felt hat, the kind of person she really felt herself to be. Margaret felt crushed. Her breath wouldn't come right. She was arriving with nothing but humiliation and emptiness behind her, and she was too uncertain now to think ahead. Her feet were just following the nonchalant, accustomed footsteps of the redcap who had her bags.

Light poured down in great slants from somewhere above them . . . and there was the floor hard and actual and interminably wide under her feet.

Margaret had a confused, exciting, unhappy awareness of the crowds. There was only time for a glimpse of foreign black moustaches, a scarlet hat with just the dashing tilt that made her envious . . . and they were past, the crowd had shifted. She paid the redcap and stood alone. The cathedral light of the station filled her with such awe that her knees were trembling. Margaret did not know why she had dismissed her redcap, or where she wanted to go. She picked up her bags herself, staggering a little, although she scorned unaristocratic behavior; and she tried to feel as if she were hurrying too—somewhere. . . . She went past shining windows of little shops, stirred by the sight of books, a red dress, a silken medley of tinted stockings—making her think desperately of all the things she wanted and didn't have—and how was she going to get them? Everything that she saw was hallowed by an irrefutable distinction because this was New York. Still trembling, Margaret came out into the brilliant sunshine of the city, blue sky above, horns snarling through the confusion of traffic. She felt a thrill of rejoicing, tentative, painful, and yet so sharp she could hardly bear it.

But at the same time she was breathless, small, insignificant, and lost. She was glad to get into the refuge of a taxi—although she could have walked and walked, walked forever. . . . She sat rigid through the hurried, swinging drive that seemed to blind her with the confusion of all she didn't have time to see.

She had another moment of breathless, stopped bewilderment when she got out of the taxi into a street that seemed high and rocky with the towering apartment houses. It was like being in some giant graveyard, among titanic tombstones, the buildings were all so high and stony and dull white. In a secret torture of fear that she might have mistaken the number, Margaret went up to the desk in the apartment house and asked for Mr. Bellew.

"Are you Miss Ferguson?"

"Yes."

The man handed her a note. Mr. and Mrs. Bellew had gone out of town for the day. They would be back early in the evening. She was to go into the apartment and make herself perfectly at home; and there was a nice little tearoom just five doors down the street. She would find the door of her room open. She was not to be worried. They would be back before nine o'clock.

Margaret was ashamed of her own craven weakness in wanting someone to welcome her first, without plunging straight into unknown, exhilarating danger. She must enter cautiously, feeling her way, clinging at first to what she knew even though she despised it. Mr. Bellew had been superintendent of schools in Belmond. Now he was taking a course at the Columbia Teachers College. To think of being a student with Mr. Bellew!—it showed how exciting and jumbled up the old pattern of existence was here in New York. Margaret felt a distant respect for the Bellews, going off on some adventure and leaving just a note, instead of being here to look after her, as people at home would have thought was their duty with company. She was glad to have her first few hours alone, even if she was afraid.

The colored boy carried her bags out of the elevator and down a stony corridor that made Margaret think of either an office building or a prison. He fitted the key into a heavy door that opened upon darkened, empty air.

"Anything else, miss?"

The imaginary picture of her room in New York—something both artistic and distinguished, drawn from novels and magazine pictures—had to change into the actuality of a plain room with miscellaneous furniture. The folks had believed that she would be "safe" with the Bellews. That was one reason why they had finally agreed to let her come to Columbia, instead of going somewhere near home. But what was she to do with herself? The emptiness of the rest of the day was frightening. Margaret's expectations seemed silly. She missed the motion of the train, the crowding excitement of the Grand Central.

It was stuffy. She managed to put up the heavy window, with an instant's slanting glimpse of the stony street far below her. Ethel Spencer, before she left Belmond, had told Margaret that she must go to see Miss Grimm. Somewhere among the jumbled towers was that distinguished figure, surrounded by "interesting people," and promising an initiation into all that meant New York. But now she seemed farther away and harder to reach than when Margaret was in Belmond. Margaret felt at once tired and restless. Even in the narrow, shut-in, old-fashioned bathroom, where she had to turn on the electric light, she was aware of the city outside. Her eyes, although tired from two nights on the train, had their glowing look, not their shadowed, dull look. Nothing was in the least as Margaret had imagined it, and yet she could feel, even here, the surrounding stir of immensity.

She couldn't just stay shut up in this apartment! It seemed wildly adventurous to go into that stony street alone. Margaret didn't know what she was afraid of—having her purse stolen,

337

or losing her way, or just being inadequate to a street in New York. There was a strange freedom in wandering about where no one knew her at all. The air was fresh in the shade and the sky still brilliantly blue. She caught a sparkle of water. She went on and on, wild to see taxis and well-dressed people and the kind of buildings she had read about. She was in New York. She was drunk with exhilaration.

But then the sun got lower. The brightness was gone from the streets. Margaret felt the stony chill. Suddenly her eyes were aching, and her new magic vitality, that had seemed to lift her into another kind of being, was gone. Afraid either to ask or find the way, she cravenly took a taxi back to the apartment house, knowing what the folks would think of the extravagance. She had the depressed feeling of still being just the same Margaret Ferguson stealing into this alien place.

She sat down beside the window and leaned her elbows on the sill. But even up here, she could get the feeling of being in New York. The quiet of her stuffy little room existed within the great tangle of noises. The white buildings of the university would shelter her for a while until she could find her own kind of existence. But after once having been in these streets, she could never just go off to some little town and be a librarian. She wanted her own kind of things, the things that were more real to her intimate self than the furniture at home—fireplaces, candles (even to light a twisted penny candle left over from the Christmas tree had given her a feeling of festival), and always, somewhere in the scene, a distinguished-looking man and a beautiful dark woman seated in low chairs, and their faces just turning toward each other in passionate surrender. . . .

The noise continued, made up of infinite variations, and yet with an enveloping sense of sameness. Lights were on now, glittering in triumphant constellations. Margaret felt as if she were caught and whirled away in the jangled symphony.

2

Margaret got off the bus in Washington Square. She had wanted to come down here by herself, without Mrs. Bellew.

338

"Some day we must go down and explore the Village," Mrs. Bellew had told her with a laughing, apologetic, and yet daring, eager air. But then they would have been two people from Belmond out to see the sights. The cold wind, with its bleak watery feeling, whipped against Margaret, so that it was only through aching, tear-filled eyes that for a moment she saw the Square with the empty fountain and the arch stony against the colorless sky. She couldn't just stand here. She walked off at random, with what tried to be a purposeful air, along one of the paths between empty benches.

She was at a disadvantage because she didn't know where she was going, but on the alert because any of the people she met might be artists. A fat shoddy woman in a shawl passed her, and then two young Jews with their eager, chilled, spectacled faces thrust forward. They made Margaret angry, because they acted as if they were out for intellectual, radical things that ordinary bourgeois people like herself, from the Middlewest, couldn't understand. But Margaret never got tired of seeing "different-looking" people in New York. They seemed to contradict, thrillingly, all that the folks thought and said, all their comfortable certainties. Once Mr. Bellew had taken Margaret and Mrs. Bellew to the East Side. "Oh, you must see the East Side! See how the other half lives." With a gratified, information-seeking air, the Bellews had gone about among these "queer, foreign people." Margaret had followed with a hangdog look, acutely conscious of the provincial flaws in her own party, and wanting to apologize for the Bellews' self-satisfaction.

It was just the same with all their excursions. When they went to the theater, Mrs. Bellew pointed out interesting-looking people and whispered about them. "That man looks like some kind of a count, doesn't he? Look! Those must be real society people—the four hundred. What do you suppose that girl is? An artist of some kind? Probably a *would*-be artist. My, but don't you see a lot of funny-looking people!" She always seemed to be ingenuously admitting that *they* had no part in such an interesting scene—and yet keeping a small, provincial, complacent superiority. But Margaret still went about with the

339

Bellews. New York overpowered her—the idea of it, because it *was* New York. She had the feeling that if she started out alone her real life would have to begin. And she still wasn't ready. She wasn't actually ready to start in today. She had her old feeling of being invisible, a kind of ghost wandering hungrily through these streets to find her habitation.

She saw the old houses along the north side of the Square, and turned and walked all the way past them, reveling in their early eighteenth century elegance. Sometimes it seemed to Margaret that her real home was in one age, sometimes in another. She used to think she might have lived in a Spanish castle, dark on the inside and burning white on the outside. But now she felt almost as if fate had turned her out of one of these houses. Perhaps elegance was what she liked most of all.

"*I* live here, you're *my* house," she said rebelliously to a white doorway.

An old childish, romantic part of her mind still connected real stories with things like white doorways and velvet hangings and the glow of a sea coal fire on a stormy night.

She came to a little alley, that she recognized with an obscure thrill as a real Village place. She walked to the end and back, with a feeling of stealthy intrusion and of almost incredible recognition at the sight of lanterns above doorways and odd little windows with the frames painted a hard Italian blue—things that she seemed to know with a kind of personal inner knowledge in an altogether different category from her actual, ground-in knowledge of plain windows at home with curtains and draperies. Artists lived here. Margaret was humble and excited. She felt that they would not accept her—a thin girl in a commonplace coat, uncertain of herself because she had had no experience, and with her eyes stinging from the cold. Yet under her cringing diffidence—the external image of herself from which she couldn't get away—she had a fiery inner certainty and resentment.

Little shops. Little odd, *different* things. They were what Margaret had always wanted and had felt belonged to her personally, as distinguished from herself having to live mixed up with other people. The bleak wind made her eyes water, and her legs in silk stockings were bitterly chilled. But she kept walking on in a cold, uncomfortable daze of happiness. Candles, in waxy colors, at last her fill of candles—little foreign things, bizarre jewelry, little bookshops with queer names where they sold the kind of books she had always supposed she was the only person in town to read, perhaps the only person in the world. . . .

Margaret made herself break through her cold glaze of self-distrust. She always tried to recall Frank Gesell to her mind, to hear his deep, flattering voice. But Frank didn't fit in here. She went unfortified down several steps and into a bookshop. A *little* bookshop, from which the books always seemed more æsthetic and daring. The warm air made her slightly dizzy. A girl with bright black hair laid in careful flat curves (Margaret was always hungrily collecting data about haircuts) and with lips painted an American-beauty red, was sitting at a desk and talking to a pretty young man in knickers. Margaret was dashed by the superior sophistication of the painted mouth. She felt an instant predatory jealousy. But she wouldn't submit to this cool, supercilious neglect of herself as a patently uninteresting customer. She asked for a new book of poems, savagely glad to interrupt the conversation. The slim volume with its purple-and-pink striped cover would add to her vicarious store. The girl negligently tied up the package in smoke-gray paper and purple string and then went back to the pretty youth. The two young people had an intimate air of knowing the place and not caring to bother with just anyone who happened to come in. It seemed to Margaret that they acted as if they were initiates of the inner secrets of art of which she, in her tan coat, was ignorant. But at any rate she had made some assertion and not gone meekly out of the place. She imagined Miss Grimm getting a place for her in a little bookshop—and then she saw herself, in a miraculously becoming haircut, talking not to a pretty boy like this but to a tall, lean artist with keen eyes and face worn by the world's sorrow. . . .

By the time she went out into the street, she could feel her spirits soaring toward that pitch of heady exhilaration where she could forget her deficiencies and commit some piece of reckless daring. It was the feeling she used to have just before she jumped from the shingle pile.

But there couldn't be anything interesting on a street that had an elevated. It was too shoddy and commercial. Margaret walked back to the Square to get her bearings; and then somehow, with another thrill of recognition, she got into the very sort of street she must see—very crooked and narrow, with the painted doors and colored curtains giving her the necessary feeling of art and oldness and oddness. But there was a shoddy actuality about the dirty, uneven painting, and about the iron grating in front of a basement window—a crudeness about the blue-green paint with its hard lumps. She had never counted on that. She had never imagined, either, big dented-in garbage cans filled with the dingy bleakness of old ashes, and poor skinny cats nosing among the scraps spilled from a broken paper bag. Down in a little basement shop, with "Ann's place" daubed in childish letters across the glass, a stubby old candle and a blue vase stood on the window sill. If she was going to be a bohemian, would she have to put up with an unheated room, cockroaches, and the awful feeling that hair and skin could have when you washed in a little cold water on a winter morning? Margaret hated the memory of the white crockery wash basin out at Grandma Ferguson's. She could picture the splintery wooden floor of Ann's place. It made her hands feel blue and swollen with grimy cold, the way they used to feel when she looked through old piles of things in the attic on a winter day.

Now the demand for luxury, so strong in her—"Margaret always must have the best!"—was frightening. Because she would have to break through that, too, unless she was just ready to give up and accept the regulation things. Margaret was afraid that she was not a real artist in spite of her dream of writing love sonnets after a great experience. She was ashamed of all those old free verse ravings, in India ink on very white paper, about "my grief" and "my sorrow" and "you." Who *was* "You"? Just a very dimly remembered Gardner Allen when he was the pretty boy in the grades, or the red-headed kid with whom she had danced in the Odd Fellows Hall, or Sybil, or

Frank Gesell at the moment when he had kissed her. Or just someone imaginary.

> "You did not see
> The hands I flung."

That was about Dr. Redmond, more or less. But he ought to have recognized her through the dark little disguise of her lonely shyness! Margaret had never dared send any of these exquisitely written and carefully cherished verses to a magazine. To herself they were significant and precious, commemorating her own life and imagination, but out among real poetry they would have no meaning.

Little houses opening right on the street aroused Margaret's old craving for some place that could be the setting of her own story. More and more she hated to go back to that stuffy old apartment with Mr. and Mrs. Bellew. It wasn't for *that* she had made the folks send her to New York. But she had been a little unsure even with the Bellews at first, because they had been in New York all summer. They knew how to use the subways. She was gratified, too, by seeing how they hand changed and become more modern. They spoke with pride of having taken cocktails at a party, and then said, "Well, you know, you have to do some things so you won't be conspicuous." Mrs. Bellew had worried for fear that Margaret would be shocked! Of course the folks were for Prohibition. The Bellews were themselves, at home. In a restaurant, Mr. Bellew had lighted a cigarette and said jauntily, "When in Rome, do as the Romans do." He had offered one to Margaret and Mrs. Bellew, but only in a jocular way—that would be going a little *too* far. At first the Bellews had dazzled Margaret with their talk of the new plays she mustn't miss seeing, and of the interesting places where they had eaten. She was impressed when she saw their progress from the way she remembered them in Belmond, living in that little rented house with the bay window, doing all the regulation things, both of them singing in the Methodist choir, and Mr. Bellew on the committee for the Chautauqua. But she soon saw that they were only jaunty and excited with their year off, and were just the same people, really—no more interesting than

343

Carl and Lillian. She, with her youth and the boldness of her secret intentions, belonged in New York. But of course the Bellews were nice to her; and one part of herself liked them and was soft to them, as just other people.

Margaret looked into the windows of all the little shops with uneven doorways, at Russian smocks with red embroidery on coarse-woven linen, and silky scarves of peacock-blue with batik patterns like brown cobwebs, like patterns formed from the smoke of cigars, or like the faded prints of great, brown, skeleton tobacco leaves . . . cringing a little at the shoddiness all around her, the cold wet smell of fish from a shop with a wet floor, the dark little children with dirty noses—and yet gratified in some secret place because everything was different, intimate, small . . . silver jewelry with handicraft unevenness, and the bizarre dark goldiness of gipsy earrings . . . with a rising excitement that burned through the pain of craving for nearly everything she saw.

Well, why shouldn't she go into a tearoom if she felt like it? What if she was late getting back to the apartment? Why did she have to be so terribly scrupulous? Because she had inherited it from the folks. The whole Ferguson tribe was like that. Dad always did business on time, and if mother had to help at the church, she must be there even before the minute and do even more than was expected of her. The Fergusons were always to be relied upon. Well, that was a good reason for beginning to practice bohemian haphazardness. . . . And why did she have to feel so afraid? Even if she didn't look the way she wanted to, couldn't she just submit herself to the new experience? Why must she go through this silly, secret torture before she showed herself to any new people? She used to go around the block rather than meet people at home. Did she honestly think she wasn't as good as other people? Then kill herself and be done with it!

Only she didn't think it. And if they supposed so, just because of her diffidence, then they were fooled!

Angrily, her eyes in a dark set blaze, and her face rigidly expressionless, Margaret turned and went back to the tearoom.

344

She wanted to go into one of the most Villagey of all. One in a basement. Something in her, something that she scoffed at, romantically craved it—just as, when she was a child, and they were all playing, she had to go back and tiptoe alone into the darkest, most creaking corner of the barn. She had noticed "Marta's" painted in fat blue letters and a candle tipsily burning between chintz curtains. She went down stone steps and through a cold, shabby hallway. With an inward shrinking for which she scornfully berated herself, she opened the blue-painted door with an old-fashioned latch, the sort people had on sheds and chickenhouses at home.

Once again the reaction from the cold made her tingling and dizzy. Margaret didn't know whether to be disappointed or relieved because there were no artists in the tearoom. But she was saved again—to her shame, her secret relief—from the great encounter that was going to change her whole life.

She sat down on a blue-painted bench. There was one of those horrid floors. But there were candles, and a feebly burning old chair leg in a straggling soft mass of dingy gray ashes in a fireplace painted the same blue as the walls. Margaret's lids drooped over her telltale, ardent eyes. The candles and the fire deeply pleased her—although she couldn't help being a little squeamish over the way the candle had dripped blobs of cold white tallow on the wooden table. But she was going to get over things like that.

She still ached with cold, and a draft from under the poorly fitting door chilled her feet. The old familiar bitterness of not belonging rose in her throat. Margaret wanted to run before anyone saw her. But she forced herself to stay on the hard cold bench, trying to get hold of the shining audacity that was hidden somewhere in her cold dullness. She had been in New York almost two months now, and she hadn't, in spite of her little excursions into tearooms and art galleries, and buying caviar and pâté de foies gras and eating them on crackers at night in her room to learn expensive tastes—hadn't stepped immediately into an utterly different existence. She was still taking her library course, and going around with Mr. and Mrs. Bellew.

345

To the people who would eat in a place like this, she supposed she would seem just a regulation Village tourist.

A tall thin girl with queer hazel eyes, wild and bright, and a curly childish mass of chestnut hair, came now to take Margaret's order. "But I couldn't wear *my* hair that way," Margaret thought enviously. She did not look at the girl directly, as she ordered cinnamon toast and tea, but tried again, by drooping her eyelids, to make herself invisible. She felt all at once dreadfully commonplace beside this girl's slightly dingy, yet charming, elfin oddity. Later, she saw the girl staring at her from the kitchen door. What was it about those eyes? They were a little too close together, and one of them was set slightly slanting—but they were attractive. Margaret stared haughtily at the wall. She supposed her clothes, or something, were dreadful. Margaret never permitted herself to think of any pleasing reason why people should look at her. Those eyes! There was something not quite human about them. Maybe the girl was a genius or something. She had disappeared into the kitchen, to Margaret's relief, but now she came in with two little fat brown teapots and a flowered cup with a chipped saucer. Margaret noticed her thin hand, attractive also but none too clean, with a very large silver ring.

"You aren't Margaret Ferguson, are you?"

Margaret couldn't believe she had heard that!

"I *thought* I recognized you!" The girl spoke in a breathless rush. Her queer hazel eyes had a bright stare. "I don't suppose you remember me. Jane Gowan?"

Margaret was excited but disappointed. She had thought this girl was some odd genius—not anyone she knew!

"I don't suppose you do remember. I was in the B class and you were in the A class. I was terribly dumb. I lived in Belmond once—until my dad had to leave town. You used to go home from school with Irene Jackson. You were playing being Lady Phyllista and Countess Dorinda. I was terribly impressed!"

The A class and the B class—Irene Jackson and the Lady Phyllista—Margaret couldn't believe such words were being spoken, in this little basement room with the candles, where

346

she had expected to find some unknown genius writing immortal poetry on the back of an envelope!

Then she did remember. That bright hazel stare, wild, and yet disarming! Only no wonder *Jane* Gowan had meant nothing! Those Gowans—that awful family, who had lived next door to Irene Jackson, in that horrid little house with tin cans in the yard . . . that Mr. Gowan who had had a fight and almost killed a man on Main Street, right in front of the bank, and people had said he oughtn't to be allowed to stay in town! There *had* been a skinny little kid named Jennie Gowan. She didn't pass in school. She was the one who had hung around, bothering Irene and Margaret, when they were all dressed in their imaginary ball gowns, about ready to enter their coach. In the midst of her amazement, burrowing back into the darkness of memory, Margaret could realize what it was now about those hazel eyes. "Squirrel-Eyes" was what the kids at school had all called little Jennie Gowan!

They were suddenly excitedly glad to see each other.

"I didn't know you were in New York!" Jane said with childish eagerness. "What are you doing?"

"I'm taking some work."

Not for worlds would Margaret have confessed that she was taking a library course! It made her feel like Vanchie or someone. Anyone who had known Irene Jackson!—had known that little off side of Margaret's childhood history instead of the everyday side! There was a queer, somewhat shoddy halo about the memory of Irene even yet. Margaret tried not to show how much she admired Jane's tall childish thinness in her odd, tight-fitting, torn black dress, and the mussed prettiness of the tousled curls.

"What are you—"

"Oh, I'm just helping Marta right now. She took me in out of charity. I'm out of a job," Jane confided blithely. "Marta!" she shouted. "Come here!" A buxom older girl in a blue smock came in from the kitchen. "Here's someone I used to admire *ter*-ribly. Margaret Ferguson, this is Marta. I don't know her last name. Guess she hasn't got any."

"Little rat," Marta said amiably.

"Margaret Ferguson lives in Belmond, where my dad had a fight and had to leave town."

"Well, sit here and curse your native village together! Excuse me, Margaret. I'm making a cake. Isn't that wonderful?"

Margaret felt the aching chill go from her hands and feet and the warm brightness come into her blood. To think of finding that little Squirrel-Eyes, of *all* people, here in New York! The unlikeliness of that made the place even more jumbled-up and exciting. Jane brought herself some tea, and sat and asked questions about Belmond, and Margaret replied with ironical answers. There was a secret defiance of the folks in this alliance with a girl who came from the wrong part of town and whose father had had a fight on Main Street. There was the exciting realization that under their ironical quips they were both working off their grudges against the town.

"I haven't heard of Irene Jackson for years!"

"Oh, didn't you know about her? It's marvelous. She married a clerk in a little hotel—and then one day she ups and offs with a rich old customer, and he died and left her all his money, and she's living in Paris in perfect grandeur. Oh, yes, didn't you know that?"

Jane snuggled down beside Margaret and squeezed her hand.

"Listen, some night I'll give a party, and you must come! I'm crazy about having you here. You're the only person in Belmond I ever wanted to see again!"

3

If little Squirrel-Eyes Gowan could change as much as that, why couldn't Margaret herself? It was a miracle! But the world was getting to be full of miracles. It seemed sometimes as if the earth was shooting off on some dizzy orbit, like a rocket, and that the past didn't count any more.

Margaret walked boldly into a barber shop and had her hair cut. The barber held up the long, shorn, black locks, and asked: "Shall I wrap up your hair for you, miss?" Panic came over Margaret. Mother used to comfort her, when people praised Dorothy's curls, by saying how long her hair was. But mother had really mourned over her straight black hair. Its length had

348

been her only pride. . . . No. She wouldn't take it. She wanted to be rid of the stuff altogether. She walked out of the barber shop with her hat too big for her and resting on her nose, and the back of her neck naked and cold.

"Why, Margaret FER-guson!"

Mr. Bellew thought, of course, that he must be facetious. But Mrs. Bellew was wistful, and talked about cutting her own hair—wispish, drab-colored hair, faded and dry; it seemed cruel to think of it in comparison with Margaret's new crop of shining black.

The hair cut made Margaret feel different altogether. She couldn't quite trust her own elation at the view, in her hand mirror, of the bold outline of her cropped head that seemed to make her neck more softly girlish. She was filling out a little, too, and beginning to look slim instead of scrawny. Now, when she glanced at the mirror in the drug store where she ate her lunch—obliquely, always, for she had never quite dared risk a full view of herself—she thought she caught the sparkling look of her eyes instead of the dull veiled look. Of course she had always intended to become beautiful.

Margaret did her library work with meticulous competence, just as she had done her school work. Her pride, and her Ferguson inheritance, demanded that. But Mr. and Mrs. Bellew, who had thought of her at first as the kind of girl who would make a good librarian, were beginning to be a little doubtful about her now.

All the time, Margaret was tentatively, thrillingly, occupied with herself; with the changes that even the Bellews noticed, the whitening and filling out of her unfledged neck, the shininess of her hair that had glints and gleams of brownish red in the black when it was washed. It all seemed to be a preparation. When she walked down Fifth Avenue, she felt an aching, rasping envy of the beautiful things in windows. After she had taken her bath at night, she went through a scrupulous ritual of tending herself, a secret, devout preparation . . . stealthily, so that the Bellews wouldn't wonder why she was still up and what she was doing.

She wouldn't admit to herself how much she counted upon

349

Jane Gowan's party. It had taken the place of the hope that some day she would gather courage to go and see Miss Grimm. It wouldn't be the passport to the world of "interesting" people —but to a kind of secret, dark, haphazard basement world through which she must pass before she could really be rid of what she used to be. She let the Bellews suppose that the invitation was from some girl in her library course. How shocked they would be if they knew she was going down to the Village to see that little Jennie Gowan! She almost wished she had told them. They called after her:

"Remember what we told you about those Villagers!"

But there was uneasiness under their determined facetiousness. They weren't quite sure of a girl who lived in the Village, even if she *was* going to Columbia. They had seen Margaret changing and getting away from them. Mr. Bellew thought he must be funny about the books she brought home. "Are you going in for these free versifiers and Russian novelists?" He thought there was something immoral about free verse and modern painting, and yet he was a little bit afraid because he didn't understand it. The Bellews had both agreed that Margaret was getting to think too much about her clothes.

It was glorious to be away from that stuffy apartment and out alone in the rainy darkness. There were just the misty ghosts of the tall buildings, but their outlines held a distant power.

Margaret got off the bus in the Square.

Fearfully she carried out Jane's haphazard instructions, going quickly through the exciting little secret streets until she came to a row of small, dark-red brick houses. The iron basement railings were coldly misted with rain. The street excited her in some minor way, just like that rutty little off-street where Irene used to live. She pressed a dubious-looking bell above a card lettered girlishly in purple ink:

Gowan-Rindemiller . . .

while she waited, shivering with nervous expectancy.

The door clicked feebly. Margaret pushed it open and stepped into a chilly narrow hall carpeted with linoleum.

"Here we are!"

Looking up from the stairs, she could just see Jane's face looking down at her from over the top railing. Margaret climbed the narrow stairway that leaned perilously to the side, refusing to let her fastidiousness take alarm at any dinginess—because she wasn't going to be shocked by anything in New York. She wanted to know the worst. She had had enough of the best, of "the bright side of things." Jane's eyes stared glittering down at her from the hanging tousle of curls.

Jane squeezed her hand.

"I was scared to death you wouldn't come!"

"Why not?"

"Oh, I was such a little perp when you knew me."

"What do you think I was?"

"Oh, I thought you were grand!"

She took Margaret into a funny little anteroom. On one side stood a wabbly dresser painted that same hard shade of blue, on the other a very dirty kitchen table with a gas plate. Margaret had to pretend that nothing seemed strange to her. Jane was wearing that funny little scant black dress and dangling earrings. Margaret wished that she had dared to buy the flaming red chiffon that she had really wanted, instead of the innocuous beige that Mrs. Bellew had encouraged her to get because it would "do for any occasion." But the red dress would have given her away. When she had started to try it on, a sort of uprising of her old self-distrust and longing to be hidden had overwhelmed the faint new audacity. Jane looked so odd and different that it was exciting to feel this queer, homelike kinship with her. As they powdered their noses at the shaky dresser, Jane with an old powder puff that was soggy pink, they felt that they were both New Yorkers and secure in their superiority to Belmond.

"You've cut your hair! It's swell. But I remember those great long braids you used to have. You could sit on your hair. All the girls used to talk about that. 'Margaret Ferguson can sit on her braids.'"

"Makes me sound like a hen or goose or something!"

"Oh, I thought they were grand! I used to stare at them in

351

school and wish I could have hair as long as that. You had the ribbon braided into the ends—a red ribbon."

"Do you remember *that?*"

"Oh, you don't know how I used to adore you!"

Jane's eyes were staring and hazel-bright as she said all this in her breathless little voice that seemed always just about to break into some gloriously exciting news.

"I always hated my hair, and my folks did too, because it wasn't curly like Dorothy's."

"Who was Dorothy?"

"Oh, don't you remember? My pretty little sister?"

"Did you have a sister? I don't remember anyone but you."

"Goodness! Nobody else would say that."

"Oh, I've never forgotten your eyes or your hair. I always thought, if I could just have eyes like Margaret Ferguson's, instead of crazy ones like mine, I wouldn't ask for anything more. Don't you remember how I used to stick around, awful little brat, when Irene tried to chase me away, because I just couldn't stop looking at you!"

"How disappointed you must be now."

"Oh!"

Jane made a horrified round of her lips.

"JANE!"

Jane said hastily, "We've got to go back to the party." She squeezed Margaret's hand again. "I invited Dr. Finkbein because of you. He's got a wonderful mind! Stella isn't here— my roommate. They sent her to Trenton. She's got a job. We've had an awful fight. I don't want you to like Stella!" She pressed Margaret's arm childishly. "They're all just crazy to meet you. I told them how grand you are."

Margaret's cheeks were stained with the clear rose-red that came only when she was excited; and she could feel, in a vivid rush, the same dashing boldness that once in a while used to make the other children in awe of her, and that she had always felt was really herself, breaking through the cold restraint of her self-distrust and thorny, fastidious reserve.

"Here's Margaret Ferguson!"

Jane made the announcement with naïve triumph. Her thin

hand with its childishly cold finger tips was still clinging to Margaret's. The small room was dense with smoke. The men were standing, and the girls, seated, were looking up with an instant, cold, feminine appraisal scarcely veiled in their eyes. One of the men had a beard. Margaret supposed he must be the "wonderful" Dr. Somebody.

A youth said nonchalantly, "Hello, Margaret Ferguson." He was sitting on the floor with his head against a girl's knees. He had silky side-burns and a petulant small mouth, and he wore an orange silk shirt.

"Get up, Rod," Jane begged. "I won't let you meet Margaret if you don't!"

"Well, I know who she is already. She's Margaret Ferguson, isn't she? I like your eyes, Margaret!"

The others laughed scornfully at Rod, and yet they seemed to approve his debonair insolence. He closed his eyes languidly, and settled his head against the girl's knees. His long lashes curled like flowers beneath the childish purity of the white lids.

But all these people were different. The girl who supported Rod wore a red peasant dress with bright embroidery. Margaret always felt jealous of any girl who wore red. Her beige dress seemed commonplace and girly-girly. Another girl had on a black evening dress. She had blond hair, and looked like Mildred Summers, and Margaret instantly hated her. It disappointed Margaret that the men seemed to be inferior in looks to the girls.

At first Margaret was mute. The couch was so wide that her feet felt funny and stiff sticking out beyond it. The furniture was disarmingly childish, like Jane herself, in its foolish pretty cheapness and inadequacy. Most of the people sat on the floor. There were two wicker chairs, one painted in streaky black and one in green, that squeaked when anyone moved. A dormer window, opening like a casement, was set in under two slopes of ceiling like those modern paintings done in geometric blocks. The room was at the top of the house. Margaret imagined herself crouching at such a window at twi-

353

light, looking across the dark, narrow, little tucked-in street, and thinking of a love affair that had ended in sorrow.

A little man with fluffy hair was bringing drinks. Margaret accepted hers with the air of cold immobility that she adopted to cover her excitement and uncertainty. Once Frank had given Sybil a bottle of port, to "give her strength" when she was getting over a cold; and every night before they went to bed, the two girls had made a deliciously private rite of solemnly clinking and sipping from two small ten-cent-store glasses. "I drink to Frank Gesell." "I drink to Red McGafferty." He was that boy on the Hanging Rock football team—the only male interest that Margaret had been able to dig up. But anyway, that was better than never having tasted liquor before.

Secretly fearful, Margaret sipped the stinging, bad, orange-colored concoction. The people all joked about the drinks and made a great deal of them. One man was a little stewed. Margaret remembered the disgraceful fact that Grandpa Ferguson had been a Prohibitionist. He had voted with the party for years, saying "they'd get a man in the White House yet." Margaret felt a burning tingle in her throat. Then her finger tips tingled. Her cold diffidence was being submerged under a heady gaiety. The apartment looked beautiful. All at once she could talk to people.

The little fluffy-haired man had come up with Jane. "So you two damsels used to know each other in earlier days?"

Jane was plaintive. "Just sort of knew each other, Daggie! I used to admire Margaret Ferguson in the distance. She lived in the right part of town and I lived in the wrong part."

"You lived in the wrong part?" Daggie repeated with gently mocking commiseration. He put his arm around Jane and rocked her consolingly. Jane laid her curly head against his shoulder and snuggled to him. The tousle of curls almost hid her eyes while her lips took on the pout of a petted woman. "How grievous that our little Jane had such a humble origin!"

"But she's among the aristocrats now!"

Lee, the thin light-haired one, who was sitting beside the light-haired girl, said that with a scornful inflection.

Dr. Finkbein waited, alert and serious.

"I want to know what sort of native village produced these two interesting young women!"

Margaret said darkly, in a rush of angry daring:

"The worst place on earth!"

She had triumphed! She was accepted. All had laughed. She had proved her right to be included in this aristocracy of exile. Margaret was dazzled by Jane's candor about her social deficiencies. She had always jealously hidden her own defects. Uplifted dizzily, she began to say things she had never dreamed of admitting except in the painful secrecy of her own mind.

"Oh, she lived in a grand house!" Jane sighed.

"*Grand house*. Why, you little liar. I despise our house. It's just absolutely ordinary. That *urn*. You thought that was grand! You mean that hideous old affair in our front yard? My dad's one idea of a work of art!"

This was the way, then, of dealing with all her guilty secrets! Margaret heard the approving laughter. Only that horrid little blond Louise looked superior and was still. The wonderful Dr. Finkbein had got up from his cushion on the floor and sat down very close to her on the couch. Margaret was afraid that she would give away her innocence and inexperience. She was impressed but not attracted by his dark Jewish looks. Still, she wasn't going to be judged any more by Harry and Carl. They would be out of place among people who lived in New York, and talked about music, and sex, and perversion. The wonderful Dr. Finkbein was interested—she could see it in the alertness of his eyes, and feel it in his body as he pressed close to her, breathing too near her face. Now it seemed that all the old values were overturned. The things that had been held against her were her assets. When she told them that she had been fired from the Normal, she achieved her greatest success.

She detested Belmond. She had *hated* the Normal. She loathed her name—Margaret! It had been her grandmother's name, and she couldn't bear her grandmother. It made her think of one of those horrid "womanly" women who were such liars and tried to please everybody at once.

"Then why not change it?" Daggie asked, with his gently quizzical smile of amusement. All these girls had changed their names to suit their features or the dictates of the numerologists. Little Jane had some sort of cast-off appellation. "I am not a member of the worthy brotherhood of numerologists, and I must confess that my arithmetic is faulty, but I see no reason why you should not answer, hereafter, to the far more suitable and decorative title of—say, Margot."

Jane shrieked ecstatically. "Christen her, Daggie! Go on, you're good, you're just lovely, you're better than any priest." Daggie solemnly sprinkled a few remaining drops of gin upon Margaret's head.

But she never, never could go back to the Bellews' apartment. Now the gin was gone and they were all eating hot dogs and drinking coffee out of chipped Italian pottery cups. Jane embraced Margaret, and hid her head, wailing. There was Lossie's apartment! Daggie had the key. Lossie had left it with him when she had got a chance to go abroad as secretary to that woman with the sandals and fillets who was going to revive the ancient arts of Greece.

It was perfectly crazy! Simply mad. Mr. and Mrs. Bellew would think that she was a criminal. She had no money and she couldn't take an apartment. The folks would never send her another cent if she dropped her library course. They had enough against her already. . . . Well, then, why shouldn't they have everything? It was a dare in which she couldn't back down, unless she were to fail in everything from this time on. There was no use in asking the folks. They would never let her do it. Library course!—Lee said. Did she want to live and die a holy virgin? Money! Dear me, Daggie said mildly, what was money to hold one back from the heart's desire?

It was like those terrible, glorious moments when she had stood—all alone in the whole air—on the highest shingle pile in the lumber yard, and all the other children down below her, shouting, "You dassent do it!" Margaret felt almost that old, backward, thrilling rush of air and the hard, welcome shock of the ground. The eyes of the other people were shining with the same startled, pleased, reluctant admiration she used to see in the faces of those children. Now was her moment. She couldn't stop for what the folks would say. It was more important—breaking out of her old bonds, asserting herself, *starting*—than any right or wrong.

But there was so much more to it than just impressing any-one! Margaret realized that when the others had left, and she was alone in her apartment. It meant that now she had cut loose from her whole unsatisfactory past. When she thought of what was ahead of her, the very floor seemed to dissolve. She would have to write to the folks, go to the Bellews' and get her things, find a job. She had just forty dollars left, and she couldn't ask the folks for more—even if they would send it to her, after this.

But forty dollars—Jane would consider that an immense amount! It seemed pretty large to Margaret herself. She would soon be making money at some interesting job, in a bookshop or a tearoom. And even if she went on the rocks—actually on the rocks!—she had at least reached out to seize the kind of life that belonged to her.

Now it was almost morning. Jane's crowd had stayed to get the room warm for her, with all the rubbish they could scrape together for the fireplace. It had all seemed to be wild fun at the time, the most fun she had ever had, but now Margaret could scarcely remember any of it. Only that Lee had gone to Tony's for a bottle of wine, and they had all drunk from the bottle to celebrate Margot's emancipation from the career of librarian, and then taken hands and danced around the room. She could see Dr. Finkbein prancing with a serious intentness to be pagan and jolly. Everyone had seemed transformed—and it was so much gayer because they belonged only to this night, she didn't know who most of them were or where they had come from, except that, like herself, they were outlaws.

Now she was Margot. This was her own apartment. Margaret went softly about the room, looking at her possessions, not yet able to believe that they were hers. A crazy little laugh seemed struggling in her throat.

She didn't have the complete elegance that she ultimately demanded. But these were the things that she wanted now. She had the floor, with its wide old boards roughly painted.

357

She had the little green table with the two candlesticks and the tipsy candles. She had the creaky wicker chairs. The low open shelves on which to accumulate her chosen books. The big old kitchen fireplace, with the soft sooty blackness, the straggle of gray ashes on top, a few warm gleams of red still softly winking. When Margot came and stood before the fireplace, in her tiptoe wandering, the crazy laugh burst from her throat and she beat her hands lightly together in a solitary ecstasy.

First she lighted the two candles with the matches Daggie had left. Then she twisted some paper, as she had seen Jane do, and made the first solitary, romantic fire in her own fireplace. She felt dark and bright and wild and free! She curved her arms in a secret dance and saw their shadows on the low wall—whirled—and then stood still and gave a queer, happy moan.

But dearer even than her fireplace, dearer than the candles, were the two deep basement windows set snugly, excitingly, mysteriously below the jangling noises of the narrow street.

4

There had been rain during the night. But when Margaret finally woke up, there was only a fresh chill air blowing in through the open windows.

It was still quite dark in the basement apartment. For a long time the roar of the trucks had been making the windows shiver. The noise enveloped her in strangeness and made her feel that she was in the very midst. Margaret thought of all the dreadful things that were ahead of her. Last night's cold gray ashes lay scattered in the fireplace, and now she had nothing else to burn. She lay huddled under someone else's half-soiled blankets in the little chemise she had worn all night, and she felt herself shivering in a dark ebb of fear.

A narrow shaft of sunshine came suddenly through the upright iron bars of the farther window. It brightened up the wide green window sill and a space of dark painted floor. Margaret knew then that she would go through anything rather than give up this place.

She didn't dare to look in the glass as she shiveringly dressed.

She felt too dreadful in her beige georgette in the morning. Everything that she owned was at the Bellews' apartment. What were they thinking now? Maybe calling up the police! Margaret thrust on her hat with only the barest glance at the mirror, for fear she would hate herself.

Outside, she suddenly felt different. The narrow streets were streaked with rain. But sunshine kept breaking through, and then the dark streaks of wet glistened. Margaret began to feel queerly happy. She had a share now in the narrow, noisy streets —the hurrying people, the dark Italians in the doorways of chilly little shops with sausages hanging in the windows, the bookshop with dirty copies of *Beulah* and of ancient textbooks on the shelf outside, the smooth handicraft tea tables in another window, the taxi skidding and pulling up in front of the small brick house with the window boxes, while all the little kids went scattering. . . .

This was the first day of her real life. From now on, she would be Margot, never Margaret any more. Breakfast had to be a kind of beautiful rite. She went hastily past the common cafés and the wagon lunches, the corner Coffee Pot with men sitting around the counter and bending down to gulp pale coffee from thick cups, the drug stores where people with jobs snatched hasty breakfasts. From now on, she was going to do what she *wanted* to do, not what was sensible. She chose an expensive restaurant with heavy, cream-colored, French-looking curtains. With an air of cool immobility, in spite of her hatred of her clothes, Margaret followed the dark stout waiter to an upholstered seat.

She felt a solemn, luxurious joy in the ceremony of her late breakfast in this leisurely, upholstered place. How did she know? This might be the last day of her life. Holding the large menu card between her hands, she languidly scanned it. Her old Ferguson thriftiness quailed. But another side of her—her own side, the *real* side—seemed to come alive and bright and gay at this extravagance. The blood came into her chilled hands and feet and she felt her movements growing graceful and slow to fit in with the hushed atmosphere. She could live in a basement, without conveniences—but when she went out to eat, she had to do it in the proper style. The folks were just the opposite! When they drove to Geneva, they took along a lunch and ate it in the park, saving the price of a meal. Margaret felt above them. She felt *richer*. There was no one else in the place except a good-looking man with a clipped moustache absentmindedly pouring amber-brown coffee from his silver pot as he read the *Times*.

The sun was out, brilliant, shining on the dark wet. Taxis darted under the long, sweeping, clanging roar of the elevated. Margaret felt that she couldn't go and see the Bellews today. It was *her* day. This was her own secret celebration. Without stopping for any decision, she turned and fled toward Washington Square, where she paused in the sunshine, among the bare wet trees, in the freshened air. Without thinking again, she climbed to the top of one of the green busses that after a moment began to lumber up the bright width of Fifth Avenue. The blue sky was narrowed by the tall buildings, and she looked down on the sauntering people with mazed eyes, as if she were fulfilling some dream. She felt crazy with happiness.

Hastily she rang the bell and went down the perilous steps. She knew that she had to buy some new clothes to suit this feeling, no matter how she used up her money. The windows of the fine shops brought back the guilty shame of her poverty. It was a physical hurt—this craving for the tinted exquisiteness of the sheer silk stockings, the beautifully done up jars of cosmetics in their expensive colors of pink and lilac and cream. With shame, Margaret hung about the racks of reduced dresses, hating the supercilious knowledge in the eyes of salesgirls. A saleswoman came toward her, with the pretense of refined speech and of obsequious enthusiasm trying to belie the open secrets of her hennaed hair, white at the roots, and the deep sagging lines and under-eye puffs beneath the dry pink-and-white of make-up. The sight drove Margaret to grasp her youth. She was twenty-seven—old enough!—and if she didn't have things pretty soon they would do her no good. Driven, unsatisfied, her money burning in her purse, Margaret could not stop until she had bought a black silk dress with unusual sleeves, and a red hat from a bargain counter. Even then, the fever was not spent—not until, sick with audacity, feeling the floor drop away from her at the fatal dwindling of the bills in her handbag, she had bought rouge, geranium-red lipstick in a silver case, a package of scented cigarettes, two little wine glasses in an antique shop, and a heavy supply of ten-cent-store candles.

Her feet were noiseless on the carpeted softness of the Rest Room in the department store. She managed triumphantly to change into the new black dress in the cramped space of one of the toilet booths. Then she stood before the long shining mirror, detesting the critical eyes of the other women, and made up her face with the new rouge and lipstick. Everything about her seemed changed, and yet more than ever her own. Her eyes sparkled darkly under the red of the hat. She seemed to have come into possession of a light, sauntering step, and she felt that now she truly was "Margot."

She went out into the bright street. Instead of feeling poor because of her extravagance, she felt much richer.

She chose a French restaurant for luncheon because it was foreign. This meal was another secret celebration. Margot slowly relished each course that she ate in her free solitude—the rich soup, the asparagus, the chicken. All seemed sanctified because they were French; although the table-d'hôte luncheon was not particularly good. She was aware of two men with foreign moustaches, and their presence made her hands seem whiter and her movements more graceful and significant; although she felt the disgrace of never having had a romance in her life, and the difficulty of working up her feeling for Dr. Redmond into anything that would do. She smoked one of her new scented cigarettes, idly and gracefully she felt, one elbow on the table, as she ate the small pink-and-white slab of ice cream and drank the bitter coffee from the small thick cup. The meal was sumptuously complete.

Still she was not ready to go back to her cold apartment and the consideration of her problems. Some part of her exuberance had not yet been given vent. She had spent all the money that she dared. There was nothing to do but go into a church.

Margot felt that this was like entering religion in a book: to

open a gate, and go past a small fountain chilly with thaw, and
into the silent dusky charm, heavy with the accumulated silence
of old beliefs, of the low, irregular rooms of the little Anglican
church on the side street. Margot had long ago decided that she
didn't believe in religion. But the high church atmosphere had
a romantic attraction for her, as a child of Puritan upbringing.
She felt that she was treading on the edges of a mystic feeling
that she couldn't quite accept. She was all the more intrigued
because this feeling was slightly spurious. Things irregular, off
the set pattern, little steps up or down, odd windows, hidden
window seats, balconies, unexpected corners—these were the
kind of things that made Margot feel as if she were just on the
verge of being in a story. Nothing was irregular at home except
the cupola on the old Spencer house. Margot walked softly down
the aisle, hungrily feeding her appetite for color and difference
with the sight of the white-and-gold altar, the woody smell,
the cushion and candle smell, the thick silence. She solemnly
knelt on a prayer bench . . . but nothing came, no answer, no
more than when she looked into a glass on Halloween; and she
left the church feeling surreptitious and unsatisfied.

The sun was clouded over again. It was colder, and the noon-
day brilliance was gone from the streets. Margot took the bus
to Washington Square. She was tired now, but only partly
appeased.

She didn't know just what to do. She stood on a corner,
chilled and jostled, confused by the overhead roar of the elevated. Someone was coming toward her. She recognized the
little beard—it was the wonderful Dr. Finkbein! Margot saw
guiltily that in the daylight he looked like a poor professor.
There was the wrinkled dreariness about him of a man who
lived in a small rented room. But they greeted each other with
enthusiasm.

"Just the young woman I was thinking about! Won't you
come in somewhere for tea? Then we can continue our very
interesting conversation."

The smoke-filled room where candles flickered was like the
inside of some dark shell. They took their place among the
heterogeneous couples sitting on hard benches and leaning their

elbows on unsteady tables. Margot felt some unsatisfactory romantic pleasure in the spurious charm of the "quaint" little tearoom made over from a stable. She played with the pretense that Dr. Finkbein might be that "older man" who had come into her imagination in so many guises, and who could form and direct her. There was a sweet, insidious flattery in the thought of being led, adored and guided—like Charlotte Brontë's heroines. It was a little difficult to sustain the idea of Dr. Finkbein in that rôle; but she felt defiantly that she had to begin to live right now, with what was around her. She tried not to meet Dr. Finkbein's earnest, empty eyes.

He was nervously responsive and delighted when she asked him boldly to go back with her to her apartment. He had already clapped the admiring label of "hedonist" upon her. All day Margot had scarcely dared believe in the existence of her basement room. But there it was—her own—below the noise and the passing, with the barred windows and the little grated door down two stone steps.

"I haven't any lights," Margot said nervously. "I'll have to unwrap my candles."

She felt Dr. Finkbein breathing too close to her. He was fumbling helplessly for the candle. Then she felt the awkward, timid earnestness of his hand on her arm. There was a moment of embarrassing hesitation. Trembling inwardly, disgusted with her inexperience, Margot tried deliberately to smile. She saw his bright spectacles—and then his kiss fell, clumsy and fervid, on her lips.

Margot pulled herself away. But at any rate she had dared! She had made her first day end with a kiss.

Why did she have to suffer humiliation just because she wanted to stay in New York and do some interesting kind of work instead of just the ordinary kind?

There was a bookshop that Margot had seen on just the kind of street that charmed her most, a piece of street that went zigzag, like going down the Crooked Street in *Old Witch*. On one side of the shop was an Italian grocery with funny cheeses in the window, and on the other a gift shop with Czechoslovakian

363

toys. Margot had gone in trembling and humble, scarcely able to raise her lashes. A cadaverous young man in black-rimmed glasses was leaning against the table and talking with a stout young Jew with fuzzy hair. The cadaverous one, the owner, had come up negligently. She had to swallow before she could speak. "I just wanted to ask you if you needed anyone here to help you." Her timidity had amused them highly. "Well," the man had said, lifting one eyebrow, while the other silently shook with laughter, "what kind of help do you offer?" Margot said haughtily, "To sell books!" "Why, my dear, I'd love it if I ever sold any!" And they both had laughed and laughed, thinking that because she looked shy and young, and had a middlewestern accent, they could be as funny as they pleased and she wouldn't really understand it. "If I could support myself," the cadaverous young man repeated, in his gently supercilious tone, "I'd love to support you too!"

The bookshops, the tearooms and gift shops she had entered, stopping outside blindly to fortify herself with the memory of all the praise she had ever had—every one had been a humiliation! The antique shop where the tall woman had come toward her from out of a tantalizing disarray of glass decanters and clocks and andirons, lifting her insolent threads of eyebrows, judging and discarding Margot as a customer not worth while. The bookshop in the Grand Central, in an entirely different New York, a kind of giant place that seemed to belong to the teeming present and not to the romantic past that lingered about the painted doorways and the iron railings down in the narrow streets. The crowded little shop had best sellers on all the shelves. There was a crisp noon smell of coffee from the tiny, nickel-bright eating place next door where all the people were catching trains. The proprietor, efficient, fresh-skinned, large-bosomed, like a clubwoman at home, had turned Margot out tolerantly but in quick order. "My goodness, I believe every girl in this country comes to New York wanting to clerk in a bookstore! If one-thousandth of them got jobs, the town would be swamped." And then the fading, literary, spinster woman with graying hair done in a braid around her head, looking like Vanchie, who had taken Margot's name and address. "Margot!

What a charming name! Are you French? I thought so, with those great dark eyes! Do you write? Oh, I don't believe that! You must come to one of our poetry readings some night. And bring some verses of your own!" She was only another example of Margot's fatal ability to attract the wrong kind of people.

Now Margot lay huddled up on her cot. A trickle of tears had dried on her cold cheeks. She still had some of the rubbish the gang had left her, scraps of kindling gathered from the sidewalks, crates thrown out beside wholesale houses. But her matches were gone. And while she didn't have a job or any money, she was ashamed to see any of the crowd.

She would tramp about answering ads as long as her shoes lasted. She wouldn't let the Bellews into her apartment if they came with a final effort to bring her back to the fold. She would never read another letter from the folks. She would stand crushed with little sawed-off Jewesses and fat Italian girls in gaudy make-up before the dirty windows of dark factories until a short dark man appeared upon the steps and shooed them off. But she would never be a teacher or librarian! Then she would die. There would be the consolation of the cold bright fantasy shed around her last moments by the poem she had copied into her red book and that now was her favorite.

> "In the dark, I shall rise, I shall bathe
> In waters of ice, myself
> Shall shiver and shrive myself
> Alone in the dark . . ."

She would leave a note asking for a pauper's burial so that even after she was dead she wouldn't be indebted to the folks!

"Margot! Let us in!"

Somebody pounded, laughing, on the window. Then there was a prolonged peal of the bell. Margot kept perfectly still. They shook the grilled door.

"Margot Ferguson!"

Her fierce sense of privacy broke down. She ran, with trembling hands opened the door, and then plunged down on her cot and buried her head in the blankets.

"Go away! I didn't tell anybody to come here. I want to die!"

Jane, who had been laughing, now suddenly burst into tears. "Oh, Daggie! Oh, don't let her!" She tried to clutch Margot through the blankets. Daggie lit a match, glanced mildly about the room, and settled his eyeglasses. He stood smiling down at them with that gently admiring and quizzical air with which he regarded all womankind. Why, assuredly, he said—while Jane wailed—Margot might have the privilege of dying. It was a privilege which he believed in extending—among many others—to all the human race. But he must remark that she would then pass to the great beyond with the honor of being the first hungry damsel who had ever turned down the offer of a meal from him.

"Jane, here, comes and suggests them herself!"

Jane made a face at him, and rubbed her cheek against his arm. He sat down on the couch beside her.

"Being a philosopher," he remarked, "you must permit a few philosophical observations. Even in the presence of contemplated death." Jane moaned and buried her curly head against his shoulder. He patted the curls. "Which," he added gently, "is dubious of action, after all is said and done."

Margot kept her face determinedly buried. With one hand Daggie stroked Jane's curls, with the other held Margot's wrist. His soft voice flowed on, never varying its mildly philosophical tone, and in the dim light from the basement windows his fluffy aureole of hair was comfortingly visible.

In the first place, he gathered, without too great a strain upon original observation, that the damsel who now chose to be called Margot Ferguson (having been gifted by Christian parents with the rather too well-worn name of Margaret) found herself in a situation far more common to members of the human race than she imagined. The circumstances, briefly, were these: no heat, no food, no lights. And to judge from the wrist which he was now holding (not entirely without pleasure to himself) the situation had been of some duration. His first suggestion was dinner—again, not without some reference to himself. A slight plumpening increase would make the wrist even more pleasurable to hold. The proposal, however, had not been well received. Strange! For in innumerable instances, some of them close at hand—Jane slapped him, and then hugged Margot—it had been used to meeting with instantaneous approval. The reason for this was—*pride*. An estimable quality, but in the present instance, misplaced. For pride in regard to "what ye shall eat and what ye shall drink" was according to scripture a characteristic of the Philistine. Consider, not the lilies of the field which were not available, but little Jane! Did she take heed as to what she should eat and what she should drink? Nay! And it was given unto her.

Jane struck him with her small fist. Daggie captured the fist gently.

The trouble with Margot Ferguson was that she was still acting the part of the no doubt far more estimable but far less interesting Margaret!

"Let me," said Daggie, offering cigarettes, "paint a word-picture of the Ferguson household of Belmond, Kansas or thereabouts. According to our authority, Jane, it is a prosperous household, even grand! Upon the spacious lawn stands a dignified urn of some cemeterial plaster resembling marble, from which vines trail in a graceful manner."

Margot gave a smothered sound of tremulous laughter.

"Say it is noon. The whistle—town has a whistle, of course? —has blown. From the kitchen where Mrs. Ferguson, a respectable lady of gracious proportions, is bustling, comes an enticing odor of beefsteak to procure which many also graciously proportioned creatures are annually slaughtered in Kansas. Potatoes are boiling merrily in the kettle, while the garden—where Mr. Ferguson takes his evening recreation with the hoe—displays a highly vitamized array of peas, beans, squash and rutabaga. This is the meal to which Mr. Ferguson, a fine old gentleman with the moustaches usually described by the term 'walrus,' is wont daily to sit down, after due attention to the blessing, with an excellent appetite."

"Dad doesn't have walrus moustaches!"

"Ah! Smooth-shaven. . . . But I'm only proving that up to this time Margot Ferguson has not known the meaning of the phrase 'to be hungry.' She invests it therefore with far more significance than the term deserves."

A little help? Why should she mind it? Consider the youth Bobbie, or the youth Rod—lilies truly. Bobbie, who held that plaid knickers marked the artist, and so attired was sharing the excellent bed and board of the ever-generous Marta, ousting —Daggie was sorry to remark—the little female Jane. Unless he, Daggie, was misinformed, Margot herself had accepted an invitation to tea from a learned and serious-minded gentleman of his acquaintance.

"Oh!" Jane breathed. "Dr. Finkbein thinks you're *won*-der-ful!"

No job? Jobs came and went. Little Jane could tell her that. It was the private life that mattered. And she, with her interesting conquest of a learned gentleman, was just beginning her private life.

Margot let herself be dislodged from the blankets. Jane, still with moans of sympathy, washed the tearstains from Margot's face, intently, as if she were tending her doll. Daggie, smiling, watched them, and flicked the ashes from his cigarette. He had found and lit the stump of a candle. The others, he said admiringly, she must have consumed, like the lost children in *Tom Sawyer*. But tallow as a diet, although its literary backing might be excellent, was hardly sufficient. Tony would supply more plumpening fare.

"So let us on to Tony's."

Daggie and Jane marched her down the street between them. Margot felt strangely weak and cleansed. It was as if the winter rain that was falling had swept away the old accumulation of grievances, leaving only this wet blackness that sent up fragrance into her heart. All the lights had rainbow haloes. They went down into another basement and rang the bell at another grilled door. The deliciousness of the steamy smell of food and tobacco that came through the noisy chatter made her head swim with hungry ecstasy. It was like coming back to life. There were red tissue paper roses on the white mantel. They were more beautiful than if they had been real. The thick brown soup sent up an intoxicating steam. The crusty Italian bread and the unsalted butter were more delicious than the image of the bread and jug of wine beneath the bough which she had once thought so enticing in the *Rubaiyat*. The bright, noisy, basement room was a refuge for difference, a sanctuary for the exiles from homes both too good and too bad. It *was* home, now.

Even after Jane and Daggie had left her, Margot couldn't go straight to bed. She crouched beside her beautiful fire on a little red-painted stool. How lovely her room was now, how changed and mysterious!—the softly flaming tips of the red candles that Daggie had bought her, the big unsteady shadows on the walls. "Here today and gone tomorrow." The words whispered themselves with a mysterious consolation. The red wine, the firelight, the candles . . . Margot sprang up to get her red book because she couldn't sleep unless she had tried to keep this happiness from slipping away.

Coming home radiant, amazed, Margot couldn't believe what had happened! And just as casually! She had seen a funny little tearoom, in a crazy little place not much bigger than a passageway; thought, "Shall I?"—and walked boldly in; said "Do you need anyone to help you?"—and the woman in the pink smock, looking up with mildly distracted, wide-apart, gray eyes, had answered, with a trail of Southern inflection:

"Yes, I reckon I might!"

Now the story of herself was beginning to come true. She was in her own basement apartment, and she was going to work in a Village tearoom.

5

Margot stepped lightly about the room washing off the black-painted tabletops, feeling gay and artistic in her yellow smock, humming as she worked. She went into the kitchen to get the lunch cloths out of the tipsy black-painted chest of drawers. She loved even the kitchen in this crazy place. The most delicious kind of cozy heat spread out from the ancient range where they had things cooking in big kettles that might have come out of a folk tale. She simply adored their huge old coffeepot.

369

She spread the yellow cloths on the black tabletops. They were of cotton crêpe with fringed edges. They had been her own idea. Mary Lou had let her paint the furniture black.

"Mary Lou!"

"What, honey?"

"I just had a swell idea!"

Mary Lou came to the kitchen door with her hands floury.

"Oh, no—I don't know—maybe it isn't. Go on back."

Mary Lou went back into the kitchen obediently. How queer it was! Margot thought—this sort of power she seemed to have over worshiping older women. They seemed to belong mysteriously to her guiding star. Mary Lou's fondness was half childish and half maternal. It was even worse than Vanchie—the utter round-eyed, trustful admiration with which she accepted all of Margot's ideas!

"I can't help it. It's my destiny."

Now came something that every day she simply loved to do. It was to go to their big old crooked cupboard in the kitchen and get out the dishes. They didn't match. She didn't want them to match. Margot and Mary Lou had picked out every one separately. She saved until the last, with sensuous pleasure, the two thick yellowish plates and cups of Spanish pottery. She was going to keep them for the little table where she and Lee would sit. If Lee came in today!

Never would she get over her joy in this tiny, tucked-in, unexpected, folk-tale place! Daggie said it had been a hangout for a bunch of Italian gamblers. Margot hoped that was true. The kitchen floor was crooked. You went down one little step. Nobody but Mary Lou could have done such cooking on the ancient range.

She hugged Mary Lou.

"What's the mattuh?"

"Nothing! I just thought about our breakfast."

"Honey, tomorrow I'm going to get us some little sausages."

Daggie laughed at them with his gently philosophical pessimism. One wild woman and one addle-pated!—he said. But all the crowd were reveling in Mary Lou's expansive maternal care. Bobbie had driven them away from Marta's. Mary Lou

370

had the money from the estate back home. All her life she had wanted a tearoom. Now she *had* a tearoom. Why think beyond that?

Every morning, they both got up late and came over to The Hole, and Mary Lou cooked a leisurely, luxurious breakfast which they ate at the kitchen table beside the warm stove. They had their own little special granite coffeepot. They used the Spanish pottery.

"Honey, what shall we have for dinner?"

"Oh, anything good."

"I might have another ham with cloves. Jane likes that. I want to put some flesh on that child's bones. Her little hands make me think of the canary bird's claws my old Aunt Nancy had. She was a little bit queer—well, *right* queer—and she didn't love anything but that skinny old canary."

An atmosphere of Southern laxity and warmth and ease seemed to emanate from Mary Lou plump and flushed at the kitchen range. She had a helpless maternal softness. Yet in the clarity of her round gray eyes there was something virginal. All those years when she had been keeping house for "papa," she had been dreaming of a tearoom of her own. If she had thought about men, it was only shyly, as a little girl might think while she played with her tea set and dolls. But she had taken the crowd for her children.

"Oh, my only precious! Where is he? How could his mother forget him?"

With her voice drenched in pity, eyes wide in compassionate horror, Margot swooped down upon the scrap of kitten asleep beneath the stove. Its black fur was brown with dust. Margot brushed it rigorously. She held the little creature up against her cheek to feel its ecstatic purr. She had found it in the alleyway—little black, mistreated thing! Starving and crouching on the edges, just as she herself used to do. It was as if her own little lost cat, the one that Carl's dog had killed years ago, had been given back to her. She was finding all that she had lost. It was a kind of symbol. A little black cat!—to wind in and out among the black table legs with lifted tail, to sleep curled up on a yellow cushion, to lap its milk while they drank their coffee—a kitten's lapping and purring, the final sounds of luxury! Now Margot could close her eyes to the other frozen, skinny felines nosing the sorry garbage cans of the Village.

"*You* aren't going to starve, you little black one," she told it passionately. "Margot has you. You're *my* kitty. You're saved."

With a glance of defiance at Mary Lou's back, she poured out a bit of coffee cream into her yellow saucer and screened the kitten while it drank with little black paws on the table and little furry neck outstretched.

"Now, little blackest, you can go to sleep."

They didn't have many people for lunch. Mary Lou didn't want many. She didn't like to work her head off for strangers, she said. The crowd all came for dinner. But it was an excitement every day to see what people might drift in. Once a Village sightseeing party had come. "Isn't this quaint! Isn't it the *quaintest* place." Margot, as she went out to the kitchen with orders, made whispered reports of the diners to Mary Lou. Those they didn't like the looks of, they gave the homeliest dishes and the poorest pieces of meat.

"That old buzzard again? Here's this piece of fat. It'll be good enough for *her*. Honey, I like that boy with the glasses. Poor boy! He looks so thin. If he comes in again, you can ask him if he wants a second cup. He looks like he needs more to sustain him."

"Hello, Princess of Darkness!"

Lee had come in again. He dropped in nearly every day for lunch now. Louise didn't know it. He was sitting at their own little corner table.

"Come on and sit down, and let's have our grouch out on the world."

Margot sat down, propped her elbows on the table, accepted a cigarette.

"This is Princess's black cat?"

"Oh, Lee! If you aren't nice to him you can't stay here.

372

Mary Lou's afraid of him. She thinks he's going to bring bad fortune."

"Sure. We Southerners are all afraid of signs. All sunk in superstition. I'm scared myself."

"My precious!" Margot moaned. She took the little cat.

"You don't want to let Louise see this cat here!"

"Why not?" Margot belligerently demanded.

"She yells if she sees one. Got one of those complexes."

"You needn't think I'm going to chase out my kitten just to suit her complexes!" Margot buried her face in the softness of brown-black fur. "My little dark angel, little blackness, I adore you. I don't care, I do!" she said, coming up, and glaring defiantly at Lee.

"I don't doubt it. You give every evidence. Doesn't Mary Lou think you're a witch?"

"No. She thinks I'm just lovely."

"Hasn't heard you go on about your grouches. Margot: Prejudices: Seventy-seventh Volume. It'd be Louise's grouch today if she knew where I was!"

"Oh, I wish you wouldn't everlastingly keep bringing in Louise!"

"You two girls don't like each other very well, do you?" Lee asked, curious and excited. "What's the trouble? Been quarreling over my attentions?"

"*Your* attentions! I've never had any of your attentions."

Lee said meaningly, "That's what you're getting today."

Margot looked at him witheringly. But she felt the exciting pleasure of sitting here with him talking inanities, beneath which there seemed always to be hidden significance. His knee pressed hers under the table. His thin hand, with the fore-finger stained deep orange, strayed, as if by accident, towards hers. There was an attraction between them, half reluctant and jeering, but more than she had felt for any man since Frank Gesell. Daggie was nicer than Lee. But she didn't count Daggie or Dr. Finkbein as men exactly, since she couldn't have fallen in love with either of them. She didn't know whether she liked Lee, but there was a give-and-take between them. Besides, she liked to beat out Louise. Louise *would* be the one to grab the best-looking man in the crowd!

"Margot, tell me, what has been your love life? Ever have any fellow but me?"

"*You*," Margot said witheringly.

"What did you do back there in Belmond, in the old days?"

"Oh—went home with boys from the Young People's meeting."

"Was there a line-up outside the church? God, don't I remember those line-ups! The church stag line. I was raised in the Baptist faith. Somebody always got away with the best girls, left me walking home alone. No wonder I took to the pool room. I never had any luck in love. Don't have any more. Unless you're going to be good to me?"

"I suppose you were in love with someone like Louise!"

Lee settled himself with relish.

"Why don't you like Louise?"

Margot refused to answer.

"If she knew where I was at this moment! She hates you. She's afraid of you. You two girls are the great antithesis, aren't you? That's why I have to seek you out. You're my only antidote. Darkness and light. Tempest and sunshine. I told Louise to go and hear your friend Doc Finkbein's lecture on Frigidity in Women. And well he ought to know! Must have been favored with plenty of it. Until Margot was kind. You don't need any lecture, Margot, beyond what I could give you. Want to hear mine?"

"I don't care to be an antidote!"

"They cure," Lee told her meaningly.

"No, merely neutralize."

"God! Even that would be something. I never could make a hit with a girl like Louise. That's why I always run after them. One of those who always love what they can't have. Look here, if you want to see what a fool I am."

"I know anyway, but I'd just as soon have the confirmation."

He emptied out his pocket on the table. Margot laughed at

374

the litter. But she felt a little thrill of excitement when she touched the things, all bitter-scented from the squashed package of cigarettes. Lee rooted about until he brought out a soiled, folded paper.

"Read that, if you want to know the worst."

Margot read incredulously. She felt a jealous fury at the thought of such words being applied to Louise.

> "She is all so slight
> And tender and white—"

"Louise isn't—if you mean her. I'd call her quite fat." Margot scornfully thrust out her own slender dark arm. Lee took it, and bent back the slim, smooth, flexible thumbs. His hand crept up the wrist. Margot felt the stealthy pressure of his fingers. She jerked her arm away. "I just don't see the application," she said disdainfully.

> "She is as gold
> Lovely, and far more cold.

That's the truth, too!

> For if I win grace
> To kiss twice her face—

And that's about all I've got for two years' straight devotion! Well, not much more than that, when you come down to essentials."

He stared at the litter on the table, then swept it back into his pocket.

"'And far more cold,'" he repeated. "That applies anyway. Well, that's the only difference there is between girls. Some get hot and messy and some stay always cool. That girl's body is always fresh and cool. Not that I ever had much chance with Louise's body! She looks to that. She's the only virgin in the crowd. Unless you're one. Are you, Margot?"

She refused haughtily to answer.

"I wouldn't answer for you. I don't know, though."

He reached out and turned her face up toward his, with his finger under her chin.

"God, but you've got beautiful eyes," he said intensely. "I could fall in love with you right now. You could get me if you wanted to, Margot. Look how those lashes curve." He described the curve with his finger. "They're immense. They're bigger than Louise's. Hers are gray, though—cool."

"The color of cool dishwater," Margot said spitefully.

Lee laughed exultantly.

"No wonder she's afraid of you! She's jealous. Do you know that? You've made her jealous already. Margot. Would you love me the way you do that cat? Daggie's going to take his protégés on a jaunt tonight. Margot. Will you be my girl?"

"No!" Margot said furiously.

She swept up the dishes and carried them out to the kitchen.

First, Margot thought that she would luxuriate in the hot bath—no matter how many people wanted to get into the bathroom . . . and then all at once she was so eager to read and write in her red notebook that she had to jump shivering out of the tub and wipe herself in a hurry. The bathroom was a funny little sawed-off room at the end of the long dark hall.

But before she opened the notebook, she had to arrange everything to her complete satisfaction. She had a ritual for these two luxurious hours at home. When it was raining, she lit candles. She would light the red candles today. Her cot was drawn up in front of the crackling fire. She had plenty of fuel now. All the gang knew about her not being able to pay for gas and electricity. The fireplace smoked, but she liked the bitter smell. She liked the noise outside her windows. Margot herself, warm from her bath and fragrant with Woolworth talcum, sat wrapped in blankets, her hair soft and damp about her neck, and all her paraphernalia around her—little cake she had brought from The Hole, her red notebook, cigarettes.

With infinite relish, eager but slow, she went over the later entries in her red book, written in hastily between exquisitely copied pieces of poetry. She was just entering upon her own youth—held back, delayed, like flowers in a cold spring.

"I tell you beauty wears an ultra fringe."

376

Let Dorothy, and Mildred, and the other girls have the ordinary things! It was that "ultra" which *she* demanded. Margot's red notebook was beginning to brim over with the poems of Edna St. Vincent Millay.

Her friends weren't just the ordinary kind. They were exiles, outlaws from home, who had found their refuge in the smoke-filled rooms in these narrow streets. They warmed themselves at the fireplaces of the past. They all had "histories." Dr. Finkbein had been born in Europe. He had suffered awful things when he was a child. Daggie had been the odd one in a New England family. He didn't consider a Dagget necessarily superior enough to the human race to be entitled to live on the labors of others, nor could he feel a spiritual alliance with the making of cheap shoes. Music being a boon to humanity, he would clerk in a music store. Mary Phipps had a sister whom she hated. And think of even Mary Lou!—soft, maternal, child-like—but suddenly, at thirty-seven, deciding that she wasn't going to be another old maid in a Southern town. Now Margot thought that perhaps her great work would be a picaresque record of a modern woman's life, enriched by the histories of her friends.

But life . . . she stopped . . . she was still upon the outskirts. For herself, she would have nothing to put in—nothing beyond her quarrel with the folks. She was a virgin. When they talked about "virgins," she blushed all over with secret shame. Jane had lived with men. She was like a thin little cuddly kitten, with half-wild eyes, snuggling down for a moment with anyone who was good to her, and then suddenly running off upon her own queer little concerns. But Jane had started with the advantage of a disreputable family! "Virgin" was the greatest term of obloquy. Margot couldn't stand it, to be shut out in her innocence, not to be free of the world. She was as innocent as Mary Lou—as Vanchie! *More* innocent than Dorothy. She was ashamed to live when her only real experience with men was confined to those awkward, overgratified kisses that Dr. Finkbein had felt himself privileged to bestow upon her ever since she had kissed him that first night. But she had ac-

377

cepted them, because she wasn't going to hide away any longer from *any* kind of experience.

Margot threw her red notebook against the wall in disgust.

The crowd came to The Hole for dinner.

Of course Louise had to be here!—sitting beside Lee, silky and cool, scarcely glancing at the other girls. Jane and Mary Phipps and Lenore hated Louise because she was only playing at living in the Village. Her folks supported her, and she let everyone know that she came from a wealthy family. Louise let out a scream. The little cat, perking up spirit to be playful, had touched her shoe with its paw.

"Lee—somebody—take it away! Oh, I hate the damned things! Scat!"

Margot swooped down furiously upon the little cat and bore it off to the kitchen.

"Lee doesn't hate it." Margot's voice was hard. "He held it on his lap this noon."

She saw with triumph the look that shot from Louise's eyes. Well, let her know that Lee had been here without her! Louise thought she needn't bother to be a rival to a little bit of riffraff like Jane. But she had to reckon with Margot, and she knew it! And Margot felt with malicious triumph that this was her place. The black tables and chairs, the color of the dishes, even the darkness of the night were on her side.

"I know I shan't come to this tearoom again if I have to have *alley* cats crawling over my feet, as well as—" Louise gave an expressive glance at Lenore and Jane across the table. "It's rather hard on Mary Lou!"

Jane hopped joyously into the fray.

"I think the little cat's *darling*. Bring it in, Margot. I'm going to let it eat off my plate."

Daggie spread a gentle, deterring hand. "I'll protect you from the beast, Louise." He lifted the kitten from Jane's plate.

"Oh, never mind," Louise said with cutting distaste. "No doubt they're accustomed to keeping the pig in the parlor."

"Oh, yes, we were!" Jane cried, in ingenuous delight. "I had the *dearest* little pig—"

378

"Sh, sh!"

"With a little curly tail—"

Daggie put his hand over her mouth. She struggled, wildly laughing.

"And the sweetest *rat!*" she shrieked.

Louise got up from the table with dignity. Well, let her sit like an outraged queen, saying her dinner was completely spoiled! *This* was the night when it got nothing for her. She still kept the notions of the petted small town beauty, who expected that things would be *done* for her, not that she would ever *do* anything. Now the tables were turned.

"Children, children," Daggie expostulated. "Don't spoil the party."

When they left the subway and came out into Wall Street, Margot tore her arm away from Dr. Finkbein's and ran off alone down the empty street. She didn't want to hear about capital and labor and the class struggle tonight. In his awkward, earnest fatuousness, he would never forget the promise of that kiss! Well, it was everyone for himself. It had to be. The tall buildings narrowed and towered on each side, filling Margot with a hard, exultant sense of power. The voices echoed weirdly in the cold, dark canyon of the street. How little they all looked between these towering walls! There was a ruthless power here that cared nothing for them and would crush their tiny lives out of them without mercy. But at night-time they could play about these stony fortresses. There was some kind of gleeful revenge in that! They could have their own lives while the world was going ponderously on—in the interstices of time and place, here in this uncharted hour of night-time. They were the outlaws.

Margot dashed up into a stony doorway and stood for a moment, panting, feeling queerly alone and sorrowful. She pressed her cheek against a cold stone pillar. She had got away from Dr. Finkbein at last.

Footsteps beat lightly up the stone steps. Margot stood in rigid wariness. Now her heart began to beat thickly. Lee pulled her out roughly from behind the pillar.

"Here, none of that! You ran off to be chased, didn't you?"

The likeness between his thin, bitter hardness and her taut rebellion quivered in their hands, with a strange, unsatisfying thrill of hostile attraction.

"And their lips met!" Lee said dramatically.

Now the others had discovered that they were missing. They heard the jeering voices from the street.

"It's the moonlight!" Daggie said.

But with his usual philosophic air of a quizzically and affectionately amused onlooker, Daggie would do nothing to check the catastrophe that was overtaking his walking party. He watched it come, as he might have stood at a window to watch a cyclone approaching.

"I want Margot to walk with *us*," Jane whimpered.

"Don't check the mating fever. Be content with your loving Daggie."

In this cold canyon between the huge buildings, where the moonlight made sharp cubes of white among the shadows, it was natural to be cruel and fierce. The fight was on between Margot and Louise. Margot felt that it was something that had been ordained since the beginning of time. The figure of Louise, in the soft gray coat with the soft gray fur, the little gray hat pulled down over her golden hair, had drawn into itself everything that was hostile. Margot fantastically piled her hatreds upon it. It was the gray and white kitten that Dorothy had chosen, that all the girls had cuddled because it was so soft, leaving out the little black one . . . all the smooth Eve women, masking their shrewd maneuvers beneath their softness . . . for the first time Margot gave herself up with wild joy to the white blaze of her jealousy.

Daggie led his flock into a corner shack for hot dogs and coffee. Louise was walking close to Lee again, silently, demurely. A pang of hot anger shot through Margot. It brought the power of her insolence, sharp and bright. She pushed past Louise, and grabbed Lee's arm; and then, from her perch on the stool at the counter, looked back with hard triumph at Louise's furious, defeated face. "Lee asked me to be his girl tonight!" Louise

couldn't take defeat straight. She was outraged. She thought
somebody else ought to do something about it *for* her.

"Let 'em alone," Daggie said. He threw up his hands.

Margot's legs were trembling. She felt a wild desire to cry,
in the perilous remorse of victory. But the smooth Eves weren't
going to have everything forever! They had their weapons—
their selfish deftness, their yielding softness that masked as
sympathy and flattery—but they had nothing to match her
insolence. Because she dared! She would give everything she had
for what she wanted. Louise sat baffled and crying in her in-
ability to go the whole way. Her care for what she would gain
was less than her fear of what she might lose. Well, they got
the soft places, the fearful ones! But Louise couldn't have this
cold, bright moonlight.

The rest of the night was a kind of hectic scattering. They
all stood shivering near the cold harbor. Then there was the
hollow, softened thudding of their feet on the wooden platform
as they hurried onto the ferry. The breath of the cold water
had a wild, fresh touch of spring. A mist of spray touched
their faces as the boat swung out, carrying them across the
dark swell of water.

Now Louise was trying for consolation and support against
Margot. She was making the others pity and surround her.
But Margot was the one who was in league with this night.
Beneath the necessity for her triumph, Margot felt a darkness,
a queer fatality. Here at the ferry railing, with the heaving
black brightness all around them, the hostility between herself
and Lee was yielding to the perverse thrill of their likeness.
They were standing against Louise together. The fascination
each felt for each—thin, sharp, too personal—was straining to
defeat, by its own assertion, all that made up their bitterness
and loneliness, from long, long ago.

They were off the boat and all crowding into the taxi.
Jane was wickedly glad that Margot was winning. She burst
into wild fits of giggles that Daggie tried mildly to subdue.
Louise sat in stony silence. Margot had beaten Louise tonight.
Lee was hers, they felt alike. She had made him admit her,
assert that likeness, admit that here *she* was the choice—not

Louise, stealthily invading even this place where she didn't belong and that she couldn't live up to.

"I'm going home with you. Do you know it?" Lee challenged her. "Louise'll never forgive me for this."

"Never forgive you!" Margot said scornfully. "She'll love you."

They stood shivering on the dark pavement while Lee paid his share of the taxi. It seemed to Margot that she was trembling on the very edge of the world. But she wasn't afraid— she wouldn't turn back now. This had to be. She fitted her key into the lock of the grilled basement door. They went into the cold room.

"You know I haven't any lights."

She heard Lee laugh. "You girls are all alike, aren't you?"

"I'm not alike!"

She felt hard and alone. The others saw her as insolent, predatory, triumphant. They didn't know that inside she was frightened and trembling, wildly at bay before all the established canons of the world. What she felt was a kind of dedication. Yes, a dedication to her own way of life! Lee put his arms around her, and the unlighted candle fell bumping to the floor. "You little mad Indian." There was a note of hard, admiring hatred in his voice. But the hatred was joy. Or almost joy. Again she felt that it *had* to be like this. Something within her was weeping, was helplessly protesting. But she fought blindly against the protest, to force out of their bitter likeness rapture enough to hold against Louise—against the world.

Margot went out into the street. The world ought to be made new. She was changed now. She was a woman of experience.

Christopher Street roared with its narrow confusion. It was dark in the rainy morning. Margot felt that she was walking through the very center of the noise, the traffic, the people, the skidding cars and lumbering old truck wagons with the heavy feet of horses slipping on the gleaming wet. Battered tin ash cans stood out in front of tenement houses. The same poor skinny cats were nosing. She was on an equality now with the heavy Italian women with the dark shawls over their heads. She need no longer bow to what mother and Aunt Louie and Aunt Ella and all the others said.

It seemed to her that a mysterious ripening had come over her slight body. Lying in the cot, alone this morning, just wakening out of a final deep oblivion, she had felt a curious upper sense of fulfillment and ripening—with underneath, something crying, fatal and lost. But it was done. At last she was entirely at home in her basement room.

She went into The Hole. Through the crooked doorway of the kitchen, she saw Mary Lou's unconscious figure.

"Honey, what happened to you? You're late. I ate my breakfast. You don't mind? I saved some things for you."

Did Mary Lou know that she was changed? There was no knowledge in the round, innocent clarity of those virginal gray eyes. Margot felt a shiver of loneliness. It would never be the same again, eating breakfast here with Mary Lou. She would never again have quite the old, unconscious wholeness. She held the little cat with its whiskers and fur pressed up against her cheek. "Little black one. You're my little black one." Her eyelashes were wet.

"Honey, I'm goin' out to buy a few things."

Under her calm, now, there was a restlessness. It was rising and taking possession of her. Margot got up from her breakfast. She stared into the wavy little mirror beside the cupboard. The coaly brightness of the pupils widened and made her eyes all black. She thought, with a fierce defiant joy, she was really an outlaw. The folks would repudiate her forever. She had gone outside and made herself a free lance, wrecked her "virtue," set herself beyond the pale. She was glad! She caught up the little cat again. They were both black ones. It was a queer, solitary, exhilarating feeling—as if she were some kind of dark, bright meteor shooting dangerously across the safe, settled, complacent orbits of the fixed stars. . . .

People began to come in for lunch. Margot felt a curious lack of interest. They were people, that was all. There was one of those parties of sightseers. Margot went in to serve them with a cool, contemptuous assurance. But she had the dramatic feeling of herself, slim and different in her yellow smock, with a dangle of gypsy earrings beneath her short black hair.

"Do you suppose she's foreign?" one of the women whispered, half shocked and half admiring.

There was no reason to be diffident with the large, handsome married woman, dressed in inconspicuous expensiveness, with the old-fashioned diamond solitaire and the thick, plain gold wedding ring pushed together on her plump left hand. Her kind of self-assurance came from having known only the tame, admitted things. In a place like this, she was superior but uneasy. Margot could recognize the high, hungry animation, the restless, shut-out ignorance in the seeking eyes of the thin, unattractive, well-dressed woman, just getting to the point when her unclaimed solitude began to seem hopeless to her. She was the kind of woman who felt exhilarated and flattered in Rod's little shop, up one flight of dark stairs, on the narrowest street, watching him handle with delicate fingers some little blue Chinese vase, while he explained its beauties, with a glint of callow, cold, dark disdain in his almond eyes. Ladies who thought Rod was such a *beautiful* boy! The thin woman giggled with nervous delight at having dared to come to such a dangerous place as this.

Lee didn't come in to lunch today. Margot was glad. But it left everything flat. The rasped, angry solitude that engulfed her made her afraid.

"I've got a headache," she told Mary Lou. "I'm going home."

It was the same as all other days, only more so, as she fitted her key into the lock of the grilled door, sidestepping the scattering of rubbish the garbage collectors had left when they emptied their cans with noisy carelessness. The cold stale silence of her room surrounded her. The memory of the night before lingered in it like the events of a dream, so vivid that—unreal all the same!—it lasts over into the morning.

What was there to do with herself? What use to light the candles—gloat over the fire, alone?

"There was a time when I was sad and lonely,
And stood in strange forgetfulness apart."

384

Was *she* "lonely for her loneliness" now? She could never go back. The torn-in-two, crying ache of this new solitude had to be assuaged—but never again by that old, rapt solitude. The icy glaze of the shell that had surrounded her was broken. Whether she loved Lee or hated him—whether it was happiness or misery—it was nothing to be here without him now.

Slowly a strange depression came up from depths below all her other feelings and settled darkly over her. She didn't take it back. She *wanted* to want him—in spite of the trembling, new humiliation of finding that another human being might be necessary to her. She felt that she had to go on to the end that she could almost see. But in everything that she did, there was always a flaw, something fragmentary and broken. It seemed as if she had only used herself to triumph over herself. She wanted to cry. But there weren't any tears. Perfection was still beyond her. She was furious at her own desires, hurting herself upon the memory of imperfection, but wanting even that more than the old enclosed unreality of a dream.

6

Grimmie asked, "Do you really mind if I go off, Margot precious?"

"Of course not—you crazy thing."

"Well, I hate to leave you alone. With those big dark eyes!" Margot hooted.

But as she sat tucked among the velvet cushions, with the book of H. D.'s poems, the Armenian cigarettes beside her, candied violets in the Chinese bowl on the lacquered stand, she felt lapped in the warmth of Grimmie's generosity; and the dark misery that still stayed, like a cold spring flowing underground, made the contrast of her comfort all the more dramatic.

"Sweetheart, are you warm enough? There's plenty of coal in that sack in the do-diddy. Don't warm up that old stuff in the kitchenette. Go out and get a good dinner when you're hungry. I want to fill out those thin little cheeks. H. D.! Oh, isn't she glorious? She simply made Greek poetry *live* for me. 'Then swam a new planet into my ken'—or anyway . . . you know. Good-bye, dearest, I have to *fly*."

Grimmie rattled more coal onto the fire from the little brass hod, looked around for cigarettes, kissed Margot—she was finally gone, with the orange wool hat that she had bought enthusiastically in a new Czechoslovakian shop (it was going to bring the æsthetic element into modern dress) tilted wildly over one ear, and a streamer of fuzzy hair flying. The way Grimmie always made her departures!

Coal slipped in the fireplace. A few sparks scattered. Black satin mules had been kicked idly under a chair. The wintergreen branches in the big black bowl had dripped red berries on the white mantel. Books lay all around behind cushions and sticking out from chair backs. The luxury of books, more books than she could ever read! Ash trays everywhere. The ash trays at Grimmie's were always full. From the signed photographs of Grimmie's friends, hanging crooked on the white-paneled walls—writers with pipes, artists with and without beards, strike leaders with tossed tumultuous hair, the "interesting people" of whom Margot used to dream—she drew again an exhilarating sense of the variety of existence. The dark, shut-in life in the basements of the Village was far away. Her room stayed as she had left it, chill and stale with old fires and cigarette smoke, when she had walked out blind with misery. The paintings that Grimmie had bought from future geniuses were striking, some of them, and some of them just crazy; but it was nice to look at them from half-closed eyes whenever she stopped reading for a moment. The one of the cypress tree on the Pacific coast, battered and twisted by the winds into a shape that had a meaning—none of Grimmie's friends got excited about that one, but Margot didn't care, for it was *hers*. It justified her own way of existence. And then the faded old brownish photograph of Grimmie's home, somewhere in Missouri, with all the family drawn up in front of a white frame house with pillars, remotely colonial, under big trees . . . in that was the comforting sense of old ties, distant but unbroken, among the colorful clutter of foreign things. From the Greek atmosphere of the verses, a faint timeless scent of hyacinths drifted through the pleasantly smoky atmosphere of the white-paneled room with its glowing fire, up above the small seclu-

386

sion of Bank Street, with the noise coming muffled from Seventh Avenue.

Here she was under the adoring protection of an older woman again! This was another way-station of her destiny. But she had to rest a while in the luxury of this feminine lavishness. The desperate impulse had been right that had sent her out at last to find Grimmie's address. Grimmie was more her mother than her *own* mother, than mama, was—just as once she had felt that Frank Gesell was more her father than dad. Grimmie's headlong kindness and understanding had slowly soothed the rankling wound of Mary Lou's defection. Yet Margot felt that she would never forget that, nor the shock of its surprise. Even now she had to go back and live again in that moment when Mary Lou had come into the tearoom to face her with flushed cheeks and round, glassy eyes. "Honey, I can't keep it back any longer. I've got to tell you. I don't guess we can work together any more. I don't believe in what you're doin'. I think it's wrong." But didn't Mary Lou know me? Didn't she care about *myself*? To me, her *in*experience was just as wrong as my experience was to her. But I loved her for what she was behind her life. Why couldn't she have seen *me* behind my life? Mary Lou had wept. She couldn't explain it. She wouldn't keep The Hole any longer. She had gone back on the crowd. Her little spurt of adventure was over. She had retreated into the innocence which was, after all, her only possession. Yes, perhaps it was her quality. And without it she would be commonplace.

But Grimmie was better than Mary Lou! All people who had made mistakes and put themselves on the other side were truly better than the ones inside the strict circle—although Grimmie's mistakes were only carelessness, and generosity, and that sort of "unfeminine" awkwardness that had worried her family and made her an exile, having a dangle of petticoat trailing, her things all pinned together. Her being on the other side was just a passionate, haphazard espousing of the cause of anything unfortunate. Margot adored Grimmie for the recklessness of her generosity. Maybe it was foolish, and solved nothing, and laid up trouble for other people in the end, as Katherine

387

Griswold said. But it was *better,* all the same, than prudence, and she would always, always say that it was!

There was comfort, also, in the false security of the folks' approval. Grimmie had written Ethel Spencer that "Margaret" was living with her. Margot had to try and keep Grimmie from writing to the folks themselves, ashamed because they would never be able to credit or comprehend the reckless innocence of Grimmie's views. Grimmie backed Margot up in refusing to do the regulation things that had nothing inside them, that were just jobs. She had enthusiastic plans in the offing. She was sure that her friend Hjelmer Jonsen could find a place for Margot on an archæological expedition; or that one of the rich women she had known off and on from her excursions into philanthropy, some of those women who had "favorite charities" and sold their best photographs to advertise cold creams, would set Margot up in an art shop.

Meanwhile, Margot had to try and calm what Daggie called "the middle-class scruples of the estimable Ferguson family," and Dr. Finkbein her "inhibitions," by accepting Grimmie's generosity. But then, Grimmie had to have an object for her enthusiasm. Katherine Griswold had said that. "Don't mind taking a few pence, child. Grimmie has to see the hope of the world somewhere. At present, you're the hope." There was something brisk and lucid about Katherine, that Margot felt as tonic, even while she resented Katherine's whole way of looking at things. Not thinking about herself in any personal way, and with men set resolutely out of her life, did leave her mind free and cool to pick out just the sensible side—kind enough, but with what Katherine called "rational" kindness, with an untouchable superiority that hurt.

"I'd never want to have to take anything from Katherine!"

At night, Margot and Grimmie talked for hours before the fire. Grimmie sat wrapped in a patchwork quilt that an old Kentucky mountain woman had given her, looking hunched and thin like a kindly witch. Grimmie had taught for six months in an experimental school in the Kentucky mountains. Grimmie's eyes, unworldly, innocently mad, took everything that Margot told her into herself and out of her warm lavishness gave it back touched with the fire of her enthusiasm. She declared that Margot's generation of girls was wonderful. They had learned a secret of life that her own generation had missed. They went out to *meet* life, that was it! They *sought*. Margot said that all the women she had met at Katherine Griswold's tea seemed bare inside.

"Now, what do you mean?" Grimmie cried with shining interest.

"Well, I mean they all go into things, but just into *things*, all outside, they haven't worked out *themselves*. I mean, personally."

"I see, I see!" Grimmie chanted joyously.

And she went around preaching the doctrine of the personal life to all her friends, until—Margot thought—they must hate me.

Grimmie appreciated Jane too. "She takes life as it happens. She takes it lightly."

"I don't want to take it lightly," Margot said rebelliously, switching away from her championship of Jane, now that it wasn't needed. "I want to take it *hard* and have everything matter."

Even now, because of what had happened to her—painful and broken as it was—Margot felt a sense of inner superiority to these women. She had felt it that day at Katherine's tea, despite the comfort of returning to that atmosphere of feminine elegance. In the room with the white bookshelves and the white fireplace, her allegiance had gone back fiercely to the chilly, sooty-smelling darkness of her old basement apartment. Nearly all the women had wide bosoms and hips, but they were briskly spinsterish. They didn't believe in using make-up, and they were interested in outside questions. Running home through the cold autumn rains, leaping the puddles at the corners of the narrow streets, Margot had felt a rush of wild, defiant exuberance and kinship with the dark.

A delicate thread of smoke went twirling up from her Armenian cigarette. Margot watched it, as she lay among the cushions. She had torn herself away from her torturing, unsatisfying absorption in Lee. But there was something still aching and un-

389

appeased in the desolate darkness—somewhere far away from this fine, gray, upward twirl of smoke.

All the time, it had been real (rackingly, acutely real!) and yet, in some deeper way, not real at all. Their brief glorying in likeness could not disentangle the hidden twists. Their hatred of each other had always been lurking, a kind of belittlement, just because they *were* alike. The knowledge that behind each of them was the guilty secret of unhappiness and early failure had only made them despise each other. But she had taken him away from Louise!—that was her triumph—that, and her superior boldness in escaping from Lee before he could escape from her. At the time, she had believed that nothing could ever again hurt her so much. But now it seemed to Margot that she was crying because it hadn't hurt her *enough*. She felt a hardy, fierce zest in the new knowledge that gleamed brokenly through her failure. She had wanted to shatter her nice-girl fastidiousness—to learn what innocent, beloved women like mother and Dorothy would never know; a knowledge that would triumph darkly forever over the deft subtleties of the Mildreds and Louises who were after their own security. No boundaries, no limits, to feel herself out in open water.

Margot heard with a secret delight the ticking of the little traveling clock on the red lacquered desk in the littered warmth of the room.

And then all at once she was beset by the feeling of the cold November outside the windows—the smoky fires behind tattered shields of rusty iron where children played in the small, dark canyons of the narrow streets—and she had to get out into the midst of it!

The dinner at Romany Marie's was the first meal that Margot had enjoyed for itself since the breakfast in the French restaurant on the first day of her new existence. There was a fresh pleasure, subtly malicious, in being all alone. An assertion of herself, and defiance of all entanglements, and of what they could do to her. A piano was banging in the other room. But she no longer felt hungry and apart at the sound of other people having a good time together. She could live up to the requirements of life in this place. Beneath her sensuous pleasure in the spiced richness of the South European food, there seemed to run a strain of low, dark music that was an echo of her personal life. Margot sat with her head on her hand, as she dreamily took her last sip of the thick sweet coffee, that she enjoyed as being *Turkish* coffee, although she didn't like it. She stubbed out the light of Grimmie's Armenian cigarette that she had brought along to match the food. The piano kept banging; and the harsh music, reckless and discordant, seemed to follow out, like the accompaniment to a dance, the entangled lives of all the people in these narrow streets, Jane with her wilding, mongrel prettiness, Rod with his perverse delicacy, Marta's fatal kindness—the reckless, fragmentary lives, and the bitter, broken childhoods that lay behind them . . .

But she would escape! As she had escaped from the motley little group of "others" at home in Belmond.

Margot ran out alone into the windy darkness of the Square. Bare trees, dark sky, dark buildings, a few stars, and winter coming. She could breathe in the scent of change!

She had *herself* again—changed, disrupted, broken into, but herself! Well, at any rate, she felt that she was forever superior to anyone like Lucille! Margot had met Lucille on Fifth Avenue one day. Although they hadn't really been good friends at home, Lucille was delighted to see her—with that provincial delight, Margot thought disdainfully, at meeting anyone who happened to come from the same place. They "must have tea together," Lucille had said. Lucille's greatest New York adventure was still to have tea with another girl at an Alice Foote MacDougall tearoom. Never, never would she have to suffer now the fate of Vanchie's withering innocence! In the cold night, in the windy November darkness big and portentous coming down upon the earth, Margot felt aching deep within her the hurt and guilty shame of all that had been cruel and unscrupulous in her history—deceiving and breaking with the folks, the way she had treated the Bellews, her triumphant escape from Lee after she had taken what he could give her . . . yes, more than anything, the secret, half-realized selfishness in her brief, discordant affair with Lee . . . It had been—

Margot recognized now, and had somehow recognized even then —just a dark, nameless, necessary prelude to her own story.

How different it was tonight from the first time she had come to creep hungrily about the edges of the Village! It was worth having gone through everything to have all this added to her. It had been for the sake of adding to that completed self which she saw standing like a figurehead at her ultimate destination. Before she had a past, she wasn't even ready to begin. The night wind was blowing her clean. Then what was coming?

On the other side of the Square, Margot saw the old houses standing dignified and withdrawn.

III. AND IT HAD A GREEN DOOR

WHAT was it that gave this queer sense of familiarity? Then Margot remembered. She used to live on this street! She used to pass this small Italian bakery every day. Over there on the corner was the pet shop before which she used to stand looking at the smoky ears and jewel eyes of the Siamese cats. Her own little cat. The little black cat. She and Grimmie had gone night after night to search for it around Mary Lou's old tearoom. But it had never come. . . . Here, in this very next house, was her first apartment! Lord, how many since? A feeling of dingy chilliness came over her with the memory of the sunless windows and the smoky fireplace. A strange distance separated her from all that had happened here. It was as if she were just beginning life again, and this time in her own real person. The days of the basement apartment had become a legend.

What had happened to the people who used to live in this house? Margot had gone only a few streets away; and yet they, too, were legends. That little wisp of a man with the beautiful, bright, dark eyes—"a hack writer with a hacking cough," he

used to call himself—who earned a sort of living writing for
the confession magazines. "I was an only child. I know that I
had beauty of a sort, and that more dangerous thing called
charm." He kept a scrapbook full of what he thought were
his real works of genius, wistful little lyrics printed now and
again in Sunday School papers or the lesser known household
magazines.

> "Through the pale evening
> Comes a song . . ."

Some of them did have a kind of dim, appealing, girlish charm.
How Lee used to despise the little fellow! Lee. It was more
than a year since she had even heard Lee's name.

Margot didn't believe she had actually realized until this
moment how much Bruce had affected her life. It was true, as
Daggie reproached her, that she didn't see the old crowd now.
Almost unconsciously, Bruce's attitude had influenced her.
They were "Villagers" in his eyes—play boys and girls who
didn't know how to deal with the actual, solid things. And it
wasn't just the Villagers that Bruce disliked and depreciated.
There was a need in him to disparage her whole way of life.
Because her recklessness fascinated him and shamed his own
solid prudence—the prudence that had got him into the dry
rut of existence in which she had found him! Nevertheless, it
was that sense of solidity about Bruce that made Margot look
back at the time in the basement apartment as shoddy and
precarious. She repudiated the image of a little thin, dark Margot in bizarre earrings and a peasant dress, crouching over a
fire of twisted papers in the smoky fireplace and getting a sense
of romantic festivity over the burning of two five-cent candles.
It was as if she were just coming up at last from the shadow
into the real sunlight.

And yet she pitied the little dark image. Underneath, she
clung to it with stubborn pity. She was the only person on
earth who would ever entirely know the painful, rapturous,
inner secrets of its history. She knew how different this history
really was, to her, from the version that Daggie, for instance,
loved to give of it, smiling and licking his nice little chops.

393

"When Margot Ferguson first came down to these parts, she was a scared little virgin from the hinterland, who had yet to taste her first strong drink." Dr. Finkbein saw it as the bold stroke for freedom of a kind of Shaw female. Margot alone could know the secret of the grim resolution to conquer her fiercely shy virginity, to break the frozen glaze of self-distrust enclosing her. But now all her earlier affairs with men seemed nothing but a preparation for the meeting with Bruce.

She turned and walked back to look at the house again. Deep down, there still lay a hurt loyalty to the old crowd, although she had forsaken them. There was something more than Bruce knew—not just "affectation"—in their refusal to admit the importance of any but intangible things. They were all lost children—Peter Pan's Lost Boys afraid to grow up— and partly because (she told Bruce fiercely in her mind) most grown-up people were so awful! His world didn't *deserve* to be fitted into. Anyone who could fit into it entirely was just a fool.

And Bruce himself—as if he fitted! Then he would never have come down to the Village, superior and curious, "just to look around," and have found her in Marta's tearoom. That day she still held in her memory as the beginning—with the darkness, the shine and smell of rain, the flicker of the inadequate fire, the muted, yearning sound of foghorns through the soft thickness of the air. Bruce had come into the room shaking himself slightly. He looked big and competent and excitingly out of place, as he took off and folded his heavy coat. His hands came cold and fresh out of his leather gloves, as he rubbed them together, and then took up the foolish little menu card. It was written in purple India ink, in Margot's arrogantly girlish letters, with curly tails to the y's and the g's. The corners of his lips drew down as he stared at the card through tortoise-rimmed glasses he put on and then immediately took off again and stowed away in a soft leather case. But she had interested him, standing and waiting in her Russian smock, in spite of the superior, distrustful, uptown amusement in his eyes! In that soft lull of between-time, with the

394

foghorns sounding in the rainy air, her real life had begun to flower.

She couldn't stay here. This street was the past. She couldn't admit her own inclusion among the Lost Boys and the Lost Girls—as she had refused to stay in Belmond and admit herself to be one of the company of local outlaws: Dr. Redmond, because he "went with other women," and was vaguely tarnished with the rumor of illegal operations; Louella Allen who had written letters to herself and declared they came from the good-looking young Methodist minister; and that queer little shy-animal man, who had left his family and gone to live in an abandoned country schoolhouse, to be free to complete a great invention.

Margot ran, leaping in front of an outraged taxi driver, fiercely determined to be done with the old life, that had never been more than partly hers . . . although a lonely loyalty to it was crying somewhere in her heart.

There was always a lingering, fairy-tale enchantment in opening a green door. The brick house, with its two dormer windows, looked private and small between the taller houses on each side.

Then there was the beautiful, sumptuous knowledge that Bruce had found this place for her. He had gone with Margot and Frances one bright Sunday afternoon to look for apartments. He wouldn't have the girls living in a gas-heated house. "Margot might take out the plug some day when it happened to be raining and she'd drunk a little too much the night before." Margot tossed her head rebelliously at the memory of Bruce's satirical tone. But at the same time a secret smile seemed to come from deep within and curve her lips. (It was the same smile that Mildred Summers used to wear, lurking and subtle, when she came into the assembly room with the knowledge that Gardner Allen had asked her to go to the football banquet.) Margot had got her job through Bruce too. He had sent her to a friend of his who ran an advertising agency. "I can't have you living from hand to mouth this way." The sense of Bruce's protection pervaded Margot's whole existence with a flattering, velvet warmth. She was the Fair Rosamund—the Dark Rosaleen—whom the king really loved and kept apart for his delight in this little house of enchantment.

She ran up the painted staircase to her room.

She stood for a moment in the warm air feeling her joy in coming out of the chilly street into the midst of beloved, significant possessions. Bruce had had something to do with nearly everything in this room. When he gave Margot her big armchair for Christmas, he had given Frances a chair, too, a dear little old-fashioned, oval-backed rocker—out of his dreadful prudence! Margot's was upholstered in rose and Frances' in blue. He had lent her the *Grammar of Science,* with a wine-stained menu card stuck between pages seven and eight, disgusted with her "totally feminine" reading. A nice big pair of shiny rubbers stood in full view near the fireplace, revealing the obtuse masculine simplicity that went along with his prudence and competence, making her laugh at him and love him.

But she must hurry! She would get a scolding for being "extravagant with time." She dashed into the little bathroom and turned on the water full-tilt.

The door of Frances' room was open—the neat, trim room, all in cool blue and white, precise as a spinster's. Margot liked having Frances this close and no closer. Frances' own continuous, although never tumultuous, love affairs added to the secret warm richness of feminine life in the crowded little apartment. Margot's history had had more exciting episodes. But Frances was upheld in her cool poise by the constancy of the "older man" at home in Cincinnati to whom she could always turn. Bruce approved of Frances. "I want someone who'll remember to pay the rent if you don't." He insisted on his view of Margot as a "night moth." Jane, the real "night moth," he abhorred. Margot told Bruce she hated thrift. She had had enough of that at home, with Grandma Ferguson and Aunt Ella roused for weeks because once mother had let them, the two girls, wear their best dresses to school! She was going to *use* her things, and not take care of them, and spend her money for what she wanted, not what she needed—with only one life to live and that "no longer than the sandpeep's cry." . . .

But the tub must be full to running over!

The bathroom was steamy from the hot water greenish and bright in the porcelain tub. Thank heaven she was living with someone who liked to keep the bathtub clean—after those awful two months with Jane in the room with the peasant bed! Margot poured in the powdery remains of her bath crystals. They were like pale, ground-up emeralds. Little white receptacles that she and Frances couldn't resist when they went to the ten-cent store were more or less filled with cakes of scented soap in various stages of jellied dissolution. The blue, of course, belonged to Frances. The rose-red was Margot's. Once more, blue and rose-red, just as it had been at home! Margot wallowed luxuriously in the bath, thinking of the awful bathrooms that she had known in her varied life in the Village. Just at this moment, nearly everything was right! She even liked the kind of advertising—perfumes, and draperies, and cosmetics—that they were giving her to do. Bruce was coming to take her out to dinner. She thought of her crazy old dream about Dr. Redmond. Perhaps it had been a sort of prevision—because now she really was having a love affair with a married man. Margot felt borne up lightly into fragrant luxury, above the fundamental precariousness of her life. The things that she had ached to possess, through all these years, were being slowly collected around her.

She ran tapping back to her room in her black satin mules. Again the warm, intimate air surrounded her. Gossamer stockings were strewn over the back of a wicker chair. On the table was her red leather handbag, alive with its soft creases, just as she had tossed it down. There was the inevitable, untidy gray sprinkle of last night's ashes in the grate.

The mirror hung above the polished chest of drawers between two tall, crimson candles. Margot saw her face stained with a rose-red flush and her throat white above the negligee of rose-colored silk. Her short hair was strewn in locks, glossy, damp and black. At last she had that miraculously "right" haircut, of which every woman dreamed. The glossy

397

wave, shaped like the chiseled hair in sculpture, fell low across her forehead, but left the tips of her ears chastely exposed and glowing now with a faint rose-red. It gave just the touch of personal distinction to her features, and her great dark eyes, and the fine bold outline of the back of her head. The liquid powder she had learned how to use, when for three months she had done publicity for that awful French singer, whitened the brunette darkness of her skin. The rouge was laid on like the pressure of two rose petals. The painted mouth was a deeper rose. In the white face between the glossy black of the hair and the rose of the silken gown, the lashes of the two great eyes were like the upturned petals of some gorgeous flower. All the angles of her body had subtly filled with smooth white flesh; and her arms, when she lifted them up from the loose rosy sleeves, were small and white and round—like the woman's arms in that poem in the *Oxford Book,* that Daggie had once read to her, smiling.

> "When her loose gown did from her shoulders fall,
> And she me caught in her arms long and small."

(But she hadn't caught him in her arms—dear, dear little Daggie!—whom she would love, no matter what Bruce said.) Yes, at this very moment, she was on the thrilling, exquisite edge of becoming the very sort of person she had always meant to be—and she liked her name, her hair was exactly right at last, she had experience instead of ignorance behind her, and there was a man—a married man!—in her life. It had taken her all these years to struggle up fiercely from diffidence and innocence and provincialism. Now—when she was over thirty—she was coming into her blooming.

> "There came a day entirely for me."

She drew the rose-colored gown closely about her, and then opened it in a soft, flushed effulgence of revealment.

All around her in the warm air of the sweetly crowded room there breathed a kind of sumptuousness of excitement, happiness, rich expectation, that was like the final ineffability of fragrance hovering over flowers.

Bruce sat in the armchair smoking while Margot put on her wraps.

"It's getting cold as the devil outside," he warned her. "What kind of shoes have you got on?"

With a sensuous delight in obedience, Margot thrust out her foot, that felt beautifully slender in its satin slipper.

"You'll freeze to death in those things, you silly kid. Haven't you got some overshoes around somewhere?"

"*Overshoes*. Galoshes! Don't make them sound worse than they are."

"Well, put 'em on, whatever you call 'em."

"You aren't planning to make me walk all the way to Carlo's, I hope?"

Margot shrugged her shoulders. Rubbers and even galoshes made her think of winters at home and being called back to the house protesting. But when Bruce told her to wear such things, she felt again that subtle, sensuous pleasure—that female pleasure in obeying, when she knew, *half* knew, that she could rule. She brought out the galoshes with exaggerated meekness and sat dreamily still while Bruce's large white fingers were fastening the clasps.

Bruce said, "Let's see you." He put his hand on her shoulder and turned her toward him. "What's different about you? Have I ever seen this dress?"

"About a million times!"

He frowned, and Margot laughed tantalizingly. She knew what the difference was that Bruce, in his large masculine obtuseness, could not name. But there was a breathlessness in her laughter. For mingled with the blooming of her power, she had a feeling of shyness, almost of flight—just what maidens were supposed to feel. She! After the "experiences" that now lay satisfyingly thick behind her. She had felt it, with a delicious surprise, when she had heard Bruce's footsteps on the painted stairs.

Bruce flipped the book on the table.

"Let's see how you're getting along with Pearson. Eighth page! Is *that* the extent of your progress?"

Margot lightly shrugged her shoulders, realizing obscurely

399

that his sardonic tone was partly a tribute to her—he wanted to pick some flaw, assert his masculine superiority, because he felt that she had power tonight.

"I'll get it read sooner or later—when I have time."

"Hmp!"

"I know what you're going to say! I'm 'subjective,' and just interested in what has a 'personal application,' and what 'titillates the senses'—"

She did a little dance step in front of Bruce before she took the book away from him. He couldn't hurt her by criticizing her tonight. It gave her pleasure, since she thought she could discern in it a defense that he was putting up. And anyway, it was a delicately perverse delight to feel that she had power to fascinate him while he disapproved of her. Or thought he did! Because men didn't know what they really felt—they always thought they felt according to their theories.

"I don't want to talk about science while I'm starving. I don't even want to talk about myself."

"It's the first time, then!"

Margot danced softly while he tried to button her heavy coat. Bruce put his hands down firmly on her shoulders and made her stand still. But she looked away sidewise, with a secret delight, thinking how all these poems and novels and biographies and memoirs that Bruce derided had their own purpose for her, all helping to make the very thing that troubled him tonight. She felt as if all her books were like a great bouquet of chosen flowers surrounding her with their fragrance; and she smiled, lightly scorning Bruce's "science" that didn't dare believe anything was said unless it was said in black and white.

"Here—come on, you young Pavlowa. Get some of that food you're starving for, and then you won't feel so airy."

Margot ran downstairs ahead of Bruce, drawing on her gloves as she went. Bruce was always very solemn and discreet, except when they were in her own apartment—probably trying to create the impression that his interest was equally divided between Frances and Margot. But at least he didn't prudently suggest, any more, that they ask Frances when they went out together! The people who owned the house, a youngish couple named Allison, he an editor of some sort and she an interior decorator, lived on the first floor. When Bruce chanced to meet either of them, he quite unnecessarily froze into his character of heavily respectable business man. "Trying to look like an uncle!" Margot thought in rebellious scorn. But there was no one in the hall tonight; and Frances was working overtime and hadn't come home.

"Where are we going?"

"Why, to Carlo's, aren't we?"

"That where you want to go?"

Margot felt almost foolishly hurt. Bruce knew it was their own special place, where they could feel hidden and alone; and he oughtn't even to suggest going anywhere else when she felt so happy. But he was so fearful of making the slightest admission that there was any understanding between them! As they stood on the cold street corner, Margot's power seemed to drop away from her, and she felt shivering and alone. Bruce's heavy figure in the expensive overcoat was like a monument of all the settled solidities that menaced everything she cared for. He looked like a family man.

"Oh, of course we'll go somewhere else if you'd rather!"

Bruce smiled at the pride in her tone. "We'll go where the little girl pleases."

"I don't please any more than you do."

"Well, I please, then."

But she had to like him again for the curt, masculine gesture with which he signaled a carefully slowing taxi, and for the sound of his voice giving Carlo's address. She tried to gather to her for protection all that she disliked: his blindness, obtuseness, terrible bulky stubbornness, the tone of amusement he used toward her friends,—as if his country club friends from whom he was running away were better!—the rubber-stamp words he used like "radicals," his insistence that the only good stories were in the *Saturday Evening Post,* and that he only read Conrad because it was "adventure stuff" . . . and yet all the while she was feeling the fine, perverse—yes, "ultra"—delight in forcing this very kind of man to admit her fascination. She was somehow incomplete with any other.

401

But the joy with which Carlo greeted them—greeted them *together*, as a couple: "Oh, Mees Ferguson, Meester Weeliams, come in, good evening!"—seemed to renew their intimacy magically.

"There's our table all ready!" Margot cried joyously.

She sat down in her own special chair close to the warmth of the big stove where she loved to see the red cinders as they fell into the tray. Carlo's was their secret place. No one they had ever heard of came here. Margot felt a childlike, blissful contentment.

"I think maybe Mees Ferguson and Meester Weeliams come tonight!"

"Why?" Margot asked eagerly.

"Oh, I do' know why, I look for them all day."

She laughed out joyously. Bruce went to hang up their coats with the serious care he bestowed on all material things of good quality, horrified at Margot's habit of hanging things jauntily askew. He wouldn't believe her when she told him that once she had been even more pernickety than he. None of the family could do anything to suit her. Now, to cure herself of impossible fastidiousness, she had run to the opposite extreme. But then, Bruce demanded that things must *have* quality. In his eyes—gray, shrewdly appraising, with a surface of regulation business man's look—there was something baffled, hurt and defensive, obscurely misled, and unlit.

Margot leaned her elbows luxuriously on the table. There was no one else here except a dark, silent Italian gobbling spaghetti at a corner table. She loved Carlo's funny Italian ornaments on the mantel—a toy lamb, a little wineglass, and valentinish things made out of red and green tissue paper. She *adored* his old-fashioned gramophone, with its far-away sound, as if the music were coming from the just perceptibly out-of-date era of fifteen or twenty years ago—funny and touching, and sentimentally melancholy, like an old summer hat with its faded gaiety of flowers suddenly unearthed from a bent pasteboard box on a top closet shelf.

"Play my waltz thing," she begged Bruce.

He smiled at her with his expression of indulgence—the nice

402

expression, not the false one that tried to belittle her. This was the way that she liked Bruce to be, just the way he was now. She loved the feeling that against the background of his strength and large indulgence she could play airily with even her whims in a willful refinement of her individuality.

"You're a funny girl."

Feeling the smiling fondness of his tone, she could sit back for a moment secretly with her enjoyment. The faded melody seemed to put her back into the undefinable time when Carlo's rooms had been the parlor and back parlor of a distinguished mansion. Now the ornate carving of the ceiling was broken and the marble fireplaces were closed. Margot liked to think herself sensuously back into the times of those old scenes in magazine illustrations she used to pore over on rainy days in the back room in the library where they kept the bound volumes of *Harper's*. One of those scenes where there was always a sort of small, insignificant man with a curly moustache, overshadowed by the great bare shoulders and rounded hips and satiny train of a Gibson Girl. At the side stood a potted palm, just partly drawn into the picture. Any scene of the past was always romantic to Margot. And here was she, Margaret Ferguson become Margot, actually *in* such a room . . . but in her scant black crêpe de chine post-war modern dress, her little pulled-down black hat, with a dangle of earrings beneath it—and she was here with a man who was handsomer than any storybook hero, and she was beginning to live out her own thrilling, half-known, half-unknown drama . . .

Bruce was asking, "What can you give us tonight, Carlo?"

Carlo, happy in the stiff, torn white jacket he had run into his kitchen to put on,—Margot adored his punctiliousness, here in this faded room—was eagerly repeating:

"I have scalopini, I have broil' chicken . . ."

"I believe we'll have the scalopini. Does that suit you, Margot?"

"And cheese!" Margot put in eagerly. "My kind!"

"All right, then, Carlo, the scalopini, and a bottle of the red, and bring the girl her kind of cheese."

Margot sat back with a contented murmur. Carlo went off

smiling. The faint music of the waltz had trailed into dying discords.

"Do you want it on again, Margot?"

She shook her head decisively.

Bruce laughed at her. "Little 'my, my, my,'" he said. He shook her slightly. "Always knows what's 'mine,' doesn't she?"

"Well, I have to! Nobody else does."

"Nobody else does, hm? Don't you think I have a little glimmering by this time?" She shook her head. "You don't? I only wish I knew my own as well!" He got up, and touched her hair. "I'm going out to discuss the subject of the wine more at length. Can you amuse yourself while I'm gone?"

"Of course not!"

She wouldn't admit that Bruce, that *any*-one, really knew a thing about her. But it was only with Bruce that she had this feeling of sumptuous excess. It was his bigness, the kind of clothes he wore, his presents, his flowers, the way he scolded her, and looked after her, the little extra delicacies of food and wine. She seemed always to be moving in velvet surrounded warmly by his care. Bruce was the only one who could give her the right to be the princess of her own fairy tale.

Margot rested her chin upon her hands and waited. The dark Italian slithered up the rest of his spaghetti and left. Even though Bruce was in the other room, she felt close to him. She could sense that his first resolve to stand out against the fascination she had for him—pretending it was all amused friendship on his part—was melting into that complete indulgence in which they were most in harmony with each other. This strange, thrilling, discordant harmony! Her time was coming. The day "entirely for her," that she must have before she was willing to die. That was what she had realized, with that feeling of delicious flight, when she had heard Bruce's feet coming up the stairs.

"All right. Got it fixed."

A shock of tenderness went through her at the familiar, mannish satisfaction of the tone, mingled with a kind of underlying heaviness of responsibility long borne. She knew what it was that Bruce had really missed and wanted, although he couldn't name it or even perceive it. He had confessed to her once, as they sat before the fire, fulfilling her old vision of the man and the woman in the two low chairs—with bashful difficulty, almost like a schoolboy—that she "stood for something he had missed." She wanted passionately to fill the blind emptiness in his life. She had never felt like this toward anyone before— not as if she wanted to *give* things. It was as if her little glazed sheath of self-absorption had suddenly cracked, letting in a kind of light she had never known existed.

Carlo came in, consciously and decorously reticent, but triumphant, with the hot dishes.

"Oh, our beautiful food!" Margot cried ecstatically.

Bruce looked at her, smiling at her eager voice. The lines of bleak dissatisfaction seemed to have faded from about his mouth. Warmth had suffused the assured, hard gray of his eyes, under which lay that lost, dark bafflement. He had to admit *her,* as she had admitted him—not just smile indulgently at her highly personal tastes, really *admit* them.

"Wait!" Carlo cried in delight.

And in a moment, he came running back from the kitchen with three of his dear, funny, squat little glasses, into which he poured the rich red port, with its hidden sparkle.

"We mus'n' have jus' common glasses. Mees Ferguson she look so pretty tonight!"

Bruce flushed. "That's right," he said heavily. "Join me, Carlo. We'll have to drink to Miss Ferguson."

"Thank you, Meester Weeliams! Tha's nice."

They both raised their glasses. Bruce touched Carlo's almost solemnly. Margot's face slowly grew hot up to the sculptured black wave of hair. She wanted to say something; but she sat mute, helpless, open, in a shyness that made her eyes burn through a mist of tears. Carlo seemed to know with them that there was something significant about the little ceremony, and to be giving them his blessing.

The flush slowly died. Carlo had left the room again. There didn't seem to be any way to keep him. They heard the homely sound of the embers falling down into the tray of the stove.

Bruce put his hand over hers. Margot sat looking down at the large white hand with its plain gold ring. Who had given that to him? His wife? Margot had always disdainfully and airily skirted the thought of Bruce's wife. But all at once she hated the woman with a blinding hatred. Bruce never mentioned her directly. Only once or twice, as if inadvertently, he had referred to his family—and once at the first, conscientiously, to let Margot know that they existed. But Margot was scornfully sure that she could imagine what the woman was like!—one of the kind who had always been her enemies. Louise, Mildred, yes, clear back to Eve—the fair, smooth, sly, complacent, deft "womanly" women, who were nothing on their own, made out of a rib of man, or pretending that they were so made to keep the man happily conceited. Even mother was one of them. Even Dorothy. Nearly every woman in Belmond! When all that they were after was to line the nest for themselves, and, by lining it so softly, to blind their mates to the wild, rapturous freedom outside. And the man plugged away, and read travel and adventure stories. But this was *her* day. She was the dark other one. Hers was the secret of the "ultra." And she felt fiercely exultant because her hand beneath Bruce's, narrow and satiny white, lay significantly ringless.

Bruce drew away his hand and pretended to be absorbed in his dinner. But from the slight rigidity of his shoulders, the way he looked away and cleared his throat, Margot could tell that he, too, realized that their "friendship" had imperceptibly, involuntarily reached another stage. Impatient as she had been at Bruce's prudence and his ostrich blindness, a kind of painful, suffering reluctance that she discerned in him, and closed her mind against—yet Margot herself relished the slowness, almost sumptuous slowness, with which this relationship had passed inevitably into phase after phase, leaving the last one behind in an epoch utterly past. She wanted to dwell in each stage by itself, experiencing its final essence, knowing that when it was gone it was irrevocable. It seemed that she had known beforehand—from the day of her birth, almost—every stage as she reached it. And yet each one was utterly new when it came, with the blinding shock of a revelation.

But now the time had arrived when both of them must see

and acknowledge where they were moving. Carlo's quaint little compliment had torn away the veil. Why should she care about that woman in the background, any more than the woman would care for *her?* The Eves had all the soft places. Everybody was on their side.

But she couldn't make a single move toward Bruce. She felt amazed, terrified at her helplessness. Not even to grasp what she fiercely felt belonged to her! It was as if she had to sit just trembling and waiting—because this was what she had been waiting for all her life. For this she had broken ruthlessly through her old bonds of fastidiousness and fear, so that she could be free whenever it came, ready for it, equal to whatever it demanded. She had lost the bold, wild aggressiveness with which she had torn Lee away from Louise. That wouldn't count now. She couldn't make a single move. Because this was the test! All the womanhood that she had acquired would go for nothing unless he proved to her that it was nothing she did, but herself, that was desired.

Bruce was looking at her, and Margot looked back at him with her eyes open in a suffering, dark, exquisite humility. He could take her or leave her. That was the truth. Nothing counted if she had to take *him.*

"It's a pretty funny thing, isn't it, that a man can go along for forty years not knowing that he wants something? He must be pretty much of a dub, don't you think?"

"Maybe it's an acquired taste!" Margot said bitterly, falling quickly into her old self-distrust.

"Anyway, I'm getting to see it's something it would be damned hard to get along without. What am I going to do about it?"

Margot would not answer.

Bruce asked her suddenly, "Where did you get those great dark eyes?"

It was a silly question. It sounded like Red Riding-hood. It was what she had heard in her childhood until she was sick of the words. "Where did that child get those eyes?" But then it had always seemed to be in a tone of reproach, marking her off from the rest of them. When Bruce said it, he marked her off

407

too—but as someone special, unique, chosen. She had been waiting all her life to hear this said to her in just this way. It blotted out the other voices with a miraculous comfort—as if Bruce had known. It was too perfect to be true. But it *was* true. It was something she could never lack again.

A strange, almost mystical sense of enlargement came over her, in another of those blinding sweeps of revelation. It seemed as if she knew herself, and, through herself, something more. It wasn't just Margot Ferguson whom Bruce was choosing— but all that she stood for, the one precious thing that had gone so long neglected, useless and yet absolutely necessary above a dead level of existence . . . the enhancement, the "ultra" . . . finally given its right to be, through her, if Bruce, with his solid masculine authority, could see and choose it.

"Margot. You haven't answered my question."

She struggled blindly to say something.

"I can't now."

Because she felt wildly that this time it must be perfect, not flawed and broken. Perfect, if it lasted for only an hour! This was part of her own story, in which every event must be true and real, and follow out her dream. It had to be as much to Bruce as to her. She knew the creed of all her friends—to snatch at happiness wherever it offered, and not think beyond: there was little enough of it in this world. But this time—the great time—must be all beautiful. Her after-life would have to feed upon it. Whatever was wrong and unbeautiful could never be made up for. It would hurt her forever. This wasn't just a "Village affair."

Some more embers dropped into the tray. Taxis passed in the street, below the windows, and an old street car went bumping and banging down there, the trolley scraping out a momentary fire.

"When are you going to answer it?"

"Some time."

Margot got up. She wasn't conscious of planning any action. There was something outside herself that did it for her. Maybe astrologists were right, and her guiding star was in power.

408

She wandered about in a soft restlessness while Bruce paid
the bill. She stood a moment at the long window. Beyond the
empty streets, and the narrow edge of the island, the whole
Atlantic lay. In the wideness of the night, she was conscious
again of that mystic enlargement. She felt her part in the universe. Her own line in history and tradition. All the powers
were in league with her, everything she wanted was coming to
her. But this time it must go slowly, like music—not hasty,
broken, snatched, and jangled!—until it reached its perfect
consummation. She went over and petted the toy lamb, feeling
childishly that it was allied with her, in her feminine world,
against all the ways of men.

"You like your supper, Meester Weeliams?"

"Everything was fine, Carlo!"

"You like it, Mees Ferguson?"

"It was the best I ever tasted."

Carlo opened the door for them, with a beneficent flourish
of courtesy.

"Good night, Mees Ferguson, Meester Weeliams, come
again!"

2

As she undressed, sitting on her day-bed, Margot let herself
have one quick glance out of the window and down at the
little back garden. It belonged to the people downstairs. It was
nothing but a square of earth not quite covered with thin-
rooted, yellow-green city grass. At home, the folks wouldn't
have called it a garden.

But the jonquils were enough. When she saw the flutter of
petals on the long single stems, pale green and tender in the
strip of damp black at the foot of the high board wall (where
a neighborhood of cats promenaded) she could feel the spring
hovering around them, wild and secret and sweet. Windows
were open in the brick houses of varying heights that faced
each other across this pleasant side street. It gave a mingled
feeling of intimacy and variety to see the warm flutter of all
the curtains—white, rosy net, bright cretonne, and some long
draperies of golden silk that blew softly out and then clung

for a moment, like butterflies, to the snowy window sills in the third story of that tall brick house. The curtains meant that all the different, unknown people were having *their* experience of spring. Margot felt that she loved New York until she wanted to leap and run and break into shouts and singing! She loved to sit on the swaying top of the green bus that lumbered down the Avenue in the early twilight toward the arch standing small, but with a hardy dignity, among the budding trees. That was when she reëxperienced the triumphant feeling she could never get over . . . I'm in *New York!* She loved the blue-gray twilights when the buildings near Central Park had the quality of old-fashioned paintings of the Whistler period, that made her think of pretty ladies in victorias, with gleaming eyes behind tiny veils, breathing the perfume of the violets that brought memories of their lovers. She loved the fragrance —the sudden whiff of heliotrope—that came from the massed bunches of yellow and white and lavender flowers for sale on the warm street corners; and to hear, on an idle Saturday afternoon, sitting on her day-bed with books of poetry scattered luxuriously around her, flicking ashes into the beloved little dish of flowered red pottery Grimmie's friend Jonsen had brought her from Mexico, and knowing that she was going out to dinner with her beloved—to hear the long-drawn-out cry of the bearded old man hunched over on the seat of his small wagon crammed with pots of pansies delicate and living in their damp earth, the wagon slowly passing down the street, the wheels creaking, the old horse stopping . . .

The folks pitied her, no doubt, for being shut up in New York! But Margot had become a city child. It was more exciting, not to see, but to feel all the bloom that was centered in one row of jonquils; the relaxed warmth of the evenings when she and Bruce walked back from Carlo's, stopping at the window of the little antique shop, and Bruce carried her jacket over his arm.

"Pastures that call from a leaf."

Because intimations were all that she could stand! And even now, she could scarcely endure the delight that she was always pressing, pressing down, in her heart . . . she would have to run out shouting—or do *some*-thing. . . . She buried her head in her black satin cushion.

But now the first beautiful time was over, almost over—the time when it seemed that her love was more precious to her for the quickening sense it brought to every tiny thing she did: putting away her clothes clean and crisp from the laundry, eating in her French restaurant at noon—even more precious than being with Bruce himself. That had suddenly become perilous. Such bliss poured through her when he even touched her hand that it left her nerveless and shattered. She was afraid. They were both afraid. Because they must wait until they were alone, just she and her lover together, in a time stolen out from ordinary existence to be their secret treasure forever. She had put off a little glaze of sophistication to learn this new thing step by step, exactly as it happened. Now, with her eyes closed tight and the cushion pressed against her ears, she could go back into it from the very beginning. The rainy day in Marta's tearoom, with the foghorns weaving their muted music, like the prelude to a great event. The dinner at Carlo's when he had greeted them together, knowing that they would come, and they had kissed, and she had had the courage to send Bruce home. The blank, awful hours when she jumped into a taxi and rode and rode because she couldn't stand it to be anywhere without him. The night when Bruce had come solemnly to talk to her, and they had seen that they must make their mighty decision, like people in a play. Only the play was real.

"Margot, you know I'm married. I don't see how this thing is going to end."

"I don't *want* to be married. I want to be perfectly happy."

"And you think I can make you perfectly happy?"

He was the only person in the world who could. Well, he could take a little time off for that!—for the gift of everything that he had missed. It didn't matter where they went, only so it was away from here, nowhere they had ever been, a place that would belong to them alone. Then when it was over, it would be over.

Margot got up, breathing quickly.

411

It was time to take her bath. But first she must dance around her room, bare feet softly thudding on the painted floor, to experience the naked joy of her own body, the movements of her arms "long and small," the rosy flowering of her breasts. Alone for the last time. No sunshine in her cool back room. She felt herself cringe away from the imperfections of earlier experience. Now she understood why a bride should be virginal. But there were always forerunners. Even Juliet had had some dim predecessor with Romeo. That was the rôle of the others, in the secret continuity of her life story, whose destiny had been to shatter her fear and make her ripe for the season of true love for which at last she was fully ready.

There was a sense of queer reluctance in having the time come. She wanted to hold it back, to stay a little longer in this cool shadow, before she must step into the open light. She could never have this time again. When it had reached its fullness, it would be over. Again she had the old sense of something irrevocable—an undertone of her own low music that made tears from a secret, lonely depth come slowly to her eyes.

But this was her own time! The day "entirely for her."

With that knowledge, she seemed to enter again into that sense of mystic enlargement. She huddled down among the cushions. Her own body was small and white at the center of a spreading darkness that was fluttering and alive with intimations she could barely touch. It was as if suddenly she could see that everything in existence was bound together.

Yes, in books, in poetry, it was beginning to be *her* kind of heroine. This was her day! It was *her* kind of clothes that women were wearing; not the girly-girly things she used to storm at; but things that were rakish, dashing, brief and colorful, eyes mysterious and dark under the pulled-down softness of the little hat brim, earrings dangling. The clothes she had had to wear when she was a girl were just a disguise. These were her self-assertion. Now shocked elderly authors felt it incumbent to write about "the modern girl"—usually landing her back in the home, of course, well chastened, but sometimes actually permitting her to triumph at the end! It had seeped even into the movies. The Mary Pickford curls had given way to the sleek darkness of the "vamps" and the naughtiness of the flappers. Bringing it down, of course, to its lowest terms! The other day she had met Lucille. With her open middlewestern face, soft and featureless as a prairie landscape, her pretty-girl clothes, and the wrong kind of lipstick, Lucille was placed and dated. It was about time for her to give up her career and enter into the duties of wife and mother, looking back on the one romantic day when an actor had taken her to tea. It was the dark, vivid, naughty heroines of the Restoration who were in favor now with the intelligentsia. They were reviving Congreve in the Village little theaters. Poetry was doing homage to Lilith instead of Eve—*Eve,* whom Margot always pictured as an opulent nude, standing in a modest position, and looking up from under fair tresses with the sly, self-satisfied glint of Mildred Summers' eyes. Even that little Harvard professor, a friend of Grimmie's, had read a ponderous sonnet to Lilith.

> "When I look into the darkness of thine eyes,
> Where dwell those sparks of infinite dangerousness."

As if any real "dangerousness" wouldn't scare him to death! Katherine Griswold, pretending to seek an ash tray, had leaned over Margot to whisper, "Child, beware!" But then, it showed! Now the triteness of the old fairy tales was being reversed; and it was Rose Red who was coming out into the sunshine, and Snow White who was banished to the shady side of the story. Dorothy had had her time. She was married, and had babies, and was living in a bungalow in southern California. Rose Red could no longer be shunted off with the prince's brother . . . because she, Margot, had been given the personal crown of Bruce's true love.

Now it was she who was getting the roses. Bruce had sent them to her last night. They were the deep crimson ones, her own kind; not the pinky-white ones that Dorothy had carried at her wedding; but roses, and not the off-flowers that were lovely, but at the side. Now she could claim the rose, the center of bloom. She looked at the red glow of her roses in the midst of the deep green leaves. Exultance spread all through her from some exquisite center of joy. "These are for you." But

413

even in those words, a premonitory sadness came over her, beautiful and dark. The undertone to her happiness sounded its own low music—the knowledge, at the very height of the moment, of its briefness, and its irrevocability.

She went to take her bath. The drumming of bright hot water into the porcelain whiteness of the tub, the reckless scattering of crystals from which a powdery fragrance rose, the peeling of thin white paper from the smooth cake of Red Rose soap—all these made up the sumptuous beauty of a feminine ritual. Care of her body was a secret religion. All this spring, buying clothes with a magnificent extravagance, Margot had told herself, "It's now!" And afterwards—who knew, who cared? Everything—she thought, as she splashed the sudsy water—everything contributed to make this her springtime. She could see something symbolic even in the weather. First, the cold; but even then, with a wild sweetness in the air. The dark March, when rain dashed against the windows, and she and Bruce sat together in front of her fire. Those days were like the first fragmentary, stormy intimations of love. The clouds were darkened and then white above tall buildings, suddenly breaking in the wind to show a cold blue April sky. And now the wonder, the warm amazement, of a May all soft and ineffable, coming with the marvelous blessing of fulfillment after the spring storms!

Margot dashed back into her room. She was warm and glowing. With the same high sense of secret ritual, she began to put on her new clothes. She must have everything new to correspond with her new existence. The silk stockings were still creased and shimmery. The little bodice and knickers of crêpe de chine clothed her in silken softness.

Everything was contributing! It was as if she stood at the center and all things converged by some natural law. Other people felt it. Men looked with blank eyes at the vacant seat in the bus and sat down by her. The old man at the corner paid her gallant compliments when she bought the morning paper. She no longer had to endure shrewd, deflating looks from salesgirls. They brought out their nicest things as if she wouldn't deign to consider any others. Even that stiff at the office began

414

to show signs of interest! Suddenly all her old friendships opened new intimacies. People whom she hadn't seen for months began to seek her out again. She and Grimmie had talked until two, sitting on the floor in front of Grimmie's fire, with sherry gleaming in the little cut-glass tumblers; and Margot had let herself go in the luxury of telling Grimmie all about herself and Bruce. Grimmie had begged her solemnly not to let this pass without fulfillment. "No matter what's in the way. Don't you let go of it. Margot. It will never come again." She saw Grimmie's face with its fuzz of graying hair, the profile that was like a kind Indian's, with a queer, mad touch of nobility; and she felt how other life histories were woven about her own in her secret, picaresque record. Years ago, Grimmie, too, had been in love with a married man. But they had parted with a single kiss. It was as if the imprint of that kiss could still be traced on Grimmie's lips, full and dark and faded, marking her out for renunciations and throwing her into vicarious generosities. The man had stayed in the Missouri town, getting fat outside and hollow inside, like all people who let the perilous, real thing go. Margot felt, with the deepened poignancy that even the slightest things awakened in her now, the sense of underlying kinship with women. Not with the smooth, safe, complacent ones, who worked underneath for security!—but with the others. "You and Bruce take your holiday. Don't pay any attention to what may happen afterwards. Everything has an afterwards." It was true that love was fatal, no matter how silly that might sound in all the little verses that repeated the same thing over and over; thousands of little voices murmuring words that someone was always finding to be true. It seemed to Margot that what had come to her was something she had always foreseen, although it was so utterly surprising in its actuality; and the unreal, shattered remnants of the old existence she had lived through just because she couldn't help it, were being cast behind her forever. Now that she had entered upon her own story!

She heard Frances' discreet little knock.

"Margot! May I come in?"

"Oh! I supposed you were at the office."

415

"I skipped out. I wanted to say good-bye."

"Oh, Frannie! You darling."

Frances came on into the room. She had on her little dark blue silk dress, and her face had its office sallowness, dramatizing the radiance of Margot. Frances conceded that generously.

"You're all ready! Where did you get the beautiful bag?"

"Grimmie's. She let me take it. No, not what you think!"

Frances sat down on the day-bed while Margot put on her tan felt hat at the mirror between the two red candles in the silver sticks. Margot hadn't told Frances much about the journey. But of course Frances knew that she was going somewhere with Bruce.

"You look grand in your new suit!"

"Do you like it?"

Margot turned around from the glass. Frances came up to her. She said in a softened, moved tone: "You look beautiful. I hope you'll be happy, darling." And kissed her.

Tears sprang into Margot's eyes. And as she looked at Frances' small face pale between the bands of smooth brown hair, she felt again that deep sense of kinship. Frances, Marta, Jane, Lenore . . . All women in the world wanted to be made happy once. Then they could afford to die.

"I want you to take these roses!"

"Oh, *no*, Margot!"

"Yes, I do. I can't take them with me."

"Goodness!" Frances tried to laugh. "I'll be buried in splendor."

She stood pale and small with her arms around the great bouquet. Margot saw her little face looking down from the head of the painted staircase. The door of Margot's own room was closed. She didn't know when she would open it again. She was leaving everything—the red-and-gold Chinese tea set, the fireplace, the rose-red chair, the books in the low white shelves, the poetry that she had been reading all over again, seeking affirmation now instead of the old hungry knowledge. But she was going away from other people's stories. In her bag, beneath the pale silk nightgown, lay the only book that she wanted to take—the little red notebook in which, on beautifully smooth

416

new pages, she would inscribe every flutter of ecstasy so that nothing, nothing, of this time could ever be lost.

She felt that she was opening the green door into her fairy tale.

It was warm and sunny in the street. One of the golden curtains hung over the window sill of the tall brick house. The roar came loud from over on Sixth Avenue. Now it seemed to Margot that all this part of the huge, thrilling city was secretly packed with her own memories—every little news stand and tearoom and shop on the narrow streets. But she was going away to some enchanted place that had never really existed before and would never really exist afterwards.

"Margot! Catch!"

One big red rose plumped down at her feet. She bent to pick it up, to wave at Frances—

"Here, taxi!"

In the taxi, with its smell of leather and stale tobacco, its scrunched-up, empty cigarette package on the floor, she had all at once a small, ordinary, empty calm.

"Where to, miss?"

"The Grand Central."

Again she crossed the interminable width of floor, with the great slants of cathedral light pouring down from the hugeness above her—she, Margaret Ferguson, who had come here such a few years ago, in that old tan coat and hateful hat she had bought at home, to enter upon her destiny.

3

They stopped at a filling station, and Bruce got out to ask about the roads.

"Better get out too. Not good for you to sit too long."

He helped Margot out of the car, and they stood for a moment in exquisite unity. It seemed impossible to part for even this tiny while.

"Be good while I'm gone," Bruce whispered.

He went into the office of the filling station, and Margot wandered off in the clear, dry sunshine.

417

But she would never again be really alone. She was doing as Bruce had told her, keeping the memory of his touch. There were some nameless white flowers growing in the rough soil. As Margot bent down to touch them, the old sensation of existing within herself came over her like the shadow of a memory. But yesterday stood forever between her and the old narrow groove of personal intensity. In the miracle of perfect union, the enclosing sheath of individuality had been finally dissolved. She was reborn into a region of pure happiness in which she seemed to move with a divine unconsciousness.

This was the region she had always known that she would find. But now that she had actually entered it, every feature of the sunlit landscape held the shock of a magic newness. Every step of the way, long traced in a dream, was a divine discovery. She had known what it was to be perfectly happy. She had had the day that was entirely her own. But instead of making her ready to die, as Margot had always supposed in a dazzled way, it had opened up further whole regions of discovery—like this cloudless sky above the plains, which, as she looked, went into depths on depths of blue.

But now she felt too happy. She wanted to seek some shelter. Besides, she was too far away from Bruce.

The car stood in the dazzling sunshine. Now it seemed years and years ago that Margot had first seen it standing—stiff, embarrassing and new—beside the platform of the suburban station where she and Bruce had agreed to meet, on that first awful day when they had started out afraid to be with each other, cold and stage-struck at the beginning of their venture, feeling as if they were asking too much of an uncomprehending and grudging world. Margot got into the car and slammed the door after her. The sound had an intimacy so deep that it filled her with unbelievable contentment, shutting her in with memories that were all alive within the small, warm silence. Yesterday. Now it had become "yesterday." But it had been. And she still possessed it. She could see the rushing, cold stream where they had bathed, the space under the pine trees where they had lain together. The brown butterfly still hovered above the red mountain flower. Margot moved restlessly on the warm, velvet seat, feeling the difficulties before her if she was to keep her memory of perfection forever secure and undiminished.

A strapping young fellow in coveralls came toward the car, with his blond hair glinting rough in the sun. He hesitated, and grinned.

"Oh, you folks are together!"

He nodded toward the oil station. His grin, with the flash of white teeth in the tanned, grease-smudged face, had an easy, friendly understanding and acceptance. Margot saw Bruce's firm, large figure, as he leaned with one elbow on the counter having an earnest masculine confabulation with the oil station man over a spread-out map; and the pride of their being together was almost more than she could endure.

The young fellow thumped a tire. He was sticking around because he admired her. But admiration came easy now that she no longer needed it.

"Not had this car very long, have you?"

Margot smiled and shook her head. In her brown tweed suit and light felt hat, and the scuffed, comfortable, easy grace of her laced Prince of Wales shoes, she had a flattering consciousness of herself as an impressively urban figure out here in the anonymous countryside.

"I saw it was a new car. It sure is a good-looking model. Going to give you a lot of service too." He nodded, and tapped the hood in appreciation. "New York! Looks like you folks are a good ways from home! Going out to the coast?"

"Just driving."

"Sure! Well, that's the way to do it."

He grinned at her again, and went off.

Margot could see the gestures of the two men inside the building. Their movements had a pleasant, earthy slowness behind the sunny glare of the large front window. With a subtle smile of feminine contentment, Margot sat back to wait and let them settle the question of the roads between themselves. Now, with her head resting against the soft upholstery, and her bare hands folded, she could feel the sense of anonymous country leisure widening around her in the sunshine. "A good ways from home," the young fellow had said. New York

419

seemed more incredibly far away to Margot than it must seem to him. Only that speeding stream of noisily high-pitched cars on the highway connected this little wayside jumping-off place with any memory of the city; and even the cars were more widely spaced than they had been. She thought of New York standing incredibly on its island, like some separate walled city, tall and feudal and feverishly modern, existing in and for itself, a crazy pattern of streets and buildings and rushing people caught in the thundering network of trains above and below. The life was a fevered, half-mad, half-splendid dream. Existing within the dream, on its own terms of terrible immediacy, people had to believe in it to the exclusion of all other existence. Get outside—and it was incredible! Margot felt the slow, beginning sweetness of a kind of reconciliation to the land. The rough dry ground smelled good. A tuneless music thrilled along the telephone wires. Now it seemed that a great space, that was more than just miles of country, lay between her and all the life she had known up until now.

She looked at Bruce, standing big, easy and absorbed, with one arm resting on the counter. She felt all over again the wonder of the richness with which his love had endowed her, adding to her what he was, filling out the empty places of her own being. All that had been rudimentary and fragmentary in her experience was miraculously fulfilled . . . even her silly old notions about Dr. Redmond at home, about having an affair with a married man . . . the need for someone big and competent in a worldly way that perhaps she had got from her old admiration of Frank and Sybil, and her dissatisfaction with the folks . . . the desire for the shock and delight of what was different from herself that had first been aroused when she had seen Jesse and Dorothy exchanging their bridal kiss. . . . At this moment Margot's life seemed to her an illuminated landscape in which all the lines were in perfect focus.

Bruce reached out and put his forefinger on a spot on the map. There was something personal in that little gesture— something that she recognized as *Bruce*—something dominating, accurate, but slow. Margot felt a sense of hot possession. It frightened her, threatening her ideal conception of love, which dictated that it must end when it was over. Her fear seemed suddenly to strike her with a distant, vicious hatred of the shadowy figure of the wife, who must have seen that very movement, who knew the brief, accurately judging squint with which Bruce "sized up" a hill before they came to it, the way in which he accomplished everything with that satisfyingly competent minimum of movement. She wanted to blast the woman into forgetfulness—to scorn her out of existence! With a piercing overflow of jealousy, Margot seized Bruce's heavy driving glove, that he had thrust into a pocket of the up-holstery, and pressed it up against her face.

But an hour of yesterday was something that only she herself and Bruce would ever know. Margot felt that it had annulled everything that went before it. The men whom she had known before she knew Bruce seemed to have been washed out of existence. Life had all been pitched into the present. It was now. It was this moment, sunny and still, in the great slow drift of time, and she was living in it.

Bruce came out still looking thoughtfully at the map. He spread it open against the wheel. Margot fidgeted in her seat. She felt a qualm of the minutely vigilant fear which still had to keep its strained hold beneath the surface of her happiness. She sat scarcely breathing. If they had already had the best of their love, and Bruce was beginning to forget about her, then it had to be, and to try to do anything would be only a violation. Bruce's right hand slipped down from the wheel and groped softly and blindly for hers. She felt the even clasp. Everything swung into focus again, the sky was brilliant, and now to sit here while Bruce made out the way was only a delicious waiting.

Margot felt the rapturous triumph of her power, of having torn Bruce out of his fixed orbit and brought him over to her side, making him admit and care for her own kind of things— the out-of-the-way things, and out-of-the-way places, that had always been discredited. Through his love for her, she had triumphed finally over Eve immemorial—as somehow she had always felt that it was in her destiny to do. The magic balm had soothed and satisfied all the ancient wounds in her vanity. Bruce was the kind of man who, until now, had always belonged

421

to the enemy. But it was more than satisfied vanity. It was lifted far, far beyond that—so far, that she could only realize, with a distant wonder, that the old cuts no longer hurt. Margot bent swiftly down to Bruce's hand and kissed it.

Then she settled happily into her place. She heard the familiar, exciting, mounting sound of the engine. The youth in coveralls, who was tinkering with a car, grinned and lifted his hand in a farewell salute. Margot waved back at him. As they drove away from the filling station, it seemed to her that she and Bruce were two free beings who had got outside all the small involvements of ordinary local existence.

"Want to drive?"

Margot shook her head. With Carl at home, she used to have tremendous battles over the car, treating all his directions with the highest scorn. But with Bruce she felt a soft, pampered and pampering feminine luxury in sitting back and letting him have the wheel. It seemed to her now as if any action of her own, anything that she did simply on her own account, would rouse up the separate individual being that was now submerged in love. Being in love was an element as far beyond control as the May weather. They were both lost in this element, and actions of their own could only distort the miraculous truth and rightness of love's unfoldment. Everything must be accepted as it came—even the moments when Margot felt herself drop into sudden bleak torture at the perception that she and Bruce were awry . . . when his way annulled her way, so that she lost her bearings, lost her being . . . when the shimmering texture of happiness was endangered. Now if an ending was in their minds, they kept it cannily hidden from themselves and each other, closing their minds to a decision that loomed somewhere ahead of them, far beyond this limitless sunshine.

Bruce was sitting in the lobby. The moment Margot stepped out of the elevator, he dropped his paper and went over to her. She saw at a single glance, with an exquisite relief and triumph, that he had been sitting and watching the elevator. His face broke into a smile that was a confession, as he stepped quickly forward and touched Margot's arm.

"Have a good sleep? I didn't either."

He grinned down at her. They could not kiss before these people. But this mute acknowledgment of their need for each other, with hands just touching, was better than a kiss. For a moment, as they stood together before going toward the dining room, they felt the marvel of being reunited. The morning became instantly radiant. Last night, lying for the first time alone, it had seemed to Margot, taut with the strain of that vigilant watchfulness, that perhaps the best was gone, and that she must speak quickly if she was to be the one to say when the parting was to be. But this morning they were happier than ever to be together. Reunion was another miraculous discovery. And only now that she had escaped it, could Margot really see into what a black pit she had been staring. But the danger was already incredible and forgotten.

"Well, we'll make it up on breakfast," Bruce said.

They went into the dining room. The head waiter instantly withdrew his hand from the chair of the table at which he had stopped, when he saw Bruce's slight frown, and led them toward the window. Several women sitting together were looking at them with impressed curiosity, and Margot had the delightful sense of their seeming a handsome and interesting couple.

It was cool and quiet in this hotel on the side street, giving the sense of a retreat. Bruce wouldn't admit it, but Margot knew that he had been afraid to take her to the more fashionable hotel. Out in the lobby, an Indian with a darkly classic face pattered over the tiled floor with baskets which he silently offered for sale. The other people in the dining room—an elderly fat man at a solitary table, and one of those inevitable parties of school-teachery women—seemed to offer almost a surfeit of safety. But there was always, even here, a slight tingle of danger in coming among people. Bruce feared this, but Margot loved it.

"How grand the food looks!"

"Does look pretty nice."

The smiles they exchanged were an admission. The magic still held, brighter, more radiant than ever, since they had learned how lost and empty it was to be apart. The fresh roses on the table, the grapefruit with their red cherries, the silver covers over the buttered toast, all seemed festive. The pleasures of civilization were new again. Last night it had been horrid and confusing coming into the hotel. Even on this side street, the noise had been hideous, after the room in the adobe house where they had slept the night before, in a small sanctuary of Spanish domesticity made up of stiff lace pillow shams, artificial flowers, family photographs, and rosaries, in beautiful incongruity with the great, pure, surrounding silence of the desert. Margot had felt as if she were bidding some kind of mournful, significant farewell when she had taken off the scuffed Prince of Wales shoes that had gone along so many beloved trails through mountain forests and meadows, leading her to the edges of silent lakes, and to hidden clumps of tall, blue columbines; and the tweed suit that kept in its rough meshes the dust of the roads and the smoke of their campfires. But this morning she felt washed and fresh and gay in her light silk suit and her shady hat. Now the noises in the narrow street had a cheerful sound. The cool room was brightened by the clear sunshine of the early summertime.

Margot looked out of the large window and felt with new delight the exotic strangeness of the place. Indian women in bright-colored dresses were passing; and she saw two men in ten-gallon hats, one of them wearing a red velvet jacket with Navajo silver belt. It was the kind of place that she could love, *her* kind. She felt with mystic certainty that they had reached a goal. After breakfast, she would make Bruce walk with her through the narrow streets looking at the silver bracelets and the Indian baskets, which enchanted her, while her ingenuous delight at the "foreignness" enchanted him, making him smilingly and teasingly indulgent, as she adored him to be.

"I *love* it here," she said.

She loved all the West. Now she had found her own country. Margot felt that all over again, when they took the car, that had been newly washed and greased, and drove out along the desert road. She remembered how it had been coming through the Middlewest, where the very sidewalks seemed to hold reminders of her lonely, dissatisfied girlhood, and she felt every minute that the big front windows of familiar-looking frame

424

houses in all the little towns were glaring at her with the same old humdrum, settled, family disapproval she was sure everyone at home would feel if they knew about this journey—and they would stop her if they could! But at the first sight of mountains, lying blue beyond the plains, she had felt that she was out of the houses' reach. It was the West, where everything was different—the land of outlaws, and bright colors, and bad women, and high-stepping horses. The soil yielded gold and silver and turquoise, instead of just everlasting "crops." It was hard and unmanageable and magnificent—*her* country—not the fertile soil the folks called "good land," moist and obedient to the plow, settling down tamely and patiently to the tasks that people exacted of it. She thought of the old country roads, as they were printed on her memory, with their rural, local look, where the marks of wagon wheels and horseshoes and of the aimless struttings and scurryings of chickens patterned the soft warm dust under a fringe of willow trees. It pleased Margot to think that Grandpa Ferguson would have said this land was "good for nothing," because it couldn't be "harnessed to the plow."

"You are useless, oh grave, oh beautiful . . ."

How she had hated "useful things" from her childhood up!— shoes that were bought "to give good service," those awful dresses, the kind Mrs. Bellew had wanted her to buy, that would be "appropriate for any occasion," houses that were supposed to be "nice" because they had regulation comforts, and the kind of dismal burgs that dad called "nice little towns" because they had the usual set-up of brick bank building and stores and churches and vile little movie house. Margot rebelled joyously against all that the folks had ever called "good"; and now, in this country, where the hills were tossed and swirled in magnificent madness, she had her justification.

At last she was in her own land. At home, it had always seemed as if everything really belonged to Dorothy and not to her. Dorothy's girlish loveliness was the only kind that counted. But Margot had always known that somewhere was the place where *she* belonged. Here, even the flowers were *her* flowers. The red and yellow cactus blossoms wore her own colors; and she felt that something in herself went with their frail, silken delicacy and wildness. And there was something in her, too, that could match and live up to the fierce splendor of these mountains—something that none of the folks possessed. She was the only one who had the recklessness to take her own way. They answered some secret she had always known. It was different from that hidden sense of personal knowledge with which she had gone creeping about the narrow streets, drinking in her first sight of queer little places and foreign things on that cold, bleak, long-ago day in the Village. That had been a kind of recognition, so private it was almost shameful—as if all that were something to which she belonged, and yet never could belong; for when she came to it, it was past. But here was something so ancient and deep and true that it went far back beyond personal recognition. It was so ancient that she felt it was eternal—the revelation of an ancient truth.

"Oh, Bruce, I *love* it here!" She clutched him, and laid her head against his arm. She gave a long, rapturous sigh.

Why couldn't they stay here where they had found the place they loved? Because it was wrong to the *real* reality, the only one she could truly own—a denial of this revelation of beauty, a cowardly failure to live up to the greatest thing they could feel—if they let themselves be governed by what other people had built around them, and succumbed to that.

The whole morning world lay before them. There was something deeply pending between them, that some day must be faced; but the gold of the sunshine dazzled it out of existence. In this strange, beloved land they were free again, with the illusion of belonging only to each other.

They turned down a long narrow road beside a bright little running stream with the tender green of poplar leaves above it. They seemed to have left all involvements behind them and to be driving into a world so old that it was all freshness. Margot thought of spring at home—herself and Dorothy gathering wildflowers in the woods near the farm—after a rain, the red maple buds on the wet, dark sidewalks. But that kind of weather had always left her aching and dissatisfied. Somehow, she had wanted to push the soft, lowering heaviness of the clouds aside, as if they were getting between her and some essence of the season. This was what she really loved! She watched a dry swirl of dust across a waste of desert. These were only the pale rudiments of the early summertime, archaic and classic both—the selected elements of eternal freshness in a world older than any of which she had ever dreamed.

Beyond the stream and the line of poplar trees lay the pueblo. An Indian was out working in the field. He did not look up as they drove past, with the familiar curiosity of the farmers at home, a little dubious of strangers but ready to be friendly, to raise the hand in a salute a little slower than the one given them. His back, in its red-checked shirt, was bent with a stern ease; and his long black bob swung forward under the red band about his head. Margot admired his indifferent reserve, too natural and poised to suggest surliness. The earth showed straight patterns of bright young corn, like the earth at home; but because this was far away, and the farmer an Indian, it seemed beautiful to Margot here. Far in the dreamy distance, the mesas reared their cut-off tops at different levels, giving a romantic isolation to the small fertile space of the young cornfield.

They drove into the open square of the plaza. There had never been such stillness—such utter, sunny, ancient peace. The earth-colored houses, with their softly rounded contours, the ladders bleached hard and firm in the dry pure air, clustered around the sunburned space. A dog the color of the tan dust was lying in a doorway. Women with twig brooms were sweeping the dry earth. The far-off, dim-blue mesas, the mountains still more dim and far away, and dark with cedars, seemed to endow the movements of the women with a rudimentary human grandeur and significance.

They left the car beside the little Spanish church behind white palings. The white wooden crosses in the burying ground just beyond were thrust up thick and crookedly with a primitive starkness. Margot and Bruce walked slowly across the plaza in its enchantment of morning stillness.

An old woman was standing in an open doorway looking at them with small, dark, unrevealing eyes. As they started to go past, she said in a level, emotionless voice:

"Come in. Buy pot'ry."

Margot looked eagerly and beseechingly at Bruce. He smiled at her, indulging her feminine weakness for looking and buying. But it was really more to see the way the place looked inside than to purchase anything that she wanted to accept the invitation. She stepped through the low doorway, looking about her in enchanted wonder. Bruce followed her and stood smilingly aside. She turned to him with an expression of delight, with a deep, rapturous sparkle in her dark eyes.

This was the room of which she had always dreamed, so exactly as she had always seen it that she could not believe she was actually here: the low room, with its dry still air, the place dark on the inside with the burning sun outside. She hadn't seen just what would be here, but now she knew that everything was completely as it must be. It was simple in an elemental way, but with a sense of true selection in the few furnishings—no clutter of what was irrelevant, impersonal, unchosen. She loved the whitewashed gypsum walls, and the hard earthen floor. The round vigas overhead gave a scent of wood and bark. The white fireplace in the corner was deeply burned inside to a sooty blackness. There were only women in this place—the old woman who had called them in, one middle-aged, and two younger. One of these held a baby with black square-cut hair and soft, black, gleaming almond eyes.

"It's a *doll!*" Margot cried in rapture. She felt that she adored dark little babies—they had none of the milkiness of the fat white ones with their light little wisps of hair. She turned to make Bruce look, turning back eagerly to the woman who held the baby, innocently unaware of the constraint of Bruce's smile.

The women looked at each other in stealthy pleasure, and broke into bubbling laughter. The sound was as soft as doeskin. Everything was soft about them—their broad faces, the gleam of their dark eyes, their almost soundless steps on the earthen floor. And yet they were powerful, more candidly strong than

428

the women at home. Nobody could deny that! They were all secret, all together. This was a woman's hidden stronghold. The intimacy of glances told enough, no words were needed. The youngest one was silently placing various-sized pieces of pottery on the floor, earth-colored, with great flower patterns. Margot bent to pick up a bowl, adoring its earthen coolness, its lovely, hand-made unevenness.

"Do you want it?" Bruce asked her.

"Of course I want it! I want everything."

He was already asking "How much?" The women turned to each other, laughing again, a half-abashed laughter that seemed to share a secret.

"Fifty cent'," the old woman said.

The soft, spontaneous laughter bubbled up again as if out of some hidden spring of peaceful, secret, deep harmony. They all exchanged glances from under their black eyelashes.

"What will I do with it?" Margot asked.

"Well, you have it," Bruce told her.

"Yes, I have it," Margot repeated blissfully.

They walked slowly past the houses.

"Oh, Bruce, I want to live here!" Margot moaned.

He smiled at her, and let her clasp his large firm hand.

She cried passionately, "I *do*."

How could she tell him? He was pleased and smiling, enjoying the strangeness, but be*cause* it was strange, and had no connection with the life that he called real. Was that the way he thought of her too? Margot looked quickly up at him in fright. But his face had a tender look, although its lines were stern. She clung more tightly to his hand. What *she* felt was, that she had found her home. These were houses that belonged to women, houses they themselves had made, not places that had been made for them: soft, uneven, standing as they had grown, not built to carefully calculated specifications. And they had stood longer than any other houses in the whole land! Maybe would stand longer still. Margot felt a sudden fear of the metal hardness that was coming into the world. She knew that she had always been afraid of it; the great iron of machinery that was overwhelming all the small, intimate, irrelevant things. If it were to be all calculation instead of spontaneity! Then she wouldn't care to live any longer. Now she thought back with horror to the great skyscrapers with their metal doors, their hard shining spaces on which her heels made sharp, resistant sound, the intricate muffled mechanism that was beneath their towering magnificence. It seemed as if women were being driven back to a place like this; and again she thought with longing of the bubbling spontaneity of the Indian laughter in the intimate darkness of that room.

"I want to live here," she repeated.

"*You* do!" Bruce gently mocked her. They were going along hand in hand.

"I do, I want to dress the way they do, and eat from bowls that I love, not just *dishes* you go and buy. I want to be an Indian woman."

Bruce was still gently mocking. He swung her hand.

"This is the way women can live."

"Women depend on the luxuries men get for them," Bruce told her sententiously. "Wait until you see your hair get straight and your teeth drop out. Then you wouldn't be so contented. What's all this grousing I've been hearing about the beauty parlors along the way, that didn't know how to cut a woman's hair—"

"That was in the Middle-*west*," Margot said with scorn.

"Maybe you can start up a beauty parlor in the pueblo!"

Margot was silent. He thought it was a joke, because these people were Indians, and so he, as a good American, had to be facetious about them. He couldn't see. No, it wasn't a joke! Bruce was within the enchantment too. She could feel the sense of happiness that was mounting, mounting . . . Bruce pretended to tease her to hold back that sense a little. Now he had withdrawn his hand and he was tightly clasping hers.

She wanted this—she *wanted* it. It was like something that had always been hers and that was lost until today. It was far more hers than home. In this enveloping stillness and peace, movements, impulses, seemed to come from the inside. At home, Margot thought rebelliously, everything was put on from the

430

outside. Even in New York. In New York worse than anywhere! She had loved it when she went there first; but now she felt that she could never bear to go back.

"But you *like* it?" she said wistfully to Bruce, feeling how different his ideas were from hers, liking them and hating them because they were so much the regulation American-man kind.

"It's nice, all right," Bruce admitted.

He gave a sidelong, appraising look about the place. There was a kind of pain in his voice. His hand tightened on Margot's. The silent, singing happiness mounted, mounted, carrying them with it—until she drew away her hand.

"Want something else?" Bruce asked her. His voice held a breathlessness. He loved to make her gifts. No doubt it was partly a sense of reparation—a desire to heap on her all he could in their brief time together . . . if it was to be brief. But she loved it just the same. The way, up in the mountains, he had stuck first a red flower and then a yellow flower into her hair—as if he could never get enough of the sight of her in different aspects, different colors. "Maybe we can find some of this silver jewelry to deck you out. A fellow told me you could run across better things in these pueblos than you can in town."

Bruce was looking around. Margot loved the air of masculine authority with which he did it, although she knew it was alien to the place, and gave them the air of foreign conquerors. She had exclaimed over the first piece of heavy silver jewelry that she had seen, feeling that it was what she had always been meant to wear; and Bruce had noted it, and been cannily turning over possibilities in his mind. A young woman was standing in front of one of the houses. Bruce went over to her, and then beckoned to Margot, as she stood waiting in the sunshine.

"This girl says she has a few rings. Want to look at them?"

The young Indian woman went through the open doorway and came back with a handful of silver rings and a necklace of turquoise which she held out in soft, questioning silence. Bruce examined the things with his usual appraising thoroughness. He held up one of the rings, squinting at it, and then

431

took Margot's hand and slipped it on her finger. She loved its heavy feeling on her hand.

"Like it?" Bruce asked. "I don't know much about these things, but I believe it's pretty good. How much?" he asked the Indian woman.

A thin, hard, brown young man had come softly out after her and was now standing behind her. She turned to him. He said something in a guttural, unrecognizable language. The young woman said obediently, in stolid shyness, "Four dollar." The young man had made her ask more than she would have had the courage to ask for herself. Margot felt that she loved the Indian woman, and hated all the white race, and all its hard acquisitiveness, always wanting to get, not to enjoy and savor. . . . All but Bruce. He had all the qualities she had said she hated; and she loved him.

"Well, now you're an Indian woman," Bruce said. He gave a quick smile at her, admitting the happiness, still holding it off. "I didn't want to risk the turquoises—rather ask somebody who can advise me about the value. Like your ring?"

"Of course."

Bruce took her hand and held it up, looking at it, looking at the ring with its lumps of turquoise. The satiny white of the slim hand was tanned now to a smooth brown. It quivered slightly, and Bruce let it go.

"So now you have a ring," he said softly to her.

Margot looked away. She felt another astounding, sudden access of shyness, of fear. She chanted: "I want to live in one of these houses, all dark inside, and then come outside into the sunshine, *this* kind of sunshine. Don't you?" She looked quickly up at him.

"If that's where you're going to live," Bruce said.

He caught her hand again, and held it closely. The open light in the square was dazzling with sunshine. This moment of happiness was beyond any that she had known before. Margot looked at the silent enclosure of low houses. Of all the places where she had dreamed of living—the Spanish castle, the old houses on Washington Square, the eighteenth century French rooms, like the replicas in the Metropolitan—this was most her home. It was not past and foreign. It was somehow real. When she looked through the open doorways into the interior of summer darkness, she could feel something like an old memory of a faraway dream just stirring. She saw before her, like a revelation, the beauty of living with Bruce. Just the simple beauty of *living*. Of course. That was always the end of the fairy tale. "And they lived happily forever after." And it was the line that she had skipped! But now she had come to it, and she knew its meaning.

They went slowly over to the car, which stood tilted a little on the rough ground, with the white church wall behind it. White walls, and sharp dark shadows. It seemed as if, for this moment, they had walked straight into the center of the morning peace. A kind of love she had never known for Bruce before, even in the wildly happy hours that she had reaped, softly flooded over Margot. It was peace. They two moved within it.

As they got into the car, Bruce drew her over to him, and held her against him.

"Margot, we *have* to be together," he said. "We can't separate—not now. I just can't let you go."

Margot felt with wonder that Bruce was trembling. His face was set in a grimace of pain. There were actually tears in his eyes. She softly, wonderingly touched his face. His hand was cold. She didn't understand, for it all seemed to her so natural. That was the only thing she could feel. It was the most natural thing on earth or in heaven; and that was what made it beautiful. It was the thing that came next.

4

Margot had found the tearoom in an inner court off the plaza, pulling Bruce through the dark little alleyway between the bookstore and the old museum, and exclaiming at the cool retreat in the shade of the piazza roofs. There were orange and blue tables looking out on the areaway paved with uneven flagstones, blinding white in the dry sun, with a center bed of cactus. But a shadowy coolness lay against the thick,

433

damp-feeling old adobe walls in the piazza with its columns carefully carved in Mission style.

"Looks kind of Greenwich Villagey to me," Bruce said. He looked dubiously at the waitresses in crisp, light-green smocks, carrying trays of tall, misted glasses of iced tea with cuts of lemon perched on the edges.

"Oh, no, Bruce!" Margot said.

She liked the Indian chair with its thong seat which Bruce held for her, and the horehound-brown Mexican glassware and the yellow sugar bowl with its childish, painted flowers. She stared avidly around the court, seeing first the groups of people around the tables, and envying the woman with the sharply cut profile who could pull back her gray hair that way, and so stunningly wore the scarlet velvet jacket and the enormous belt of round silver Indian discs. If they stayed here much longer, she *must* have one of those jackets and one of those belts, to go with the ring and bracelet and heavy silver earrings that Bruce had bought her. It was the kind of dress that fitted this country and fitted her, and she could already feel herself, like that woman, boldly making her own the brilliant color and the heavy ornament.

Margot's eyes roved to little shops around the court, in the windows of which she saw the Indian and Mexican handicraft, etchings, drawings, paintings, and all the various loot of the region. She felt the group of people as intimates of the country, who made this a meeting place; and she was confirmed in this when a young Indian in a square bob and orange shirt padded across the court, and they began talking to him familiarly in a mixture of Spanish and English.

"When will there be the Eagle Dance, Juan?"

"Mebbe Buffalo."

"Quando?"

"Mebbe next week. You come Thursday," the Indian said with calm friendliness.

They were standing about him, examining his strings of turquoise and bracelets as he stood stolidly impervious to their patronizing remarks.

434

"No, Juan, not good," drawled a thin youth in a béret and a red sash. He negligently handed back the string of beads.

Margot was looking at the youth when his eyes lazily met hers. He detached himself from the group and came toward Margot's table.

"Margot Ferguson!" His large eyes examined her familiarly, and there was no mistaking the curling lashes. "It's time you were coming here, Margot," he drawled.

"Hello, Rod! I didn't know you'd come out here. This is Mr. Williams—Mr. Pingrey," Margot said a little coolly. She had no desire to meet Rod here. Somehow it put the wrong kind of color on the group from which he came, about which she had been weaving an exotic and envious interest.

She heard Bruce's chilly "How do you do," as Rod, with an insolent familiarity, turned his large eyes from one to the other of them.

"Margot, how charming you look. There is that *je ne sais quoi* about you, as of a properly cherished woman. I congratulate you—both."

Margot saw the way Bruce stiffened as Rod rolled his eyes toward him. Rod's silky black side-burns, coming down from under his béret, were lower than ever, and his blue velvet trousers were gashed with red at the bottoms. He had gone artily Spanish.

"What are you doing here, Rod?" Margot said quickly, to cover up the stiffness she knew Bruce was feeling. "I haven't seen you for ages."

Rod negligently picked up Margot's hand from the table. "Not bad, the ring," he drawled. "It's an old pattern. But you got hooked on the bracelet. Factory. Me?" he asked. "I'm quite established." He made a wan motion of his hand toward one of the shops. "Mexican things. The best in Santa Fé. You want to be careful of the stuff around the hotels. You should meet Everett—most valuable person to know here. Look, he's the man in the linen trousers. Knows when every dance is going on in the pueblos. One of the few people who have really seen the Penitentes."

Margot saw the short, fat man with the gray mop of hair,

like an old actor's, and the hanging pouches under his large eyes, sloppily dressed in an old velvet coat and thin white trousers. Poor Vernon, what a successor! But he could probably support Rod more thoroughly than she had done.

Rod said, with an intimate smirk and roll of his eyes, "Everett and I are very good friends, you know. He owns all this place. Listen, why don't you come and meet these people? Going to be here long? Everybody stays longer than they expect to. It gets you, you know. You ought to know some of the real people."

Margot looked at Bruce. He was sternly cutting his salad with his fork, with an air of heavy distaste which she could recognize.

"Oh, I guess not, Rod," she said quickly. "We're just staying quietly here, not seeing anyone."

Rod's eyebrows arched. "Oh, of course. Pardon me. Just one of those things—I understand. Well, you'll probably be dropping into the shop some day. I cannot know you from Adam —and Eve, if you want," he said, with a roll of his eyes. He languidly walked away.

"Margot, let's get out of here," Bruce said from a tight mouth.

"Oh, Bruce, before I finish my salad?"

But she saw the determined set of his jaw and knew when it didn't do to oppose him. She folded her napkin, trying to look nonchalant, while Bruce paid the thin, very refined woman at the desk.

"Bruce, I'm terribly sorry," she begged, when they got outside. "That awful little squirt of a Rod!—who ever dreamed he'd turn up?"

"Just the kind of place you'd expect to find him in," Bruce said. "With that gang of would-be artists. I didn't like it from the first."

"Well, we won't go there again. I'll do the cooking myself."

"Yes," Bruce said, mocking her. "On the good old-fashioned range!"

"I don't have to use the range. And anyway, this is different."

436

It did seem different. When they had driven back through the narrow winding street, that looked as if it had grown from an old Indian trail, and had climbed the sandy arroyo to the place where their low-lying adobe house sat into the hill under the poplar trees, with the piñon like a dark fuzz beyond, and beyond that the blue mountains which seemed so intimate, and yet were twenty miles away: Margot felt a secret little ecstatic sense that this was their home. She almost resented the fact that it belonged to a wealthy artist, and not to them. He was away for the summer, and they had rented the place a month ago through a real estate man. She had come to love the white interior, that was like the pueblo rooms, with the rounded fireplace in the corner, the woody vigas in the ceiling, and beautiful furniture which the artist had made himself. Even Bruce approved it, and said it was not so arty as the painter's house with the blue wooden gate and the old Mission bell above it. They were both affectionate toward the tiny stream that flowed in front of the house between its little thrown-up banks, and which was now a dry trickle, and again a miniature flood of pale brown water—depending on how much of the flow the irrigation farms up the valley turned aside, Bruce said.

The kitchen was warm from the slowly burning range and fragrant with the beans which had been cooking since yesterday. Margot went to the olla that hung from thongs, and was cool and dewy with the water in it, and poured herself a drink into a little pottery mug. She loved the faintly earthen taste of the cool water, and the porous feel of the cup at her lips. She loved to get a drink from the olla—just as water seemed to taste better when she got it from some out-of-the-way place, such as the spring in Stumpf's pasture, next to the Ferguson farm at home, where the clean sand bubbled in the bottom of the spring. Then she went to the range and lifted the lid from the kettle of beans, which had now turned a rich brown. She poured them into the big, irregular Indian cooking pot, with its zigzag design, added water, and set them in the oven to bake. Maria, the young Spanish-American girl who came in to clean, had taught her how to make the beans and chile. She had got to love the sensation of the fiery red sauce, which reminded her of peppery and reckless Spanish qualities. Maria brought in the flat, round tortillas, about which Bruce joked, calling them stacks of cardboard, and declaring that Margot would disdain them if they were served in American restaurants. But he liked them too. He had learned to scoop up his beans with them, the way they had seen a family of Spanish-Americans doing, all solemnly seated under a cottonwood tree near a stream, with their ancient, high-pockets of a Ford parked near-by.

There was an electric stove, beside the range, on which Margot made their breakfast. She loved the intimacy of the long breakfast hour, Bruce pouring himself three cups of coffee as they lingered; the lucid freshness of the blue southwestern morning, with the mountains dim and dreamy beyond the long windows. She even liked to give Bruce the best half of the Albuquerque paper, which Bruce always bought, with a somewhat shamefaced look, saying "it was more of a real town than this tourist's dump"—there were better baseball items in the paper. In fact, Margot was getting quite a housewifely feeling. Mother and Dorothy would never have believed it! But she felt that it was different, because this was Bruce. And it wasn't a stodgy marriage. They were to get what there was in it, and then let it go. Only there was so much in it—so much more than she had dreamed. Margot was a little fearful of the attachment that was growing. Yet she was fiercely resolved *to* get what there was in it. It had come, now, to the very heart of something sweet, and she realized that it needed this daily life together to bring it to full flower.

As she worked in the kitchen, it seemed to her to have a flavor and simple dignity of something fundamental, with the scrubbed, unpainted pine-board table upon which a loaf of bread ought to stand—a jug, a loaf, and thou. She felt the same revulsion as Bruce at the sort of arty, "atmospheric" tea-rooms and bizarre eating places for which she had had a girlish weakness until now. But she seemed to have outgrown all that. She was disgusted at the thought of Rod and his whole gang —that awful Everett in the sloppy pants!—and she meant to stay far, far away from the Mexican shoppe. Why did Rod, of all people, have to turn up here, with his beautiful insolent eyes, reminding her of her past, of Lee, and the smoky basement room—here in this sunshine? She gave a little shudder.

She heard Bruce moving about in the other room, and looking up, she saw him standing at the door with an amused, fond look.

"Well! What a charming little hausfrau."

"That doesn't bother me a bit!"

"Doesn't?"

"No." She came over to him and gave him an ecstatic little hug. "I *like* it. For you." She pulled him possessively into the other room and seated him on the low couch, with its old Navajo blanket of faded rose and white and black. "You do think our place is lovely—*per*-fect, don't you?"

She could never get Bruce to uncover the real depths of his feelings, and she didn't expect it. She knew how he liked to keep a masculine playfulness on the surface, as he let his lavish care for her stand for profession, imply his feeling underneath. She was content with the half-playful, half-painful look that came into his eyes as he squeezed her arm and then stared through the window.

"We won't go to that goofy little place again. I don't like it any better than you do. I just want to stay *here*, Bruce. I'd like to cook all our meals—honestly, I would. We can get Maria to come in when we want her. And then we wouldn't have to run into people, but we could drive to the pueblos—I just haven't *begun* to get enough of the country. Have you? Bruce, answer!" She shook his arm. "Oh, Bruce," she said, with a sudden sweet overflow of feeling, "did you ever think it would come to as much as *this*? I didn't know anything could."

Bruce shook his head.

Margot felt her eyes swimming as she looked intently at his face, the structural lines of which had become so familiar and necessary to her. She felt the imprint of his features like something bred into her. There was a sudden strange yearning inside of her, quite different from simple desire. She said in a wondering voice, "I can even see why women want children

439

—of someone they really love." She held to his arm and searched his face with her eyes.

Bruce was silent. Margot quickly felt that it had struck a wrong note. She was angry suddenly, and frightened. The silence throbbed between them. Bruce got up, drawing away his arm, and walked gravely about the room.

He stopped and looked down at her with a tightened face. "Margot," he said with difficulty, "look here. We've got to . . . decide some things pretty soon."

"Oh, Bruce! Why did you have to say that right now?" The tears in her eyes overflowed. She felt a willful anger at the thought of making decisions. She hated them. They seemed wrong. She wanted events to decide things of themselves.

"Well, I've got to say it some time."

"Bruce—it was just that little bastard Rod!—You've been rattled!" She couldn't believe that this was touching the thing she dreaded!

Margot sat silent. She looked at the wicker wastebasket and saw the corners of water-color paper sticking out of it.

"Bruce, you haven't thrown them *away!*"

She ran to the basket and retrieved the pictures with a little moan. Bruce's painting had been one of the reasons they had given for their stay here, for their taking the house. He had always wanted a free space in which to do the things for which he had never had time. Margot had been happy seeing him set his small easel on the terrace, and she had watched with little cries of appreciation as his tentative brushes labored at reproducing the look of the mountains or the rambling Spanish farms across the valley. But now, as she looked up, and saw the faintly cynical look he bent down on her, she checked her lamentation.

"They're junk," Bruce said. "It's too late for me to go in for that sort of thing. Even your friend Rod could do better. Earlier I might have—I don't know. But now it's just make-believe."

He took the water-color sheets and tore them across, and threw them at the wastebasket.

Margot couldn't say anything. They weren't good. She knew

440

it as well as Bruce. But he might do something good if he kept on—she felt now as if Bruce could do anything. Anyway, she had been happy feeling that Bruce was having this period when everything that he had missed in his too-early taking on of responsibilities would come to a perfect flowering—and through her. She felt a crushed sense at Bruce's turning on it, and she couldn't protest. Tears overflowed again in her great, staring eyes.

Bruce made an uneasy movement. "There's too much make-believe around here, anyway. It's beginning to get under my skin."

Now she looked up at him tragically. Yet she knew that she held power over him, and she said, daring him to deny it, "But what we have together isn't make-believe. Is it?"

Bruce winced a little and his face turned color. "No," he said, "I'm afraid it isn't."

"*Afraid?*"

"Margot, look here—"

"I don't want to look here. I don't want to see you tear up pictures and tell me I'm nothing but make-believe. Like Rod, I suppose. I suppose you think I really belong with him!"

"Margot—"

"Oh, please don't say anything." She clung to him again, and he held and kissed her remorsefully. "Not today, not today—not when everything's so beautiful. Not unless you don't love me any more. I don't care *what* you say then."

Bruce admitted, after a rueful moment, "Then I guess I'll have to keep still." She looked up at him. He was smiling. They kissed again, in a long, silent reunion. But the vigilant fear, which had been lulled for a while by their happiness in this place, was all awake again, strained and quivering inside her.

When Margot heard Bruce walking around she knew that she was not surprised. Neither of them had slept. For a little while, they seemed to have made up, to have been happy together. But it was not true, and both of them knew it. Their supper of beans and chile, which she had meant to be such a

441

success, was a failure. Bruce had been indrawn, with a far-away look in his eyes. And afterwards, when she had told him that he needn't help her with the dishes, he had said, "All right"—with relief, it seemed to Margot. When she had gone into the studio, he was reading his mail, of which he had got a great batch forwarded this afternoon. He was thinking of either his business or his family, she didn't know or care which. But anyway, it had come between them, and she hated him.

She felt him coming toward her.

"Margot, are you awake?"

"Yes," she answered curtly.

The room was almost dark. Bruce, in his robe, sat huddled on a chair by her bed. Margot's heart began to beat heavily. It choked her, so that she was afraid she couldn't speak. She didn't want to hear—she wouldn't listen . . . but in horror, she couldn't help it.

Bruce took a deep breath. "Listen here, Margot—we've got to break it up." They were the words that she had dreaded. She was hearing them now. "We . . . we can't trust ourselves any further."

Those monstrous words had been spoken—and by Bruce. Margot lay like a black living coal of resentment. Once she had meant to speak them—if they were to be spoken. But now it seemed wrong that they should be said at all. When Bruce tried to touch her, she drew away bitterly. They felt so utterly different about this, as about other things; there could be no mutual understanding.

But in spite of herself, she was touched when Bruce, sensitive to her angry withdrawal, said brokenly, "You think I don't love you, because I'm saying this. If you knew what this takes!"

Yet her resentment flamed again, as she dwelt sullenly, broodingly, on what he had said. He couldn't love her, as she knew love. He couldn't feel that it could be put aside this way, after what there had been between them. It mattered to her more than *anything*. It wasn't love if it didn't. He couldn't understand as she understood what it meant to "give all to love." Bruce was talking, and she felt the suffering in his voice, but she was set against him inside, and hardly heard what he was saying. She felt sealed up. There was no use talking or trying to explain. She gave a little moan and buried her head in the pillow.

"Christ, if it was only that I didn't love you! I'm crazy about you. You pulled me clear out of my orbit. I don't know myself any more—that's the truth. You needn't think this is just a business man's pastime!" Bruce said accusingly. "I never was the kind who went in for pastimes. You know that, don't you? Yes, you know it well enough! You made me feel from the start it was something different. That was why it meant so much to me. It was something I never expected to find in this life."

"*Was* something," Margot said bitterly. She didn't care whether she was fair or not. Her heart was too sore. "You just want to put it away, get it over with now. You *can't* love me. Because I'm willing for it to go on, and you aren't."

"But, Margot. There is some difference between us—in circumstances. Don't you see?—I feel all the responsibility."

"You're no more responsible than I am!" Oh, those were Bruce's old notions—still between them. "Don't you suppose a woman takes a chance?" She felt her fierce recklessness, the thing that had made her rebel against all the Ferguson cautiousness. "I take *every* chance, I'm glad to! It doesn't mean anything to me if it isn't *every*-thing. But you . . . when I said that to you—this afternoon . . . you were scared."

Margot sobbed, as if she had been holding her breath too long. Only now she saw—she began to see—of what he was depriving her. It could never, never come to the perfect final flowering. Not now.

Bruce sat humbly. "Well, call it that," he said after a moment, very quietly. "You see, I have a wife and two children, Margot. You have to know what that means, what it lets a man in for."

"It couldn't stop me, if there was something else I wanted more!" Margot said fiercely. But she was stiff with anger at the mention of his wife. The word made her hate him.

There was a beseeching note in Bruce's voice—and a little of

443

hurt resentment too. "Margot," he told her, "you've got to see
it a little from my side. I don't think you realize how little
you go outside your own feelings. You hold up love as if it
were something apart from people. That's all right for you.
You can do as you please. You haven't anyone else to think of.
It *can't* be just the same for me. You've never been willing to
look at my situation. Or what it meant to me, what I was
doing. I've tried to do what would make you happy—what
you said you wanted. You said you didn't want marriage."

"I don't! It isn't that I'm talking about. It's just . . . after
what we've had, we ought to stay together—not let other things
come between."

But Margot felt the hurt of what Bruce had said to her.
The folks had said it too. "Margaret thinks her tastes are sacred."
She could set herself against them, and disregard what they
said. But when Bruce said it, it jarred her with a shock of
truth. It was as if she were all tender and vulnerable where
he was concerned.

"It was all for you," Bruce repeated. "Every bit of it. And
ever since I knew you. You knocked me clear off my base, I
tell you." His voice rose in suffering. "I've gone with you as
far as I could. Now you won't see how it is with me." He
stood up abruptly. "You've never looked at me," he accused
her. "Just at the man who could make you happy."

Margot cried furiously that it wasn't true. But, in torture,
she felt the fear of its truth breaking into her, leaving her
without resources. She fought blindly against it.

Bruce had been walking about. Now he went out of the
room. Margot felt herself alone in a pit of raw suffering.
Without Bruce, she simply did not see how she could live.
Everything was gone out in blackness. She could bear the sight
of nothing, now that she had seen all the living world illuminated by his love for her. She felt wildly that it *was* something
truly beyond her—not in glory now, but in a paralyzing fear.
She didn't know what she could do. She would rush out to
him—change him, make him accept her feelings as his. But
she couldn't move, no more than in a dream. She lay trying

to subdue her torture to the mere possibility of existing from moment to moment.

After a while, Bruce came back. He tried to lie down beside her and take hold of her. She felt his wet face against hers.

"Margot," he pleaded, "we can't keep on like this. We're fooling ourselves. It's going to get beyond us."

By now, she hated him too much. She felt again of what he was depriving her. Even *Lillian* could have children! Bruce didn't want a child by her.

"Because I know all about this," he whispered. He tried to stroke her hair. "Don't you see, Margot? We can't just go into things like that. You made me remember that I have children. I can't go back on them. I'm their father. They trust me. I can't tell you what that means. Not if you can't see it. And I don't suppose you can."

Margot was silent.

"Well, I had to have this much of you," he said brokenly again. "Whether I did wrong or not. I don't know. I can't help it. Haven't I given you some of the happiness you wanted?"

But she was still stiff and silent against him. After a while she whispered, turning away from him, "But you told me you loved me better than anything in the world, you'd never known what love could be."

"That's true."

It couldn't be true, Margot felt wildly, through a torture of whirling darkness. To speak of parting now was a betrayal of the revelation of their love. The only right there could be was to go on and follow it through to the end. She didn't care if they died together! She would rather die with Bruce. She began to sob.

"If it had meant to you what it did to me, you *couldn't* go," she tried to tell him.

"All right." Bruce was crying too. "Think it doesn't mean the same to me."

Margot muttered sullenly: "It can't mean the same to a man. They don't know what it is."

"I knew enough to risk breaking my whole life to pieces

445

to give you what you wanted most. My business—and everything else."

Margot was silent, feeling again the fear of admitting that as truth.

Bruce got up. She was listening to him with a terrible acuteness. He seemed to be talking to himself.

"But I can't go on with it. I can't go back on them. Maybe I don't put love as high as you do. I know I can't go back on my children, for another child. And that's what it would come to—would have to. Don't you see, I couldn't be anything afterwards, no good to you or anyone . . ."

"You said we could live together."

She saw the sunshine on the earth-colored pueblos . . . the peace in the plaza square.

"Well, I meant it. God knows! But, Margot—"

"Now if you go I'll *die*."

It wasn't a threat. It had said itself out of her anguish. She couldn't look into that blackness with Bruce gone. It made her scream out in fear.

"Margot, don't torture me that way!" Bruce was crying again. "You don't want me if I'm all broken to pieces. I couldn't undertake to be anything to you—not if I . . . I'm afraid of what it would do to me. I couldn't stand up under it, Margot, if I lost all my self-respect—and trustworthiness . . . I can't just do it for my own happiness."

But for her, happiness was the criterion! It was the only thing that was right. And *she* was to count less, just because she had given him happiness—had let him into that heaven they had shared together in the mountain stillness! He was against her. He was not hers. He belonged with other people. He was walking around the room now, blindly.

"Go *now*, then!" Margot screamed. "I just can't see you any more."

"I will." He stopped that blind walking. She had made him do that, anyway. She could hear his heavy breathing. "I've got to go now. I may not be able to do it. I've got to. You see that, don't you, Margot? I'm just myself. I'm what I am. I can't help it."

446

"Oh, go away. Don't talk. Not a single thing matters."

Bruce went. Even while she was driving him away, she hadn't believed that he could go. Margot sank back into that pit of suffering. She believed, quite truly, that she was dying. She did nothing to stem the tide of her suffering, and there was nowhere else that it could bear her. But still she lived on from moment to moment.

Then the din of her own inner pain seemed to fade out and leave her in an acuteness of listening. She heard Bruce packing in the other room. Margot rose up in her shock of resentment at that impossible actuality. She could almost feel the feverish trembling of his haste. A shoe dropped, and she heard him curse. His clothes—*hers*, the things she loved, the dark green tie that gave a sea-green tinge to his eyes, the rough tweed coat— how could they be the property of a woman he loved less than he did her? Why was the one most loved the one who must suffer? Bruce could actually leave her. Margot felt alone and hideously insignificant in the great blackness that was left all around her. The blackness surged over her, in helpless waves of agony. She had meant to "know suffering"—but not suffering like this. Not raw and actual, piercing to her marrow, turning her bones to water and her flesh to agony. Then she leaned on her arm again in that hideous acuteness of listening. Every tiny, actual sound she seemed to have to hear. And yet she couldn't hear enough! When finally Bruce came toward her room again, toward her, she felt as if her hands were beating the air and she was shrieking "Don't come near me!" although the whole time she was lying fiercely still.

Bruce came in and stood beside her in the semi-darkness. "Margot." She heard the strangled suffering in his voice. Was glad to hear it!—and then suffered herself because she couldn't comfort him. He sat down on the bed and tried to take her hand. He had something of his old protective, responsible manner back. He was telling her what he had thought of for her. "I want you to keep on this house. Stay here just as long as you want to—just as long as you can. You said you loved the country. If you want to stay out here altogether . . . why, I guess I can manage that." She made a movement of denial.

447

"I'm leaving some money for you. It'll see you through for some time. Now, listen, Margot, while I tell you where it is."

"I won't listen!"

"You've got to. I won't go away and leave you flat. You can't ask it of me. I won't do it." She had to hear, although she tried to hold her hands against her ears. "And I'm going to leave you the car too."

"You can't. I won't have it. I don't want to *see* it."

"All right," he said, after a while. "I'll take it away then."

"If you don't I'll take it out and wreck it!"

"Margot. Margot, *please!* Don't torture me more than you have to. By God, I don't think I deserve this!"

She feebly beat at him. "Go away!"

But he stayed, and tried to make her promise—she would write him if she needed anything, she wouldn't be cruel, would look after herself. He trusted her. She thought *that* much of him. And they both had this time to remember—just as she had said. Margot tried to be deaf. She hated his care—hated him to think of these little things, when he could do the final cruelty to her. At the last minute, she took hold of him. He had to break away from her. She heard, in horrified amazement, the sound of his great, broken sobs.

"I have to do it. Oh God, I can't if I stay any longer. Margot, let me go. I can't."

He got up, went blindly to the door. She heard him still crying—a man's fearful crying, that rocked the universe. She listened to it with her eyes open in horrified amazement. After a long time, she heard the sound of the car.

She got up, and struggled after him. Bruce was gone. She would stop him, throw herself at his feet and beg him to stay . . . anything . . . she couldn't stand it alone, that was all. . . .

She ran along the road a little way, slipping on the ruts in the darkness. After a while, she couldn't hear the car any more —nothing but the little stream, and the night-time rustling of the cottonwood leaves. She stood in horrified loneliness, listening to those sounds.

Then she felt her drained weakness. She couldn't get back to

448

the house. She couldn't even throw herself into the stream and let the shallow water cover her. Bruce's words stopped her—the sick remembrance of the suffering in his voice. That was more to her than her own impulse. But she didn't care what she did. She was beyond that. It seemed to her truly that the end of the world had come. She lay flat down on the rough ground in the chill mountain night while her suffering seemed to bear her somewhere—she didn't know where. . . . She dug her fingers into the earth.

There was a tinge of light over the mountains now. Cars were going past. Someone would look over and see her—perhaps try to come to her aid, ask her what was the matter. She felt dragged out now, not alive. But if she were going to die, she didn't want to be found here. She got up, sauntering as if she had just come into the garden for some flowers, went into the house and stealthily closed the door, and lay down on the bed.

IV. AFTER THE END OF THE STORY

MARGOT woke up with a sense of rest. It was like a dream to be back in her old room. Her own curtains were at the window, carefully laundered; and the rickety little desk stood locked as she had left it. The folks had kept everything for her exactly as it had been before—hoping, she supposed, that she would finally come home. She felt the blessed ease of lying in her bed and letting things go. The shaded room, with its closed door, now seemed a refuge.

But this half-pleasant sensation lasted for only a few seconds. Now she was awake, and already the sharp grind of pain was beginning—in her mind, in her breast . . . somewhere. She felt the empty horror of lying here alone. Hunger for Bruce consumed her. She would have screamed out if she could —only it was too sharp and absorbing for her to make a cry. It took all the life she had just to lie and feel and contemplate its completeness. There was an interval when again it seemed to Margot that she simply could not live on from moment to moment. It passed—more or less.

Suddenly she got out of bed. She had heard sounds downstairs. Bun dashed into the house and out again with a slam of the front door. The sound hurt Margot, wounded her with its careless ease. It said that to Bun this place was home. And to her it wasn't. No place could be. She sat hunched in pain on the edge of the bed seeing the white walls of the adobe house that no longer belonged to her—not the house, nor the dreamy mountains, nor the little shallow stream. There was no use in dressing, in doing anything, with Bruce gone from her life. It had lost both center and background. Every time that Margot looked at her existence she realized more the extent of the devastation.

But another sound made her get up quickly again and act to herself as if she had been dressing all this time. If she didn't hurry, mother would come up to see what was the matter. Anything was better than breaking down before the folks. That painful, hard determination was all that kept her up now. It was all that was left of her pride. She knew that her mother didn't entirely believe in her account of the trip, although mother tried and pretended, resolved to have everything beautiful between them this time. She had told mother that she had gone West with some friends of Grimmie's. "How nice!" mother had dutifully said. If she could have seen this last crowd—! Hec, her gallant suitor, who had expected to spend his nights with her, thinking that of course he could do as he pleased with a girl from New York who was running around alone out West. Rod, no doubt, had told him about Bruce, and put his own sweet interpretation upon the story. And no doubt about Lee, too, and a few other things . . . Ugh! When Margot had been with strangers she had longed for someone of her own; but here at home, meeting all these eyes, she wanted strangers again.

She dressed as quickly as she could, shuddering away from her memories of this room. She had thought that now she was forever superior to those memories. But she wasn't. It seemed

to her that she had gone back into the old chill, shaded loneliness. She felt too hideous for any but her oldest dress.

And of course she had to find Aunt Ella downstairs with
mother!

"Well! You must have been having quite a sleep."

Aunt Ella's dull black eyes were looking at her curiously.
Since Margot had come home this time, Aunt Ella seemed to
regard her partly as a stranger. Half the time Aunt Ella was
formal, the rest of the time too familiar.

"That's just what I want her to do," mother said, with a
quick, anxious, conciliatory smile.

"Well! Let's see how you look by daylight. I ain't had a
peek at you yet except by night. I want to see if you look as
stylish as you did over at our house. I was afraid to speak to
you! Well, you look a little older," Aunt Ella observed with
satisfaction. "I don't know how all the girls manage to hide
their age these days. But it's beginning to show a little round
your eyes."

"She'll look better when she's rested," mother said again
quickly, smiling.

"Haven't got much more flesh than when you left. What's
the matter? Run it all off? You ought to have quite a lot more
heft to you by this time. You ought to see Edna Mae Fawcett.
Wasn't she one of those girls you used to play with? My, she's
getting an awful behinder on her! I was just noticing that
when I saw her going down the street."

"I don't care for a behinder, thank you!"

"Oh, well," mother said, anxiously smiling again, "she'll have
several more pounds before we let her go."

Margot went on into the dining room. Mother had a woman
out on the screened porch, ironing, and so her place had been
set in here. Any walls were better than to be left to the awful
vacancy of the outdoor light. On her first day at home, there
had been a sort of freshness of renewal. It had seemed as if
here she could hide and rest. It had been grateful to her to
get away from that awful crowd, whose belated antics she had
long ago outgrown, with the very beginning of her love for
Bruce. She remembered her dry despair at the idea of returning

to *that*. Hec, with his gin and his hang-overs and his pumped-up hilarity, the unwelcome zeal of his disappointed love-making! For a few sweet hours, she had felt at home in this place and renewed by its innocent charm. But now it was just another restless sojourn. It was too late to make up the old quarrel. Too much had happened between. For a moment she almost pitied the folks and their transparent efforts, mother's anxious kindness, dad trying to make up with her and pretend that nothing was ever wrong. She felt as if she could have cried over their innocence.

Margot sat down and stared at her glass of orange juice. The perception that mother was using the prettiest dishes for her only made her feel worse; the pathos of these little conciliatory efforts, as if she, Margot, were still a child. It was useless, if she had to go on without Bruce, to do so much as lift her hand to her mouth. She drank the orange juice quickly, with aversion, so that mother would see that the glass was empty. But she couldn't get farther with the breakfast than slightly to move her spoon back and forth in the bowl of cornflakes and rich cream. Thank God, Aunt Ella was still there so that mother wouldn't come out and offer to cook her an egg! She saw that mother had given her, for her coffee, the little spoon with the calla lily handle. Her dry eyes ached with the effort for tears. Margot pushed the spoon aside. It belonged to Dorothy. Yes, she thought bitterly, she had come to admit it: Dorothy was the one who had everything.

Margot sat staring into dreariness. The crazy trip with that lousy crowd had dazed her, kept her in motion, held at bay the actuality of her pain. But now it only sickened her to remember the falsity of the whole thing. It made her angry with herself that she couldn't be worse than she was. But she had proved one thing that she thought fiercely she would like to tell a few of these people who were writing books: when a woman had really had the man she loved, if she did *love* him, she needn't think she could work it off with a bunch of others. No wonder women in the old days had become nuns! She wished she could hate Bruce—oh, she wished she could *hate* him. But when she dreamed of forgetting him, the world seemed to revolve dizzily and leave an abyss. She clung with both hands to the edge of the table. She could have nothing else while she remembered—but there would be still more nothing if it all were gone.

She heard mother and Aunt Ella talking in the living room, and it made her detest them. It made her feel wild and at bay. If they really knew about her, they would put her out of the house. It seemed cruel, simply too cruel, that Aunt Ella should be able to keep Uncle Ben, when they were bickering all the time, just because she wore a wedding ring!—while she herself and Bruce, who loved each other, had to be apart. The folks would call it "too bad"—the eternal bickering—but they would think it perfectly right for Aunt Ella and Uncle Ben to be together.

The front doorbell rang with sharp carelessness. Margot's heart literally did stand still. Her hope, discredited even while she felt it, hurt so that she began to hum loudly, in order not to be able to listen. But there was no sound of Bruce's voice. She heard Aunt Ella's exclamations of wonder; and then her mother called, "Margaret!" When she had first come home, it had been good to be greeted as "Margaret" and to drop back for a little while into her girlhood. But now when she heard mother call her that, she hated it, for it seemed to ignore and annul all her life as "Margot." And she hated the folks because she couldn't tell them about Bruce.

But there was still a little grain of sick hope left. When she went into the living room, and saw the long flower box, the hope grew suddenly so immense that it choked her. The boy who had brought the flowers read out loudly:

" 'Mar-gott Ferguson!' "

Margot saw their bewilderment. Aunt Ella said, "Here, we can't make this out. Seems to be for somebody we never heard of! Still, they ain't any other Fergusons in town."

The boy said the flowers had come "by telegraph."

"Hurry up, Margaret, open 'em up," Aunt Ella said. She was all eyes. And mother was just as eager although she was trying to subdue it.

Margot opened the long box. Her hands were cold and she

felt that she was trembling. She tried angrily to beat back her expectation. But she was sick all the same when she took the card from the shiny green tissue paper and glanced at it. She had known even before she looked! Yet the disappointment was so terrible—and so absurd!—that the whole room was swimming around her. She threw down the card.

"Aren't you going to open it up?" her mother asked.

"Maybe she don't want us to see it," Aunt Ella suggested. "Must be pretty serious when it comes by telegraph."

Margot saw how excited they both were.

She languidly laid open the green paper and took out the huge bunch of bright pink roses. Bright baby pink!—the very shade she hated. She had a wild impulse to laugh. This was such a perfect offering from Hec! But she remembered the deep red roses in her room—her *own* roses—Frances standing with them at the head of the painted stairs. . . . The world was too awful to endure. All that was gone.

Margot could scarcely bring herself to glance at these hideous flowers; or even to hide her pain from her mother and Aunt Ella. Mrs. Entwhistle had come into the room, doubtless hearing the commotion, and she was staring too in admiration.

"My—but aren't they pretty!"

"Do you remember Margaret, Mrs. Entwhistle?"

"Oh, yes, I remember *her*." Mrs. Entwhistle nodded briskly. "She's the one that used to be in the library!"

Margot tried to smile, to make them think she was properly delighted—to hide herself from them. It seemed as if the room was filled with women. But there was a dreary solace in their excitement. She could see that now they looked at her with increased respect. Even mother! To mother, Dorothy was still her colleague, and Margot was still the spinster daughter.

"Aren't you going to tell us who these came from?" Aunt Ella demanded. "What about that card? Don't you think she ought to pass it over to us? You know anything about this, Annie?"

"Not a thing." Mother looked at her half timidly, but smiling.

"You can see it," Margot said carelessly.

She flipped the card onto Aunt Ella's lap. Let Aunt Ella make what she could out of it!

"Oh, no, I guess we better not," Aunt Ella protested, somewhat scandalized.

"Go ahead!"

Aunt Ella read aloud ponderously, " 'Bee-reaved without you. All nature mourns. Hec.' Is that right? That's what it says. Is that a name?"

"Kind of a one," Margot said disdainfully.

"Sounds funny."

"The real name is Hector."

"*Hector?* Is that a man's name? I thought it was a dog's. Why, Roy Hatch has got a dog named Hector."

"Well, there isn't much difference," Margot said, with acid pleasure. But she was remorseful, seeing mother give her a confused, anxious look.

Aunt Ella repeated, "Well, anyway, it must be pretty serious when he telegraphs, whatever his name is. Annie, we want to look out. Margaret may surprise us by getting married yet." She frankly surveyed Margot.

Margot shrugged her shoulders.

Mother was still puzzled. "But how do you suppose they got your name like that?" she asked.

Aunt Ella chimed in again. "Yes, ain't that funny! 'Margott.' Whoever heard of a name like that? It's worse than the other. I should think the greenhouse would have known who you are."

"Well, I expect maybe the telegram—"

"Yes, but the greenhouse ought to have known who she was. Cliff Taylor ought to have lived long enough in this town for that."

Margot said impatiently, "That *is* my name. That's what people call me!"

" 'Margot'? Who calls you that?"

"It isn't 'Margott.' Mar-*got.*"

"Well, it's got a *t* on it!"

"Yes, but that's the way it's pronounced. It's French."

"What you got a French name for?" Aunt Ella demanded, very humorously.

Margot shrugged her shoulders again.

"I think it's a very pretty nickname," mother said.

She had to endure the excitement of all the three females over getting the flowers put into water. Margot hated these roses as she had the geraniums that little red-eared Eddie Whitby had given her once at school, in the days when she was making up romantic stories about the beautiful Gardner Allen. But she felt again that dreary solace in the uproar that the whole thing caused. It had raised her status quite definitely, she saw. Aunt Ella was trying to get her to explain, mother wanting to be told, and hurt because she wasn't.

Margot said, "Well, I'm going back to my breakfast."

"I should think you'd want your flowers with you in there!—where you could see them. I would, if anybody sent me a bouquet like that."

"You can look at them," Margot said pointedly.

"Well, she takes it coolly," Aunt Ella observed as Margot left them. "Must be used to getting flowers." She stared again.

Margot stayed in the dining room until she was sure that Aunt Ella was gone. Then she wandered back into the living room. There was the same quivering dreariness everywhere, without Bruce. His absence seemed to stop all action at the center. Margot sat down to the piano, played a few bars, and stopped.

"Oh, go on and play," her mother begged her.

"I don't know anything any more."

"Didn't you ever play in New York?"

"I didn't have any piano."

She got up restlessly, wanting to stave off questions about New York. Mother was hurt because Margot told her so little. But it couldn't be helped. Margot turned on the radio, getting bursts of sound from various stations, as she moved the indicator carelessly. A woman's hard, bossy voice blared out, disguised under a specious sweetness.

"And of course you will want the recipe for the ice box cookies, if you do not have it already. I know that each and

456

every one of you swears by her *own* ice box cookies. But even so . . ."

Margot snapped off the radio.

"Horrors, what a female! How can you stand it?"

"She gives very good recipes sometimes. I don't like her voice very well, either," mother admitted. "But they all talk that way. It isn't so good in the mornings, but in the evenings we get lovely concerts. Dad likes the Eskimo Band."

Margot flopped into a big chair. It was a pain to be spoken to, a pain to be forced to give her attention. But when she was alone she couldn't stand the leaden dreariness.

Her mother said, "I wish we could have some of the girls over while you're here."

"What girls?"

"Why, Margaret, the girls you used to play with. Your old crowd."

"I never had any crowd."

"Why, yes, you did," mother said, pained. "You used to play with Edna Mae and Lucille. You've seen Lucille in New York. It's too bad she isn't here this summer. Of course the other girls are both married."

"Can't they get out?" Margot asked ironically.

"Well, I just meant, they're busy with their children. And Edna Mae hasn't been very well." She went on quite unconsciously to talk about Mildred. "She has three *very* sweet little children. Of course I don't see much of her. That young crowd don't do much but play bridge. But we'll probably see her at the picnic tonight."

"Is Gardner Allen in the Rotary?" Good heavens!

"Oh, yes, he's been in some time. He took his father's place."

He would be!—Margot thought sardonically. But she couldn't, even now, avoid a twinge of jealousy. Mildred was no doubt the perfect small matron, and had everything she wanted!

She got up restlessly, saying that she was going out on the porch.

"All right," her mother called after her, happily, "I'll come out with you after I've looked at my cake."

Margot sat down in the swing. The slight motion sickened her. She couldn't bear to look out on the lawn—to see the tree under which Dorothy had stood to be married. Mother was constantly lamenting, "It's too bad you couldn't have seen Dorothy while you were out West." "Well, mother, I couldn't say where to go." "No, of course not, if you were with other people." For a little while, she *had* thought of going to Dorothy's. They had always been different, and yet allies. Dorothy's house had seemed to her her refuge. But after all, Dorothy was married, she was one of the enemies—Margot could feel Dorothy judging her in advance. She couldn't bear to be "Auntie Margaret" and palaver over the children. And she couldn't endure to show herself to such an attractive man as Jesse in any light but that of being radiantly successful. To Jesse, she would still be only the unmarried sister—a kind of Sister Anne! There wasn't any refuge. Not anywhere. New York—but the old crowd had none of them liked Bruce, they would welcome her back in glee as one who had learned her lesson.

She heard Bun go tearing into the house again. "Where'd you get the flowers? Gee! She must have a boy friend." He said it carelessly, and tore out again, wrapped up in his own concerns. It made Margot feel old.

There was nothing she could bear to do, nowhere she wanted to go. She dreaded getting outside the confines of her own lot. Here, Mrs. Morgan was always nice to her, in her funny dry way, because she was a Ferguson—although Mrs. Morgan liked Dorothy best. And Mrs. Viele was sweet to everyone! The people in the rented house next door didn't matter. But Margot had met Vanchie one day on the street, had stopped—and Vanchie had scarcely greeted her. Vanchie had never forgiven her for deserting the Bellews and not going on with her library course. Why should she have cared so much about Vanchie? But she did. She had felt stripped and ashamed, losing that old fond adoration. Just as when Mary Lou had gone back on her! She felt that she could show herself to Vanchie only as careless and successful—not maimed and marred. Everywhere, now, she had to go unsupported by the knowledge of Bruce's care. She felt a shameful dependence on those silly flowers, which would get her by with the family. The morning sunshine was pleasant on the lawn, that was fresh and green after the late summer rains. The asphalt was dappled with leaf shadows. But she was out of tune with it. She had never been in tune.

Margot was dressing for the Rotary-Ann picnic. What a dreary joke! But nearly everything now was a dreary, sardonic joke—on her. Her reluctance of the morning had changed to a hard, cynical determination to show people in Belmond that she wasn't just Margaret Ferguson any more. She heard her mother busy about the house; and she felt, with an envy that was both painful and contemptuous, that she would put romantic ideas of love out of her life—that was the way to be successful—she would charm some roaming widower at the picnic and settle down in a home in Belmond. She would be what the folks wanted. It irked her that all these women still spoke in guarded tones about married life before her: Mrs. Viele, the other day, saying archly, "I don't know whether we ought to be letting Margaret hear these things!" Margot didn't believe in her resolve even while she was making it. All the same, she wanted to show people. She put on the white silk sports suit with the yellow hat, yellow stockings and white sandals. Yes, earrings, whether they suited this costume or not! She remembered, with an ironic twist of her mouth, how she had always meant to come back to Belmond in long earrings. Her Indian jewelry, though, she would never wear again. Never the ring which Bruce had put on her hand! *She* had a ring, as well as all these ladies, and far more exciting than theirs—but of course they wouldn't see it! She made up only her eyes and lips. She supposed it would kill the folks if she smoked out there! They accepted smoking now, as long as she didn't do it before other people. Bun had broken them in to all such things.

"Margaret! There's someone to see you."

Mother's voice was pleased and excited. At last someone had called on her! Mother had been hurt by Vanchie's coolness. It couldn't be Bruce—or mother's voice wouldn't sound that way; so it couldn't possibly be anyone she wanted to see.

459

Margot went slowly down the stairs. This morning she had had to fight against reluctance to see a soul, and to tear herself out of her painful absorption. She knew Aunt Ella had gone away saying, "Well, she ain't any better-natured than she used to be, even if she *is* better looking." Aunt Ella couldn't get over it that she was better-looking, Aunt Ella's expectations had been so low. But this afternoon, Margot felt hard, bitter and easy, competent to deal with anything in a sort of contempt of its lack of significance to her.

"You have a caller," her mother said, pleased.

A tall, rawboned girl in a badly hung dress was standing just inside the hallway, with her mouth open.

"Do you know me?" She gave an eager, awkward laugh. "I guess you remember Ada Rist."

As she heard the excited, foolish pleasure of the tone, Margot was ashamed because she couldn't feel anything better than relief that it wasn't somebody worse. For a moment she had had an awful vision of Hec following her here. But it was too easy to impress Ada! She saw the glisten of admiration in Ada's vacant eyes.

"Well, I should say I do," Margot said easily.

Ada laughed again, abruptly, too pleased, when Margot shook hands. She gave another laugh, and then moistly kissed Margot's cheek. She seemed delighted because Margot hadn't ordered her away.

"I wouldn't hardly have known you," she said now; and added with naïve enthusiasm, "You certainly do look great. I guess it agrees with you there in New York."

Ada's eyes glistened still more. For a moment Margot felt a cynical happiness, as she thought that here was one person with whom she wouldn't change places even to get rid of her misery! She used to endure Ada hanging around, see her only as a satellite, as if Ada were actually non-existent except in relation to herself; but now her own pain opened up to her a vision of Ada's life as it was in itself, with its meager personal pleasures and its vicarious excitements. Evidently Ada still adored her. She stood holding Margot's hand, fumbling it in her clumsy fingers. Margot heard the foolish eagerness of her

460

laugh. What a mess the world was! This was only another instance of the way she attracted a person who could mean nothing to her. Anger at the craziness of existence forced her to smother her impatience, and smile. But she couldn't really think of a thing to say, the encounter was so meaningless to her.

She asked at random, "What are you doing now?"

"Oh, I keep the books at the implement works now," Ada said proudly. "It's a lot nicer being at home here where you know folks and have someone to go around with than being off there where I was." Apparently Ada took it for granted that Margot had been keeping up with her history. Margot hadn't the faintest idea where "off there" might be. "Aren't you ever coming back here?"

"Doesn't look like it," Margot answered.

"You must like it there in New York," Ada said with her foolish laugh, staring with admiration.

Margot smiled. But again she had a troubling vision of Ada's life, making her interest out of the events of the town from the outskirts, going with "the girls" to the movies and afterwards gorging themselves on chocolate sundaes at the less popular drug store where they could hide the shame of their aging solitude from the blithe callousness of the high school chits, excited by their adoration of their favorite female stars and hiding their crushes on the male stars, buying the movie magazines to read about "the love affairs of the stars." Margot perceived, with a good deal more irony and less pleasure than she had once expected to feel, that to Ada she herself was what Ada doubtless had learned to call "glamorous" from the movie magazines. But it did give her a slight revenge for Vanchie's flustered ability to hold to her disapproval and stay unmoved by the fascination Margot used to exert. Margot felt almost warm toward Ada—as warm as she could feel toward anyone, when her heart was so dry. She felt the irony of being appreciated at just the value she had wanted to give herself.

"Why do we stand out here?" she said with vague cordiality.

But Ada wouldn't go into the living room. She answered

461

with awe, "Oh, no, I don't want to make you late for the picnic."

Evidently Ada regarded the Rotary picnic as too lofty a social event to aspire to. It made Margot think of the old days when Ada would stand waiting in mute, awkward adoration, after school, until she saw whether Margot was going off with "the girls" among whom Ada was too humble ever to think of including herself.

"You must come again, Ada," Mrs. Ferguson said now.

"Yes," Margot repeated somewhat vaguely.

She pitied Ada as much as she could anyone when she herself was so sore. But did mother actually think she could be excited by a call from Ada Rist? Well, she would show the folks this afternoon. She would do *that* much.

Bun was out in front now with the car, honking loudly. Dad, as usual, was afraid they wouldn't be on time, and mother was afraid they would forget the baskets. It seemed to Margot she had known all this from the beginning of time. She went out and got into the car beside Bun.

"You the driver?"

"Yeah, if I can get dad into the back seat. I can make half an hour better time than dad and he won't know it. It's a trick." Bun grinned. "You want to drive?" he generously offered.

Margot shook her head. The words struck on a very tender spot in her memory. She felt the pain of being in any car but their own roadster, hers and Bruce's, driving through the sunshine toward the blue mountains. What if she should startle the folks by telling them that a man had bought a car for her! But they wouldn't believe her, probably. They still thought of Carl and Dorothy as "popular" and Margaret as "unpopular."

Bunny, however, as they got out of the car at the picnic grounds, showed a certain pride. Margot felt that mother was rather uneasy about her looks, about what people would think. Maybe she was a little too exotically "smart." Bun took her arm and led her forward, and Margot could feel that, even if she was his sister, he was half shyly pleased to appear with her before a crowd. It helped her vanity greatly and made her

462

feel suddenly a sort of barren gaiety that would prove capable of anything she chose to do.

Oh Lord, but how familiar was this picnic grove!—the long tables under the heavy trees. What would the old crowd say if they knew she was attending a Rotarian picnic?—and looking forward to it with some excitement? Margot felt her old impatience at the familiarity of the middlewestern atmosphere, the dark green leaves, the concentration upon food, the fat men already licking their chops, and the matrons stooping broad-beamed over the well-filled baskets. The Rotary Anns were entertaining the Rotary boys. But at least Margot was pleased that the foks had got this much more secular. They were worldly, in fact, compared to what they used to be! Yet she had an outraged disbelief. How could she be here? For a moment she struggled with it as if it were a nightmare. She seemed to see, beyond these heavy oak trees, the sunny peace of the pueblo on a cloudless day.

There was the first slight embarrassment of facing the group. But she saw instantly that she was the best-dressed woman there, the most striking. It gave her a rather pleasant feeling of cool world-weariness above her pain. Her mother was saying nervously, with a little laugh, not quite knowing whether she dared to be proud of this daughter, "Of course you know Margaret!"

There was some consolation in seeing the surprised, interested eyes, the calculating glances of the women, no doubt wondering "what she had done to herself." Most of them hadn't known her well, thank God. Dad had become a Rotarian since her day in Belmond. It showed how the folks' prestige had increased that the club had made a pretext of dad's handling of estates to bring him in as well as Richard, two from the same bank. But Ethel Spencer greeted Margot with effusion, taking both her hands.

"Why, Margaret Ferguson! I've been hearing about you from Grimmie. She's wild about you. Isn't she a dear old thing?"

Ethel's bright eyes had taken her all in and approved. Margot had a subtle feeling of being accepted as a confederate in the great business of man-charming. She saw with mixed dismay and satisfaction that even Ethel was not so pretty as she used to be. The gray in her hair was pretty, like the powdering for a fancy dress ball, but the lines in her face were deeper, and the muscles of her throat sagged. "Oh God, does everybody have to get old?" Margot remembered what Aunt Ella had said this morning, that had caused her bitter moments before her mirror. She felt a cold breath of fear. It was not so much satisfaction, after all, to find that she was prettier now than Ethel Spencer.

However, she approved of Ethel's blithe forgetfulness of the duties of women. Ethel had set out the things for herself and Richard, and now she left the other females to decide on which end of the table to place her cake. She thrust her little hand through Margot's arm and went off with her, saying:

"Have you seen everybody? Let's get away from those tables. Aren't these things deadly? My dear, you've saved my life by coming! You look absolutely grand."

Ethel was walking her cleverly nearer the men who were grouped together, loudly jesting, and making sport of being pampered sultans. Mr. Viele was calling out loudly, "Let the women do the work!" Someone else was saying that this was his idea of feminism. "Say, if it is, let's have it every day in the week!"

Ethel murmured, "Have you seen Richard?"

Now he came up to them with alacrity. Margot felt a slight, sardonic smile on her lips. Richard had been eyeing her from a distance.

Ethel said with a subtle intonation, "You remember Margaret, don't you, Richard?"

"Margaret?"

"Margaret Ferguson."

"Well! For the love of—Little Margaret Ferguson! Why, I thought you were just a small child."

"Oh, no, I grew up before I left town."

"You did? Well, where were you hiding? I never saw anything like this!"

She said pointedly, "You never saw me at all!"

464

"What's that?" Richard seized her arm. "Well, I'm going to make up for that right now. Hear that, Ethel?"

Ethel smiled sweetly and ambiguously. Her eyes were wandering, but Margot wasn't interested enough to follow where. They were calling everyone now to come and eat. Some man with glasses and a fat face was getting up and bawling in stentorian tones. Some of the old notables of the town were here— the Vieles, the Hoaglands—but the club was at least half made up of what the folks used to call "the younger married set." It was funny to see the folks among them! Margot herself, when she was a child, used to think of them as almost unholily "fast." But now they looked staid enough.

"Ethel, is this our table?" Richard said significantly.

He drew Margot down beside him. Margot saw that she had been placed in a select group. Mother was looking a little anxious at Richard's attentions. But it must be all right with Ethel there! Ethel did not seem disturbed. Margot didn't know, or remember, who all these people at the table were. It was the "gay table," obviously. But looking down it a little way, she saw a head of white hair that disturbed her with its familiarity. All at once she knew who it was. It was Dr. Redmond! The hero of her dreams. But Richard was keeping up such a barrage of compliment and jaunty innuendo that she hardly had time to look around her.

"Does everybody know Margaret Ferguson?" Ethel asked sweetly and inclusively.

"Sure, everybody does!" Richard answered.

"They don't. Or *I* don't," Margot said to him in a low voice.

"Don't tell me you want to be introduced to anyone. I couldn't stand it."

"I don't. But I do want to know, where's Gardner Allen?"

"Gardner Allen? Hah? What's the heart interest there? I don't believe I'll show you. Well, there he is. I trust you, Margaret. The gentleman at the next table beside the chocolate cake."

Margot looked. *"No."*

"No, she says! What does that mean? Want an introduction?"

465

"I'll kill you if you attempt one. There's no heart interest. None at all. But he used to be the prettiest boy in our room at school."

"Is that a fact?" Richard asked with vague geniality.

Then he put several sandwiches on her plate, telling her that she was his partner's daughter, and he must look after her.

Gardner Allen! That fat slob! Margot knew that it had lain stealthily in her mind all day, hardening her and making it possible for her to stand things enough to go to the picnic— the thought of carrying off Gardner Allen before the eyes of Mildred. That was the reason for the mysterious eye-shadow, and the yellow silk stockings, and the yellow hat. But when she looked at him now, it seemed too much of a punishment. Yes, he had turned into a sloppy small town slob, with receding hair and rimless glasses, and a deflated, bewildered look. Mildred, of course, was too much for him. Margot remembered that mother had said Gardner wasn't doing so well with the store. Evidently he was not accepted among the élite of the Rotarians. But all the same, she bet it *was* because Mildred was too much for him! There was Mildred herself. And she was just a youngish small town matron. She, who had long been to Margot a symbol for a type of femininity, spurring Margot on to greater efforts! Nevertheless, Margot saw from her eyes, from a certain uneasiness and animation in her glances, that she was still capable of cutting up and was far from resigned to being no longer very pretty. She didn't like it very well, having to sit beside poor Gardner. He was quite out of the hilarity of the "gay table." Margot was confused between feeling sorry for him and still feeling jealously that it was his own fault. Mildred was sore because they had been placed where they were! If she watched, Margot thought, she could no doubt see with whom Mildred was having an affair or whom she was after. She could forgive and even approve that in Ethel Spencer. But not in Mildred Summers! Mildred was up to her old tricks! Margot thought she hated these women most of all who played both sides. But again it was not interesting enough to seem worth while to put herself to the trouble of watching.

Dinner was good, of course. You could count on food at

466

home, if nothing else. All were loud in their praises of the Rotary Anns. Margot was excited, after all, by Ethel's subtle implication that they two were banded together to have a little feminine delight apart from the housewifely herd. It was pleasing to have Richard's attentions, even while she discounted them. He was jaunty as of old, when she had stared after him, highly impressed, as he went down the street swinging the only walking stick in town. And she had always liked him, in spite of what she knew was the folks' unspoken disapproval, because he had said that she would "work havoc." Well, she hoped that now she was working it!

When they got up, Ethel again thrust her hand through Margot's arm and drew her away. "Tell me about Grimmie," she begged. They went off toward the creek. Ethel said ingenuously, "I love to wander in the woods, don't you?" Margot was amused at the dreamy look of absence with which she contemplated the other women getting to work at the tables. But Margot defiantly approved of it. She felt a savage hostility toward the housewives, and imagined that they were all regarding her with stern condemnation. As a matter of fact little Mrs. Cummings was saying wistfully that she wished *she* could wear yellow; and Mrs. Ferguson was flushed with praises from Mrs. Viele and Mrs. Hoagland in regard to Margaret's improved appearance.

"I always thought Dorothy was a lovely little thing. But I didn't know you had *two* such beautiful daughters! Somehow, I didn't seem to know Margaret so well."

But the men soon drifted near, as always when Ethel was around. Margot thought she saw now that Ethel was tightening the reins on Richard in a subtle manner. Her effusiveness toward Margot had not decreased, but now it was imbued with a certain defensive alertness. No, Ethel never gave herself away, either! She never really got in wrong. When four of them went strolling beside the creek, it turned out to be Ethel and Richard and Margot and Dr. Redmond. And then Ethel thought of something that she wanted in the car and Margot and Dr. Redmond were left together. To be regarded in Belmond as a dangerous woman! She supposed it was a triumph. It afforded her no particular pleasure; but all the same, she wouldn't have been without it. For a moment, she contemplated going out for Richard and giving Ethel a genuine scare, feeling slightly angry at the sense of Ethel's maneuver. But it didn't seem any more worth while than to pretend to the folks that Hec was someone she might marry. Where had he ever got the money to send her those roses? He must have done it when he was drunk. She hated Bruce, because he hadn't even left her the poor satisfactions of her vanity.

Still, there was an ironic pleasure in contemplating the fact that she was in what had once appeared to her as a romantic position, strolling on the river bank (or at any rate, along the edge of the creek) with her old hero Dr. Redmond, while his wife was left laboring among the housewives. Dr. Redmond pretended that he remembered her perfectly. But Margot knew he didn't at all. They made conversation out of this. And she had thought that he would be a romantic lover! Probably because of the ice cream pants, she now thought sorrowfully. There was a curious embarrassment in his manner, which Margot only partly realized came from his uncertainty with her. She seemed to him too young and too well-dressed to consider him very seriously. He felt himself old and shabby beside her. It made Margot angry. She didn't want the person who had once represented all the romance that Belmond had to offer, now to be showing himself such easy prey as this. He laughed nervously at all that she said; and he was only too anxious and pleased when she suggested that she was in need of a drink.

"Come on," he urged her, seizing upon this. "I've got a flask in the car. Probably not so good as what you get there in New York, but it's guaranteed bourbon."

"No. I don't think so. It would be too much of a blow to my folks."

"They won't see us. There are lots of woods around here, aren't there?" He gave a foolish laugh.

"No, I can't be such an undutiful daughter."

"Come, now, don't tell me you're always so dutiful. I've heard about these girls who live in New York!"

468

"Yes, but haven't you heard you shouldn't believe all you hear?"

"Oh, come now, you've raised a thirst, don't go back on me."

"I may have raised it, but I can't satisfy it."

"Oh, yes, I think you could," he said significantly.

Margot suddenly felt angry, disgusted, and she wanted to laugh. He was a sickening old owl, at that! But it was simply too tiresome for her to go on with it. She would almost rather be back with the Rotary Anns than go on with this. Sorry to dash the good doctor's hopes, but—

"Listen! There must be something going on."

He was reluctant in none too delightful a fashion, but Margot insisted brightly that she must see what it was. "Of course I must!" She was interested in *any*-thing that could happen at a Rotary Ann picnic. Not anything, the doctor reminded her with significance. But she walked quickly out of the woods as if she were a prim virgin disgusted with "advances." Anything to get away from this sorry anticlimax of disillusionment! As she saw the crowd of wives settled to watch the men pack up the baskets, as had evidently been hilariously agreed upon, she thought all at once of her own little kitchen where she had puttered around during the sunny hours of the morning while Bruce painted on the terrace. Her pain was too great for hatred. But it seemed to her that she was shut out from everywhere.

And the villain still pursued her! She told him pointedly that he ought to be packing his basket. He refused to do it unless she helped.

"I help?"

"Well, you're not one of the Rotary Anns."

"No, but I'm exempt. I'm only a daughter."

"Daughters have to work."

"Oh, no, they don't. You must pack your basket, or I'll think you're not a good husband."

Well, it served him right! He had turned all colors. She was disgusted with him, anyway. She saw his wife, suddenly remembering her, a thin, embittered woman with dead eyes; and suddenly Margot wanted to be on her side. Yet she couldn't be on her side, either. Oh, everything was a mess! Margot sat down on the bench beside her mother, glad all at once of mother's soft, bright innocence.

Mildred was there too. Suddenly she caught a glint of nervous hatred from Mildred's eyes. Mildred was sitting and loudly joining in the women's mockery of the men's basket packing. But if Mildred happened to glance at Gardner, her face grew vacant and she looked away. Life was turning out to be even crazier than Margot had supposed it could be! That one little look had told her that Dr. Redmond was now Mildred's Great Moment! That explained his extra gallant and reckless air. So she had now beaten out Mildred after all! Well, she was going to enjoy it. She *would* enjoy it, although her flesh crept with disgust, exactly as if she had been one of the worthy matrons. Oh, yes, Mildred was still in the running! Now coarseness made up for the loss of subtler attractions. It was a poor triumph! A mess all round.

Mrs. Viele said archly, "Margaret, how does it happen you haven't anyone to pack a basket?"

"Oh, we don't know what Margaret has up her sleeve," Mrs. Hoagland said.

She could see that mother hadn't been able to refrain from telling them about the roses! There was a kindly, interested look in the women's eyes, as if they thought they scented a wedding.

Dr. Redmond sat down near her again. Margot ignored him. But he was uneasy about Mildred too. He didn't want to lose out there. He had long ago ceased even the pretense of thinking about his wife. Margot hadn't heard, but she had seen—with a shudder, she could imagine—the dry little colloquy between them when he had gone belatedly to pack the basket.

There were shouts a little way off. They were getting up some races. Bun was at the head of them. He had constituted himself the leader of the crowd of youthful daughters, high school girls, and even younger.

"Oh, I guess the younger set are up to something," Mrs. Hoagland said, settling her bulk contentedly.

Margot watched idly. She felt a sudden searing jealousy. In the light of it, she hated the whole crowd with whom she had been eating and playing, who ought long ago to have forfeited their threadbare title of "younger married set." She saw Dr. Redmond's dissipated middle-age in heartless clarity. Even Richard's jauntiness was affected by a brilliant display of bridge work when he smiled. And she fancied he was using stuff on his hair. She remembered again what Aunt Ella had said to her that morning. Trust Aunt Ella for such sweet remarks! Margot had a cold, senseless fear that life was over. And as she watched Bun, she was acutely jealous of his easy youth, that had come into all the best of things; of his nice, ingenuous face, with the thick mussed brown hair and the freckles, the sleeves rolled up on his arms brown from swimming. The little girls standing taut and set for the race looked unbelievably slim and fresh, in their brief dresses, with their sunburned legs and casual socks. Margot felt all at once marked and dissolute. She looked in cold disgust at her slender, stained forefinger. She felt as if she had played out her part, and another show was beginning.

"Ready! Get set! GO!"

One little girl sprang ahead of the rest and won. Bun brought her up to get her prize from Mr. Viele. Bun was brotherly to all these girls, although slightly patronizing as a college youth. Margot felt again, as she looked at him, the happier auspices under which he had grown up—the kid brother—taking all the privileges she used to crave without suspecting anyone had ever had to fight for them. She saw that the eyes of the matrons had turned from her now and were fixed with smiling admiration upon this little girl. She was a hard little thing, athletic, in socks and sunburn, with her hair pushed carelessly back. Margot remembered how she herself had adored Grimmie, the person from away. But this child was cool and competent, she didn't even see the exotic stranger.

"Who is she?" Margot asked her mother.

"Why, that's Frankie Weyant. Addie's cousin. She goes to our church."

"Goes to our church!" That made it all the worse. Frankie Weyant had sat down with Bun, and was scratching a mosquito bite. As Margot stared at them, and at the next races, she had a

471

strange feeling, like that old feeling of mystic enlargement, and yet different . . . as if the world, while she was not watching, had made another mysterious revolution, and was already turning from her own kind of girl—she was no longer standing at the center—but the light was shining prophetically, like the long light of morning, upon this fresh little hard figure with the tossed-back hair.

The light got dimmer in the grove. It took the folks ages to pack up. Bun was going swimming with the other kids, and then to the movies. Although he had been proud to make his appearance with Margot, she was too aged to be even considered. She would have to go home with mother and dad. As she waited in the thick twilight, she felt as if all the crowd around her were marred and scarred and past anything new. The heavy leaves shut out the sky, and now the mosquitoes were beginning. She had had what she wanted. Nothing could ever take it away from her, but nothing could bring back the wish. Now, at this restless moment of impending dusk, she would have wanted something new if she could . . . only she was impaled on the old, she couldn't . . . She saw ahead of her another night to be got through without Bruce. She had everything, even the belated admiration of Dr. Redmond—with Richard's attentions thrown in for largess—all because she didn't need them now, she supposed, and no longer cared for them. What forces had she set moving, down what mysterious pathways, when she had wished those wishes long ago? Now it seemed worst of all to remember that once she had had "the time and the place and the loved one all together" and could never have them in the same way again. Her fatal faculty for flawed experience—she had dropped back into it again. Those hidden forces, so cruel and so sweet and so hideously just, were no longer working for her. She tried to imagine a time when Bruce would come to her and she would no longer want him. She had to imagine something for the future—find some oasis in that dreary waste. But this wouldn't do, for it would poison, obliterate, make meaningless the happiness she had possessed. She would rather go on wanting him forever. Was that all that lay ahead of her? She thought of the thin, dark, hungry girl

472

who had lived in this place hidden and alone. She felt that girl avenged. And after all—all the happiness, all Bruce's love—that seemed to be the only satisfaction she could really feel . . . and that, so faintly! She remembered the admiring glisten of Ada's eyes. She saw that she had become, more or less, what once she used to dream of being, in those stuffy afternoons at the library, reading other women's poetry—she was returning home after what she used to think of as a great, tragic experience, knowing how she wanted to dress, wearing long earrings. . . . But this was how it really felt. Margot bent down and killed a mosquito viciously. Why didn't the folks hurry? She had pictured herself sitting somewhere, beautiful and torn by life, dressed in filmy black, and writing sonnets that recorded the great experience of her life. She couldn't write of this grinding reality. It possessed her too completely. What was written about had to be held away . . . and if she *could* hold it away, that in itself was a kind of defeat.

The voices sounded like voices on the stage. And yet everything seemed local and small and actual. Margot stared at the women talking together, at the Hoaglands climbing into their big car. All her old ideas, so long, so intensely and jealously cherished, seemed suddenly to go to pot. She admitted to herself, in deflated bitterness, that she wanted nothing but to be with Bruce, and on any terms—she could even have been a Rotary Ann if *he* had been packing her basket. Was that what it came to?—being completely in love with someone? No, she didn't admit that. She still believed that she had had something beyond what these women had experienced. She had taken her love for what it was—anyway, for a time. She shuddered at the perception of the long, bitter, pitched, marital battles, and pressed to herself the sweet, painful knowledge of her love. She felt herself obliterated by it. That had been an exaltation. But if it left her to this blackness . . .

"Well, Margaret, ready to go home? You got sort of left out," Mrs. Hoagland said, coming back for a spoon dropped in the grass. "Whew!" She straightened her back. "I guess all of us wish we were young enough to run races. But I don't think even a prize could tempt *me*."

It was very different—the feeling of reaching New York this time. No one knew that she was coming back. Margot didn't know why she was, herself, except that she couldn't stand it at home any longer. The atmosphere had begun to get strained. Mother couldn't understand the telegrams and special deliveries from Hec—silly ass!—when Margot assured her that she cared nothing about him. She had tried to tell mother carelessly that he was a man she had met on her trip. But mother saw further than that—although not as far as the truth. "But do you think you ought to hear from him so much if you don't care about him?" The folks had pretended they wanted to keep her in Belmond; but actually, if they had ever told the truth, they didn't very well like the prospect of having a grown-up daughter on their hands. The folks had a social life of their own now. They no longer seemed to exist solely for the sake of their children. The folks had accepted it now that Margot had cut away from them. They actually liked her better for it! Dad, now, when he spoke to her, took an entirely different tone. But of course nothing could really bring up her stock with the folks except getting married.

Margot looked drearily around at the other people. A fat woman in a wrinkleless black crêpe (so well corseted that she probably didn't acknowledge she was fat) was now putting on her fur coat. Margot felt set apart in her brown tweed suit. She was returning to New York in the same suit and hat she had worn when she came away. She had gone with her mother and Mrs. Viele on one of the shopping trips to Geneva which were part of the weekly schedule now in Belmond; but long, long past were the days when she had considered buying a dress at Schauffler's Department Store as having attained the heights of fashion. The brown tweed seemed to keep woven within its rough texture the dust of the roads and the smoke of the campfire and the pure sunlit air of the desert. She wore it like a hair shirt. It kept reminding her of all that was past.

There was no interest, only a shuddering aversion, in getting back to New York. The recognitions that she couldn't help making hurt her. The train was passing through the great Jersey marshes, and soon it would reach those awful miles of suburbs. Margot couldn't bear to look. The waste, empty marshes were too symbolic of her own life. She had got past the first stage of acute suffering, and now she seemed to be entering this phase of emptiness. She looked at her love affair from outside, noting all its stages, as if it were a long-drawn-out disease. But when she thought of the cure, everything in her protested. She could not imagine life with no thought of Bruce at all. She tried to tell herself that she had no hope, and she knew disdainfully that her fairy tale was shot to pieces; but she was aware still of a little living, smothered thread of interest because Bruce was in the world.

She picked up her bag and went into the dressing room. Her face in the glass had a darkened, sallow look. Frowning, she took out her cold cream and her cleansing tissues, and then slapped her skin revengefully with a cloth dipped in astringent, according to the best beauty advice. But her face didn't come out all new, as the advice promised. There were dark places still under her eyes. And now for the first time she noted a faint hollow under her chin. No—it wasn't just that she wasn't feeling her best, that she was tired. These things were marked to stay. What Aunt Ella had said was true. She didn't look so young as she used to! She had begun to lose her looks. In a struggle of wild revolt, Margot thought in horror of what this would mean: no longer to rejoice in the tingling smoothness of her body when she rubbed it dry with a great Turkish towel, nor to feel that every change of color in a hat or scarf brought out another aspect of her dark charm. . . . She had thought that everyone could get old but herself. That it was something they could help! Now she felt the dry terror of that inescapable encroachment. The signs had begun. She fell into a hideous re- counting of all the marks and ruins of age that she had noted— the way Mrs. Viele's hair had turned white underneath with rusty streaks of red on top; Vanchie's withered, long, delicate throat, yellow and pathetic; the mole with the stiff black hairs and the other hair patches on Ada Rist's heavy chin; the harsh, colorless fuzz on Mrs. Morgan's bleak face; Aunt Ella's hanging jowls . . . Mrs. Lowrie's lumpy figure. . . . All these horrors seemed to be lying in wait for her. She saw just how they went. No! She would be an exception. . . . But even now, she wouldn't have dared to toss back her hair carelessly like that child Frankie. She would never look any better than now—and even now she didn't look as well as she had a while ago. She could only hope to stave off, not to improve.

Margot could scarcely bear to look at the mirror as she renewed her make-up. This face didn't represent her any more than had the dark little unfledged face she had seen in just such a glass as this the first time she had come to New York.

She went back to her section to endure the rest of the journey. That dreadful session with the mirror seemed to have killed even the one little spark of feminine interest she had felt that morning when she had noticed that the somewhat good-looking dark man had halted at the entrance to the dining car and at just the slightest look from her would have come to her table. She knew that he was looking at her now. And for a moment she was able to recover a slight, romantic consciousness of herself, dark-eyed and somber, a mysteriously experienced woman sitting alone. But she felt perversely that the doom she had seen for herself was already upon her. Margot felt a queer sense of almost hysterical gratitude at his interest in her, mixed with scorn, as if he didn't have the sense to know that she had begun to lose her beauty. "You ought to see Frankie Weyant!" she had a crazy desire to tell him. Why couldn't she have given him that look? She perceived him as a married man temporarily on the loose. Or why couldn't she have seen him on her first trip when she was dying to create interest in somebody? She felt again that she hated Bruce. She wanted to hurt him by developing an interest in someone else. But because other men weren't Bruce she wasn't able to trump up even that much interest in them.

No, she couldn't stand it, she couldn't live. . . . Before, even when she was miserable, she had always seen the shining outlines of some great experience ahead of her. Her misery was because she had despaired ever of reaching it. There had always been expectation. On her first lonely journey, everything had been before her. Now it was all behind. She couldn't think of anything in the world she wanted, because it wouldn't be equal to what she had had. She could only play out the same story over and over in more and more debased versions, like an old artist repeating himself. That was all, now, that any love affair could be. And when she thought of one so entirely different that it would create experience, the wrench from what she had known was too great. Even her wishes couldn't encompass it. She had wanted to love to the height of her ability, and now she did, and she was bound within those brutal limitations. She could feel nothing beyond a savagely bleak desire to act on necessity. She seemed to see things only for what they were—a flat vision, like that of all the middle-aged, ordinary people she had always despised. Either she must keep this hurt forever chafing, and live with it, or accept the flat emptiness if she tore the image of Bruce out of her heart where it was embedded.

She couldn't bear to look at the other people, who were now closing their bags and putting on coats and hats. She didn't want to have to think of them—her own pain was enough. She felt herself too well informed of the various signs of frustration and contentment.

The train reached the station. Margot stood up in the aisle with the other travelers. If she could be sure that Bruce still loved her, she could feel herself dark and sad and marked out with tragic experience from among them; but if he didn't, then she seemed to be nothing, not even alive. The fat woman in the fur coat was crowded up behind her, eyeing her with curiosity. Margot's eyes, grown hideously sharp, had spotted the drooping lines superficially erased by massage. She believed the other woman was noting with the same bleak, shameful fellowship the marks under her eyes and the new faint hollow under her chin.

Now they were leaving the train. She was coming back all alone, as she had come the first time. But it seemed now as if that had been the romantic entrance—not this. Whom did she want to see? Hope and interest was gone from every encounter. Yet as she stepped down, with the aid of the porter she felt a dizziness of excitement, a sickening alertness, because she was again in the same city with Bruce. She followed the redcap along the noisy platform, unsteady and strange from the long journey. The sense of Bruce was all about her . . . and yet hopeless, almost as if he were someone who had died. She was walking alone and blindly. She had a panic sense of not knowing where she was going.

Margot came into the great light station. The noises of the footsteps dinned in her ears, and the voices surged around her, an indistinguishable uproar. She was here! She was back in New York.

But she couldn't think of anywhere to go. And there was a queer sense of change. She had not yet followed it to its source; but it was as if the light had shifted from morning to afternoon. Her apartment was no longer there. Or at least it was no longer hers. Frances had decided to marry the faithful lover in Cincinnati. Queerly enough, it was Margot's journey that had brought Frances to that! Margot's furniture was in storage. Once again she was a bird of flight. She couldn't have endured to go back to that house and open its green door—to see the chair that Bruce had given her, the bowls that had held his flowers, the books of poetry that had all taken on meaning from his love.

In a sudden fever of impatience, she paid the redcap—just as she had done once before. She sat down on a bench with her bag at her feet, trying to make up her mind where to go. She felt herself dark and alone in the midst of the crowd. Alone, and she could not call on Bruce. Tears were coming to her eyes . . . as they used to come at odd moments, on that hideous after-journey, whenever the noise subsided. Margot touched her eyes with her handkerchief. She remembered that she used to get pleasure even from the choice of a handkerchief in the morning! It seemed to her now that these were the things it was hardest to lose—all the little, irrelevant things, that once had been infused with happiness, that now were only tedious necessities, if Bruce was out of her life. It was this emptiness that was the worst! She seemed actually to realize it for what it was, as she sat alone in the great station, knowing that she was in New York but that Bruce was nowhere near. Even the acuteness of suffering, when Bruce had left her, the hours of agony when she had lain alone under the cottonwood trees, had been something to fight against. Then, at least, she could hope for alleviation. What was there to hope for or fight against now . . . in emptiness?

Yet she knew guiltily, deep within her, that she had stared into the emptiness, but not yet entered it. Not truly. It was the sight that appalled her. It was disappointment that made tears keep coming to her eyes. She knew the source of this sweet, sickening excitement, from which her limbs were trembling. She was back . . . she might see Bruce. . . . Wherever she looked it was with the unreasonable hope of seeing him. And she felt bitterly torn between the desire for him and for the recovered sense of life it gave her, and the need to wrench her thoughts and her love away from him entirely and submit to that great emptiness that might slowly bring change and renewal. After all, her life was set in a narrow groove, and not in the wide freedom of eternity—as she had felt after the first fulfillment of love . . . that which had seemed the beginning, and had already been the best. That was where she should have stopped, if her love was to be classic, a perfect memory. But now she cared more for imperfection.

Her heart was beating in a heavy expectancy. She opened her handbag and took out her thin silver compact. She remembered the day she had bought this, before setting out with Bruce—the counter at Best's, the heavy crystal through which the silken scarves, the ribbon corsages of satiny green and orchid, had seemed so magically springlike—and then the crowds, the sunshine, the mingled eagerness and warm languor, the blue sky above Fifth Avenue . . . if she lost Bruce and his love for her, she lost all of these. Having love, you were *part* of things, had the right to walk the earth anywhere. Another memory came over her of a moment when she had taken this same compact out of this same brown bag. It was on top of the pueblo at Tesuque, where they had gone to see the Eagle Dance. Margot could feel again the dry golden heat of the southwestern sun, an Indian sun, burning down on the dusty desert that surrounded the low square of flat-topped Indian dwellings. She remembered

479

the very feeling of opening her purse and taking out the compact—as if the shiny leather were alive with warmth, *belonging* to her. It seemed as if nothing could ever belong to her again—for all things were marred, spoiled, meaningless, if she was not in love. Reality was still in those places where she had lived with Bruce. Margot seemed to herself like a superannuated actress, living in early triumphs, disdainful of aftermath.

She wouldn't be that way! Bruce couldn't have that triumph over her. Not when he had been able to leave her! She would avenge herself by living afterward!

Suddenly she felt how tacky she was in her brown tweeds. In the interval, everything had changed, even the fashions. She perceived with horror the women around her, as if a new race had appeared and preëmpted the city, a race to which she didn't belong. They *were* wearing longer skirts. Almost the hated skirts of her girlhood. It was true! She had seen the dreadful things even on the simpering wax models in the windows at Geneva, but she had refused to believe in them. As she noticed the decorous hang of these smoothly molded skirts, with their reactionary primness, Margot struggled with rebellious fury. They were not *her* clothes any longer. She was horrified at the new make-up, the faces smooth and bald as eggs, with sun-tan powder and purple lips. It made her feel both contemptuous and dated. She clung fiercely to her own individuality.

But all the same, the deep rose-red of her lipstick seemed wrong beside this obnoxious purple. Her legs looked awful to her helplessly displayed beneath her short tweed suit. She saw Frankie Weyant's face again, under the tossed hair, as Frankie turned away after receiving her prize, flushed with running, but hard in structure, like her firm little spine and legs and arms. She saw the cool way in which Frankie ran off with Bun, untouched by her triumph, taking it as a matter of course. It made Margot feel herself by contrast battered, marred, vulnerable. She had had her time. Frankie had the future. But she couldn't even find solace in hating Frankie as she used to rejoice in her hatred of Mildred Summers!

Margot stood up. She must go somewhere. She couldn't stand this inaction. In a bitterness of impatience, she thrust her compact and handkerchief back into her brown bag. There seemed to be a hard, competent insolence in the way these new women passed her, never glancing at her, leaving her out. What she would have given for one of those sharp, appraising glances, perceiving her at once as a rival, someone to be reckoned with—! Now she needed her lover in a new way—his love to make for her a refuge against this strange hateful world in which she no longer belonged. Yet she knew, with a sickening shame and helplessness, that she dreaded to leave the station and go into a room and shut the door, into a place where she would have to be sure that there was no chance of Bruce's seeing her.

A redcap cruising alertly held up his hand and came toward her on a slide. Margot let him take her bag and started to follow him. Suddenly she knew that she could never stand to see that compact again. It belonged to the past. The touch of it was poisoned. She took it hastily out of her purse and hid it behind a crumpled copy of the *Times* near her on the seat.

"Taxi, miss?"

"Yes."

As she followed her redcap, going along with such nonchalant competence, Margot seemed to be walking into panic. Where should she go? Her green door was forever closed to her. She had to follow the boy just as if she were not crazy. They came out into the noise of Forty-second Street. Margot experienced a moment of intense homesickness for the sunny silence of the desert. It was not brilliant today, only cold, with a dead gray sky, people going along shivering, a day that meant nothing.

The taxi driver swung open the door and looked back at her. She had to think of something to say. The only place where she could go was to Grimmie's. She felt the irony of her return to that often-used retreat.

"Bank Street. Do you know where to find it?"

"*Yes*, ma'am. Ain't that over by Seventh Avenue?"

"Yes."

She supposed he *didn't* know where to find it. Taxi drivers always said they knew. Anyway, he was driving her in the right direction. She would make him take her straight to Grimmie's door. She could not bear to walk through any of those familiar streets.

Margot stared out with hard eyes as they drove down Fifth Avenue. She felt a bitter hatred of the noise and the hugeness around the station, making her think of how she was to earn a living. She couldn't go back to her old place. She had stayed away too long. She was unable to look ahead now. She seemed to have lost the thread of her own story.

The taxi went along with jerks and impatient halts. Everywhere, Margot seemed to see these smooth, metallic girls whom she hated. They were like the modern buildings, not individualized, but stylized—with their small smooth heads and necks, like those of the figurines with the gilded or silvered hair in the shop windows. She bitterly pictured Frankie Weyant among them, groomed into urban smoothness. They were the culmination of the metropolitan era. She herself was an individual. "Different," "strange," were words that she had always loved. She could never belong.

It was New York, her city, but all seemed changed. It was full of the noise of tearing down and putting up, the dust of plaster flying. Margot saw with helpless indignation against "business" and "progress" that one after another of the old beloved landmarks was going. They "needed the space" was what people said—the men with brutal mouths and shrewd slits of eyes pictured in the rotogravure section of the *Herald Tribune*. A great wooden framework was built all around the old Waldorf. The interminable noise of feet on the wooden walk under the temporary roof seemed to exterminate the fragrance of violets worn on mink coats that had risen like an emanation of the nineties whenever Margot had walked lingeringly by this place. She felt lost in the mighty steel and metal implacability of this commercial world that cared nothing for her own sacredly held feminine values of beauty and romance and association. She would go back to the pueblo and live with the Indian women. She felt a grinding homesickness again for the uneven, handmade softness of the adobe walls with their rounded corners and their crooked doorways grateful to the hands and the feet. But she couldn't be there without Bruce. Each of those soft-voiced women had her mate. Then where could she go? The expatriates were returning from Europe, driven out by the bitter breath of strange, approaching storms. She was a Middlewesterner. New York had been *her* coast of Bohemia. She seemed to see her little cluster of confederates scattered and put to rout among these stony towers. Jane—where was she?—with her wild, little-girl face faded and brutalized. Frances—turning back to prudence and stability. Marta—defeated by her own generosity. And she could see even Grimmie getting older, a nuisance to these hard young people in the new causes, with her enthusiasms . . . She could have wept over them, in fear and rebellion, the lost children of this ruthless, blind, stony world, who for a few brief years had found among the narrow streets of a left-behind village a kind of tawdry make-believe of the sort of world *they* would have chosen.

Margot felt a wild impatience for the small retreat of Bank Street. She directed the taxi man brusquely. That, at least, kept a kind of twilit dignity. She wanted to see the house where the "original owners," or their descendants, still lived, those almost mythical beings—where every day, behind the clear glass of the front door, stood a great basket of formal flowers. But she felt at bay, in a wild fury, when even here she came upon the noise of riveters and the dust of tearing down and building. It was the old apartment house on the corner with its square, dignified windows, where people said that Willa Cather had lived, and that always made Margot think of the cool clarity of Willa Cather's prose. She shut her eyes. She couldn't bear it. In a tone of suppressed anguish, she told the driver to stop at Grimmie's door. She got out blindly, went up the steps, and rang the bell beside the beautiful tall white door with its carving and its rounded panels. She rang again. There was no click in answer. She felt in despair. Then she heard footsteps in the hall. The door opened. Margot started eagerly to speak, thinking that it was Herbert, the smiling colored janitor. She had a feeling of almost hysterical gladness, that changed into shock, when she saw that it was not Herbert, but a small hard-bitten white man with suspicious eyes.

"Do you know if Miss Grimm is here?"

"Grimm? She don't live here."

"Yes, she does," Margot retorted, with angry impatience. "Don't you see her name on the bell?"

The man came out and looked at the bell.

"Yeah, I see the name. But that apartment's empty."

Margot went down the steps and stood idly for a while on the sidewalk, then walked blindly toward Seventh Avenue.

3

For a little while, the musty retreat of this small room in the old-fashioned hotel on Twenty-third Street seemed to be a refuge which Margot could accept. The long windows had white inner shutters and there was a dark red carpet on the floor. The decorous dignity of the elderly clerk seemed to hold away and make of small account the noise of the riveters all over the city; and the faintly British atmosphere with its deflating coolness, its refusal to perceive what it didn't wish to perceive.

Margot lay across the bed. She had closed the blinds and shut herself into the half-provincial air of the room. She had a sense of bitter triumph over Bruce, since she would never see him in a place like this. She pictured herself living in one of these superannuated streets, in one of the houses with dilapidated bow windows, going to a small, left-behind church with a beautiful ritual, and being noticed by the rector. But even daydreams were no consolation if they did not somewhere contain the figure of Bruce—and hurt too much if they did. She could have stayed where she pleased. She had the thousand dollars with interest that dad had solemnly handed over to her, no doubt having given up the hope of her getting married. He had given the same to Carl and Dorothy at their weddings. The folks seemed to emphasize the fact that they were treating her the same as the other children, if she *had* disappointed them. Margot remembered the forty dollars with which she had first set out to "live her own life" in New York. Now she knew that even a thousand dollars wouldn't last. She still had something left from the money order that Bruce had sent back to her in Santa Fé, and that she had cashed because she couldn't help it; but this

484

she didn't want to spend; she only wanted to keep it and look at it mournfully now and then, hurting herself in various ways by the thoughts derived from its possession.

The sense of loss was too acute! Margot felt she had to get out of this place as out of all the other places since she had left the adobe house by the stream—their home. She put on her felt hat, that now looked unbelievably out of date compared to the sort of winged skullcaps she saw other women wearing. In spite of the cleanly quiet given by the long windows, she could not bear to stay in this silence that quivered and hummed with her restlessness.

Margot felt too confused and disheartened to do anything but sit in the lobby. She had been grateful at first for this old-fashioned atmosphere in which she didn't feel herself such a relic. But now she was aware of the dreary people all around her; old ladies of a past vintage, their white hair done up with shell pins on top of their heads, wearing dark dresses with lace collars, looking like old Englishwomen, narrow, dried-up, old-fashioned, and assured. She felt stifled by age, and she wouldn't accept it. It was like an actual, physical smell of corruption that made her sick. She went out blindly into the open air. For a moment, she was grateful for the noise of the taxis and the street car on Twenty-third Street.

But now it seemed to her that she couldn't bear to stay among *any* people. She felt a wild beast need of solitude. She would find a place where she could be "alone with her memories," she used to picture herself. She would seek her own way of living— she wouldn't submit to new conditions.

The seminary always gave a feeling of seclusion to Twenty-first Street. One of Grimmie's friends used to live on this street, and Margot had dropped into her apartment occasionally for tea—a woman who was following Gurdgieff after having outlived a stormy affair. Margot felt slightly better. She began to see the faint outline of an after-career for herself. In this street with the seminary chimes, a sort of hiding-place, she could live out the tail-end of experience writing her sonnet series before an 1820 open fire. These houses were not pretend-old, as most of the Village houses seemed now, on streets the names of which

485

had once shimmered in a romantic haze, but now brought only dreariness, visions of little fruit stands with the refuse thrown out beside them, of the poor skinny cats around the garbage cans—Barrow Street, Commerce Street, Grove Street, now she hated all of them. But the numbers by which *these* streets were called seemed to make them anonymous.

The place, however, was *so* genuine that it was depressing and impossible. Margot's fastidious nostrils curled at the ancient smell of frayed linoleum and horrible curtains and bad cooking. The fat, regulation landlady, who snuffled and asked if she was "a single woman," humiliated her by even supposing that she would consider living in that hideous room with the round dining table and the felt cloth and the folding bed. Margot thought sadly, as she left, that she must want the pseudo after all. She turned with a sense of guilty relief at a place with all the familiar marks of inner shutters, arty curtains, and tearoom below.

"Ring Bartholomew for Apartment."

Margot rang. How often had she done this? She was back in the old feeling of being a New York woman on her own. It was what she had always wanted to be. But now she felt horror at its iron grip of familiarity.

A woman—Bartholomew, doubtless—leaned over the dark banisters and called:

"Do you want to see the apartment?"

"Why else would I ring?" Margot wanted to ask.

She went up the sloping, slightly perilous stairs, fighting down and refusing to recognize another of those uprisings of the sensation that she had done this before.

Bartholomew was waiting for her. She wore a faded green smock and drill riding breeches.

"You want to see the apartment? Right-o!"

Margot had to say yes, since she had come this far. But she felt an instant outraged repulsion at the dry, cynical sound of Bartholomew's voice, with its false, bright, valiant cheer, trying to make "the apartment" sound attractive. She hated the whole affair, as in mute derision she followed Bartholomew into the all-too-familiar large front room, with the long windows and the white inner shutters, the white fireplace, the floor with its wide boards painted a dark shiny brown. Too well she knew this woman's gay, sensible, "free" suggestions with their careful note of casualness. "Yes, I know all about it, old girl, you might just as well drop it, we're just buddies together." The smiles which they could not help exchanging revealed with dreadful embarrassment that both were all too experienced in the matter of New York apartments and that each understood too well what the other was up to. Still, they went on with the silly business, Bartholomew brightly overriding Margot's cynical objections, as if the idea of Margot's taking the place was already settled.

"Now it has this little kitchen."

Bartholomew opened the well-known closet door revealing the two-burner electric stove on the shelf, with a crumpled, half-used breakfast food box and a coffee can on the shelf above it. It was apparent that the usual burner was out of commission.

"It's rilly all that one person can use—if you're alone. There's an *aw*-fully good tearoom downstairs. I know the woman who runs it and she *does* have very good food. This is all we need for two, and we have even cooked chicken on our stove!" Now Bartholomew was trying to put over the advantage of *not* having a real kitchen, knowing well that neither of them believed it. "Gas is rilly unsafe in these old houses. And we do all insist on our old houses!" Margot gave a loathsome, answering smirk. "Electricity is so much cleaner, and we like it *so* much better. It's awfully jolly to cook this way, everything within reach, you know?"

And seeing a protest coming, she added quickly, cheerily, "And I must say the fireplace does work!"

Why make a protest, anyway? The poor female had saddled herself with this house, thinking doubtless she would have "freedom to write" or something of the sort, and now her living depended on finding all its disadvantages enticing. And what was the use of a kitchen when Bruce would not come for dinner on a rainy night, folding his thick coat smelling woolly of moisture, and drawing off his heavy gloves as he had done that first afternoon in Marta's tearoom, smiling at Margot's little card table in front of the fire with the red and black fringed cloth and the black candles? Margot mutely let the demerits of the place be shown to her, although she disliked it more and more bitterly.

Bartholomew admitted with wistful archness, "Now, there isn't a private bawth. But there are only three of us to use it. It's rilly the same thing, you see. We do try to be coöperative."

The carefully hasty glimpse which she was vouchsafed of the littered "bawthroom," with the copper blossom of the electric heater about the ineffectiveness of which she could be told nothing, finally enabled Margot to find a handle for refusal. It was apparent that in spite of the "coöperativeness" of Bartholomew and her partner, Bartholomew was all too used to having a refusal on these grounds. She had a fatalistic, although martyred, smile, suggesting that Margot had done her great injustice. The door of the room which "we" evidently occupied was open, adding to the sum of Margot's distaste, with its sight of a feminine domestic life in the midst of wabbly painted furniture, unwashed teacups, and India prints.

At last Margot was able to flee this place also—to get away from her unadulterated understanding of the life of the two women, with whom, thank God, she wasn't going to coöperate! This one, in her drill breeches and her synthetic accent who was taking Margot's "I don't believe it's what I want, I don't care to share the bath" with that martyred smile, was valiantly upholding the part of the man. Margot refused to admit the sense of Bartholomew's pathos in that rôle, her unripened body in the smock and the riding pants, her thin little hands with the skin darkened, the deep orange stain on her delicate forefinger, the hair chopped off straight across the forehead in a Dutch cut too young for the faded face beneath it, with dark circles of perverse dissipation beneath eyes that embarrassed Margot with their look of suffering intelligence—like the eyes, somehow, of that awful dog at home, that kept coming over from next door, and that mother detested and pitied too much to drive away, with the eyes begging you not to observe the femaleness wished upon her all too generously by an unkind God . . . except that the dog's eyes were dull and mute and Bartholomew's were so bright with painful intelligence. Margot fled down the stairs, away from even the memory of the crêpy thinness of the delicate throat above the mannish collar of the smock, the small, distended cords that made Margot ache with a sense of strain— as if the love which infused this person was too rarefied, too thin, felt on the naked nerves. She was only less awful than the sight, for a moment, of her "coöperator" in the doorway of "their" room—full, soft, discontented, babyish and faded, with cheeks that had once been a blooming high school pink and were now cushions of tiny red veins intertwined in a minutely intricate leaf-veining, the fuzz of fair hair pushed back in the girlish dishevelment of 1910 which had set the type for this girl . . . as a later time, Margot felt with horror, had set it for herself.

"O God, I couldn't live there!"

To live in a place like that, and no longer to have Bruce! Now she was oppressed by the seedy quality of Twenty-third which used to make it romantic. Those windows with diamond panes in shoddy rooms, with each a large bed with dubious covers, a gummy gas-plate set on an old commode, inhabited by broken-down actors!

Margot felt damp with horror at the thought of all these places. Their familiarity was not a refuge but a kind of disgraceful admission. That aging atmosphere, the wide boards so hard to sweep, in which fluffy strands from the rugs were always dingily caught, the gritty dust collecting in the panels of the shutters, the drift of cold ashes under the grate—she had felt that she was getting away from all these things (which vexed the fiercely orderly instinct inherited from Grandma Ferguson) when she had left with Bruce.

And yet there was nowhere to go. She was lost. She didn't seem able to think of anywhere else to look, and she couldn't bear the idea of the hotel—that was shot. To find new life!— in this cold, bright air. But she seemed too dull to seek for it. There was only Twenty-fourth Street left, a final hope. Perhaps she could stand a lonely life in one of the little brick houses with iron-lace balconies. There was a small dark green one that she remembered. Margot trudged over to Twenty-fourth Street, although she was tired and cold, and her head ached. But when she got there, the cupboard—no, the whole block was a gaping hole!

Margot went back on the run. But she had the sight of a hag on a street corner, and although she went quickly past the old woman, she had seen with horrible acuteness the marks of hopeless, shifty age and failure, as the poor creature wheedlingly held out pencils that she knew no one wanted to buy. Margot could feel already the end of her thousand dollars. She saw herself in varied hideous form in all the superannuated women she passed. And Chelsea was full of them! With face set, she took her key from the dignified clerk. She went up to her room and threw herself again on the bed. She thought of the people who had been for a brief time her companions in rebellion—all the Lost Children—like pigeons ousted from the old buildings where they had built their dubious nests and felt for a little while at home. Now she saw Bruce as belonging to the brutality of the money-making side, and she felt that he was a stranger.

She couldn't live in one of those old places, anyway. That was outlived. There would be no more romantic joy nor meaning in making one of them her own. Margot felt a desperate need for something new and selfishly satisfying to blot out of the faces she saw the stamp of unfulfillment, that she recognized, and would not share.

She lay quiet on her hotel bed. But now she loathed Bruce's wife with a deadlier hatred than she had ever known. She started up, damp and trembling—almost with the sense of having committed a crime. She would never give Bruce children. He didn't want children from her. She was something else to him. She was just what she had wanted to be. The fragrance, the disturbing gleam, the thing that was "different." Why must these things come back upon her, when she had lived through them once with so much pain? But she felt now, far more bitterly than before, the depth of the wound which Bruce's reluctance had given her. . . . She craved something new, something that had none of herself in it. She had given herself away and she didn't care for the thing back. She understood why women wanted children, when their own beauty

490

was going, their own lives were lived out. She could have endured Frankie Weyant, if Frankie had been her own, succeeding to the throne which she had vacated willingly, because the time had come.

No, she wanted nothing. She hated all feeling. And what good had *she* ever done mother?

Margot sat up on the bed. She looked around the room with eyes of hatred. She was fooling herself with this atmosphere of preserved decorum. She was one of the outlaws.

She hated herself too much to be alone. And it would be an anticlimax to make way with herself, now that she had outlived the night when Bruce had left . . . after all her fine feelings then, that now she seemed to have forgotten! But whom was she to call, when she couldn't bear the sound of any voice but one —and not that? It was a queer fate she had suffered so far, to be defeated by having every wish come true! If Bruce came back to her, would *that* turn out to be defeat? Anyway, it was too late for victory. She felt too far away from all the old crowd. But those whom she had known later, when she and Frances used occasionally to step out together, seemed too easy and successful—the Yale boys who were Frances' friends, who all had good jobs, and wore the right kind of neckties. They would be in favor of the "progress" that was ruining *her* city. Or, if not exactly in favor, they would run easily along with it, too well-bred to care.

Margot sat down gloomily before the telephone. Suddenly she thought with longing of Daggie's little apartment where she had spent other wretched hours. She sat a long time in front of the telephone until she was afraid that she could never take down the receiver. It was like calling a dead letter office, almost. But the number suddenly said itself from somewhere in her mind. And then, she heard Daggie's mild voice answering her.

"Daggie! This is Margot."

"*Margot?*"

"Yes, I don't blame you if you've forgotten me." Her lips trembled.

"Why, my darling, to forget you is beyond my powers. Where shall I find you after all these barren years? *Where?* No, sweetheart, I don't ask how you got there. That you call me again is the important point. Well, be as hideous as you like." Tears overflowed her eyes as she listened to his comforting tone. "I'll put on my worst tie. We'll be hideous together. Anyway, I love you for your beautiful soul. Sit in the lobby among the old ladies, and await your escort, who is overjoyed. You will recognize me by the red carnation in the buttonhole."

They got out of the taxi in front of the house where Daggie lived. So much in New York had changed—but there it was, just the same as always, the decrepit old red brick house.

Margot cried, "Oh, Daggie, I'm so glad you still exist!"

The times that she had done this before were around her like a dream—when she had stood, just as she was doing now, shivering a little, and waiting while Daggie fitted his key into the heavy door. "Hurry, Daggie," she begged childishly. "I'm freezing." She was eager to get up to his apartment. Now it seemed that *there* was her true refuge. She had always come to Daggie when she was downhearted or out of a job. After a party, in those ancient days of Christopher Street, she had come and roused Daggie, because she wasn't ready to settle down yet, had made him get out of bed and listen to her experiences with his amused, gentle, Olympian tolerance. She was returning to her old haunts. It made her think of that queer little nest of elderly people that she and Mary Phipps and Rube had turned up once in a basement on Fourth Street when they were out to make a "tower" of the Village.

Margot followed Daggie up the rickety stairs at which she had always fastidiously wrinkled her nose.

"Well," Daggie said, looking back at her, "the old place still hangs together."

"I think it's enchanted. It was ready to fall to pieces when I left, and it's at exactly the same stage now."

"Thank you, my dear, for suggesting that I exercise the spell —as I trust you *are* suggesting. Or perhaps you are likening me to a Sleeping Beauty? These rooms have sheltered many a sleeping beauty in distress. Sometimes, I do admit, the soundness of the sleep helped on a bit, by sundry potations."

Daggie opened his own door, the ugly, brown-painted door with its horrid little paintless scars. They stepped into the dark little hole between the living room and the kitchen that Daggie called "the antechamber."

"Welcome back."

He turned and put his arms around Margot. She lifted her face gratefully. As she felt the touch of Daggie's lips, tender, appreciative, with the reserve that came from the wide, unassuming knowledge that he could not step out of his fatherly rôle—something sadly humorous about it—she broke into crying and hid her face on his shoulder. Daggie was the one person on earth whom she didn't mind knowing how miserable she was. How *anything* she was. They stood for a long time in the antechamber. Daggie took off Margot's hat and gently stroked her hair. She could confess everything in her tears—her loneliness, the predatory solitude in which she lived, what she hated and feared in herself and yet stubbornly clung to and defended, her happiness and her disillusions. Here was the one touch of continuity with what she had left. She felt—for the moment—that she had come home.

"You mustn't go away again," Daggie chided her gently.

She shook her head against his coat. She had wet his flowing tie with her tears. But Daggie wouldn't mind. He would lend coat, tie, anything, to the needs of distressed damsels. Margot was ashamed to speak. But she was confessing in silence her knowledge of Bruce's influence over her, of how she had forsaken Daggie. It was all that Daggie would ask for. The red carnation that he had worn when he came into the lobby of the hotel—handing her its mate—was the one little humorous touch of rebuke, delicately suggesting that it was so long since they had met she might not otherwise recognize him.

"Not entirely away," Daggie added.

He gently lifted Margot's head. She sought blindly for her handkerchief and he gave her his.

"I always have a fresh handkerchief for my lady friends. Never can tell when it may be needed."

Margot gave a shaky laugh. Daggie turned on his light,

493

shaded with the same foolish pink silk scarf, which he said he had put there to give a softening glow to tear-stained faces.

"I'm going to use your powder, Daggie. I see you still have some."

"The supply is from time to time replenished."

Margot combed her hair and powdered her face, remembering, with loneliness and remorse, the silver compact she had left at the Grand Central.

"Now, while the lady is repairing the ravages caused by emotion at greeting her long-lost friend, I, according to promise, will investigate the cellar."

Daggie came back, after a few moments, with a gilt-tipped handsome bottle, saying that the occasion demanded his best. Margot turned away from the mirror with quick, defensive self-distrust.

"I look like a hag!"

"Oh—no, no."

"What is it then?" she tragically demanded.

Daggie put his small fingers under her chin and tilted up her face, which he slowly considered.

He admitted, "You're changed a little."

"I told you I looked like a hag!"

Daggie set down the bottle. He put his arms around her again. He had less of his humorously dispassionate manner than Margot had ever seen. She felt closer to him.

"You do look changed. You aren't the little thin, dark, intense damsel who used to climb these stairs. You always seemed to have a fiery coal hidden somewhere, ready to burst into flame. Well—now it's burst! And a few things have succumbed to the fire."

Margot looked down, brooding. Her sullen lips quivered. She felt gratitude for his understanding, along with the old rebellious sense that no one but herself *could* understand.

"Why, Margot," Daggie said, chiding. He shook her slightly. "You were a girl—now you aren't. It's what you asked for."

She shook her head, thinking of that hard little untouched face of Frankie Weyant's. The old rebelliousness flared up.

She said in sudden bitter jeering, "*Men* don't think so. They

494

want girls to take experience, so long as it's with them, but never to show any sign of it in their looks! Why do you suppose those awful women talk over the radio, telling how to keep *every line* off the face—to be just as smooth as a piece of paper —the way girls' faces have to look in those awful hats they're wearing this year! No. Men want to *give* a girl experience, and then cast her off for a new one if she shows any of the results!" Margot stopped, confused—because *she* had been the new one. But all the same . . .

Daggie shook his head, making a face. "Why hit me? I'm on your side. Scratch any girl these days and you'll find a feminist."

"Scratch Louise and you won't find one—you'll find what men really like!"

"Tut, tut!" He gave her a little shake again. "That was long ago."

After an angry, shamed moment, Margot reached for the handkerchief again.

"Wasn't it what you wanted, my dear?" Daggie asked her gently, commiseratingly.

She said fiercely, "Yes, it *was*. That's just the trouble! I know what you want to think of Bruce, and you're wrong. But the Louises are the ones who always get men in the end! You can't beat their game.—And I'm not thinking of Lee, either, with any tender remembering passion, so you needn't think that!"

"Well," Daggie said, "they haven't got your old Daggie. He belongs to the other hussies."

Margot turned and hugged him fiercely. He gently put her arms aside.

"Never mind, Margot. I don't count myself. You are safe with me," he added, taking his old tone. "Come." He gave her a little push. "We will have our liqueurs in the drawing room."

They went into the shabby old living room. As Daggie made the fire with neat care, Margot wandered around emptying ash trays and shaking up pillows.

"I never can see," she scolded, "why, when you can mix drinks perfectly and make such a beautiful fire, you can let your house get into such a mess."

495

"Ah," Daggie said. "That's where it needs a woman's care."

"But you *do* make a lovely fire," she said luxuriously.

"Yes, I'm real handy," Daggie admitted, as he sat crouched on his heels. "That's why my family's ashamed of me. I take after the ne'er-do-well uncle who became the village handy man."

"Did you really live in New England, Daggie?" she marveled. "I can't believe you *ever* lived anywhere but here."

"Thank you, sweetheart. But some day, no doubt, you can ponder the dates of my entrance and exit in a New Hampshire burying ground. The tallest stone in the cemetery is marked 'Daggett'! I fear I shall attain to the family dignity in death."

Margot was staring at him soberly. Would *she* end up in the family lot at home?

"But let us not think of my demise," Daggie said. "Let us be cozy."

Margot waited while Daggie drew up his old couch in front of the fire—that old couch with its faded blue velvet cover, on which so many rebellious girls had sat, had wept so many tears, had received the comforting clasp of Daggie's small, neat hand. This place was just the same, yes, just the same. Margot felt a sad rejoicing to see the old chairs with their hollowed seats, the books overflowing the shelves and piled up on the floor, the ancient battered ash trays. And yet there was a queer, New Englandish sense of order about it too. The dilapidated, tumble-down house was a little center of stability and security in the shifting Village world.

"Come. Let us seat ourselves and be Romans," Daggie said.

He forced Margot gently down on the couch, and again put his arm around her. The blue cover was pitted all over with tiny brown cigarette holes. The ashes ground into the velvet were turning it to gray. But this room, and wherever Grimmie lived, Margot thought mournfully, were the only retreats to which she could come. At home she was a visitor on good behavior. The firelight flickered over the couch, seeming to hush even the noises of the cars in the street outside. Daggie ripped the gilded tip off the bottle of cointreau and filled the two small glasses. Margot felt the bliss of the first keen, orange-flavored sip. Daggie set the little glasses and the bottle comfortably on the table beside them. The thin blue smoke rose from their cigarettes. Margot gave a sigh. She stretched out and lay with her head in Daggie's lap. She felt that in that first embrace her wretchedness had been confessed. Daggie stroked back her glossy hair. He might come upon that first white hair for which she was always looking, Margot thought with an inward shudder. But she didn't care. There must be one place where she could be simply what she was. Daggie told her to make the sign when she wanted more cointreau. He would hold the glass to her lips.

She murmured at last, "Where are people? What's become of everybody? I don't feel as if anything in New York is the same." She stared tragically up at Daggie; and he smiled, partly at the tragedy, partly at a pleasure of his own in following the petal curl of her lashes.

Daggie said, "It is one of those periods in the course of human events when the elements order a scattering. Something is upon us. I know not what, I'm too old to know. I have decided to settle down quietly in my superannuation and hope for a visit from Margot now and then."

"But isn't anybody around?"

"Nobody. You were the disrupting force, Margot. When you left, the crowd broke up."

"Where's Mary?" she asked. She let her hand hang over the couch, watching idly the smoke of her cigarette, listening dreamily to Daggie's account—upon which he was very ready to start—told with the kindly, enjoying pessimism with which he treated all mortal affairs.

"Mary? Mary," he said, "has gone, so to speak, the way of all flesh. She has joined the great company of American matrons. In short, Mary is married."

"Not Rube?" Margot said, with big eyes, "Not the pro-*fes*-sor?"

"*Not* Rube. The professor is the man. After youth's fitful fever, Mary will find her solace in faculty teas."

"I don't blame her," Margot said bitterly. "Rube thought she could dangle around him forever."

"Is this our upholder of anti-matrimony?" Daggie marveled.

"I'm not an upholder of *mat*rimony. I hate it. Only . . . I like to see *one* man get the wrong side. But I can't bear Mary," Margot said, in quick revulsion. "I know just what she's like by now."

"Tut, tut," Daggie said again, and stroked her hair.

"Well, go on," Margot said grimly. "I want to hear all the worst."

"The affairs of our friends out in Croton," Daggie said, with a slight effort, "are, I regret to state, in one of those tangles that can only be described as a mess. Hammie—you have never known Hammie?"

"I know Bobbie."

"Then you more or less know Hammie. And you can guess the rest. I trust I may even be excused, by your inference and intuition, from going into the details of the great new venture by means of which Hammie is to nurse his genius in a secluded room on the proceeds of the tearoom which Marta has instituted in Croton? New place, new man, new art—in this case, the genius is a musician. But the tearoom remains. Hammie, it is doubtless unnecessary to remark by this time, being the central figure of what I referred to as the mess."

"And if you want me to, I can imagine the mess!"

"But wait. Others of our friends come into it."

"Others?"

"Several others. *I* came into it at one time, although not, of course, as a principal. I am never a principal," Daggie said reflectively, with a smile. "That may be why I look forward to my funeral. And even then, I shall be only one of the Daggetts —the one who hasn't been at home for a long while. Well, that will be my distinction. . . . But our friend, Marta, with another of her generous impulses which, as ever, proved ill-advised, suggested that little Jane come out to add to the upkeep of the tearoom—and the musician—Marta being overcome by the fact that Jane had fallen out of her one hundred and fiftieth job. Needless to say, Jane went! It was then with great expedition discovered by Hammie that music needed inspiration as well as mortal sustenance. Jane proved compliant. The matter was then discovered by Marta. Shall I add, with the most intense surprise?

Tears, tempests—in fact, many things followed, including a very unfortunate infant, which—I have not yet unraveled the sex, and what matter, since it is born to trouble, whether or not —but which appeared to me, while I was still acting a minor character part in the mess, to be brought up entirely on cigarette smoke and dubious milk."

"But Daggie, Marta's infant?"

"I believe, Jane's."

"Don't you know? Didn't *any*-body know?"

"I believe I took it as part of the mess. At any rate, the little child brought another generous impulse out of Marta's all too capacious bosom. When I withdrew—more firmly than has often been my wont—the household in Croton was composed in some involved fashion of what appeared to be the following: Marta, Jane, Hammie, the infant, an unfortunate but none too savory damsel named Vi, a sad kitten, a hungry police dog, and in some way better not to be examined—and I believe, at a little distance—Bobbie! At that point I withdrew. Music and poetry must fight it out."

"But you'll have Jane back on your hands!"

"No doubt. I may even have the infant. Little Jane has a great capacity for lighting upon her feet."

"Until she begins to get older!"

"Oh, if you're going to think about what happens when damsels begin to get older, you should never have left Belmond, Iowa."

"Poor Marta," Margot said, brooding. She gave a little shiver. "I suppose she supports the crowd."

"To the point that they *are* supported," Daggie said judicially, "yes."

"People ought always to set a price on everything they do, I suppose!"

"Well, love is its own reward, like virtue."

Margot shuddered. She threw her cigarette into the fire.

"And a mess," Daggie continued thoughtfully, "is all too frequently the reward of freedom." He had his small, Olympian smile.

"Can't you tell me something more encouraging, Daggie?"

499

"What!" He looked down at her. "Has Margot come to ask for the happy ending? Is *that* the outcome of experience?" She moved restlessly. "Oh, yes, I can tell you many a happy thing. Your old friend Lee, for example, I recently heard by round-about methods, is out in Hollywood, waxing—and probably waning—rich. He writes that stuff in the gossip sheets."

" 'Is Garbo's Seclusion a Hoax?' " Margot asked satirically.

"That's the stuff. Tells how Jean Harlow in real life is a flower with the gold dust still intact. Meanwhile, it gives him a chance to dine with lovely ladies and hear how their marriages are going on the rocks. A very fine life for Lee! There's your happy ending."

"Well—" Margot muttered, staring at the fire, "Louise didn't get him, anyway!"

"You vicious little hound!" Daggie said with pleasure.

"Well, I can't help it."

Margot lay looking back at that old unresolved discord. She was surprised to feel that it still faintly rankled. Lee had always despised himself for not being the American big business man he loudly derided and that the sensitiveness in him hated. And he had wanted Louise because she was the business man's prize—wanted her, and groveled to her, and despised her . . . and now it was easy to imagine him in Hollywood growing fat upon his surrender to cynicism.

Daggie repeated, "Come, come, that was long ago." He tried again to look into her face. "If you don't like that happy ending, I can give you another. You have not forgotten the good Dr. Finkbein? Then you will be glad to hear that the worthy gentleman is flourishing. The old house in Thirteenth Street was finally sacrificed to the path of progress, and the Doctor —of Philosophy—forced to seek another home. At that time, with the proceeds of an amazingly successful book having to do remotely with the subject of the sexes, the Doctor suddenly decided to take an apartment, and—although without the customary female aid—discovered within himself an unsuspected taste for domestic life. I hear that he purchased his domestic tools in the ten cent store, so many that he had to convey them home in a taxi, thereby reducing economy. Now, I believe

—although I have evaded bringing it to the test—the Doctor
is occupied in asking his friends to dinner. It would be worth
your while to go, if well fortified before you start. If for no
other reason than to see the apartment! It is beautifully, even
magnificently furnished—in spots. The principal adornment,
for no reason that I have ever discovered, is a pier glass belonging to the Astors. Imagine our Doctor arranging tie and beard
before the pier glass in the morning. I never saw a bed in the
place. I don't know where, or if, the man sleeps. He is writing
a book, of course! Now, isn't that a pleasant story?"

Daggie looked down. He said tenderly, "Margot, you're
sleepy."

She shuddered and grabbed hold of him. "Oh, Daggie, I can't
bear to go back to that hotel!"

"Don't go back, darling." He rocked her. "Many a damsel
has sheltered here in distress. I do have a bed—even if no pier
glass—and I will go even now to prepare it for you."

"I don't want the bed," Margot protested childishly. "I
want to stay here on the couch. Can't I?"

"Certainly, my dear. But I will wake you up when I go
through in the morning. Remember, I am a business man, and
up with the clock."

"I don't care. This is the only room I can stand."

Daggie embraced her gently. She saw that he looked pleased.
His cheeks were even a little flushed. He laid his face against
her smooth hair.

"I'm glad to have my little Margot back. All my other damsels have forsaken me. I was beginning to look forward to a
lonely age. Are you going to stay now?"

She leaned against him, but didn't answer.

Daggie had gone to bed in his little room that contained
just a cot, a chest of drawers, and an improvised closet. He had
given Margot a pair of his pyjamas, with surprising lavender
stripes, and left the bottle of cointreau near her "for consolation in the morning hours." Margot lay on the couch watching the last of the fire. The firelight played on the piles of
books, on the cointreau bottle, on the unexplained picture of

an austere New England woman that hung, framed, on the wall. Was that what had given Daggie his wistful, humorous tenderness for all the rebellious girls, for Jane with her wild, tawdry prettiness . . . the firm, sharp, unrelenting outline of that face? Daggie's own history was shyly hidden within the placid incongruities of this room, with inherited reticence, only a gleam of it shining here and there. The paintings done by Daggie's friends were all bad. About all his friends—even herself!—there was that chosen touch of tawdriness. Yet the room itself was somehow cool and clear. There was a mysterious consolation in the place.

But all the same, she was restless. The feeling of having come home was leaving her. She felt torn apart from Bruce. The physical need for him stamped the night with anguish. Daggie thought that her affair with Bruce was over. But it was never over. Any more than Daggie would ever really extricate himself from Jane's messes! His secret had shone for a moment in the strangely shy tone of his voice when he had hardened himself to bring in Jane's name—a secret that he himself looked at with quizzical dubiousness queerly infused with reticent pain. Margot looked again at the austere New England face in the dark oval frame. Perhaps Daggie needed Jane to complete himself, as she needed Bruce.

She turned from side to side—picked up a book, read a little—impatiently put it down, bitterly recognizing something grotesque in her suffering. She hadn't provided for this—and had thought herself so darkly wise! The early gray light came in on the battered ash trays, the aged couch cover, the chairs with their deep hollows, the dingy floor. Daggie was a thread with the past. But the thread was frayed, the past itself discredited; and now only the central pattern mattered. Daggie had won, by his philosophy and restraint, an eternal place on the margins. This was no refuge, either. Margot left a note for Daggie, and went out into the flat, mysterious chill of the early morning air.

4

Margot went straight on through the living room and into the bedroom, dropped her packages on the dressing-table bench, and flopped into the easy chair. She closed her eyes for a moment with a feeling of rest. She could shut herself in from that tormenting alertness she felt whenever she was out on the street and had to fight, angrily and yet fearfully, against the hope and expectation of seeing Bruce. Now she felt a sullen, deep pleasure in being up here hidden and alone.

Last night, it had seemed as if she couldn't bear it here in K's apartment. She felt as if she had thrown the die and thrown it against herself. Coming here seemed to mean that she had accepted all Katherine Griswold had said, the day when they had luncheon together—not in one of the old candlelit tearooms run by romantically ambitious women, but in the dining room of a Madison Avenue hotel. Naturally—K's treat.

"Well, Margot," Katherine said, with what sounded like satisfaction—funny how many people seemed to feel satisfaction about it!—"you're back. I heard something about it from Grimmie. Well, my dear, you don't expect those things not to get out. We all know everything about each other." K gave a hasty sweep of the hand.

"Take it as that," she went on. Katherine did always have to be didactic, but with such crisp assurance that her friends sat mute, impressed at least for the time being. "You've tried it once and got it over." Margot's eyes shifted. Her sulky lips trembled slightly. "Let me tell you, Margot—" K took a fat English cigarette, moderately expensive but plain, out of her smooth leather case, and tapped it efficiently. "I've been through it all once. It's a good thing to have done, and then—that's that." Margot's dark red lips took on a sulkier curve, as K leaned on her elbow and calmly blew smoke. But she couldn't help listening, with a kind of resentful fascination, while K went on with the trenchant platitudes that were her stock in trade. "Better to have learned now than later that we all have to depend on ourselves ultimately."

When it came to "the sweet," as K had learned to call it, after various vacations abroad, each one making her more disgusted with the way things were done "over here"—K had looked and refused, making Margot feel still more guilty. Katherine was thinking now of her figure. After years of brisk altruism, and early excursions into social work, K had now decided to become strictly commercial, rationalizing the decision, of course, in her usual convincing way. She grew confidential—for Margot's good—as she drank her coffee and smoked another of her well-packed, firm cigarettes.

"I'll tell you, my dear, I went through a very difficult time last spring. Of course, it was a transition period. But I came to several new conclusions. And I hope you perceive the result."

The chief conclusion being—platitudinous as all the others, but just as crisply and convincingly uttered—that we live while we live.

"I think Grimmie helped me to it."

"*Grimmie?*"

"Yes, in effect. I mean I have an aged parent too. I am also the unmarried daughter. I made up my mind right then and there, when Grimmie toddled home, that when the call came for me, I was going to be in such circumstances that *I* could dictate to my brothers. I'd send more than they did to mother, so they could have no kick coming, but as for going back to the little gray home in Michigan, it wouldn't do. Just one argument would work with them, and I was going to have it. I was going to be able to say to them: Look here. You boys earn so much? Well, *I* earn *so* much. And it would be enough more to shut those boys' mouths and make their eyes bug out. Let me tell you right here, Margot—that's the only talking-point that counts."

And then K went on with some more of her original wisdom, under which again Margot sat recalcitrant but dumb. We were living in a mechanical age. All right, quit hugging old fireplaces, and have the benefit of it. Her friends could keep their India prints and their rickety four-posters. But as for her, she was going modern. She was going to reduce her hips and never be caught in a peasant dress again. Suddenly she had waked up to the fact that she wanted an electric refrigerator, not a box outside the windows, and plumbing that could work without gasping out a whole symphony of tunes. First she had thought she would be psyched, when she had begun to get dissatisfied. Then she had found that a modern apartment and beauty culture were a lot more fun and no more expensive. She had set out to beat the game.

"You see what's happened to Grimmie. Come back? Pooh!" Katherine snubbed out her cigarette. "Her mother will outlive her. I don't care how old she is. She'll live to be a hundred and fifty if need be. After successfully getting rid of her ugly duckling, by pecking at everything Grimmie did, she now plays the one trump card to draw her back in the end. If Grimmie'd had a real job, she wouldn't have gone. She could have laid down terms. Oh, yes, there are half a dozen others, all living nearer by. But they're married, my dear, and 'have their homes.' The old lady would have to knuckle to *them*, not they to her, and well she knows it. That's the only job of the single woman of the family! She's always lying around loose, supposedly, to take care of those who've already had full lives. No. Each man has to go out for himself *some*-how. You're none too young to get onto that, my dear; and my advice to *you* is, to start right in. This is the psychological time."

"I did go out for myself when I went away with Bruce."

"Pooh!" Katherine pushed back her coffee cup. *"That's* not what I mean."

Margot slowly opened her eyes. Her feeling of refuge was shot through with the irony that gleamed, now, through everything. The inevitable older woman had appeared ready to shelter her in one of her transitions—most strangely, this time, in the form of K Griswold. God moves in most mysterious ways His wonders to perform. Margot had met Katherine, just as once, years ago, she had met Grimmie—and here she was, dwelling in luxury in K's apartment, and all fitted out with a new costume and a new job, and—supposedly—a bright new set of convictions. Because, of course, K wouldn't bother with her if she didn't think *that*.

It was light in Katherine's apartment high up above the street. For a moment, as she saw its chaste, hard, modern simplicity (which she had now presumably accepted) Margot felt that same old grinding, romantic nostalgia for the dark interior of the pueblo with the pattering feet and intimate, soft, bubbling laughter of the Indian women. She wished she was back in Grimmie's room with the candlesticks and clutter of "little foreign things," the helter-skelter of cigarette boxes and used wineglasses on the table, and the paneled walls with the paintings all hung a little tipsy. She couldn't go back to Daggie's. It made her sore and guilty when she thought that she hadn't called him and told him she was here, thus evading his gentle belief that she had returned to the old rebel fold. But she had to keep hold of this brittle new promise that had half dragged her out of her pain. She suddenly felt with panic that she had entered this modern hardness. She felt of her new sleek haircut. She already had a job! The first craven relief had begun to die, but Margot took a desperate clutch on it. She had gone to see Sarah Rosen, as Katherine had suggested—had done *all* Katherine had suggested, as if K's latest sermon had her hypnotized. K had called up and made the date—after that of course it was up to Margot. Sarah, a large, brilliant, black-and-white-effect person, was all for business, kind, but hard as nails. Still, she showed her femininity by the decorative and intimate nature of her small advertising business, specializing in commodities that appealed to women; by some providential chance, the very thing that Margot had done. All the time that she was giving a creditable imitation of a crisp young woman who knew what she was about, Margot had had a guilty feeling that Sarah Rosen *must* be sharp enough to see through its falseness. But she seemed to have taken Margot on her own terms.

Katherine had told her to go and get some new clothes first.

"And spare no expense, my child. A ladylike shabbiness will not appeal to Sarah."

So now she had gone in for "success." From this time on, she would have to blot out the thought of Bruce in which she lived—this sense of quivering readiness that would not permit her to pin herself down, even to ambition.

She felt that sick flutter again. She got up impatiently.

She stood and looked at herself in K's grand mirror. K, deciding to go in for clothes and looks, *after* she had decided to cut out men! Margot's big dark eyes grew hard as she stared at the somewhat unfamiliar figure in the glass. Aunt Ella ought

to be satisfied, she thought. In this close-fitting dress she
seemed to have developed all kinds of new protuberances.
However, some of the same hard exultance came back to her
that she had first felt when she had seen herself in the svelte
new dress that changed her from the Margot of the brown
tweed suit, of the scant black satin dress she used to wear—
with red earrings—to Carlo's. After making her purchases and
spending too much for them, she had felt the usual exhilaration. In the "modernistic" shop, with its glass and angles, and
sleek metallic figurines, one pair of red shoes and gloves laid
beside them "effectively" displayed in the expensive simplicity of a long counter, Margot had sat and smoked with
arrogant carelessness, her knees crossed like those of the other
women, one narrow foot dangling. These were the women of
a period of hard drinks and strong manly cigarettes—no longer
the epicurean liqueurs procured in fusty back rooms and the
scented girlish cigarettes voluptuously smoked in candlelight
before an open fire. Margot saw herself now as a kind of feminine misogynist, making use of men when she wanted them,
but no more romantic about sex than about liquor.

She took off her clothes. At least she had the luxury of this
glorious little bathroom, stocked with smooth fat cakes of
soap and brushes from the kind of glittering little shops that
were called "Chemists" instead of drug stores. But she knew
that this was not like her old stay at Grimmie's. She could
have it all and welcome while K was in Bermuda. But K would
expect her to have found a place of her own by the time K got
back. The thought seemed to harden her, to bring before her
the conditions on which she lived now, a glittering ease mixed
with an alert danger, hard, metallic and cold. This was sym-
bolized by the shock of the shower in place of the old soaking,
luxurious bath.

Margot went back into the bedroom refreshed, stimulated,
with a feeling of cold freedom.

As she dropped the negligee from about her, and felt her
own body, an arid bitterness went through her at the thought
of going unloved. Never to have one kiss on the white space
between her breasts, nor a hand cupping the breast in joy,

507

delight like the taste of sweet sharp liquor burning through her—while she looked on in wonder, contented yet amazed, outside as if apart from herself. She couldn't be alone, like K and Sarah Rosen. She *would* not be alone. She felt a black desire to rush out and degrade what had been beautiful, throw it all to the winds, and harden herself to this degradation in contemptuous triumph.

"I shall be treading these grapes—"

She shook back her loosened hair in anger. She would have no more poetry. She didn't know what was ahead of her. She didn't care. The whole world was falling into a sickening slump. In disdain, Margot hooked herself into the svelte new corselette that she supposed she would have to wear if she was going in for these form-fitting gowns. "Now, my beloved Aunt Ella, talk about behinders if you can!" She cast off a bleak thought of Frankie's hard little unfledged figure. Well, she had hated herself, had felt inferior when *she* was unfledged, and at fifteen had worn ruffles on her chest. Here was another wish come true! She saw before her a mournful future of tap-dancing, dessert-cutting, standing after meals, exercises to the radio, like that upon which K had belatedly entered. She wouldn't be left behind by these other women if she was going to take her place among them. Now Margot felt in herself, almost to her surprise, that almost untouched stratum of meticulous Ferguson competence, that had caused her to keep exquisite notebooks in school and bring home good marks on her report cards. How queer to have that old despised family quality to fall back upon! Yet—midwestern, firm and sound— it lay beneath hedonism, and she knew it. She made up her face carefully with her new cosmetics, and foresaw another mournful future. The old egoistic joy had gone out of having shampoos and facials, when they had seemed a mystic preparation, like a long-drawn-out bridal toilette. Now they would be only necessities—"the smart thing to do," as Sarah Rosen said. Margot had seen at once, with the sharpened acuteness that had sprung into life with Aunt Ella's comment, exactly what Ethel Spencer was doing to her face—and what was undone! The married ones had to do it too! She felt an angry desire to hunt out Bruce, beat out that other woman, show her she wasn't so secure!—get the security for herself . . . but then she would have to work and strain forever to keep it. And what would it mean, with all the best gone? She felt the hard challenge of her own solitude; no longer with defiant exhilaration, but with stark brutal actuality. But if she was going to push through, she must have money, and if she made money she must put her mind to it, crush out the old sensitive readiness, follow a steely course. She heard the hard click of women's heels on the floor of the lobby in the tall building where Sarah Rosen had her office. When you got older, it was money, money everywhere! She felt a sudden, impatient, contrite sympathy for her own father, with his caution and his steady, astute looking toward future safety. At least, when the folks lost their teeth, they could afford to get good false ones! She *would* be successful. She wouldn't fall back on the folks some day. They could never, never get her in the end. She wouldn't get faded and valiant and intelligent and philosophical. Another tag-end of poetry came treacherously into her mind.

> "But me
> They cannot touch,
> Old age and death, the strange
> And ignominious end—"

Death might touch her—but age she would fight with teeth and nails—why, she had always really supposed that she and youth were synonymous! She did yet. And she remembered how she used to admire Aunt Louie, for being pretty and unused, and think that she herself would be like *her* and not like mother. She could have what she was after now, because inside she hated and disdained it. That was the strongest, meanest armor.

Margot had had dinner with Sarah tonight, after having stayed late to finish some work. Sarah had evidently regarded that as a great favor, which would keep her flattered and wildly industrious for about a month. Margot pulled down her mouth sardonically; but all the same, she liked the thought that she had made good with the boss so quickly, and remembered, with considerable pleasure, the look of envy and curiosity in that blonde girl's eyes.

Now, Margot had a cool, easy feeling as she sat in K's low armchair, reading a little, but too tired to take the reading seriously. The time was about to come, no doubt, when she would be the perfect tired business woman, disdaining literature that disturbed the brain, and reaching for a detective story every night. She had carefully refrained from touching K's beautiful little pile of expensive wood. This was her next-to-the-last night in the apartment. Tomorrow she would have to begin the good old search for a place of her own. But this was the first night, Margot realized, when she hadn't minded being alone. She thought, again with that sardonic twist of her lips, of how people in books, after some great sorrow, "plunged into work" and came out bright and new, finer than ever, with something gained—a deeper note in the work. "I wonder if I'm putting a deeper note into cosmetics!" Well, she didn't find that quite such a simple recipe as it was cracked up to be; and yet, now that she had got started, and hadn't taken to drink, or followed the plan of *The Green Hat* woman, *pour le sport* (which once she had regarded as quite romantically effective), it seemed as if she *could* work, and a little better than before —out of a kind of disdain, as if to prove to everything in general how little she cared about it. The feeling gave her a bleak but slightly cocky superiority.

The telephone rang.

"Oh, damn!"—when she had just got decently settled in K's chair. If it was Daggie, she would harden herself, and tell him she was too dead to talk to anyone tonight. She was ashamed—but she didn't want to go back to Daggie. She didn't want to be intimate. But doubtless it was just somebody else calling for K.

All the time that Margot was telling herself this—as if she were repeating it to convince someone invisible—she was aware of the same discredited expectancy underneath. She "told herself" these things, but they were only stagy. She lifted the

French telephone, deriding herself for the way her heart had started beating. Oh, if she *still* had to be such a fool! It was just something left over, meaningless now, like a horrid effect of an old disease.

"May I speak to Miss Ferguson?"

"This is Miss Ferguson."

"Margot——"

The world seemed to turn in a slow, dizzy amazement. The miracle had happened. Bruce was calling her. Margot didn't know whether to be glad—or what to feel. She didn't feel in any way, except that she was trying to right herself in this dizzily turning universe, and to choke her heart down to where it belonged instead of letting it beat in her throat.

"Margot, this is Bruce. I want——"

"How on *earth* did you know I was here?" Margot demanded. Her voice broke in absurd indignation. All at once she could have cried for rage.

"Oh . . . I tracked you down."

"But—for heaven's sake! I don't see *how.*"

"You don't seem exactly pleased." She could hear Bruce's laugh—"mirthless," a book would call it.

Margot didn't seem able to think of anything to say.

"Listen, Margot. I want to see you."

Margot felt moments go by as she kept on sitting at the table. She sat there in transfixed silence, as in one of those dreams when she found herself unable to make a move at the crucial instant.

"Did you hear?"

"Yes, I heard."

"Well?—you haven't answered."

The moments went by again—almost as if they were marked and separate, and she could feel each one in itself, an entity. But she couldn't seem to get her lips open. Under her frozen muteness, she had the wild realization that if she was to save any of her pride, and the possibility of the new existence, now was the time when she would have to say something bitterly, decisively final. This was her chance. But she was pierced by the humiliating knowledge that she couldn't do it—she was

511

going to be unable to hold out against Bruce. The most she could do was to give in as slowly, grudgingly and temporizingly as possible—and she was almost too weak even for that!

She said foolishly, in a girlish-sounding voice, "I don't know just why you want to come."—Furious because it sounded hurt and lofty.

"I want to see you," Bruce repeated.

"You don't know where I am."

"How do you suppose I called you?"

Silence. Margot's face burned with the childishness of her retort.

"Margot—" Bruce insisted.

"Well, I . . . suppose you can see me."

"I'll be up in a few minutes, then."

Margot put back the telephone. She had a ghastly desire to laugh at this picture of herself sitting like the heroine of a movie who had just received the great message that brings on the happy ending. She got up, pushed back the little chair angrily, groaning in self-contempt and humiliation as she felt with what ease and swiftness she had succumbed. Her pride was hurting as if it had been an actual living tissue which had received a physical wound. It wasn't that she had let Bruce come—but that she couldn't help herself!

Yet all the time her blood was singing in a terrible jubilance. Bruce had called her—he hadn't let her go. She would see him and be with him. She felt—oh God, she didn't know how she felt! All seemed to converge toward a center of sickening fear. Why was Bruce coming?—why hadn't she asked him? demanded to know before she had given him leave? Because already she had built up an immense edifice of expectations. What if he wanted only some little thing? If he still had something of hers that he wanted to return?—or to get back something of his that *she* had? Margot wrung her hands and groaned again, jeering furiously at herself. But still . . . he must have gone to an immense amount of trouble to find out where she was, with no clues at all that her imagination could discover. She wondered again who could have told him. But when her mind started to go over the possibilities, it seemed to stop in a bitter impatience. The fact that Bruce had called, was coming, and that she didn't know what he was going to say, was an immense obstacle against which every other thought stopped dead.

And now there was the dreadful problem of getting through the time until he came. Margot walked back and forth through the rooms, into the bedroom and out again, into the kitchen, wringing her hands, moving a chair—anything to get through this gap of time. She tried to find some way to harden herself against anything she might hear. Against hope, first of all; and the sickening fall of disappointment. She didn't even know exactly *what* she hoped! She wanted to be cold to Bruce, and to tell him that everything was over in exactly the way that would hurt him most . . . and all the while she was trying to keep herself from the wild belief that miraculously this *was* the happy ending! She was listening with painful acuteness for the sound of the bell, wishing she could get where she couldn't possibly hear it, but afraid to end the torture that way. For a while she stood staring into K's mirror. Then she threw down the powder puff. She wouldn't let Bruce think she had got herself up for him. And what did it matter, anyway? She could never look prettier than she *had* looked. Not even so pretty. Now it seemed to Margot that the little marks under her eyes were stamped with such a hideous sharpness that they were all anyone could see of her. She went back into the living room and sat down again in K's chair.

Her mind went over and over what Bruce had said in a fruitless effort to be prepared. She felt with a sort of awed joy that there had been a suffering reluctance in Bruce's voice underneath a dogged decision. She tried to ward off any treacherous sympathy at the perception. But she couldn't keep her mind from ranging to the limit of the possibilities of what his coming might mean. She knew now, no matter what contempt of herself the knowledge gave her, that she couldn't bear to let him go again. She wanted Bruce to marry her.

But even that couldn't be a happy ending. Not now. Too much had passed. Too much water had flowed under the bridge. Nothing could be quite the same after that night of solitary agony when she had lain out on the ground. Time had worn at the love between them and laid scars upon that shining tissue which nothing could erase. What had happened was irrevocable. Yet Margot felt, with she did not know what mixture of rebellion and deep emotion, that the frayed fabric of love still held. And it was better, in some way, marred and tarnished as it was now. She looked back on her day of perfect happiness, and the happiness seemed shallow. She could not put away this deep undernote of pain. She had thought that she had learned then what it was to love; but she hadn't known until now, when she actually could not help herself, and was letting Bruce have his way against her will.

"Now love has bound me, trembling, hands and feet."

Horrible fool! She hadn't got rid of poetry even yet. It had sprung up again, like "the purple flower which the heel has trampled" . . . and everything around her was quiveringly alive.

The bell rang. It was pressed lightly and quickly, but the sound was piercing. Margot felt the restlessness of her terror suddenly leave her. She could walk forward quietly and easily. But her hands were cold. She opened the door. When she saw Bruce standing there, she suddenly felt that she was in the paralyzing center of fear—and that was why it was so still.

"Oh, hello," she said foolishly.

Bruce didn't answer. But he stepped quickly inside. When Margot saw how solemn he was, her heart began to thud with heaviness. She was too concerned with controlling herself really to see him now. Each was paralyzed with fear of the other. Margot stood aside, while Bruce turned and took off his coat, folded it carefully, and laid it on a chair with his hat on top. It was just as she had seen him fold his coat a hundred times; and she had a dizzy feeling that they *must* be in the old apartment in the little house in Twelfth Street. It was crazy that they should be here together—and yet in terror of each other, and apart. They could somehow annul all that had happened, if they would.

Bruce turned back. He looked at Margot now. He smiled

514

slightly, and she saw his lower lip tremble. Her resentment and constraint melted.

They stood facing each other, and their eyes met in naked helplessness. Margot felt instantly, in a rush of sympathy and truth, that pride was shameful and petty, it was left behind. She saw that it had been as hard for Bruce as for her. He, no more than she, could keep apart. Perhaps less—he had come to her. This time had a strange solemnity. Margot did not know which one made the movement that brought them together now. Both seemed to do it with a single, spontaneous impulse; to be drawn together by something inevitable and outside themselves. Their kiss was strange and solemn too; and Margot, trembling, felt that Bruce's lips were cold, although now her whole face was flaming. There was fear, reluctance, confession, gladness in the kiss. But again Margot felt that the depth of this emotion made up for the loss of the old pure happiness.

Bruce shifted his position a little, as they stood there together, and then led Margot over to the couch. All this time neither of them had said a word. They had reached each other again. That was enough. The feeling was so solemn that only now a little realization of bright joy was beginning to make its way through the first emotion of reunion. Bruce slowly drew her up to him more closely.

"Margot, we can't separate like this."

She murmured tremulously, "I know it."

"Yes. But what are we going to do?"

They had turned toward each other again. Margot heard with a shock of incredulity that tone of suffering reluctance in Bruce's voice; and now she saw the same thing in the hurt, strained look of his eyes. She had a moment of panic. Her lips opened and at first she could not answer.

"It isn't fair to you," Bruce said heavily. Now he was staring straight ahead. "I knew damned well I oughtn't to come up here. But I couldn't help it. That was all. I've been crazy."

He turned toward her again, with a dazed, bewildered motion, as if he had lost all comprehension of himself. Margot struggled with a sudden wild pity. Perhaps there was a love

515

even beyond hers, that would be still more merciful, and set him free. But she closed her eyes to it in the force of her own jealous passion. Bruce drew her up against him almost roughly. She sat weak and dizzy in his arms. She knew now that for the first incredibly blissful moment of reunion she had believed that they were to be together for ever and ever. But now, bit by bit, the comprehension that Bruce didn't mean that had been forcing its way through her. Margot could only wait, while her heart beat in suffocating disappointment and suspension.

"You ought to put me out," Bruce muttered bitterly.

He turned away from her and put his face down upon the smart, square, new cushions at the end of the couch,—as crisp and cool in their linen freshness as K's own common sense. It made Margot feel that she was defending Bruce against Katherine—against everyone. She felt a fiery impatience with the way K looked at things, mixed with an angry suffering at being herself drawn away from that clear coolness.

She waited. What Bruce had said to her just now Margot felt as a slow hard blow that was gradually opening up a whole undesired vista of comprehension. Irony was returning to her, after her brief belief in the miracle. Her "great passionate love affair" was flawed and fragmentary—after all, it was her own! And the person who really pursued her, and could be wax in her hands, was Hec! No doubt even Dr. Redmond wouldn't have propounded divorce nor offered marriage!

Then she felt her heart thudding, and understood why it was. Bruce was crying. The sound seemed to enter and open up the very center of her heart, with a piercing pain that made her helpless; just as long ago (so she felt it now), on a beautiful lost day, this same man had reached the very center of her physical life and brought her to ripeness in a single hour. She had thought that then, finally, she "knew love." But this was something deep under that ecstasy of gratitude—this feeling that the sound of Bruce's crying was within herself, was more hers than her own. It made the earlier happiness incredibly shallow and immature.

516

She whispered, "Don't, Bruce. Don't. Please don't. I can't bear it."

And that was true—literally true. She felt wildly, like a mother with a hurt child, that she would do anything to stop it —with a quick disdain of herself, as if against that sound she no longer counted. She took Bruce in her arms, and tried to console him, by any words she could find to say—anything was better than having him away from her.

Bruce finally drew away from her, wiping his face, and trying shakily to get back into his character of a responsible man. He said:

"I know it's damned wrong. But I can't get along without you just the same."

Margot was silent. She felt the painful sweetness of that confession wrung out of him. She waited. But she realized that he was not going to say anything about his family. She felt with wild bitterness that it *was* unfair. She resented the assumption he was tacitly making that they stood together in comprehension, both taking it for granted that he must be what he called "loyal" to his family, that all that was settled, and she agreed and would be resigned to taking the small end. After all, in spite of the realms of golden air they had reached and dwelt in together, Bruce was himself and she was herself. He *had* taken that time as something really set apart; had never understood or shared with her (except humbly, tentatively) her own religion of love—that, if it *was* the best thing mortals could know on this earth, they were cowards not to make it take precedence over all lower things; and now he had slipped down, with some disappointment, pain and loss, and yet with bewildered relief, to the old regions that he knew better. But there was nothing to do with her bitterness and resentment except to let it turn in upon herself. Because, all the same, this was the man she cared for; the only one who, even by his imperfections, could make her feel to the utmost of her capacity, and a little beyond. By the very thing for which she had asked, she was entangled now—on the off side, to be sure— in the ordinary world of mortal love from which she had fled. She couldn't bear to be without Bruce.

"Well . . . it looks as if we can't help ourselves, that's all."
He heard the tone of bitter derision in her voice.

"Did I—bust up something for you, Margot?"

"Oh—" she laughed. Bruce looked at her almost timidly.
"Just the fond notion that I could get along by myself."

Bruce took her hand, and kissed it. He said humbly:

"Well, I had that idea myself. I wouldn't have believed I'd
come after you again, after I'd once had the guts to leave you.
I guess I simply couldn't stand it any more."

Tears sprang into his eyes again. He made a grimace, and
looked away from her.

Margot had to swallow the implications of that statement.
But after a tiny space of cold, hurt aversion, she put her arms
around Bruce again. Tears were thick in her own eyes. Even
as she fondled him, there was a wounded resentment deep
within her, that some day must bear some kind of fruit. Bruce
hadn't wanted children from her. He didn't think of her "in
that way." Again it was what she had asked for—it was what
she had asked to be to him. The trouble was that *now* she
wanted to be all things . . . as he was to her. She understood
that the fight was not ended, even after she had won a victory. Again Margot had that larger sense of a turn of events,
making the light shift and fall upon another space than that
in which she moved, leaving her in a different kind of shadow
than the cold earlier one. Her figures of Lilith and Eve were
eternal combatants. The contest was never really ended. But
Lilith, Margot felt bitterly, was always getting a little the worst
of it, was always getting submerged at the close. The old weary
battle was on again. But Lilith could put a finger in Eve's fine
pie!—and she had her victories. Well—she would snatch what
she could. She wouldn't retire tamely from the contest. What
she had must always be snatched and fragmentary, it seemed,
even after she had reached fulfillment. And here again, as if by
the turn of the ball, the old fatal flaw was revealed.

"Well, I guess I'm a fool," Bruce said. He tried to grin at
her.

But he had accepted her fierce consolation. If she was willing
. . . why, then it was all right.

"I've got you again, anyway," he said, putting his arm around her.

There was an obtuse masculine fatuousness in those words. Black sparks were in Margot's eyes. Did he suppose it could be just the same again? That they could go back to their old relationship, when she had lived in the little house on Twelfth Street, and he had come to see her there? The meaning would be gone from it now—from the little meals she got ready for him, with the card table and the candles—if now he was to be hers only on the difficult precarious terms that he was making. She sprang up, ready to deliver herself of not a few bitter words. Yes, he thought he could have her just as he wanted her! But it couldn't be the same again. He needn't think that. He had broken off their love when it was just at its best, and let her get through it, and now he came back for just as much as he pleased.

Bruce listened doggedly. But his face was set in that way Margot knew, and which made her shake inwardly. Even her anger was crippled at the center by the knowledge of how necessary he was to her.

"Don't think it's easy for me, either," Bruce reminded her. "You always think how things will affect you, and how they're going to suit some idea you have beforehand. I tell you, this business is harder for me in plenty of ways than it is for you, Margot. I thought I was putting myself straight that time I left you. You think I'm gypping you! Maybe you think I haven't given you anything. I've busted up my integrity, if that means anything. It does mean something to me. Not that I blame you—I did it myself. But I can't give up all my responsibility," he repeated stubbornly. "It's just one thing I can't do." Tears started to his eyes again. "I tell you, we're in this thing together."

Margot sat and stared at him. She trembled, knowing that she could not lose him. His words sank into her, bowing down her head. Her defenses against him seemed gone, now that that hard little enclosing sheath was broken.

"I still love you better than anyone else, whatever you think," Bruce said.

Margot looked away, biting her lip and clenching her hands, and then looked back again. She saw Bruce, all at once, as Daggie and the others used to see him. A bald light shone upon their whole relationship, stripping it of any special and peculiar claim to romance. Bruce was just like other men. He wanted his wife and his mistress both, and he would keep them both as long as they would let him. But all that he said, his dogged insistence upon his "responsibility," no matter what incongruities and injustices it entailed, was making him all the time so fearfully much more valuable. Margot loved him unwillingly for his conscientiousness, aware of her own ruthless lack of scruples, in which at times she gloried; and at the same time she felt bitterly that he hurt her more than by an act that could be despised. She loved him because she couldn't overthrow him. And yet she *did* despise him, because he couldn't let love have its way—love that was like genius, greater than either of them. Only lovers who so felt it could act out a great and fatal drama. She and Bruce were different, and theirs was half-and-half.

"You can tell me to get out if you want to," Bruce said. "You've got the right to. I know I had no business barging in again, at this late date. I was the one that started things this time."

Margot's lips trembled at the queer, conscientious gallantry of that admission. But it didn't make it any the easier! She could see that before, when she had thought she was in love with Bruce, "crazy about him," she had been taking him really as the partner who could best bring about the fulfillment of her fairy tale. Now he was himself to her. That was less, in a way, but it bound her to him even more tightly. She struggled even now for a complete and perfect ending; but she couldn't bear to give up to the other woman; or to face the emptiness if Bruce went away. Life was going on again—only it was on his terms, not hers. In that there was a kind of deep-lying, wry justice, as if slowly the balance must be righted, if at last they were to stand for a moment in perfect equality. It seemed to be a law which she felt a racked, sacrificial consecration in fulfilling. She had asked for a "fatal" love—and here it was.

She had wanted it to be her whole life, and now it was. Here was where her fine hard independence went to pot! She felt herself again transfixed in that painful, humiliating readiness, which was yet too sweet to be given up. Nevertheless, the stratum of Ferguson practical ability in her was real, under all her romanticism; and now that she had fallen back upon it, it would keep demanding its right to assertion. Margot could already feel herself struggling to weld the two needs together, knowing that they were eternally opposed. She acknowledged the bitter justice of her plight. She felt herself looking down that long vista of which she had had a glimpse before, seeing the tortuous ways of her great love affair. But what she couldn't see was any ending.

"Are you going to let me stay, Margot?"

Margot was still sitting half turned aside. Now she turned back to Bruce. Her lips were helplessly parted, her eyes darkly strained with the sense of all she couldn't communicate.

Oh, yes, she was going to let him stay!

This slow, mute embrace was not like the first joy of re-union, with its false rainbow miracle of promise. Beneath it lay reservations, resolves, reluctances, streaks of hardness, half-estrangement. After they had once made the Great Renunciation, it seemed a little silly, even, to be getting together again. Margot felt silly, as if she were going on acting after the curtain had come down. All the same, this embrace had a mutual quality they had never quite felt before. Perhaps in guilt, perhaps in defeat—anyway, it was there, and it joined them together. The painful sweetness of desire was awake again; the broken habit of intercourse demanding its conclusion. They were ashamed, joyous, defeated, proud—all within the compass of that mortal bond, which for the time being at least, was stronger than anything. They had recovered life—on what terms it seemed they could—although it was jumbled and precarious, touched with derision, and they no longer knew where to find their footing.

Part Five
The Youngest

AN agent selling silk stockings rang the bell at the Ferguson house. No one answered, and after ringing again and waiting, he retreated. Only when he had got past the place, he saw "the lady of the house" out in the garden talking to a workman. He thought of seeking her there. But the poor fellow (who had started out as a preacher in a humble denomination) was secretly glad of an excuse that allowed him to cut any house on his beat. He had never overcome his stiff reluctant shyness, his nervous dread of intrusion, in spite of needing the money. So Mrs. Ferguson escaped, as Mrs. Morgan, frankly looking out of her window to see where the fellow was going next, observed with satisfaction; and the agent himself doubtless missed an easy sale to a soft-hearted customer.

The "workman" was Uncle Ben. Mrs. Ferguson had just mentioned, after the service last Sunday, that they must get hold of someone to put in their garden; and Ben had said he would come over. She wouldn't have thought of offering her brother-in-law this little bit of wages. But she could see that Ben really wanted the job. In his few bleak years of retirement, he had grown increasingly lonely for the work on the farm. Sometimes he went out there, but Ella didn't like it, and twitted him. "What do we give part to a renter for if you're going to go out there and do all the work for him yourself?" When Ben had first appeared this morning, Annie had noticed how aged and disconsolate he looked. The eternal bickering between him and Ella, once a joke among the relationship, had grown to bitter proportions now that they were housed up together with so little to keep them busy. Ella got after Ben for sitting idle, and then she scolded him for all his meager activities— going over to one of the neighbors to do a little tinkering, fussing over the storm windows, wandering off downtown to stand on the corner and talk with the other retired farmers. Ella had grown fat and complacent since they had moved into town; Ben, older and grayer.

But now he was more like himself. He loved to work in the earth. Even Grandpa Ferguson had admitted that Ben was a natural born farmer, although he was almost too slow and careful ever to get things done. And this was the very kind of work he liked best, small and puttering, where he could take infinite workmanlike pains. He and Ella had their own garden of course—a model one—but Ella always had to come out and pester him for being so slow. He and Annie could talk things over together. Since Annie had more on her hands than Ella, she wa'ant so pressed for time, Uncle Ben thought with sardonic pessimism.

"Well, now, Annie, I'll tell ye. I dunno as I'd put any small flowers right there, for they'd be a little too much in the shade of those cosmos later on. Ain't that where ye have yer cosmos?"

Ben had brought over the fork that he had been using on his own garden. 'Twasn't hardly worth bringing in a horse and plow from the country for these little patches o' ground, he said. Easier to do it by hand. But he was in no particular hurry to get to work. He was enjoying his sister-in-law's company. The spring air was somewhat chilly, but the sunshine was bright, and the ground had a good loamy smell. Mrs. Ferguson had put on her old coat with the worn beaver collar.

"Annie, do you remember that sociable out to the old schoolhouse where Joe Brownback got you for a partner in Wink 'Em, and wouldn't let go of ye, and Fred was so mad? I dunno's I ever saw Fred so mad."

"Oh, he can get mad!"

"Yes, sure, I know he can—wouldn't be a Ferguson otherwise," Uncle Ben said with feeling. "But 'tain't so very often Fred right outs and shows it like he done that night. I thought they was going to be a real fight between them two boys before the evening was ended. Well, they wa'ant the only fellows liked you pretty well, Annie, in those days."

She laughed and colored. Tall, his big shoulders bowed, in his ancient brown vest and work pants, Ben with his kind slow voice took her back to her girlhood days when she had come out to Buck Creek as the pretty new teacher whom all the fellows tried to get a chance to meet. She remembered the small county fairs where "the young folks" drove together, with the big farm horses snorting as they climbed the hill. She thought of the oak grove behind the little district schoolhouse;

of the polished brown leaves littering the hollows in the fall. A vision of these things overhung the April garden.

"Well, Annie, I'll tell ye, I'll get the ground ready today, that'll be a fair morning's job, and tomorrow we can decide for sure where to put the flowers. I s'pose *she'll* want me this afternoon."

Shivering a little, Mrs. Ferguson went back to the house. That bitter touch at the end made her sad, remembering the days when they had all been young people together.

The house seemed modern and warm and bright after standing out there in the garden with Ben.

The Fergusons had been a little slower than other people of their financial status in doing over their house. Fred had held off, with characteristic caution, until the children were pretty well accounted for, and he could exactly see his way. Then at last the place had undergone the prescribed metamorphosis of all the well-to-do homes in Belmond: with the parlor and living room thrown into one, the old downstairs furniture relegated to the attic or bestowed upon Essie Bartlett and her mother, new fixtures in the bathroom, new flowers and a trellis on the lawn. The warm easy atmosphere of the living room seemed an age removed from all that Ben had been talking about—seemed almost to be in a different world. There was an early American quality about Ben that Annie could recognize and yet had never really known: something sylvan, like the homemade hunks of maple sugar his cousins back in Pennsylvania used to send him every year, and that he would slyly take out of a special drawer in the back porch (supposed to be hidden from Aunt Ella), pounding off with a hammer a sharp-edged, crumbly, dark golden piece for some child who had come to woe, warning "Don't ye let the others see it!" The rustic air that had lingered about him even in his prime was enhanced by his retirement. He was an anachronism, authentic but of the past, here in Belmond. Ben was an old man. But she and Fred were not old people!

Now that she felt the spring in the air, the bright exciting change of the season, Mrs. Ferguson realized how pleasant this winter had been that was nearly over. There had been just

527

enough to do, with club work, church work, the little journeys to and from Geneva, the happy break at the holidays when Bun had come home from the university and they had had "Carl's folks" here. The snowy winter, "an old-fashioned winter," people called it, when they had put up the car during the coldest months, had taken on just a flavor of old days . . . If hard times were around, they had not struck Belmond; and Mrs. Ferguson believed that it was somehow protected from them—just as it had never had a cyclone. Life seemed to be running along its appointed way, only with natural prosperity and well-earned comforts added. Now their peaceful, secluded, winter routine would be broken. But pleasantly broken! Soon the little excursions would begin, with the Lowries or the Vieles, the Fergusons taking along someone else who would enjoy the ride, like Mrs. Dunn or Ada Rist, and all of them bringing lunch. People were beginning to look up all the little waterfalls and odd-shaped rocks and interesting buildings that this good farming country could offer in the way of "scenery." Summer would be busy. Some of the children would come for visits. Bunny might drop in for any week-end now. He had a third-hand roadster which dad had let him get—dad remarking with dry humor that Bun had raised them to the status of a two-car family, they could count themselves among the big bugs now.

All at once, Mrs. Ferguson felt the old hunger for her children. She put down her magazine and went up the back stairs to look into Bun's room and see if it was ready. She thought with a shudder of Ben and Ella and their barren life in that narrow frame house they had bought on a side street. This had been Carl's room before it was Bunny's. It was still really "Carl's room" to his mother. Her gladness at having Carl so close—the only thing she admitted to other people—was over-shadowed by a deeply hidden, sympathetic knowledge of his dissatisfaction, and the outcome that seemed to be confused between defeat and victory. Now, in the empty chill of the room, with the back window overlooking the garden patch in which Ben was slowly moving, she could stand alone with the pain of comprehension. She thought of Carl as he used to be,

528

with his bright, confident, too sensitive eyes. How was it that she couldn't go to him?

But Bunny was always happy. When his mother thought of her youngest, a smile of fond contentment curved her lips. She could truly say that he was the one of their children who had "never caused them a moment's trouble." Coming late, he had seemed just to fit in quietly, with a mixture of affectionate youthfulness and queer, understanding maturity. Perhaps it was because he was the last—a gift suddenly vouchsafed them when they had given up thought of other children—that she and dad had both felt from the first they could relax their responsibility and simply enjoy him as their baby. Now it seemed to her, if she could *have* a choice (and of course she couldn't, it would be treachery to her mother's heart), she would say that the last was the best of all. He was *theirs* in a peculiar way that the other children weren't. Carl was hers, and Dorothy was her father's. Margaret—whose *was* she? Too much her own to be anyone's! The thought of Margaret brought guilt, hunger, frustration and pain. Her visit last summer had been really no assuagement. The mother's soft face took on secretive lines as she stood looking into the springtime vacancy of the room.

Well! Margaret took her own way. Mrs. Ferguson gave a quick shrug of her shoulders. She made up the narrow cot that Bunny preferred to a bed, as more rigorous and manly, smiling to think that she still had her youngest.

The telephone rang. That was a regular thing at this time of the morning. Fred always called up from downtown to ask what he should bring home for dinner. Some of the men stayed down at noon now, eating the forty-cent Business Men's Luncheon in the redecorated dining room of the Belmond House. But Fred liked to come home, except on the day of the Rotary meeting. Hotel fare tasted stale compared to mama's cooking. Now that they were alone, they could go back to the old country custom of having the main meal at noon—much to the girls' disgust if they had known it.

"Hello, Annie. That you? What do you want me to bring

529

home this noon? I wondered how about a little steak. They've got some that looks pretty nice here at Helmholz's."

"All right. Yes. Bring that if you want to."

But she pursed up her lips and then laughed as she hung up the receiver. She didn't doubt that dad had the steak already bought and tied up in a package. "That you?" Who else did he ever think it could be? And his asking what he should bring home was about as cut and dried as one of those Republican meetings in the courthouse to elect county officers. The men had once chosen Mrs. Hoagland as one of the delegates, out of courtesy to the ladies, after woman's suffrage had come in; and Mrs. Hoagland had gone there all ready to nominate Fannie Allison for a county office, because the ladies had agreed she needed it more than some of the men. But the meeting had slid off like greased clockwork, and before Mrs. Hoagland knew it had even started the same old ticket had been confirmed. "All in favor say aye, opposed no, motion carried, Mr. Brownback is our nomination." Those men had the whole thing fixed up before anybody went there.

Mrs. Ferguson turned away from the telephone. In the dimness of the closet, among the umbrellas and rubbers, some of the children's old things were still hanging. The big jardinière for flowers was empty. Margaret used to keep that filled.

"Well, if I'm going to have dad's dinner ready—"

She hurried out to the kitchen to fix the potatoes. Dad always wanted mashed potatoes with his steak.

Still, there was no need to hurry. There was fresh lettuce in the ice box, but Fred actually preferred canned vegetables. He was incorrigible in some ways! Soon they would have their own garden stuff—he liked that. Mrs. Ferguson looked out of the window. The garden soil lay freshly turned. Ben had gone home. Ella would raise a big to-do if he wasn't there strictly at twelve, just as if they still had all the work to get through on the farm! A bird settled on a rich black clod. Mrs. Ferguson looked more closely, thinking for a moment it was a new variety. She and Lillian now had a mutual interest in birds, vying with each other in the number of varieties that visited their lawns, the earliest that came back in the spring, the number that stayed over winter. Now, though, if Margaret would have consented to stay at home, they would have let her have a cat!

The clock struck dimly in the empty living room. Soon she wouldn't be able to leave her meals until the very last minute. As long as the steak was good, dad was satisfied. But it would be nice to have to set the big table in the dining room again. It was still a little too cold for the porch; but Mrs. Ferguson had arranged a breakfast nook, just for herself and dad, near the sunny kitchen window. She set the painted table with the green and white linen cloth she had bought at a sale in Geneva —she and Lillian had got some just alike. Then, feeling a little sentimental because they might not have many more meals out here together, she looked around for some flowers. The bouquet of straw flowers seemed dusty and stale. She might as well cut the last red tulip from the Easter plant that her Sunday School girls had given her. She put it in the little old twisted green glass vase she had got down from the top shelf of the cupboard, where it had been stuck away among other supposedly superannuated ornaments that had come from the division of Grandma Ferguson's possessions. Some of those despised things were turning out to be treasures! The girls would probably want this vase if they saw it. But she didn't know whether she was going to let the girls have any of Grandma's things or not!

While she was mashing the potatoes, Fred came into the house.

"Annie!" He came on into the kitchen. "Oh, I didn't know where you'd gone to!" He always wanted her right where he could find her. "Got your frying pan hot? This steak won't need any extra grease."

The steak hissed in the iron skillet, and the good smell went through the warm kitchen mingled with that of the coffee. Fred must always have his coffee. Fred washed his hands at the sink instead of going up to the bathroom. And he always used the toilet in the cellar by preference. He waited with his meal until she sat down. He was never willing to eat or sleep without her.

"I see the garden's plowed. Ben come over?"

531

"Yes. I hated to have him do it."

"Oh, I guess he wanted to. This is good butter. Rolfe bring it in? I don't like that butter you get downtown."

"Why, dad, it's nice."

"Well, it ain't like the homemade."

"Goodness! Nobody churns any more."

"Vina does."

"Well, she thinks she has to, you make such a fuss if you can't get butter from them."

"Ella did her own churning. All country women used to, and plenty in town."

"Yes, but you know they don't any more, Fred. How can you act as if they did? And you're a great one to talk, dad! When you won't even mow your own lawn."

She knew he still felt guilty about that self-indulgence. But he had got used to counting on the boys, and when they were gone he couldn't make himself go back to those old chores, as he still called them.

"Well, we don't have to eat the grass."

He felt satisfied at having got it back so neatly at mama. And he didn't worry about Vina. He gave her plenty for all the little extras she did. The steak was good, and so were the potatoes; and he had selected both. He still ordered the staples for the household. He was better at a bargain than mama. She looked after the rest of the stuff.

"Pretty nice dinner," he said.

It never failed to please her when he mentioned that her cooking was good. A dim pink flush returned to her cheeks.

"Fred, do you think you could get home just a little bit early? I'd like to drive out to the greenhouse and get some pansy plants this afternoon."

"Well . . . yes, I guess maybe we'd better go. May not come many more such good days for setting things out. Four o'clock suit you?"

2

After dinner, Mrs. Ferguson went upstairs to take a nap. This still gave her an almost guilty feeling of self-indulgence and luxury—for to lie down in the daytime, when a body wasn't sick, Fred's mother had always regarded as little short of a crime. Ella wouldn't do it yet. She would putter around all afternoon at nothing rather than—as she called it—give up and lie down. Mrs. Ferguson took a book along with her, as a further luxury, one that she had heard reviewed in the Woman's Club in Geneva when she had gone there with Lillian. Perhaps she herself would review it in the club here at home. This last year or two, she had begun to pluck up courage and take quite an active part. She had made a hit in the club with a portrayal of Ruth in a pageant featuring "Women of the Bible." Mrs. Hoagland—large, assured, pleasantly dominating —was the Naomi; and beside her Mrs. Ferguson, with her innocent conception of the extremely efficient character of Ruth, had seemed tender and almost maidenly. The words "Entreat me not to leave thee" she had always thought the most beautiful in the Bible. Beneath her shy, gentle, somewhat tremulous voice as she spoke these lines had run a secret strain of personal feeling that gave them a frail, touching sincerity. They made her think of the early days when she had entered the Presbyterian church with Fred, forsaking the ways of her parents. Her parents, long dead—the little Ohio town in the spring—the peaceful graves in the small burying ground, wooded and far away. None of the family lived in Woodbine now.

She dropped the book, feeling not quite up to it, and reached for the household magazine that she had sneaked along with her "instructive" book. First she dutifully looked over the recipes, then turned to a lushly sentimental story which she began to read in comfort. In the midst of a love scene, she drifted off to sleep.

She heard sounds outside. A car stopping. Then footsteps coming up the front walk. The screened door banged; and Bunny's voice called:

"Hello, mother!"

Mrs. Ferguson sat up. She hadn't really expected Bun today. The flurry of feeling her plans changed—and being still only half awake—upset her a little. Bunny came running up the stairs. Mrs. Ferguson got up and put on her kimono, and opened her door. When she saw his smiling, young, sunburned face, she was truly pleased.

"Well! We didn't expect you before tomorrow!"

She kissed him. Then she saw that there was someone else standing downstairs in the hall.

Bun, seeing her glance, said slightly abashed, "I brought Charlotte Bukowska along with me."

A girl?—and what a funny name! Bun ran downstairs. But then, Bunny liked all the girls, he was friendly with all of them. His mother smiled.

After a few minutes, she herself went down, nicely dressed. The low, intermittent sound of voices in the living room stopped. Bun stood up as his mother entered; and she noticed that slight awkwardness about him again. A girl sitting in the big chair got up too, after a moment of hesitation. Mrs. Ferguson felt a slight shock as she went forward to greet this guest.

"Mother, this is Charlotte Bukowska. I thought I'd bring her along with me—give her a chance to taste some good cooking." Bun grinned.

Mrs. Ferguson smiled. She shook hands graciously. But all the time, it seemed to her that she was barely covering that shocked feeling. The girl was large—that was partly what made her seem so strange—with frowning, heavy eyebrows. Black hair was combed from a solid broad forehead and fell in a heavy shock almost to her shoulders. The touch of her firm, large hand was strangely evasive and cold. After the introduction, the girl stood there awkwardly. She wore a careless sweater and old wool skirt, with crumpled white socks and low heelless shoes. She might have dressed a *lit*-tle more carefully if she was coming to visit people she had never seen! But what struck Mrs. Ferguson most was the strange ice-blue of the eyes under those frowning, unfeminine black eyebrows. There was something almost frightening.

What a funny girl for Bun to choose! Mrs. Ferguson couldn't help thinking that, although she instantly tried to be hospitable. She had always encouraged Bun to bring his friends

534

home, feeling that they had made a mistake in that way with Margaret. But her smiling manner covered deep uncertainty. There was a queer air of tension and smothered hostility. Or did she just imagine it?

She said nervously, "We thought Bun might be home tomorrow. But the earlier the better! It must have been lovely driving today."

"Pretty swell," Bunny answered.

"Well, it's nice you could get through in time to come."

The girl did not speak again. She sat down at Mrs. Ferguson's smiling request. She was looking around from under straight frowning brows, letting Bunny and his mother talk together. Mrs. Ferguson began to feel an uneasy, wounded hostility, based on she couldn't have said just what. This girl seemed so big and strange . . . rough, almost. There had been a frightening indifference in the touch of her hand. But Mrs. Ferguson kept going back to that sensational contrast between the blue eyes and the heavy black brows and hair.

She tried to keep up the right air of cheerful welcome.

"Let me get you something to eat. You must be hungry after that drive."

"Children," she had almost said. She would have said it happily and naturally with any of Bunny's other friends. But with this girl—she didn't want to, and she didn't dare.

Bun said with embarrassment that they had stopped on the way for lunch.

"Wouldn't you like a little something more? Some fruit— or a piece of cake? We have some sponge cake. I was counting on Bunny to help us eat it up! Dad and I eat so little."

Bun glanced obliquely at his guest. "Like something, Charlotte?" She signified mutely that she didn't. "I guess we've had plenty, mother. We'll wait and keep an appetite for supper."

"It's too bad you didn't get here a little earlier. Dad brought home such a nice steak."

Mrs. Ferguson tried to give a quick smile at the guest, but it met a surly blankness. The girl was looking down now, and

535

her mouth was sullen. Mrs. Ferguson began to feel upset and resentful.

The uneasiness grew until they were all silent. Finally Bun broke this silence with an obvious effort.

"I guess maybe we'll take a little drive," he said to his mother. He tried to smile. "I'll take Charlotte out to see the farm."

"Dad will be home in a little while."

"Well . . . I guess maybe we'd better go now, though, while it's warm."

"I expect that would be nicer," his mother valiantly agreed. "Well—" she tried to smile too—"you'll be back for supper, both of you."

When they left her at first she felt in a kind of daze. At least she would tell Bunny that he might teach his friends better manners! Not that the girl had really done anything, but she was so—just so. . . . And now Mrs. Ferguson thought she would have to call up dad and tell him that after all they couldn't go for the pansy plants. That little excursion was spoiled! She made a quick calculation about supper. She wanted to make something nice to impress that girl. Why did Bun bring *her* with him? Mrs. Ferguson was half provoked with Bun. It must have been charity. Those scuffed shoes, and that old skirt and sweater. The girl couldn't really be a *friend* of Bun's! But Mrs. Ferguson felt herself trembling and strange, judged somehow by alien eyes. She felt those cold blue eyes, remote as mountain water, still upon her; and there was a sensation she had never experienced before, as if she were being taken to task for all her innocent words and actions. She was almost glad to have them out of the house!

Bun and Charlotte walked out to the car. Bun felt with despair that they were far apart. He wanted to break down the fierce reserve into which Charlotte had retreated. But he seemed impotent and weak.

They started out in silence. Charlotte could take the custard pie for silence, anyway, Bun thought, half resentfully, half wistfully. He stole another of his oblique glances at her. He had just experienced the sensation of seeing his home through totally alien eyes—and it didn't make him comfortable, either! It seemed as if he ought to apologize for its easy bourgeois comfort. He had never realized before how complete that was. It had everything that belonged in the picture: radio, victrola, piano that nobody used any more, overstuffed davenport. It might almost have been a cartoon! And yet a stubborn adherence to his own people, an understanding of them that he could never communicate to Charlotte, a hurt perception at his mother's loyal and confused attempt at kindness—kept him still.

But he thought, damn it! He understood Charlotte too. He saw that her face was pale. Beneath a faint tinge of sunburn that had lingered through the winter, it had a sick greenish cast. Bun knew that Charlotte was weighing the possibility of their union all over again, and coming to the conclusion that it was no go. She was lumping him in with all of his household. He felt sick himself. That sense of impotence held him. And yet he wouldn't submit to it. At bottom it wasn't true. Bunny veered away from the straight blankness of despair. With fond guile, he began to plan a course of winning Charlotte from her surly muteness and from the decision before it was actually made.

They had been driving for about three hours today. Nevertheless, Bun felt fresh again. Perhaps it was fear spurring him on and giving him his second wind! He couldn't help taking his old, affectionate, tolerant, slightly cynical interest in these familiar things. He wanted wistfully to win Charlotte to some interest. At least, to make her *see* these things. But he knew that to her all towns were alike—places where the jobs were a little better or a little worse; except for a queer, inalienably American hope that each new place might somehow prove to be the Promised Land! Evidently she didn't think that of Belmond.

"Why the stern silence?"

He got a fiercely cold glance from those blue eyes. Charlotte looked straight ahead. No use to point out any of Belmond's spots of interest to her—"On your right, madam, the public library, presided over by Miss Vanchie Darlington, Belmond's most distinguished spinster—

> No such record of strict virginity
> Has ever been known in this vicinity."

That old gag the kids used to whisper when Vanchie sent them out of the library for disturbing the peace! Bun realized with a grin, half rueful, half like a naughty schoolboy's, that he didn't dare risk breaking into Charlotte's fierce concentration with any such trivialities. How different their tradition was! If you could call Charlotte's a tradition. If it was a tradition not to allow any tradition! None of these homely, intimate, small town things on which he had grown up meant anything to her.

"Your mother doesn't like me."

She announced that out of the blue. Bun felt indignation rise in him. It put him on his mother's side. He wanted to say, "I shouldn't think she would after the way *you* acted." No wonder Charlotte had seemed formidable to his poor mother! She did even to him. She was built altogether on a different scale from anybody in the Ferguson family. Margaret could certainly raise the roof at times, when the folks and she disagreed; but beside Charlotte she was a fragile flower. Bun felt an angry dismay. It was no use talking to Charlotte! She had one track and she went ahead on that like a locomotive. Went ahead with such force that she left the opposition paralyzed! Looking at her, he was aware again of her intense monumental seriousness, of a kind he had simply never met before, and about which Bun's tricksy spirit was forever playing, partly because he did respect it so tremendously . . . and as always, ever since he had known Charlotte, queerly and almost wryly mingled with his admiration and passion for her was a sense of her pathos. What he kept seeing in her—but only in flashes—was a frightened, sullen child at bay. The impulse to combat her head-on faded. Instead, Bun put his hand on her knee and shook it slightly—with the old thrill, bitter-sweet, at the touch of that firm flesh.

"That's not half as bad as you think."

He could feel that his touch had slightly weakened her opposition, although she still sat locked away from him in that
blue-eyed silence. But he believed that he knew the methods of
gradual beguilement against which, in her stormy simplicity,
Charlotte was never quite proof. It made Bun smile wickedly
to himself, pitying her because he could outwit her, loving her
because he pitied her—and yet aware that he had to go very
carefully, all the same! Perhaps what he liked best of all was
the danger.

"You had mother scared," he told Charlotte. "Yes, you did,
you had her regularly buffaloed. It scares anybody when you
turn on that scowl."

She still sat sullenly dumb. Bun was unhappy. She muttered:
"I don't see why you brought me here."

They drove nearly a block before Bun answered. "Well, because," he said slowly, "I told you. I'm going to let the folks
in on this. This isn't going to be any sneak business."

"I don't know what difference it makes."

"I know you don't. But I do. That's just the difference."
Charlotte's face was hard. Bun said, "You can't expect to sit
there like an Indian from a hostile tribe and have mother fall
for you. You've got to give the folks a *lit*-tle chance. Mother
was nicer to you a damn sight than you were to her."

Charlotte was still staring straight ahead. Yes, his mother
had *acted* nice, if Bun expected her to be fooled by that! But
Charlotte felt the essential firmness, under the boyish tenderness and easy gaiety, that always brought her up with a thrill of
hard respect. She slowly, almost shyly, put her hand on *his* knee
and returned his pressure. He watched her large mouth curve
into a lovely smile.

"Well, gee—I felt like a roughneck," Charlotte admitted, like
a surly truthful little boy. She turned away her head.

Bun was suddenly joyous. He grabbed her hand and held it
hard. Charlotte could stand up to it. You could always count
upon that. It was one of the things that made him love her, that
good hard realistic intellect of hers, with its infusion of the
loftiest idealistic passion (whether she admitted it or not)—all
her strange, half-crude, half-seasoned mixture, at the same time

539

so childish and so experienced. His thin boyish body quivered to her strong attraction. But whether she realized it or not, he was a match for her. She had given him the shock of his life, but she hadn't overthrown him. Even if he wasn't one of those tough eggs she used to know! His kind of wily steel was out of her ken, so that it almost made Bun ashamed at times to triumph over her. It *did* make him humble, in a way he couldn't explain to her. Still, he'd better not talk—he hadn't triumphed yet!

Charlotte suddenly and passionately caught at his hand. They frankly pushed against each other in the car like two young animals. And it was perilous fun for Bunny to keep driving fast ahead just the same.

Now there was an almost delirious happiness in the brightness of the early afternoon—the scudding of white clouds across the blue April sky. The country earth smelled good. Town was pretty small, but it was big out here. They seemed to have the road to themselves. A few cars passed, but somehow didn't count. If only they could be alone together like this always! They could understand each other then. But they couldn't. This sense of there being no one but themselves alive in the whole spring world had only a transient truth. Bun knew that, young as he was. Just the same, this little time was theirs. And he intended to make use of it. He slowed down the car.

"Well, here are the Ferguson ancestral acres!" he announced.

He felt Charlotte's instant frown, which he had meant to provoke. He stopped the car after grandly circling the windmill.

"Come on," he said. "It's pretty nice, if the folks do own it."

He stared impudently straight at her and grinned disarmingly. Charlotte had to smile again, reluctantly bewitched by his casual charm, which she was aware she didn't quite fathom. She could feel that she was being maneuvered, but she got out of the car and went with Bun across the driveway. There was a look of distant reservation in her ice-blue eyes.

Bun took hold of her arm and pressed it up against him. "Have I made you sore?" She wouldn't answer. "You know, Charlotte—" He stopped. "I'm not making fun of your ideas. Jesus Christ, I more than—! I love you for what you believe."

He could feel Charlotte quiver. Then she turned to him and passionately raised her full red mouth. Their embrace almost overwhelmed Bun's slight, tall, boyish frame. But he held his ground. "I just want to make you live too, my sweetheart. I want to *have* you." His voice broke with earnestness. She gave him her lips but never her eyes. It seemed for a moment, in despair, as if there were too many things around them, and between them—as if they were caught in a network of circumstance that would defeat them in the end.

But he wouldn't admit that—didn't. He gave a sly glance around to see if Rolfe or Vina might have been watching. It would have been a nice eyeful for them if they had! Bun slightly shrugged his shoulders. Charlotte was like the rain and the sun. You had to take her favors when they came. He had an admiration, deep and humble, for her untutored simplicity that could ignore surroundings. But it brought his impish spirit up again.

"Well, come on," he said slyly, pulling her along with him. "Let's see what a mess things are under private ownership. Then we can have some direct action, kid."

He grinned, not expecting a response. But he was uneasy too. Beside his beloved, he felt himself mild, unseasoned . . . beside her adventurous, embittered young life, without rules, uncharted, nomadic, now here, now there, the code all different from the bottom up . . . And yet he felt himself so much older! His mind could see around her elemental simplicity. He knew what Charlotte was feeling. But she could never seem to fathom him, and this, although it sometimes pleased him, left him solitary. She didn't try to do it. He had never really impressed himself upon her, after all. Perhaps he couldn't. He was just too slight. He felt that way even beside his brother Carl (whom Bun considered pretty much of a mess psychologically) just because Carl took things so damned hard. Bun felt a touch of that despair again.

Right now he could see that Charlotte was disturbed. She could never meet his oblique playfulness. It was out of her range. She was scowling. To her it seemed trivial and indirect. She was used to going straight at things. It was the only way she knew. Bun had a fleeting, tender, remorseful perception that his manner sometimes made her feel clumsy—and naturally she didn't like that, poor kid. Perhaps he had unwittingly brought up old memories of her childhood, some of the things she had told him about, speaking in a flat, hard, matter-of-fact voice, when they had sat huddled up together in that old deserted tool shed they had discovered: of the time when she had started to school, a little Russian peasant girl among the American kids in a western town. He didn't want to be joining in with those little devils, some of his girl's first enemies! But if she only knew what she made *him* feel like about half the time!

Charlotte walked a little distance ahead of him. Bun let her have her way. He knew he hadn't actually made peace with her yet. The trouble was that what she thought about the folks was true enough—and yet it wasn't true. Charlotte ruthlessly simplified everything. Bun saw the complexities of every situation. He had artfully put a leash on her. And yet it didn't make him any more sure that he possessed her. He felt the thrilling challenge of that. Their feeling for each other must be true at every instant, not just in the long run, or all things considered, or in a general way. If ever the truth died out of their union, she would not have him. The ceremony in itself meant even less to Charlotte than it did to him, and that seemed little enough. He felt the perilous, striving, moment-by-moment integrity of such a union as he was attempting—a different kind of integrity from that of the folks in their taken-for-granted partnership, and one they would never grant or understand. Yet he intended to snare his beloved—forever, if he could. Bun followed, smiling to himself. There was a queer, old subtlety in that boyish face. Charlotte, his new Atalanta. If her beau—Atalanta's—wasn't such a whiz of a runner, still he had his technique of overcoming his girl wonder. Bun felt he had Charlotte bothered, all the same.

He had to smile again at the thought of the classical instance compared to this almost stern modernity. He saw Charlotte's scowling face above her old white sweater, and her strong bare legs with the crumpled ten-cent-store socks. The shock of black hair was held back with the sort of Alice-in-Wonderland comb that just now the girls were using. Russian ancestry showed in the height of the cheek bones and the width of the face. But she was a good deal more American than Russian. Bun felt in her something so new that it was crude. And yet something that he thought of as pre-classic. Archaic. She was a young archaic goddess of some genus never met with in the world before.

Well, it was a good break that Rolfe and Vina weren't around! Bun had slyly ascertained that their car was gone. They must have driven into town this afternoon. Charlotte didn't seem aware that anybody *might* be here. She looked at the old place, so familiar to Bun from his childhood, with a direct, refreshing impersonality. The whole countryside seemed deserted in the spring sunshine. No, not so much deserted as never yet inhabited. The farm lay off the main road and not many cars went past. It purified everything—this sunshine, alternately so chilly and so warm, the trampled bare ground of the pigpen, the broken pale cornstalks, the dark water in the tank. It seemed to Bun at this moment that he was following his sweetheart into a morning world.

The big barn door was closed. Bun pushed it open with a running shove, the kind he had always loved to give it when he was a kid, feeling very proud of himself. The semi-dusky interior, both impressive and homely, was nearly empty. That gave a strange feeling, too, of walking in a pre-dawn stillness. Some calves looked up with soft, dark, watery eyes from a bedded stall. The girls—Dorothy and Margaret—would have gone straight for them. Almost any girls he knew. But Charlotte glanced at the little buggers with a sort of troubled reserve, and said nothing. Two were lying down, one stood on knock-kneed long legs. Bun himself, as he passed, gave a hasty caress of the knobby baby head between the two soft ears. It was all right. They didn't have the calves here for pets.

He led Charlotte artfully on to the machinery. Rolfe kept the things he wasn't using conscientiously under cover. Dad always told Aunt Ella that Rolfe was about as good a renter as she could hope to find. If Aunt Ella had chosen to descend upon the place this afternoon, and give Charlotte *that* example of private ownership, it would have been all up with Bun Ferguson! Aunt Ella was too much even for dad.

"Here's the stuff. Hm?"

The big binder gleamed in the dusk. Charlotte went straight to it with frowning, direct interest. So this was what took his goddess's heart! Bun grinned trying to imagine his mother and sisters making for a binder! They could look at it a hundred times and still not know what it was for—or even ask. It made him feel tender toward them, and even more tender toward Charlotte. Well, what was funny? Charlotte came by her interest honestly. Those long blazing days of her childhood, out in the beet fields, working by hand, had ground into her a kind of respect that the university intelligentsia who were talking now about "the machine age," either praising or damning it as their temperaments demanded, simply didn't comprehend. Charlotte stored up fine photographs of machines (most of them torn out of library books and magazines, he must admit) just as Margaret, at one stage, used to collect Perry prints of the Old Masters, and colored reproductions from the *Ladies' Home Journal*. Bun saw that it was an idea Charlotte had got from reading about the new Russia. She had a bunch of proletarian magazines published in obscure places. . . . Let her look at her machines. Here in the dusk of the barn her lover felt her womanhood. He had not yet got into the very center of that rich, potential warmth. He was still on sufferance, he knew.

Bun let her look for a while, and then pulled her away, feeling jealously that he wanted this day for himself. He foresaw that the night would be difficult. He felt with a quick desperation that he must make her his or lose her, after all. He had only this little hour vouchsafed him. He had brought his bride into the midst of alien conditions, half knowing the danger, and now he must make her feel that in spite of them he was closer to her than anybody else in the world. It put him on his mettle. . . . Of course she *was* his—just now. He had won passionate response from her. But he knew that their love must rest on something more. She had given response to others, according to her code; and although she had yielded to him, fascinated, perhaps partly bewildered, she had not yet acknowledged him

544

as standing alone from all the rest. Charlotte made no secret of the others. Bun had to hear about them and bear it as he could. He would use any method if he had to, he realized with sudden grimness. But no, he didn't want to! It would be half defeat. He felt in her somewhere an untouched purity that matched the blue mountain coldness of her eyes.

"Come on. You've seen enough."

He pulled at her, with a grim insistence beneath youthful boisterousness.

He was surprised at the meekness with which she followed him along. But Charlotte had these funny moments of docility. She had told him once about an English teacher who had had a great influence over her for a little while in a college in Missouri that Charlotte had attended for about six months. "She was going to make me lead a new life. She wouldn't let me cuss any more. I was going to be a true woman." Bun grinned, recognizing the authenticity of the quotation. But the funny thing was that Charlotte didn't cuss. Her language was soberly stripped of even schoolgirl profanity. Sometimes it had a queer awkwardness; almost—if anybody but Charlotte had spoken that way—prissy. Charlotte reminded him at times of a bad little girl trying to talk grown-up people's language. Humorously, but lovingly, Bun secretly cherished these contradictions in her.

"Now we're going over and look at the ancestral pile."

The old rock house stood pale gold and cool in the April sunshine. It seemed to Bun to have a sad dignity. The window glass glared disconsolately over the drawn green shades. Bun tried all the doors.

"Can't get in. All locked up."

Charlotte was standing back, still docile, and waiting. She asked in a queer awe:

"Is it empty?"

"Stark empty."

Bun was going on to explain the situation, but it didn't seem worth while. The familiar middlewestern routine of starting out farming and then moving into town meant nothing to Charlotte. It was such a matter of course to Bun that it simply

545

signified "American." It was funny, when he came to think of it! His Grandfather and Grandmother Luers had been born in Germany, and his Grandma Ferguson in Scotland. Yet Charlotte was "immigrant" in a way that he wasn't, that he couldn't conceive of his family as ever having been. He had always thought of his ancestry as just ordinary American, when he thought of it at all. Charlotte would cover the complications of his family history with the one scathing word "bourgeois." It was so much more mixed up than that, that Bun didn't seem to have any recourse except to fall back on facetiousness.

"*We* can live here next summer. Or next winter. You can run the binder for Rolfe and I'll take photographs." He stole a sly glance at her. "The folks own this joint."

He grinned. But he didn't know that he wasn't half in earnest. Well, this had been a pioneer home, and Charlotte was a pioneer—more than any of his grandfather's descendants!

Charlotte was still staring at the house. She said soberly, "I would have called that a mansion." Here it was—just standing empty. She thought of the little tar-paper shack on the plains where all of them used to be crowded,—blazing so in the heat of the western sun that it was one shimmer when you looked at it from a distance. The whole family had worked in the beet fields together, except the baby, and he almost did—the mother had to take him along because she was nursing him. Bun always talked as if he, and his folks, were American. Well, that was American too! She had told Bun about her father, and the way he used to lick the kids to make them all work; but when Bun had started to get indignant on her account, Charlotte had turned around and defended her father. "He had to make us earn our bread." Now, remembering, her mouth had a cynical hardness. She looked with hostile eyes at the empty house. A mansion!—a palace was what it would have been. She hated Bun and the whole Ferguson family.

Bun knew it. He felt that there was nothing he could say. Her experience was out of the class of his. But he wasn't going to let her feel separated from him, all the same. He at least knew enough to appreciate the way things were. With a kind of timidity, he put his arm around her. Charlotte's body yielded

546

to his touch, unconsciously, it seemed. Her eyes looked into his with a stricken appeal.

But she had to pull herself away and say again, "I'm going to be free just the same!"

"Sure. So am I."

Bun grinned to see the passionate flash of her eyes and the clenching of her hands. He felt inside the quivering sweetness of that fierce possessiveness she could show. All that he had felt up to now seemed shallow and colorless. Last summer he had thought he was developing a case on little Frankie Weyant— slightly detached and humorous, because she was such a kid. In fact, he had liked her being such a kid. It gave him a lot of time! He had dallied with a romantic fancy that he would wait for her to grow up and then come back for her. The appropriateness had appealed to him as idyllic. He could see that the folks were pleased at the idea of his falling for Frankie. Bun had always liked every girl for what she was. His sensitiveness had a peculiar faculty of finding out the hidden symbol in each of them, which his detachment had permitted him to appreciate at its full value. He had gathered girls, transiently loving each for what she signified to him. But Charlotte was the strange new element on which he hadn't counted. There seemed to him a sense of distance and of potential magnificence about her that bowled him over. He found his vague but changing social values —first aroused in that summer when he and Joseph had gone bumming West—suddenly concentrated and personified in this girl, with her hard, alien experience. But he couldn't say that Charlotte was just this or that. She seemed to him unique.

That was what had first interested him when he used to see Charlotte in his English class last fall, sitting miserable and silent, but sullen and hard. She wouldn't recite, because she had been shoved into the class by the registrar and didn't care anything about the subject. To the other students, she had been just a nut—their easy classification of anything incomprehensible. But her surly ability to stand alone had wakened Bun's admiration, mixed with the compassionate understanding he always had for neglected elements—why, his friend Joseph always said was contrary to all psychology, since if anybody had an easy time it was Bun Ferguson! Bun had wanted to explore her strangeness. All girls whom he classed as interesting, according to his own special exactions, excited Bun's curiosity; but Charlotte—well, it did seem, uniquely. If the fellows thought it was a queer choice, and that he was getting out of line, let them go ahead and think so. They had learned some time ago that Bun Ferguson wasn't as amenable as he looked. The reason that Charlotte had given for coming to the university tickled Bun. She had been hitch-hiking, and she had hit the university town just at the opening of school. She had entered the best hotel to go to the ladies' rooms (Charlotte's entire experience of good hotels was confined to these democratic refuges) and in the lobby she had picked up a blurb put out by the Commercial Club stating that this was "the chief agricultural state in the Union." Charlotte had the idea of going some day to work on a communal farm in Russia—when she got put out of the country, she said. So she thought she might as well stay here in the chief agricultural state and see what she could learn. She told the fellow with whom she was traveling —he was a salesman for hardware gadgets—that he could go on without her. She guessed she'd stay and go to the university a while. The Dean had been interested in her and had found her a place where she could work for her board and room. That salesman had actually lent her enough money to pay for her fees. Of course she wasn't taking a single agricultural subject! They were trying to give her "culture." But partly out of the fatalism that was blended in her with a fierce and lofty enterprise, she had thought she might as well stay until her money ran out. Bun was tickled, too, because at the little denominational college, she had told him, the one where she was going to be made into a true woman, she had raised a great rumpus by registering herself as "Charlotte Corday." Hadn't she known they'd spot that for an alias? Bun had asked her. The faculty had made her give her "real name," of course; but she had stuck to the Charlotte, discarding her own stereotyped Russian name, Sonya or Marya (she wouldn't tell him what it was), and now she passed as Charlotte Bukowska.

"Why didn't you go to the agricultural college?"

548

"Have they got one?"

"You're a prize!"

She was like no one else he had ever known on earth, and he wasn't going to let her get away from him. But he felt the difficult necessity of explaining her to the folks, and reconciling if he could the two elements. He knew what he meant to the folks as their youngest. Bun suddenly felt as if he had too much on his boyish shoulders. As if he had started to carry the whole weight of a changing world.

But now he wanted to stop thinking. He wanted just pagan revelry in the spring sunshine . . . his girl's magnificent body. . . . Charlotte was still brooding over something; and Bun divined shrewdly that it was the meeting with his mother. Charlotte stuck to her guns. But there was still—when she encountered someone like his mother, with her fine unconscious gentility, the soft evidence of an easy life—a hurt uncertainty, almost humility, that bitterly shamed her. It was what had kept her docile under the teacher in that little school.

"Come on. Let's wander."

Bun caught hold of her hand and made her come along with him. Her face had grown pink in the chilly wind that was tossing her black hair. She looked again like an archaic goddess. Charlotte had told Bun once why she had chosen that name— because once in a library where she had gone to get warm, and where the librarian kept watching her, distrusting her looks— she had seen a picture of Charlotte Corday: one woman, she said, who had guts to up and kill a tyrant—even if she did wear silly-looking ruffles on her cap. It made Bun laugh—and yet he didn't laugh. At the center of his feeling for Charlotte, deeply and shyly hidden, was an acknowledged adoration for some element of the heroic that he felt in her.

But she was as much little girl as goddess. More, at this moment, when she suddenly broke away from him and went racing along. She stopped, panting, turned toward him. Her eyes had an open clarity, although her lips kept their sullen line. Bun had noticed that before—her mouth had been shaped by experience; at times it had a spread, sensual look; but her eyes were those of a cold pure child. Her woman's spirit had

549

been only half brought to life. The brutality of her childhood was ground into her, making her forever distrustful, setting her always on the other side. It made Bun tremble with inchoate wrath. The thought of it was mixed strangely, religiously, with his love for her. Now he felt that love drenched deep in pity. He no longer wanted to enjoy her body. That seemed like an old treachery committed too often before.

"What are these trees?"

"Oh, this is a little stretch of timber that got left."

"Does it belong to the farm?"

"It does."

"I suppose we can go in, then," Charlotte said with such obvious sarcasm that Bun had to grin.

"Yes, we have the entrée."

All along, Bun had felt Charlotte's wariness in committing herself to any expression that might denote approval or even pleasure. It griped him, the way Charlotte lumped things all in together. The folks were "owners" in her vernacular, and that was enough. He didn't suppose she knew the difference between a nobleman's estate of the *ancien régime* and this middle-sized middlewestern farm! The things she knew were the craziest mixture of the bitterly realistic and the utterly romantic that he had ever come across!

"Oh—it's got a fence around it!"

"Sure. Do you want the cattle to get in?"

"I wouldn't care." She gave her shoulders a shrug.

"You're a swell agriculturist! You're going to teach the Russians a hell of a lot when you get over there." She scowled. It made her look big and clumsy. Bun took hold of her shoulder. "Come on, kid, don't be sore." He was a little sore himself. He had looked forward to bringing her out here. He respected the pattern of her life. She might be just tolerant to his! He could see all at once how his own history went back to this farm and was held—so far—in simple unity of design. But Charlotte's experience had been broken, outrageous, un-unified, made up of brief sojourns in unrelated places. It seemed to Bun as if he had taken Charlotte's experience into himself; and now already a profound break had come in that old feeling of unity.

He was looking at this beloved patch of timber as if from a distance.

"Come on. You want to see the woods. There may be some flowers up by now."

"I don't care anything about flowers."

Bun gave another of his sly grins. But he felt that this hour was somehow momentous. His hands were cold as he unfastened the loop of wire and pushed the wooden gate scraping back so that they could squeeze through. He let Charlotte go ahead while he fastened the gate. She was waiting for him now at a little distance. Bun felt the stillness all around them; and within the quiet spread of land, suddenly the fresh, bright, new magic of a wordless but admitted intimacy. He put his arms around Charlotte, and they made it up silently. She was the foreign bride, he thought, whom he had brought to this place from a strange land. Nevertheless, it was he, the almost despised stranger, who had divined the untouched spring in her that had kept her whole through deteriorating experience. She seemed again childish and pure at this moment. She had never really given herself, for no one had yet found her. Bun felt his hunter's instinct sharp and alert, crafty and deep, wanting to waken what no man had yet roused from slumber.

"Come on. This time you'll have to let me go ahead. You're liable to lose yourself in here."

The old sunken tracks of a wagon road led into the small stretch of timber, that seemed so dense, and was so brief. Bun remembered how, when he was a little boy, he always used to feel something mysterious in this patch of woods after the openness of the fields and pastures. He felt it now. The trees grew too thick and bushy. Nobody had taken the trouble to thin them out. The season was still so early, and the sunshine so scarce in here, that some of the trees were barely budded. The old fallen leaves made a mat, soggy underneath, that covered the cold, black, watery, springtime newness and ancientness of the ground.

The wagon road had petered out, and he and Charlotte had to go single file along a little path Bun well remembered, where their feet sank into the leaves and broke the flaking sticks with

551

an Indian-sounding stealthy crackle. It was like one of the old games the kids used to play. Bun went ahead and held back the branches for Charlotte, snapping off the dead ones. It pleased and touched him that she followed him with docility. He had the feeling that this place was his, and that in bringing Charlotte here he was revealing a precious childhood secret to her alone.

Charlotte's eyes had that look of clarity. It made him feel again how the ancient—the dawn-ancient—and the half-formed new were mingled in her. In this strange, this unique creature, whom he alone had discovered. It was her ignorance that touched him so, along with her hard-bitten wisdom. His friend Joseph could say what he pleased, and Bun knew himself that she spelled plenty of difficulty—but he felt that all other women would be forever tasteless and trite beside her.

He let her wander around just as she liked now. It was fun, but it was pathetic too, to watch her. She made him think of a child catching sight of something beautiful and not knowing what it was. She put both hands against a tree trunk and leaned her forehead against it. She was used to roads—perhaps the stillness and the trees of this little place he happened to be able to offer her seemed like a refuge. At home, in the house, she had looked clumsy and out of place. But here she seemed beautiful. Bun loved her at this moment more than he had ever dreamed of loving anyone.

He called, "Charlotte!"

She went over to him in plunges through the mold and the leaves.

"I've got something for you."

She looked up at him, wondering, reaching up to settle the comb in her black hair. Bun drew back and made a little downward motion with his head toward a clump of leaves at his feet. Charlotte bent down and touched the white blossoms that the leaves sheltered, looking up at him again.

"What are they?"

"Bloodroots."

She touched the white petals, almost in awe. Bun was going to laugh at her, and tease her a little—he thought she didn't care about flowers! But he didn't feel like doing it now, as he watched her. Her touch showed a girl's peculiar love for flowers, different from any man's—something intimate, personal, akin —it was something he recognized, although he couldn't have explained it. But it was strangely touching to see this feminine revelation in Charlotte. Bun reached down and picked one of the bloodroots. The orange-red juice stained his fingers, making him smile to himself.

"Here—this is your flower."

He took hold of Charlotte's hand and put the bloodroot blossom into it, closing her docile fingers around the bleeding stem. The flower seemed strangely alive in the cold white purity of its petals.

Charlotte looked away from him. He saw her bite her lip, and tears come into her eyes. But he felt that he knew what she was thinking. His love for her seemed to make him almost clairvoyant at this moment. He knew without words what she wanted to tell him—that this was what she would rather have had said to her than anything in the world. He had found her hidden symbol, and by finding it, had given her to herself. She looked at him now, and gratitude overflowed in the tears that brimmed her eyes, washing out distrust. That color, that depth of pure blue, was imprinted on his sight. Bun shyly touched her. Her whole splendid body was yielding and soft. Humbly, with gratitude of his own, and proudly, Bun felt the mutuality in this embrace, different from their others. How simple it had been!—the gift she had wanted.

"Shall we go back?" he asked finally.

Charlotte nodded. She followed him blindly out of the woods. When they were in the car, she still had her flower, and he saw her fold it carefully and softly in her handkerchief.

The nice supper promised was almost ready for them when they got home. The table was laid festively in the dining room, with a spring centerpiece of jonquils and narcissus. It was too early yet for fries; but dad had been able to get hold of a nice fat chicken to cook with hot biscuits—Mrs. Ferguson remembered that Bun liked chicken pie almost better than fried chicken.

There was still a glow upon the two young people when they took their places at the table. Their faces were fresh from the spring air. A new unity held them together. It showed in their voices—although Charlotte's was muffled—and in the quick, radiant glances of their eyes. The surly line of Charlotte's lips was indefinably softened. Bun's mother had caught the meaning of this at once; although as she talked nervously, asked them about the farm and urged them to eat, she was struggling to deny it. The pleasant warmth aroused by the consciousness of having got ready a lovely meal for Bun and his guest was struck with horror. She had divined that this girl was older than her boy, exaggerating the actual three years that lay between them. She was aware, too, of experiences of which she had no real knowledge, and they both repelled and intimidated her. But she tried to tell herself that Bunny had always liked all the girls. It had never been serious. And this would be the same . . . although she knew already that it wouldn't.

But gradually Bunny saw Charlotte's light dimmed. She was silent again, awkward, and obviously out of her element. She ate the good things almost timidly, trying with childish care to curb the frankness of her appetite. He had never seen her so uncertain and downcast as this. And he divined why it was—he had won her to him, and so dissolved her strength. Now she could no longer stand on her surly independence. She was softened, bewildered, and on the defensive. He could almost have cried as he felt her shy, awkward efforts to make herself acceptable to these "bourgeois," whom until now she had always been able to regard out-and-out as her natural enemies. It was as if she had just become conscious of her old sweater and scuffed shoes as things of which to be ashamed instead of proud. And he didn't want that change! He felt to blame. She was awed by the pretty dishes and the filet lace which his mother— ironically!—was using in her honor. The large hands that had learned hard work too early were pitiful now handling clumsily the best silver and the delicate cup—were clumsy instead of splendid. Bun felt again what lay ahead of him. It was hard.

perhaps not to be done . . . In a sense, he was giving away the freedom of his youth.

Seeing Charlotte here at his own table made him realize all over again how different she was from any other girl he had known. He despaired of the folks ever understanding her—or why he had made this choice. He remembered how pleased they had been when he had brought Frankie back with him once last summer, after he and Frankie had taken a hike together. They had treated her almost like a daughter then!—his mother had given her the pretty red-and-gold cup that the girls had always loved, and his father had trotted out his array of dry little jokes. Now they were even more bewildered by Charlotte than she by them. But Bun kept to his stubborn determination to give the folks their chance.

After supper, there wasn't much to do. Charlotte never thought of offering to help with the dishes. Maybe she didn't know that it was required of her. They sat down in the living room. Mr. Ferguson tried to make conversation by asking a few questions about the university.

"What course are you taking?" he said to Charlotte.

"Not any, I guess." She reddened.

Bun turned on the radio, turned it off—played a Paul Robeson spiritual on the victrola.

"Why don't you find something more lively?" Mr. Ferguson asked jestingly.

Mrs. Ferguson called to him then. For a while, the folks scrupulously left the young people to themselves. Bun went over and sat on the arm of Charlotte's chair. He put his hand on her shoulder, but he couldn't think of anything to say. He was restless with the sense of what lay ahead of him. He got up and went over to the piano and played a few meaningless chords, trying to work himself up to his announcement. His strained uneasiness showed in every move. Charlotte looked curiously subdued and disheartened.

Then his mother came into the living room, dutifully smiling, and saying that she would show Charlotte to her room.

Bun got up from the piano stool. His freckled face was pale.

"I guess I might as well break the news," he said.

Dad had come back into the living room too. In the silence that had followed his announcement, Bun heard the steady ticking of the clock on the bookcase. He saw the suspended anxiety on his parents' faces.

He went over and put his arm around Charlotte, and faced them. His face had a strained, appealing look, both boyish and old, as he tried to smile. The words seemed to him now almost more than he could speak.

"I gave myself a kind of birthday present, mother, a few weeks ago, that I haven't told you about. Charlotte and I got married."

He could see the shock in their faces. It was worse than he had thought. His mother looked actually as if she had been stabbed!—and as if she was just beginning to realize that it was her son who had done this. Bun felt himself trembling all over. He still forced himself to keep his strained smile. But he could feel that it made his face ghastly—and foolish. He stood his ground with gallant courage. He needed it more, it seemed to him, than in a stand-up fight, for he could perceive the blow that he was dealing them, and knew they wouldn't retaliate. And he knew how it must seem to them, this sudden flat announcement, with nothing to precede it—as if they had been betrayed. That was just what his mother was feeling, and he realized why. He felt for a moment as if he would break to pieces, beset on all sides. There was so much that he just couldn't tell the folks . . . how he must take Charlotte when he could get her . . . and how it was partly for their own sake—he was trying to be above-board. He couldn't give Charlotte up, no matter what happened; and yet he had been determined, when he saw that his love was not a momentary affair, to have it in the open, so that the folks would know—would hear it from himself and not from others. Mother was thinking, doubtless—he could see it—that Charlotte had lured him into this! And he would never be able to make her believe how little Charlotte had cared about the marriage. She had only gone through it to please him, half shrugging her shoulders, and believing that he was incomprehensible. Bun could have laughed. Now he was scrupulously bringing Charlotte home, to introduce her to the folks, as he would have done with any bride.

After a while his father said slowly and carefully, "Well—this is quite a surprise!"

His mother couldn't speak. Her hands were trembling.

Bun gave a shaky laugh. To have them say anything was a relief!

"I suppose it is!"

He had seen his father's eyes turn toward his mother, in uncertainty, to see how she was taking it. Dad expected mother to give the cue, and she wasn't giving it. Bun felt that he had to blunder along, in that awful hush, now that he had begun the thing, and go on scrupulously with the account he had so long been preparing in his mind. But his face had got red with the guilty realization that he wasn't so scrupulous as he was trying to make himself out to be. Because he had counted on their affection, and indulgence—he had known that if the marriage was all over when he came to speak to them, there was nothing they could do but accept it.

"Couldn't you have waited till the end of the year?" his father commented finally.

Bun colored again. "Well, it didn't seem as if we could. It seemed as if we were wasting our time when we weren't together." He tried to grin, but got no response. "You can't always wait." He put his hand on Charlotte's shoulder, and felt that firm flesh.

Charlotte was pale under her sunburn, and dumb.

Still those awful silences followed everything he said. It seemed to Bun again that he was going to pieces. Anger flared up in him. What was so terrible about this after all? They had tacitly trusted him to do as he liked all his life—and now he had made a choice, and it didn't suit them. Why should the folks be pitied? Their lives had gone smoothly, they had never run into any but minor troubles . . . except, perhaps, with Margaret—and Bun had long ago shrewdly decided that that was as much their fault as hers. But it was just *because* they were so innocent of tragedy that it seemed he had to pity them —and because it was he who was giving them their first actual

557

blow! All his tenderness for them suffered. At this moment, it was *they* who were the children.

His father asked at last, "Where did this take place?"

Bun told them bravely, "We went to the justice of the peace."

He could see his mother's horror at that. Her eyes turned for a moment toward Charlotte. To the folks, there was something wrong in the very sound—something hasty, secular . . . well, that was true.

Bun felt with shaken relief that he could talk to his father, however. It was all turned around—mother had been the one to whom they had gone to interpret things and set them right with dad. Bun looked at his father in appeal. His mother had not spoken all this time. Bun saw her wounded eyes and trembling hands. At last she had been caught off her guard, struck too deeply to keep the situation smooth, as she had always done before. Bun knew well how all this seemed to her! The blow came from his hand—but he couldn't help it. This was his first actual experience of what it meant to make a choice. It might sound heroic—but, actually, it was a tearing in two.

With dad, queerly enough, there was almost a feeling of sympathy!

"What'll the college think of this?" Mr. Ferguson asked now.

"I'm not going to tell them," Bun said.

"Well—is that right?"

"Maybe it isn't, dad. But I can't help it." For the first time, Bun felt his lips quiver. He kept his grin with difficulty. "They can find out for themselves. But I wanted you and mama to know about it."

The clock ticked again in the suspended silence. Bun could feel that he was bathed all over in a cold sweat. He felt for Charlotte's hand. It was numb and unresponsive. She was almost cowed. . . . This was his appeal. It was the only one he had to make.

"Well," his father said finally, "I guess you're twenty-one, all right." He permitted himself a smile. His look tried to take in Charlotte too.

But Bun could see that even dad was mystified and hurt. He felt now that he could never make them understand. The most he could hope was that they would believe he had been taken off his feet, and "wasn't responsible"—and they must make the best of it. All at once, the future of their youngest child had got out of their hands, and out of their comprehension. Bun had always been aware of a certain inner detachment from his family—as if already, young as he was, he had a maturity that the others didn't have, and he must get things worked out in his own mind. That was why he had chosen the university in the first place—because none of the others had gone there, and he had felt the necessity of taking some step outside the family paths. He had met mild bewilderment, mild argument. But he had never encountered genuine misunderstanding before. It made him feel strangely helpless. The lines of existence were drawn far more sharply than he had ever known—and just tenderness and tolerance for all concerned wasn't enough. He could never make the folks see what Charlotte meant to him. He shrank with horror from the thought of bringing that deeply hidden personal secret to light. He would rather have them misunderstand him! They couldn't feel his hot haste to live all of his life that he could with this strange girl whom he had found. His world wasn't the same as their world had been when they were young, and had felt that they had all the years before them. Now—who could tell? But in that summer when he had struck out and left them, he had felt the ominous first thunder. They didn't even understand his desire to bring them and Charlotte together! His mother thought that Charlotte was "designing"—it was the old, primitive explanation, and mother had fallen back upon it, although it was unworthy of her. Yet in a way he had to accept it, since it was her special love for him, her youngest, that had thrown her off her balance.

Anyway, he stood clean before them. Now they must just make what they could of it! He trusted, half with relief, half ashamed, to their kindness, which had never failed him.

He saw his mother pull herself together. She had always so hated any suggestion that the whole family didn't stand together in perfect harmony!—and she couldn't bear that before Charlotte, this stranger. She managed to call up a wavering smile.

"It *is* a surprise," she said.

They all felt the inadequacy of this faint remark. But they accepted it with relief. Bun saw his mother give him and Charlotte a strange glance; and now for the first time he couldn't tell all that was in her face. But she came up to Charlotte, trying to smile.

"Bun is our baby, you know. It's hard to believe he's really married."

She said this in appeal—but perhaps, too, there was a deft touch of spite. Bun was all at once aware of depths of feminine craftiness struggling with feminine tenderness. But the tenderness was too much—the gentleness, the life built on affections. It broke her down. She kissed Charlotte gallantly, but in defeat, with her eyes full of tears.

"Your folks don't like it."

"Yes, they do."

"They don't!" Charlotte looked at him, outraged by the falsehood.

"Well," Bun pleaded, "we had to expect they'd be taken by surprise."

For a moment, he was afraid of the storm that Charlotte might raise. His mother had put them in the guest room— Dorothy's old room. The pastel-colored furnishings, the dainty curtains, still seemed to breathe the soft fragrance of his sister's tender placidity. He wanted to rest here now. He couldn't go through much more.

But he saw that Charlotte had been hurt through her hard youthful armor of sullen defiance. There were all the old hurts in it too, which he wanted to assuage. He thought of telling her that she had made no response, had forced his parents to do it all. But he couldn't. He could only soothe her.

When he put his arms around her, she turned to him passionately, and he felt the savage innocence beneath the hard coating of experience. *She* claimed him now. Her kisses annulled the other claims.

"Your folks wouldn't want me if they knew what I was like,"

she told him bitterly, turning against herself. Her eyes were wild.

"Well, it isn't my folks. I'm the one that wants you. Don't you believe I'll stick by you?"

"You can't," Charlotte muttered, looking down. Her sullen mouth quivered. "All bourgeois stick together."

"Charlotte, you don't mean that. Not about me," Bun pleaded, holding her tightly.

He couldn't get her to look at him, and he was hurt.

"Wouldn't you have wanted me to be decent to *your* parents?"

"No."

"Well—" Bun said with difficulty, "I *do* want you to be decent to mine."

But how could he go on even seeming to upbraid her? His own heart was sore from the dubiousness of the folks' welcome, although he might comprehend the cause. And he felt remorseful in a queer way. A few weeks ago, Charlotte would have laughed off such a meeting with bitter carelessness. But now, in her bent head, and her eyes that wouldn't look at him, he could feel her humiliation. She had wanted the folks to like her after all. She even cried a little, biting her lips, but yielding helplessly to the tears. Bun felt a painful tenderness at this evidence of the very human side he had awakened in his goddess, bringing down her old defenses. Now the natural girlish desires which he had discerned with excitement beneath the strength of her harsh independence were alive in a sensitive confusion. Charlotte *wouldn't* have asked him to accept her parents. Neither he nor she would have cared whether they accepted *him*. But he had tried to draw her into his home circle, where once again she was made to feel solitary and at bay. There was nothing he could do about it except to make her feel his own love again. Exhaustion gave him a feverish strength.

She was more yielding than she had ever been before—more yielding, more concerned, straining toward him now as he toward her, seeking a confirmation of the gift he had made to her when they were alone together. But even in the moment of fulfillment Bun knew that their first passion had changed. They

561

had let the world in on it. It was no longer all their own. The moment could not stand for what it was in its own rapture of the present. The future lay in it too. Bun knew well how little the fact of marriage meant to Charlotte. She couldn't understand what it had been to his parents, the kind of mutual thing —with her own father a brute, her mother a drudge, the sweetness of passion gone long before she was conceived. But he had grown up in the accomplished placidity of that mutuality. Bun felt with humiliated uncertainty that perhaps he was "bourgeois" after all. His marriage would mean to him all that he could make it—although he would take it as he must. No one would ever know or love Charlotte as he did, anyway! Surely that would always be a bond? He couldn't help struggling toward permanency. It seemed again for a moment, in a still more impotent despair, that the forces against him were too much for his slight powers. .

"We're going to make a go of this," he whispered brokenly to Charlotte as he held her. "I can't let you get away. That's why I took you when I could. You mean the most. Charlotte. Don't you believe that? You mean the most."

He had convinced her, for now at any rate. He let himself rest for a little while in the splendor of her body. Yet even while he felt her strength, knowing it superior to his, there was in him the self-respect of his own comprehension that enveloped her.

Charlotte, satisfied, went to sleep. But Bun, after a spent shallow interval, was awake again.

Now the difficulties so unlooked-for in his easy, happy youth were heavy upon him in this dim hour. The future was clouded by them. Bun lay frowning. The fresh night air came in through the sheer curtains and centered in the little bowl of crocuses that his mother had placed scrupulously on the guest room table. There was a fragrance too delicate to be defined. Life was turning out in a queer way—a jolt had come in the early simplicity, and things no longer hung together.

He could feel in Charlotte an alien force that drew, repulsed, and held him. With a sigh now he relinquished the old idyllic thought of Frankie, youthful and cool as this fragrance in the night. Yes, he saw now, in another moment of clairvoyance coming this time largely from exhaustion, that he had really cherished the idea of some day—when she was older, when it suited him!—loving her. All would have been so clear and straight and easy then. This strange force had come suddenly between them, new, unpredicted and unpredictable. . . . That summer in the West had been the first of it, when he and Joseph had worked in the factory—that had been his first actual glimpse of what lay outside, after his gay easy boyhood and his warmly cherished childhood. He hadn't been really contented ever since. Something kept drawing him out from the old pleasant ways. That queer maturity of which he had always been conscious, that oldness in his youth, which came from being the youngest—an after-thought! Bun smiled wryly—had endowed him with a comprehension that wouldn't let him turn back. And now Charlotte's bitterly matter-of-fact stories of her child-hood hardships had somehow made them his own. They repulsed him, in a way—the hard brutality—but he could never turn his back upon them. Her wandering, inchoate youth, after Frankie's that was clear and fresh and all of a piece—struck deeper. The folks had made his inheritance *too* pleasant, and that was why he couldn't accept it. That summer experience of his seemed kiddish and shallow after the harsh realities upon which Char-lotte had been nourished—the immigrant childhood, the long broken journey West, the dawn-to-dark primitive labor in the sugar beet fields, the good old American attempt to rise ending this time in bitter resentment . . . and now the dream of a new Promised Land rising far away and slowly superseding the old dream of America. . . . He was meeting something, per-haps his match and more. But he felt stubbornly that he had something to give, something still fresh and inimitable, that couldn't be relinquished.

He felt the strangeness of Charlotte in this pastel-colored room that had belonged to Dorothy with her bright girlhood and her traditional marriage. He remembered that marriage now, on the radiant June day, out under the maple tree on the lawn; he himself so proud of his station as best man; all the church people and the relationship gathered around in a close and still unbroken circle. Already that seemed to exist in a past golden day which had been the culmination of the life here at home.

Bun raised himself on his elbow and looked at Charlotte asleep. His lips curled irresistibly at the thought of her loftily ridiculous name. Charlotte Corday Bukowska. This was his bride. His—Bun Ferguson's! The romance of this strangeness gave him a secret youthful joy. His lips quivered sensitively and settled into a troubled line. Charlotte's black hair was tossed back from her face on the white pillow. The heavy scowling eyebrows were serene in sleep. The startling ice-blue of the eyes was veiled by the smooth lids, and what he noticed most was her mouth, marred and blurred by experience . . . now she had the drooping lips of a hurt child.

He looked at her for a long time, with the feeling of tears burning behind his eyelids.

He turned restlessly away, thinking again of his easy youth, in this favored place—the warm home, the little local town in the pleasant shade of maples and elms, with the great rich country surrounding it. He felt an almost religious consecration in the vision of making up to his beloved for all that she had been made to suffer, and he hadn't—and the thousands of whom he was aware through her, of whom she had given him his revealing glimpse. His shyly hidden religious feeling could flower in the night. It was something which even the folks had never suspected. The old religion had never meant much of anything to him, although he had cheerfully admitted it and made allowance for it as a fixed fact in his parents' lives. All his own turned to this girl, the symbol of what he felt in the world outside. He himself was slight, young beside her—with her three extra years, her hard-bitten experience—but old, much older too. He wanted to take all this that was alien on himself and somehow absorb it. He felt the failures of his own family—Carl with his childish clinging to the old ways marked by sharp defensive irony; Margaret with her passionate exile leading nowhere. He, Bun, coming later, had escaped the need of these. It seemed as if all the elements of his home and family were lodged in his mind and affections to be held and comprehended by him alone;

564

and that somehow he must make a synthesis of them. But his home would never be the same to him after tonight. His easy life as the youngest was over. His beloved would lead him along very strange ways; but he had to go, holding all the while to things of which she was unaware and which he had inherited, fusing the two in some difficult reconciliation . . . perhaps impossible. He seemed already to be far from the folks, although he would never relinquish his youthful love for them, his tender, comprehending appreciation. He and his bride were the inheritors of a stormy future, even here in the pleasant fastness of this middle-aged frame house on the familiar local street with the tall trees all up and down the asphalt.

3

"Hi, Fred."

"How-do-do, Harry."

"Aren't walking, are you?"

"Yes, I had to leave my car at the garage."

He had got so out of the habit of walking that the familiar street at this hour looked almost strange to Mr. Ferguson. It was even stranger to have his acquaintances greet him just as always. He turned and looked at Harry Burbank as if it were someone he didn't know. Town was noisy with all the cars going home. But it seemed to him to lie within a hush of unreality. The pause that had intervened between those last two brief, momentous statements—his, "Well, Richard, I guess the time has come for me to pull up stakes," and finally Richard's, "Well, Fred, that's for you to say—" persisted still. After those words had been spoken, reality, the old reality, had ceased.

He passed the brick hotel building on the corner. The Rotary met there in the dining room on Thursday noons. Mr. Ferguson did not glance at the familiar windows. He had stepped out of his place. He was no longer one of the business men. The sound of his own footsteps had no meaning. He felt himself walking in vacancy.

He turned off from Main Street, so he wouldn't have to meet so many people.

Of course, there was no reason to feel any shame. It had been his own action entirely. It ought to be, really, a matter for pride. His affairs were in good shape. This was a day supposedly, to which he had been looking forward all his life. But a certain shame persisted. At the conclusion of his talk with Richard, Mr. Ferguson had got out of the bank as quickly as he could, not wanting Ray and the other employees to know.

Now he began to be really aware of the pain of that break; and yet running surreptitiously through it a strain of relief. He knew now that it wasn't just because of Annie. For a long, long while, he had been silently, secretly preparing for just this day. When he looked back, he could see that it had been inevitable from the start. He and Richard had never really pulled together. It was a wonder they had got along for as many years as this! He, Fred Ferguson, was an inheritance from the Old Man Spencer's day, too valuable for Richard to discard, but a drag on him all the same. There was a new order of business to which he didn't belong. Richard said that he was afraid of expansion; that he wasn't willing to meet the new prosperity on its own terms. He was the old style of banker, he could now admit that freely to himself. An account to him was a trust rather than an opportunity. His money he had expected to make through his own investments, by a slow shrewd adding of dollar to dollar. He had gone too far now from Main Street to be able to see the bank even if he had looked back. All at once the image of the new building had become dim to him; he knew that he had never been at home there; the dark interior of the old building, narrow and homely, was again the reality to him.

He looked around him at the stream of cars speeding past on the asphalt. The town lay in a bright summer light. He hadn't realized all the building that had taken place within the last few years. They hadn't seen much of it on their own street, which was long settled, and belonged to an older day. At another time he might have regarded all these evidences of growth with a natural pride. They were what he himself, along with the other business men, had hoped for and had helped to bring about. But now all at once, as he looked at the bright new glaring oil station opposite, and the roar of the cars hurt his ears, he had the feeling that things were getting out of hand. He started to

566

cross the street and stepped back nervously out of the way of a car. What did the fellow think he was doing, anyway? They all thought they had to go just as fast as they could, these days! Mr. Ferguson suddenly found himself on the side of the pedestrians. For the moment he felt confused, outmoded. He had to realize that now when it came to walking, he wasn't so spry as he once had been. He felt a helpless outrage at the noisy indifference of that fellow who had made him jump.

"Don't he know there's anybody but himself on the road?"

Well . . . it looked as if Richard had the town on his side. The rush of cars, the glitter of sun on the red gasoline tanks, the smell of mortar from the tearing down of the old brick house next to the corner—all spoke for Richard. A woman going past said brightly, "How do you do, Mr. Ferguson?" A flutter of chiffon and a scent of powdered fragrance seemed to linger after her. Mr. Ferguson stared. She had spoken to him, but he didn't know who she was, all dressed up that way. He passed the Hoagland home, a large brick house with heavy porches. Young Bert Hoagland and a tall girl in white were playing in the tennis court. Their voices had an easy ring, their movements a summertime casualness. If the Hoagland bank, "the other bank," actually was in trouble, as some people thought, it didn't seem to bother this young Bert any! Mr. Ferguson thought he didn't know, maybe he was sorry he hadn't made more use of his opportunities to get as fine an establishment for his family as Henry Hoagland's over there. It was less than an hour since he had given up his place—but now already time had flowed past, and he couldn't have gone back to it. A great syringa bush near the walk was heavy with fragrance. The summer brightness pulsed with activity. A truck went roaring and lumbering past piled with brand-new furniture for somebody. All seemed fair, and more than fair. And yet all the same, he didn't trust it. There was some presage of a storm that he could smell far off in the air. There was nothing but his native canniness to back him up—Richard had all the arguments, so far as anyone could see.

But everything was so much the same on the surface that it was hard to realize he had done something irrevocable.

567

He thought perhaps he had better stop at the manse before going home and inquire about Mrs. Lowrie. She had been ailing a good part of the winter, and last Sunday she hadn't been able to attend church. It wasn't anything serious, Mr. Lowrie had cheerfully insisted; but then, they might feel hurt if folks took them too much at their word, and nobody stopped in to inquire. The way Annie had been feeling, he didn't like to ask it of her.

The street on which the church stood was older than his own. It had a look of shabbiness, with its rather small frame houses. The manse itself was in need of painting. Mr. Ferguson was ashamed to see it like this. It seemed to proclaim the dwindling meagerness and poverty of the congregation, and to be a slur upon himself. But he couldn't do everything! Once the ladies would have attended to such matters. But now the real workers were dying off, or getting old, and the younger ones, it seemed, weren't willing to bother with bazaars and big suppers. Besides, the church had got into the habit of counting upon him for everything. Well—he wasn't in business any more. He would have to think before he put his hand into his pocket. It was a queer sensation to know that now he had as much as he was ever going to make.

"Maybe I shouldn't have stopped."

He knocked, but nobody answered. The paper lay out on the walk. Mr. Ferguson picked it up and put it carefully inside the screened door. Reverend Lowrie had mentioned once last winter that if Mrs. Lowrie didn't improve, he believed they would drive over to the clinic in Geneva; and so perhaps that was where they had gone today. That would mean she was pretty sick, then. Mr. Ferguson felt a sense of heaviness, touched with shame, because he didn't want anything to happen before he and Annie got away—if they were going.

While he was here, he thought he would go around and take a look at the cistern that Mr. Lowrie said was leaking. It was at the back of the house, near the back steps. Mr. Ferguson lifted off the wooden top and squatted to peer down inside. He saw that the whole thing needed recementing. Yes, things were in poor shape all round. The barn had some shingles loose, and the doors were rotting. The church had never had the barn made

568

over into a garage. It had stood empty for years. Reverend Lowrie was the first minister who had owned a car. He used the building just as it was. Mr. Ferguson had a sneaking feeling, snooping around this way when the Lowries weren't at home; although of course it was justified, since the repairs were up to him. Mr. Lowrie always put in a neat garden. But it wasn't so nice this year as in other years. "I guess his wife took up a lot of his time." Mr. Ferguson shook his head. He didn't see how he was going to get away. It had been one of the chief accusations against the old Montgomerys that Mr. Montgomery hadn't known how to make garden, and to manage. Mr. Lowrie had been active and thrifty, a small town man, keeping things up fine at first; but now it began to look as if his time was running out, like that of all the others.

Mr. Ferguson turned away with a feeling of sadness. He ought to go over to the church, too, and have a look at that stain in the plaster the snow had made last winter. He looked at the faded brick church, the narrow Gothic significance of the pointed windows; and felt he didn't want to go in there and see some more things that needed doing. The heavy leaves seemed to darken the street. The little spurt of renewed activity after the war, when they had first got Reverend Lowrie, was petering out. During the winter, the congregations hadn't been so bad, but now that summer had come they were smaller than ever. Mr. Ferguson was uneasily aware that the old talk about disbanding was going around again. Everything devolved upon a few—Mrs. Dunn, the Weyants, Essie Bartlett, Mrs. Rist and Ada—all of them willing enough, but the paying was up to him. For years this little band had fought all talk of joining the Congregationalists. But how would it be when they were gone, when the question was left to the young people? Mr. Ferguson felt he couldn't say much, since his own children had stopped coming to church. Now that he had dropped one load, it suddenly seemed as if this other was too heavy. There had been a pride and consolation in being the mainstay. But now he felt that he was carrying the whole church on his shoulders. The pain that had begun this afternoon spread and deepened. If folks didn't want the church, or the bank as he would run it, then it was time for him to leave. Let them get along without him! He could feel how much it had hurt when Richard had let him drop out with so little argument—and with a sly off-glance of the eyes that said he, too, had long been thinking. What was the use of keeping the church up for a few, at his expense, if the young folks didn't care about it? Mr. Ferguson felt that he'd like to make these repairs that were needed, and then get away from the whole thing.

He was tired, he wasn't used to walking. All his mild elderly aches and pains had come to the surface, and he went along slowly.

Mrs. Ferguson had stepped out into the back yard, and Mrs. Morgan saw her and called to her:

"How's the bridal couple? Aren't they coming back here this summer and let us have a look at them?"

She tried to speak brightly. "I don't know!"

But she knew very well! She went back into the house, and automatically finished the little task that she had begun, laying the flowers that she had cut on a newspaper on the kitchen drainboard, and with trembling hands picking off some of the leaves. She kept hearing that question over and over in her mind, and the strain of pretending was simply more than she could bear. The eyes of her neighbors, she felt, were upon her all the time, penetrating beneath the falseness of her smile. Oh, for Louie—somebody!—Fred was no use. All he did was try to soothe and console her—just as false with her as she with him! For the first time the smooth surface of a beautiful family life that she had always been able to keep, even when they were having so much trouble with Margaret, was cracking and straining. Before people in town, she could never let down for a moment from being Mrs. Ferguson, a fortunate woman, satisfied with everything just as it was. Once she had gone over to Mrs. Bird's, with some vague idea of talking to her—Mrs. Bird didn't belong to their church, and she was different. But Mrs. Ferguson simply hadn't been able to spoil the dear old lady's image of her as the happiest of wives and mothers, completely fulfilled in her beautiful brood of children. She was just barely able to restrain herself from sweeping flowers and paper together and throwing the whole thing into the wastebasket: acknowledging to herself by this out-and-out act that there was no use in making pretty bouquets, her home and her whole life had gone back on her. She crowded the flowers hastily into any kind of a bunch, stuck them into a vase which she reached for blindly on the cupboard shelf, and then left her bouquet standing there, and went on into the living room.

She sat down in the big chair. Her hands went lax on the arms. She lay back in a luxury of suffering, now that for a little while she didn't have to keep up before anyone—feeling almost as if she were drowned.

But the silence was too much. She was afraid of it. She had to do something. She walked around the room for a while, and then out into the empty hall. Without knowing just what she meant to do, she went upstairs, and then blindly into Dorothy's room for comfort. The dainty motionless curtains kept the room in a summertime hush. But this was the room where those two had slept. She had forgotten that when she came in. And Dorothy was too far away! Mrs. Ferguson wrung her hands.

She went out into the hall again. The door of Margaret's room was closed—just as Margaret's life was closed against them. Mrs. Ferguson couldn't bear to go into her own room. No help for her there. She dreaded to have Fred go off in the morning and leave her to face the blankness of another day; but in the night she was in a fever of impatience for morning to come. She lay outwardly relaxed, so that Fred wouldn't suspect, but inwardly she was hard and closed against him. She had to keep practicing her old code even now. Oh, if she could tell Fred how she did feel, let him into the awful blackness of the emptiness before her!—but her voice seemed to be drowned under years and years of womanly silences and bright pretenses. At the same time, she kept struggling to preserve her old attitude toward him, to withhold her secret from him, in which he had no share. The once that she had burst out at him, although it hadn't begun to rid her of pent-up grievances, had made him uneasy and strange with her ever since.

She went downstairs again, took up a magazine, and for a

little while felt quite calm again. The Vieles had spoken of getting up a group to drive over and see the Hanging Rocks, and momentarily Mrs. Ferguson was able to look forward to this. But then she thought of how Bunny used to do the driving for them, when he was at home, taking along little Frankie or some other girl. The pain of Bunny's marriage was what still filled her mind. She felt the marriage as a cross-blow that had struck at the roots. When Fred tried to get her to say just why she was taking it so hard, she couldn't admit her real feeling about it, she could only give the surrounding reasons: the girl was older, she was so rough, she wasn't their kind. Fred just didn't see how alien the girl was. Her terrifying strength!— against Bunny's youth, his slightness, his tender rearing. Mrs. Ferguson herself didn't understand the girl, couldn't make her out; but she had an intuition all the same that she was drawing their boy away to some threatening distance. There was a sharp blade of fear cutting into her confused hostility toward this alien. She couldn't give Bun's wife a name, she could only say "that girl." Bunny had chosen that girl . . . and now some hope—something—was dead.

Her youngest. She could stand to lose any of them but him! She had somehow known that she must give up the others— but never this youngest! Her last, and she would have no more. She felt that with blinding, piercing bleakness, as she wandered in anguish through the empty rooms. She had never taken in its significance before. Because they had Bunny, their gift to comfort and complete them, to throw a light of youth over their age. They had loved him in a bright security—and if *that* was gone—! Now there was no one but herself and Fred.

Terror came upon her. The whole house seemed unreal. The familiar furnishings were all around her but they had lost their meaning. She dreaded to have Fred come home, because it seemed as if he, too, meant nothing to her now. He had things outside, she charged that up against him—the church, the bank. She had nothing. All her pleasant activities, the club, the efforts at civic improvement, existed only on the circumference of her life. Her children were at the center. The home was nothing without them, she knew it, and she knew they were gone.

Now a deep resentment seemed to be struggling through her fear and emptiness. She was fighting to get back the memory of her girlhood. Then she had seemed to exist in herself, not to be dependent upon other people. Locking up the schoolhouse at the end of the day, going down the road with some of her "scholars" clinging about her, hot moist little hands loosely clasped in hers —out drying her hair in the sun, spreading out the shining light brown strands tipped and feathered with gold—she had been happy, and needed nothing else. She used to go after flowers in the woods and make careful little copies of them in water colors. This had seemed to afford her a lovely satisfaction, precise yet dreamy . . . but now she couldn't even recall what the satisfaction was. She couldn't go back to making water colors! She thought of the time when she and Fred were in love . . . the picnics in the woods, when the buggy wheels crushed narrow paths over the moist fresh grass, and the others sent them off to get the water for the coffee out of the spring beneath the big rock . . . and the cool breath from the stones, the hot sunshine in the open picnic place, had been illumined with a marvelous significance . . . which had never quite failed—until now. It was not just a sentimental saying that this love had crowned her life. It had blossomed in marriage and borne the fruit that she had craved. She could never say that her marriage had not been happy, in spite of all its secret failings. Nevertheless, her own separate life had gone down beneath it; and now that she needed that life again, she could no longer find it.

The whole town was empty. She had come into it a stranger, and now it seemed that she—she *herself*—was a stranger still. She had pretended to accept all kinds of things she had never actually accepted. Now when she tried to look ahead, there wasn't anything that she could see. The children hadn't known her as herself. Fred, either—or if he did once, he had forgotten. Maybe there *was* no self any more. It was all dissolved and lost. She had gladly given it away—but now she felt defeated.

Mr. Ferguson came within sight of his own house, substantial and roomy on its nice piece of lawn. The hedge of bridal wreath was still in bloom, which they had put in between their yard

573

and that of the rented house next door, hoping it would keep out the dog and the children without need on their own part to keep shooing them away. There was no sense of heaviness here. All lay serene in the late afternoon light.

But as he approached the house, Mr. Ferguson was aware of a sense of emptiness that couldn't have been guessed from the pleasant exterior. The old home life had changed, and something vital had gone out of it. Ever since Bun's marriage, things hadn't been the same. Their pleasant, settled ways of living were upset. Sometimes he came home and found that Annie hadn't got any supper ready—an unprecedented thing! She didn't feel like cooking just for the two of them, she said. It wasn't worth the trouble. Well, then, they would go down to the restaurant, he told her. But neither of them enjoyed that very much. Gradually he had come to feel that there must be a change, something must be done for mama; and now that the change was upon him he felt relieved. He had a hurt feeling when he looked at the house. His old, constant satisfaction seemed to be gone. He traced it to the thought that his own children had pulled out—there were none to succeed him, in the house, in business, in the church. All at once he understood fully how mama felt. What was the use of keeping up everything just for themselves? Mama said he didn't feel as she did about the marriage. Maybe he didn't, just as regarded the girl herself. Her healthy robustness appealed to him, and she couldn't be so bad, he thought, or Bunny wouldn't have chosen her. But he realized now how he had counted upon his youngest son. He had always had the idea of setting Bun up in some business here at home, that would appeal to him—maybe something that he himself, when he got ready to leave the bank, could go into with Bunny. He had never supposed, any more than Annie, that they would lose Bun.

He opened the screened door and went into the house.
"Mama?"

No answer.

At first, he felt furtively relieved. He could put off the fuss of his announcement a little longer—make up his mind what he really did want to do about going away.

He went out as usual to get himself a drink. He always liked to do that when he got home. He turned off the faucet but for a few seconds the water slowly dripped. Now he began to feel heavily the silence of the house, that had only seemed to him a peaceful quietness before.

"Annie. Mama!"

All at once he went quickly and stealthily upstairs; and it wasn't until after he had opened the bedroom door, and seen the room unoccupied and in order, that he felt the heavy beating of his heart. This was where he had found her that Sunday morning, after Bun and Charlotte had left, lying huddled up on the bed and crying in such an abandonment that he had been terrified. He was only now realizing just how deep that shock had gone. At first he hadn't known what to make of it. He knew the marriage wasn't what they would have chosen, but he thought they had agreed to make the best of it. Hadn't mama reproached him often enough for not seeing the children's side? And now it seemed as if he had learned that lesson and mama had forgotten it! When he had tried to talk to her, how she had flown out at him! He couldn't get over it even yet. All at once she had opened up—mama!—and let out grievances against him that he saw she must have been cherishing for years. It had seemed to turn everything upside down! No, he *didn't* take on as she did—that was what she had told him; and it was because he had never cared for the children in the same way. "If you did, you wouldn't have to have things pointed out. . . . You know Margaret was with some man last summer." He hadn't known it. Mama had never said so before. Had Margaret told her? "Of course she didn't tell me! Do you suppose she'll ever tell us anything?" And then she had gone back years, while he had stood there dazed and bewildered—until finally he had realized that now she was blaming him for the way he had treated Margaret when she was sent home from the normal school. That had hurt him terribly. It hurt him still. Because he knew, and had long ago come to acknowledge, that maybe some of the things he had said then had been a mistake. But he had supposed at the time he and Annie had felt just the same! Of course he had been the one to do the punishing, since Annie was no good at it; and it was partly because Annie had felt so bad . . . he was going to see that this time Margaret knew what she had done. Last summer, when Margaret was at home, he had tacitly tried to make up for their mistakes, giving Margaret her money just the same as he had done with the others (he had given Bun his money too) and not even suggesting what she ought to do with it. The pained, guilty feeling that somehow they had failed with Margaret had made him more lenient to the others. He had tacitly come over to mama's side. And this was all that mama saw of it! Talk about *his* not understanding—! An old hot stubborn anger that he hadn't felt in years had flamed up in him, and he had turned and left mama to think what she pleased, and gone downstairs. There he had sat for a while, grasping at the arms of the chair, and trying to get hold of his anger. It was hard, painfully hard, for him to admit it—but he had never felt right about Margaret. Maybe, when you started wrong, you couldn't get the wrong undone. All right—if Margaret *was* carrying on (so he thought of it), then he guessed he was ready to bear his share of the blame. Still, that was a reason—so he wanted to tell Annie—why they oughtn't to make things hard for Bunny and this girl. The things Bunny had said—his arguments against the social order he knew his father had helped to build, his resolve to go off and start somewhere with Charlotte all on his own—these had hurt, and hurt still. They had driven the first wedge of doubt into Fred Ferguson's conception of things. But he and Annie ought to stand together, not apart. He hadn't been able to stay away from her long, or to keep his anger. It made him guilty that he *didn't* feel this quite as she did. She had always been more to him than the children, and he felt humbly that he wasn't more to her.

"Annie, we oughtn't to take sides on this. We ought to stand together."

She had agreed—or seemed to agree. Nevertheless, ever since then there had been a feeling of separation.

He felt suddenly lost. He hadn't the business, he hadn't the

children any more to build and make plans for. Only Annie—
and he would do anything to get her back.

Again he felt that unreasonable fear. It turned him cold. He
went hastily downstairs again, and through the house. Then he
saw her working among her plants in the back yard. In that
one moment of terror, he knew how much she counted with
him—yes, when you came right down to it, more than anything
else ever had or ever could. He had proved it at last, by leaving
the bank, something she hadn't believed he would ever be
willing to do. He felt the desire to go off, to let everything
else slip—just to be together, and to enjoy themselves, before
it was too late.

As he crossed the back yard, he knew already that he was
leaving. He saw all the familiar things with incredulous pain—
the garden, the old workshop long empty, their apple tree. The
beauty of the summer light of late afternoon lay over it all,
more beautiful than he had ever seen it. He saw her small figure,
in the thin summer dress, the gentle, fine movements of her
little hands. He felt a surge of lonely anger against the children
for hurting her. What she had said, the way she had chided him,
although she had seemed to repent it with tears, had sunk into
him deeper than she knew. Once she had told him that he never
did anything just for her. "Anything extra—anything just for
me." The accusation held justice and injustice both. Maybe he
was jealous of the children, now that he saw how she missed
them. But they were themselves as well as "the folks."

Yet when he came to make his sober announcement—the first
time he had spoken it to anyone but Richard—it sounded incredible in his own ears.

"Well, Annie, I have something to tell you." He saw her
startled face. No, it wasn't about the children, either—not this!
"I'm going to close up my account. I've decided to leave the
bank. . . . So I guess you and I'll go off and have a good time
together this winter."

Part Six
The Folks

ALL this week it had been warm. And yet, most of the leaves were gone, showing that it was almost November. The trees stood branching dark against the blue, and around the heavy trunks the leaves lay thick, yellow and yellow-green, still soft, almost tender, and freshly fallen.

But it had been pleasant like this for such a while that Mrs. Morgan didn't feel she ought to trust the weather much longer. Now was the time to look after her plants.

Anyway, she wanted to be out here so that she could be sure to go over and say good-bye to the Fergusons.

At first she hadn't been able to get down to work, expecting them to come out any minute. But the car stood empty in the driveway between the two houses, ready for the journey. Of course, it always took. folks longer to get off than they had planned.

Mrs. Morgan was bending down over her flower beds with her back to the street. "Funny she cares so much for flowers. It don't seem to go with the rest of her," Mrs. Viele had once remarked to Mrs. Ferguson. Mrs. Morgan didn't really care for flowers in the way that so many women did; or if so, she stood apart from that naïve delight, regarding it with dry harshness touched by humor and holding a strangled sense of defraudment: perhaps most of all with a stringent shyness. She knew it wasn't in keeping with her looks. She could tell herself that better than anyone else could tell her—she wasn't going to give anybody else the chance. People wondered why she had so much nicer flowers than others! Well, because she made a business of it. When anybody suggested that she must have "the knack," Mrs. Morgan scoffed. She said she guessed the knack was just hard work and doing things when they had to be done. She didn't wait around to get Loren to do the hard part for her. She wasn't afraid of getting her hands dirty. A slightly contemptuous, slightly shamed knowledge of these things was always in Mrs. Morgan's mind when other women exclaimed over her flowers. When she worked with them, decorating the lodge hall, or one of the churches for baccalaureate services, she felt awkward and never seemed to fit in; but at any rate, she could supply the decorations!

581

She also took a dry, sardonic pride in keeping the Old Lady Morgan's grave beautifully decorated—who had lived with her and Loren, and who *had* shown herself plenty feminine.

Mrs. Morgan had become so absorbed in her work with the dry, brown, matted plants spread fernlike on the sunwarmed ground that she almost lost the sense of where she was in time. Then she would look up and see the Fergusons' car out there in the driveway, and realize that her neighbors were leaving her. Mr. and Mrs. Ferguson! It didn't seem as if *they* could have reached the well-known stage of being left alone, with all their children married, or at any rate gone from them, and now getting ready to close up their home and go out to California! Mrs. Morgan had seen plenty of changes come over her street during the thirty-five years she had lived in this house. But it wasn't until now, when the Fergusons were leaving, that she felt the first real shock of time and change, and thought, It won't be the same any more.

A sense oppressive, and yet half ghostly, of slow, subtle, inevitable alterations was all around her, as she stood up, straightening her back, and protesting. It gave her the feeling all at once that so much and so little had come to pass. There had been so few marked happenings in the Morgans' own lives that Mrs. Morgan, with a kind of bleak curiosity, avid, caustic, and yet at bottom not censorious, because of her inner shyness, had noted outside events all the more clearly. She was very likely the most just observer on this street. But this morning all that she saw, in reality or in imagination, was made heightened and strangely moving in the light of her neighbors' departure.

She thought of the street as it used to be, years ago, and as she had scarcely realized until now that it had ceased to be. In the warm, deceptive beneficence of the October sunshine, that time was more real than now. She felt around her the air of that day, preserved only in glossy old photographs, and in memory.

Here stood the same houses—and yet how they seemed to have changed! Her own house the most of all. Photographs again, in a woven Indian basket given Mrs. Morgan as a Christmas present years ago, were the only things to recall the low frame house, plain and spare, with the hard-coal burner in the front room, into which she and Loren had come to spend the difficult, constrained first years of their married life with Loren's mother—years of which Mrs. Morgan now secretly thought with a harsh but half-resigned embitterment that had never received any answer. They had done nothing to the house until after the old lady had died. But now it was already a good while, as local history went in Belmond, since the Morgan house had worn this modern aspect, standing low on the ground, dampish under heavy trees, the porch blackly screened, and the rough coating of cement darkening through the changes of middlewestern weather.

No, not all the same houses. But it was a good while, too, since the old Grandma Davis house had been slowly carted off on wheels, to the great diversion of all the children, and the squarish frame house built next the Fergusons' on the other side, where renters with varying supplies of children had lived, but always it seemed with a yelping dog of one breed or another to endanger Mrs. Morgan's yard and flowers.

The white house across the street seemed not to have changed so much, although the old Gilberts who had built it were dead and it, too, had been given over to renters. Large, rambling, remotely and coldly Maine-style in the touch of classic severity given it by the doorway, not even the tourist sign in the front window had entirely bereft it of its native dignity. But the beautiful Yankee neatness of the woodpile in the back yard was gone—the ring of the ax on frosty mornings—the sight, sad in its sense of age, of belonging to another time and place, and yet in those very things somehow stabilizing and dignifying, of old Mr. and Mrs. Gilbert sitting silently together on their porch in the summer evenings. For as long as he could get about, Mr. Gilbert had gone muffled, limping, but true to his duty, with a shining little tin pail down the icy walk to the creamery on Saturday mornings. The sense of that long evening of life of the old couple, homely but formal, almost a work of art in its precision, could never quite leave the long sad windows and the chill whiteness of the closed front door.

The history of the Brattle house in the next block had a tragic tone out of keeping with that of the others. Someone regarding it—not Mrs. Morgan!—might have put the whole story together in the form of a drama called starkly "Pride," and almost too clear-cut in its pitiless unfolding. This story, however, had values beyond Mrs. Morgan's power of plain judgment. She was able to regard it only as a moral lesson—to be learned chiefly by the protagonists themselves, one of whom was now beyond learning. Its outline was too hard and recent for the drama to have sunk back into the softening light of memory that shone over the Gilbert place and the shortcomings of reticence and thrift on the part of old Mr. and Mrs. Gilbert. It was long enough past, even so, with the house standing empty on its big corner lot, for the gray-white paint to have faded, the fancy balconies grown precarious and dingy, the shingles begun to roughen and curl on all the silly little toboggan slides of roof, and the wooden ball from the front porch railing to have fallen and lain cracked and half embedded in the grass. The house stood now like an ugly monument to the played-out pretensions of an early aristocracy in Belmond. It would soon be a disgrace to the whole street.

Pride was the beginning and the end of it. And what good had their pride done them?—Mrs. Morgan thought with an outraged, rankling resentment. It had caused those two to marry in the first place, and then had been the means of keeping them apart. There had been no merging in that marriage, even less than in hers and Loren's, in which each stealthily recognized the solitude of the other. None of the home girls were good enough for Lawrence Brattle, and he had had to show the town his superiority by choosing this girl "from away." Pride on Ida's part had never permitted her to yield to the life of the little town which she had entered unwilling and contemptuous. On Lawrence's part, it had forced him to despise and defend the town which he had never been willing to leave, since that would have been yielding too much to Ida. It had made him both overcareless and overfastidious about his legal cases, always spending more money than he earned, until his practice had become the worst pretense of all.

Well, anyway, it wasn't true, Mrs. Morgan could think with feelings too mixed and far-reaching for analysis, that to have children was the one thing needed to make a marriage real! It hadn't worked that way with the Brattles. But it seemed as if their one child was more the outcome of pride than of love. Each claimed her above the other. All the feelings that should have gone out to each other were concentrated on Virginia, forcing *her* pride too; until, by the terrible overemphasis of their love for her, they had lost her love for them. That was how the shrewdest observers were now making out the story: a story of tragic check and balance ending in blasting negation. Lawrence had seemed the winner for a while. Showering all that he had upon his one daughter, making her the justification for all, refusing to be separated from her, sitting with his arm conspicuously around her as if to warn every rival away—some people had thought that relationship "beautiful," but Mrs. Morgan had always doubted it, the excessive quality of it had offended her. And the result had finally been to make Virginia break away from the confines of his love, go as far from him as she could, and end by loving no one! The father whom she had overidealized at the start, she hadn't been able to forgive, as she might have forgiven one who had meant less to her. The whole idyll of his love for her had seemed tarnished and falsified. So that perhaps Virginia couldn't be blamed so much after all (as the strict notions of filial duty still prevalent in Belmond did blame her) for refusing to leave Paris where she lived all by herself, Ethel Spencer had reported, in a dubious little hotel, and come back to her stricken father, or to her mother left penniless and alone. But Ida had gained no more for herself by her immaculate virtue. Perhaps even less. Ida had been too proud to turn to anyone! Virginia had loved her father too well to forgive her mother either. This was what Ida Brattle had got for keeping *her* child so scrupulously apart from the rest of the children, nothing but white good enough for her to wear, nothing but expensive and distant schools good enough for her to attend—Mrs. Morgan could remember when not even the Ferguson children were good enough to play with Virginia Brattle! After Virginia had left them, Lawrence couldn't stand the bleakness of his home. He couldn't endure Ida's contempt without the exquisite support and retaliation of Virginia's preference. It was as if all his emotions were left stranded in helpless and chaotic agony. So it was no wonder that he had turned to a more easy-going woman to give him ease and sustenance—or a pretense of them; one who still thought that a Brattle *was* somebody. And then, after his whole quivering, shameful history of domestic and financial failure had been uncovered to "everybody," that same pride had forced him to cut his throat; and when that had failed, like everything else he had attempted—hadn't even brought back Virginia, had kept her away in fierce fastidiousness—to die slowly, and bitterly, away from home, where nobody knew him, in some cheap sanatorium. Of course Ida couldn't stay here either. Ethel Spencer had reported (with some pleasure, since Ida hadn't even quite accepted *her*) that she was acting as a kind of companion, or nurse, nobody knew just what, in a wealthy family in Chicago. That was how she had finally got away from Belmond! She had left Lawrence to cut his throat, and to win at least the pity of his neighbors for himself, and their chief condemnation for *her*-self—and to lose her child just as irrevocably as Lawrence had done.

No, sir, Mrs. Morgan decided firmly, it didn't do for any man to think himself better than his neighbors. If he did, it just showed that he hadn't the good sense to know where his own weakness lay. The neurotic values of the decadence of an aristocracy, however small, however local, were only a fading overtone in the life of such a town as Belmond.

The Ferguson house was the one that was always the same. Mrs. Morgan looked now, and saw it standing there on its familiar lawn, that was narrow on her side near the driveway, but wide on the side toward the rented house, with the big maple tree under which Dorothy had stood to be married, and that urn that had come to be one of the landmarks of this street. The house was nothing special. Both the Brattle and the Gilbert house had overshadowed it in their day. But now they had lost their glory; and the Ferguson house, freshly painted in its light clear yellow, the lawn always so well kept, the porches screened, the barn made over into a neat garage, all finished and settled and looking as if it belonged where it stood, shone out among the other houses. Other families had moved away, or died out, or lost their money. But the Fergusons, although they had their faults like others, were the kind of people who could always be counted upon. When Mrs. Morgan occasionally said, "Yes, we have some pretty nice folks living on this street," she really meant the Fergusons.

And now if *they* were going—! When Mrs. Morgan had said in her first dismay to Mrs. Ferguson, "This town will just be lost without you folks," she had meant something real. The hard times that were beginning to be felt around them had not yet touched Belmond. When the Morgans had heard of disasters, of banks failing—they had always had the feeling— well, *their* bank was safe as long as Fred Ferguson was there. Mrs. Ferguson wasn't the managing kind, like Mrs. Stark, or Mrs. Hoagland, but she had her part in almost everything that went on in Belmond. She was the one neighbor whom Mrs. Morgan trusted to understand that she herself meant more kindly than her manner might sometimes lead folks to think. Mrs. Morgan felt that now she knew why, when the town had lost its character, when too many folks had died, and control had passed to the younger ones who could never seem to measure up to the older, people who could afford it just went away, to spend the days they had left out there in the sunshine. But somehow she had never expected the Fergusons to go! Their full, busy, well-fixed household had always been a kind of center. She felt as if the house next door had stood in the full bright glow of a long noon sunlight, and that when it was empty, that glow would have passed away from the street, and twilight come.

Mrs. Morgan saw Mr. Ferguson come out to the car laden with suitcases. She carefully wiped her neat green trowel and laid it on the porch step. Then she went over to the driveway.

"Well, looks like the baggage man is here!"

"Yes," Mr. Ferguson said, "I guess we'll get loaded up now." He opened the door of the sedan and began stacking the suitcases neatly on the back seat. There were already some boxes in there. Mrs. Morgan stood watching him, wanting to help, but feeling awkward about it.

"All that stuff looks as if you were going away for a long while."

"Well . . ." Mr. Ferguson would never quite commit himself. "It's hard to tell just what we're going to need."

"Yes, I guess so," Mrs. Morgan agreed.

Much as she hated to see them leave, she began to feel buoyed up now by the excitement. There was a shout, and they turned to see the Vieles crossing the lawn, Mr. Viele raising his hand in jovial salute, and Mrs. Viele with arms hugged tight around a package. That gave Mrs. Morgan a qualm—she hadn't thought of giving any present to the Fergusons! Mrs. Viele was the kind who always remembered such things.

"Well, we thought we'd have to see the travelers off!" Mr. Viele was announcing, panting. "I see there's somebody here ahead of us." Both the Vieles cheerfully greeted Mrs. Morgan. "Where's the missus?"

"Oh, I guess she's still inside there primping."

Mrs. Ferguson came out now, wearing her fur coat, and a new hat that she must have got when she and Mr. Ferguson were in Geneva last Saturday. It was a small folded toque with a little veil, and gave her a curiously festive aspect.

"*Does*-n't the lady look sweet!" Mrs. Viele exclaimed.

She went over to Mrs. Ferguson and put the package in her arms, hugging her and whispering to her. It made Mrs. Morgan feel more remiss and awkward than ever. "Oh, you shouldn't have done that!" she heard Mrs. Ferguson exclaim; while Mrs. Viele made the proper protests, saying it was just a little to nibble on if they got hungry—and to remind them of home.

"We don't need to be reminded of that!"

Mrs. Morgan said, "You folks ought to have let me give you some breakfast."

"Oh my, no!" Mrs. Ferguson cried. "It was just lovely of you to think of it, but Ella and Ben want us to stop in there—I guess they begin to think by now we aren't coming!"

"Well, these things always take longer," Mrs. Viele consoled her.

"I could have heated you up a cup of coffee, anyway," Mrs. Morgan said.

"Oh, no, we both had a cup when we got up, and we feel just fine."

The three women stood aside while the men were busy loading up the car. Mrs. Morgan felt chagrined because Loren hadn't stayed to help his neighbors get started. But he thought he must be in that store by seven-thirty even if the sky fell. As Mrs. Morgan said with dry bluntness, nobody with good sense came into a hardware store any more in these days of ten-cent stores. But Loren still took a stubborn pride in the excellence and wearing quality of all his tools and cutlery and gadgets. Mr. Viele always seemed to be able to get away from his office!

"My, don't we hate to see them go!" Mrs. Viele mourned.

"I do, all right. I guess everybody does."

"Oh, well, we want them to have this lovely time too," Mrs. Viele cried, putting her arm around Mrs. Ferguson.

And it was true, even if the others couldn't go along, and enjoy the sunshine, nobody begrudged the Fergusons their winter in California. They had earned it, if anyone had. It was coming to them, Mrs. Morgan thought—even if she and Loren did have to stay here and shovel coal as usual. The Vieles had had lots of trips—nobody need pity *them* if they had to stay at home this winter.

"Can you get this in somewhere, dad?" Mrs. Ferguson asked, holding out her package to Mr. Ferguson. "Put it where we can get at it."

"What's this? Still more?" Mr. Ferguson demanded.

"Why, it's a whole lot of lovely things to eat that this naughty woman went to work and got ready for us."

"Well! Looks as if we weren't going to have to buy many meals on this trip!" Mr. Ferguson exclaimed.

The people in the rented house were out in the back yard keeping an eye on proceedings. The children were getting a little farther all the time over the boundary line into the Fer-

589

guson yard. They didn't feel quite the same as the people who were settled and owned property on the street.

Mrs. Morgan said, "Just wait a minute!"

She went into her own house, and into the dining room, where she kept some of her best plants in the sunny south window. She took a bright little scissors out of the buffet drawer—all her tools were first-class, they got *that* much, anyhow, out of keeping a hardware store!—and cut off the two beautiful purple blossoms from her famed gloxinia. She had never done such a thing before for anybody. She searched through the soft flannel leaves of her housewife until she found a long black-headed pin the right size—"Wonder I'd have it!"

The folks were just getting into the car when she went back to them. She took Mrs. Ferguson's arm and drew her aside.

"Here—let's decorate you up!" she said gruffly.

Bending, so that Mrs. Ferguson couldn't see the tears in her eyes, she carefully pinned the flowers onto the collar of the thick fur coat. Mrs. Ferguson craned her neck to look down at them.

"Why, Mrs. Morgan! Just see what this woman's done—"

She stood back, so that they could all see her decoration. They were as lovely as orchids!—Mrs. Viele cried. Mr. Viele was hearty in his appreciation. "You ought to keep those, somehow, till you can get out there, show those folks what kind of flowers we can raise back here in Iowa." Mrs. Ferguson's cheeks were flushed. She couldn't say how pleased and moved she was. She knew how Mrs. Morgan hated to spoil any of her sacred plants.

"She looks like a movie actress!" exclaimed Mrs. Viele.

"Fred, you must feel like you folks are going off on a honeymoon."

"That's right," Mr. Ferguson proudly agreed.

They all laughed. Mrs. Morgan, turning aside, managed to brush off the tears that had now overflowed, and gave a sniff and a cough to cover the proceeding. She didn't have a handkerchief in the pocket of this old jacket—she never had one when she wanted it—and now her nose was beginning to run.

She contrived to wipe it with her sleeve, pretending that she was scratching it.

"Well, sir," Mr. Viele now said, "looks like we've put in all we can."

"Yes, I guess she's pretty well loaded."

"Now comes the season of sad farewells. Well, Fred—"

"Well, Melvin—"

The two men shook hands.

Mrs. Viele, smiling and tearful, embraced Mrs. Ferguson. Mrs. Morgan was standing awkwardly aside. She dreaded this. But now her turn came. The soft fur of Mrs. Ferguson's collar brushed her face. "Well, I just hate to see you folks go," Mrs. Morgan muttered. She couldn't keep from crying again, or help folks' noticing it this time. Mrs. Ferguson gently patted her shoulder. Much more than could be spoken was expressed in that embrace. The years of neighborliness—all the little visits, the gifts of cookies and melons and slips and flowers, the helping out at this time and that. Mrs. Ferguson's fine little face, with its delicate wrinkles and gentle eyes, and her little veined aging hands with the wedding ring and the old-fashioned engagement ring with its thick gold hoop and tiny stone on the small ring finger, seemed so tenderly feminine to Mrs. Morgan that she felt a compassionate, adoring patronage toward Mrs. Ferguson, as toward a young girl. Now Mrs. Ferguson's face was flushed, and that, with the fashionable hat and the wisp of veil, gave her a kind of after-glow of girlishness setting out on her journey.

The Fergusons got into their car. Mrs. Morgan had to turn aside, grimacing, from the embarrassed sympathy of the others, and accept the handkerchief that Mrs. Viele pressed into her hand. Mrs. Viele's own tears flowed so easily that they embarrassed no one—certainly not herself.

The Fergusons were now nicely settled, with the lunch box, the handbag, the rug in case of need, all disposed of, with Mr. Viele's help. The people from the rented house had come over too, now, and were standing back from the others, the mother trying to restrain the children.

591

Mrs. Morgan, her face still drawn into a grimace, said, "I'll take care of the plants."

"Oh, I'm sure *they'll* be taken care of! I expect I won't know them when I get back!"

"Oh, you'll see such flowers when you get out in California," Mr. Viele told her, "that you won't look at your own when you get back." They all laughed in relief. Mrs. Morgan blew her nose. "Now," Mr. Viele warned them, "we don't want any of those pictures of picking roses in February, when we're buried in snow back here!"

"That's just what you're going to get," said Mr. Ferguson. "You didn't spare us any when you were down in Florida. And that was about the coldest winter we had!"

"My, it was lovely there," Mrs. Viele murmured aside to Mrs. Morgan.

"Have you got everything, Annie?" Mr. Ferguson was asking. Yes, she had. "Well, you want to be sure. Though I don't see how we'd get much more in this car."

During this last week at home, Mr. Ferguson had been depressed and taciturn, making Mrs. Ferguson turn often to say to him, "Well, Fred, if you don't *want* to go—" But now he seemed to have drunk of the excitement of departure. Usually on pins to get started when they were going anywhere, now he was ready to sit here and exchange the usual banter with Mr. Viele—even if Ella was waiting for them, and they hadn't had their breakfast either.

"Remember, they're not to keep you out there!" Mr. Viele cried above the sound of the engine starting. "They're great ones for trying to keep folks when they get hold of 'em, those California-ites."

"Oh, I guess we can get away from them when the time comes."

"My, I hope it's this nice all the way!" Mrs. Viele said. "But you'll soon be away from the cold weather." She nodded brightly.

Now Mr. Ferguson was getting anxious to start. Mrs. Ferguson sat smiling, reaching up once to wipe her eyes. Love to Dorothy, they were all telling her. "Kiss those dear children for me," Mrs. Viele cried.

"Remember, you're coming back! You tell Dorothy and that man of hers they can't keep you. Say hello to those grandchildren. I expect *they'll* want grandma and grandpa to stay."

The loaded car moved slowly out of the driveway. The neighbors were all waving. The woman who lived in the old Gilbert house was standing in her doorway now. She waved.

"Drive careful, Fred!" Mr. Viele shouted.

Everybody laughed. The whole town knew Mr. Ferguson's caution.

"See to it that the folks get you well fed up—you'll have to live on oranges out there in California! . . . Guess he didn't hear that."

They all waved hopefully again as they watched the car drive off down the street where the yellow leaves were sprinkled. They still stood for a little while.

"Well, they're off," Mr. Viele announced.

A momentary friendship seemed to have been formed among the neighbors. They were all being left behind. "My, don't we hate to see them go," cried Mrs. Viele tearfully. They all said how lonesome it was going to be without the Fergusons—but how nice they *could* go.

"Not everybody can these days!"

Certainly it seemed to make the street very empty. Already the Ferguson house had a closed-up look. Another empty house on this street! What was happening to it? And the Ferguson house had always been so busy, so full.

The others left, but Mrs. Morgan and the Vieles still stood talking together, as more intimate friends of the Fergusons. There wasn't much to be said now except repetitions. Mrs. Viele hinted at how badly Mrs. Ferguson had felt about Bun's marriage. It was a dreadful blow to her. And after Margaret . . . But Mrs. Morgan, somehow, didn't want to say much— she felt as if she knew more about the family affairs, living next door, and she didn't want to betray them, even to Mrs. Viele. She felt too lonesome and sore, with the Fergusons gone.

"Well, sir," Mr. Viele said finally, "I wish *I* was going to California."

Mrs. Viele said with smiling loyalty, "Well, we've got just as good a place as any right here."

They all agreed—Mrs. Morgan a little doubtfully. It didn't seem very good with the Fergusons gone. Yes, she guessed they hadn't so much to complain of—except the snow.

"Oh well," Mr. Viele said, "a little snow don't hurt us. Keeps us limber, shoveling."

But whatever they said was an anticlimax now. Mr. and Mrs. Viele agreed that they'd better be getting home. "Business goes on for the rest of us as usual." Mrs. Morgan went slowly across the driveway when they left. She had taken off the old gloves she had been wearing while she worked among her plants. The finger tips had been cut off, and now she noticed that her own fingers were dirty. She expected Mrs. Viele had been noticing that too, for all she was so soft-spoken and nice!

She went into her kitchen. It was not much like the Old Lady Morgan's kitchen of other days—this fresh room with the bright linoleum, all the modern appliances. The breakfast dishes were still on the table. Mrs. Morgan gathered up the silverware and took it to the sink.

She stood a moment, and then went into the other room.

Mrs. Ferguson's plants were in the front room. Mrs. Morgan fingered the lacy fern. It made her think of Mrs. Ferguson, it was so dainty—and of all the warm, busy life of the house next door. Well, she'd have plenty of time to look after the plants this winter. Loren was getting so he liked less and less to drive anywhere. Her house seemed bleak. Its neatness was no comfort. It was years, now, since she had got things fixed the way she wanted them. The memory of those first years under the supervision of the Old Lady Morgan had left bitter dregs. But even so, without that . . . maybe she just wasn't the kind. She didn't know as she could blame either herself or Loren. But now she couldn't help begrudging Mrs. Ferguson a little, much as she loved her. If Dorothy was the fairy-tale princess of the street—yes, she and not Virginia Brattle! with her rich handsome husband, her beautiful marriage, her lovely home—Mrs. Ferguson seemed to Mrs. Morgan the queen. She had all a woman could ask for. Family troubles, which Mrs. Morgan had noted more shrewdly than her manner gave any indication, only made her life more rich and deep and full. There was a dry shame in Mrs. Morgan's own heart.

Mrs. Morgan went back into the kitchen. She detached the shining toaster from the wall and carried it to the sink. All these shining appliances made her think of Loren. Thin, grayish, noncommittal, his natural taciturnity grown upon him during all these years in their trim, silent house—neither of them talkers or readers or people to go—and wearing an old gray striped coat that didn't match his pants, Mr. Morgan was as much a part of the hardware store as the bright scissors of graduated sizes in the showcase and the washing machines at the back end of the room. When someone would remark, "I don't see how hardware stores make much money these days," Mr. Ferguson would reply with a worried, dogged belief in the business excellence of his town, "Oh, they do it on their stoves and wash-machines." Mr. Ferguson was one of the kind who still wanted the tools he bought to be of the best and to last when he got them. But folks like that got fewer in Belmond year by year. And the hardware store, such a good business when Loren went into it, now was getting dusty and left behind. It seemed that they were going to have less instead of more as they got older. The best years, meager as they had been, were left behind.

"I'm not going to wash those dishes until I feel like it."

Anyway, they had their own place. They could do as they pleased. Now there wasn't even a neighbor to notice.

Mrs. Morgan went outside again. She wouldn't look at the Ferguson house. She felt ashamed and disgusted at having broken down and shown her feelings to all those people. There was a flatness, now that the folks were gone.

"Whoo! Scat!" Mrs. Morgan said suddenly.

That nasty dog—well, anyway, it had traipsed a little too far this time and lost out on the proceedings. Mrs. Morgan always hated to be as fierce toward the animal as she felt, for fear of what Mrs. Ferguson would think of her. But she couldn't bear to have the ugly beast around.

"You get out of here and quit leaving your calling cards in my yard!"

2

Even before they finished breakfast, the skies had begun to cloud over; and by the time they left Belmond, it was plain that the weather was in for a change. Later in the day, it had begun to rain. Going down through the southern part of the state, the autumn fields had turned dark and sodden, there was a patient, local, reproachful look about the wet frame houses and the farms with their leafless groves. The dark brooding sky seemed to tell the Fergusons that winter was coming on, and that never before had they been away. It gave them a feeling of shame and of flight which they never quite lost all through the alien stretches of the desert country. Their last view of home should have been that happy one of their house and their neighbors in the sunshine; but instead it had been of the little group of relatives and church people—Ben looking old and stooped, Mrs. Lowrie frail and faded—standing out in front of Ella's narrow frame house, shivering and left behind, under a darkened sky.

Through all the earlier part of their trip, the Fergusons had felt like strangers in a strange land. The scenery was splendid, of course. But Mrs. Ferguson had been nervous on the mountain roads. She didn't really trust dad on roads like that, although she sat tense and still, and wouldn't have told him. She longed for Bunny. The pain of that—to her—incomprehensible marriage dug its way even deeper into her, as if it were a wound that was slowly spreading from nerve to nerve. She had been afraid crossing the desert, where it was so far from town to town. The few people whom they met were dark and alien. At the Indian pueblo where they stopped, in the late afternoon, almost twilight, a chilly wind blew across the open space of the plaza in swirls of dust. The earthen houses looked stark and bare, the whole place ominous and strangely deserted, as if it belonged to another age. They didn't see how Margaret could have said she wanted to live there! "Oh well, Margaret likes anything that isn't what she's accustomed to." At the Grand Canyon, of course, it was wonderful. It was glorious, they soberly admitted that. But Mrs. Ferguson had drawn back from the railing, trembling a little. Dad could take refuge in statistics. But his arm was her only protection against this feeling of mightiness and of her own terrifying insignificance. There was something about that uncharted sublimity that dwarfed and threatened all the sanctities that she held dear. In her secret heart, it was not only terrifying, it was distasteful. Had she told the truth—which she would never do!—she would have admitted that she hated it.

But the moment they crossed the California line, the Fergusons had a feeling of safety. This was novel and strange, but it was an extension of what they knew. It was where Dorothy, and Louie, and many of their old friends lived. The word "Arizona" had a foreign sound—a western story, or a movie, Indians, or a health resort—but the word "California" was rich with familiarity. The desert all at once became friendly and interesting; and in the blaze of the far-famed sunshine, that last dark vision of home faded away.

It seemed as if things *did* change at once. They found such a nice tourist camp, even if it was out on the desert. With its neat stucco houses, with the fine windows and the real curtains, and the cactus garden, it was almost like a little town.

"Well, mama, maybe we better stay here tonight."

"Oh, yes, this looks nice," Mrs. Ferguson replied happily. "It doesn't look like that other one."

They pulled up at the office building. It was almost evening. But fear had fallen away from Mrs. Ferguson now. She was only a day's ride from either Louie or Dorothy. A very nice man owned the camp.

"Yes, sir, I've got a cabin for you—showers, toilet, kitchenette, everything you could ask for. I try to have the best there is going. Now if you folks'll just sign the register—"

Mr. Ferguson signed.

"Ioway, hm?" the man said, looking at their car. "We get

597

a good many folks from out there. M'wife and I used to live in Missoury."

"That so? Well, that's a pretty good state too," Mr. Ferguson conceded.

"Yeah, it sure is, it's a pretty good place. But *we'll* never go back there."

"Like this better, do you?"

"Well . . . you don't have the cold weather."

The man took them proudly to their cabin. Mrs. Ferguson exclaimed over how nice it was. It had bedding and all—good bedding. "You can count on it," he told her, "that bedding's clean. M'wife sees to that."

"Oh, I can see that," Mrs. Ferguson said happily.

It was nicer than a hotel, she thought. It was really like a little house of their own. Before this, she and dad had disliked the tourist camps, with all the noise of people coming and going. But now the time had come when she was ready to be pleased with anything. Their holiday was actually beginning. The man was telling them, why, some folks stayed a week or more—they'd had one family stayed a month! Said they liked the camp and might as well just squat here. Oh, this air was fine! There was nothing like it. "You know, folks pays a lot of money for desert air, in Palm Springs and those places. These scientific fellows are saying now it's got more of these vitamines or whatever you call 'em in it. Here, you can have all of it you can breathe for a dollar and a half. And if you've once breathed it, you'll never be satisfied with any other."

Mr. Ferguson listened silently. The fellow was kind of a boaster, he had decided, but he had a nice place here, so maybe he had a right to talk. There was even a relief in this familiar loquacity after the dark taciturnity of those Indians and Spaniards. At least it was language they could understand, like what they heard at home, only more so. If Annie was satisfied . . . Now Mr. Ferguson stepped in to ask if there was a place to eat.

"We can fix you up right here! Steaks, ham and eggs—whatever you want. M'wife's a good cook."

Mrs. Ferguson was happily sure of that. Well, then they'd try it here, Mr. Ferguson said. They washed their hands in the nice little bathroom. The water *was* hot, just as the man had said. The supper was nice too. Mr. Ferguson enjoyed his steak for the first time in days. Mrs. Ferguson, not wanting such a heavy meal, had chosen bacon and eggs. She was pleased with everything here. She felt at home among these people. The little waitress was nice about getting her more hot water for her tea. A pretty girl too, although perhaps with hair a trifle too golden. "You folks had all you want?" the girl asked sociably as she made out their bill; and the proprietor's wife, a perspiring fat woman with scanty bobbed hair, came waddling out to ask anxiously, "Was everything all right?"

"Oh, yes," they assured her, "it was fine."

After they had eaten, they decided to walk around for a bit. There wasn't much of a town, they could see, but the oil stations were all brightly lighted up, giving it the semblance of a metropolitan air. At this hour, the place really seemed more imposing than Belmond! Now Mrs. Ferguson felt that she could enjoy the novelty of the desert. The air was colder now, but it *was* wonderful. She looked with pleasure at the delicate colors of the sky. They didn't care to walk along the road, because of the cars; so they turned back toward the camp. Mrs. Ferguson stopped to look at the cactus garden; and Fred was interested too, since this wasn't just pretty, but something of a curiosity. Must take a lot of watering, though, he observed. He was wondering if this camp business was profitable. He could see that it took work and meant quite an outlay. Well, if they just didn't get too many of them, and run each other out of business—

"Look at this, Fred! Isn't it pretty?" Mrs. Ferguson touched the soft white plumes of a tall pampas.

"Better not touch it, mama. These cactus things have spikes."

"Oh, well, this hasn't," she said, stepping back nevertheless. "Oh, and see, this is pretty too! I didn't know cactus could *be* so pretty. Those huge big things looked so awful when we were driving along. Still, I wouldn't want things in a garden, it doesn't seem, that I had to be afraid of."

Everything was beginning to seem to her interesting and amazing. She had a childlike trust in the wonders of California.

The air was a little too chilly now, so they went inside. Mrs. Ferguson took out her knitting. She was making a little sweater for Rosemary. She had thought she would get it finished on the trip, but until now she had been too tired to work much on it in the evenings. Fred said he thought he'd step over to the office and see if they had a paper. He was gone quite a while—perhaps he was talking to the man. But she didn't feel lonesome or afraid. She worked happily away at her knitting, taking delight in its tea rose-pink, picturing the harmony of this delicate shade with Rosemary's brown eyes and fair hair. Pleasure had suddenly opened up again to her in her old diversions and there were new ones ahead of her. The little kitchenette painted in apple-green was so pretty that Mrs. Ferguson almost wished they had been staying here long enough for her to do some cooking in it. She was anxious, of course, to see Dorothy, and Louie, and all the folks. But in this place, she had a strangely blessed sense of being far away from all anxiety and trouble, and contented in a way she hadn't been for months.

Fred opened the door.

"Annie, you ought to come outside," he said. His voice was proudly excited. "Just come and see what a big moon there is."

She put down her knitting without protest, and went out with him, feeling excited too. He led her out behind the cabins of their snug retreat, away from the brilliant showy lights of the road. It seemed strangely wide and still—the noise of the cars was far away; and the moon was so marvelous it made a kind of fairyland. "You can see to read!" Fred exulted. Yes, it was certainly the biggest, brightest moon they had ever seen. All the desert was bathed in silver. And she could enjoy this beauty—because this was California, their goal, and she felt that the dangers of their journey were over. Fred put his arm around her; and just before they went into their cabin, standing in the dark little space between the doorstep and the car, he reached down and pressed his cheek against hers.

"Are you having a good time, mama?"

She nodded.

"Well, I don't know as I'd like to stay here, though," he said, after they were in bed—referring to the proprietor's assertion that he wouldn't go back to Missouri. "I guess you'd want something besides air after a while."

The next morning, after a good breakfast and fine coffee, they started out on the last lap of their journey.

"Well, stop again on your way back, folks," the proprietor of the camp told them.

"We'll certainly do that if we come this way."

"Everything was lovely," Mrs. Ferguson called back brightly.

The air was as pure and clear in the morning as at night. They were in California at last. It gave them an elated holiday feeling.

The towns were bigger now—different, of course, from those at home, but the difference was the kind they had wanted to see, not something to disturb them. They were looking at everything with eager eyes. They drove through a whole forest of branching cactus—"Joshua trees," a man at a filling station said they were called. "Well, sir, I didn't know there were so many kinds," Mr. Ferguson kept repeating. "My, there's a lot of waste country, though," he soberly added. "I don't suppose it's good for a thing but these cactus and stones." Mrs. Ferguson said nothing. She was already so pleased with California that she wouldn't agree.

Every moment now the landscape was changing. The long hard stretches of the journey were past. They felt as if they had been set free in the light golden sunshine. Now they were driving along a sort of avenue between tall palm trees and orange groves. They were beholding that, to them, almost miraculous sight—oranges growing! The globes of the thick-skinned fruit were still green-gold among the dark glossy leaves. Mr. Ferguson felt better now that he was where he could see things growing. Although the ground was hard and dry still—it must all take a lot of watering. He liked places that were settled, he said. But the mountains were not so terrifying and strange beyond these pleasant homes. Everywhere there was evidence that people—their own kind of people—were living just like anywhere else; and yet it seemed to the Fergusons, on this bright morning, that the whole land existed in the midst of eternal holiday. Old anxieties, stringencies, responsibilities seemed to be gone. The estrangement of the last few months had been magically healed in the moonlight. They felt that particular happiness in being together, which, close as these two were, only visited them at rare unpredictable intervals.

They passed enticing roadside stands with oranges and figs and nuts for sale. Everything seemed to have a kind of theatrical, festive air. The beautiful fresh dates!

"Do you want to get some?" Mr. Ferguson asked.

They stopped and got out of the car. Mrs. Ferguson was pleased at Fred's easy readiness. He was always "good" to her of course, but now he seemed to stand back, anxious to make her happy . . . almost like the old days of courtship, when he had driven her into town with the best team of horses, and wanted to buy her ice cream, popcorn, everything they saw, in order to beat out the other fellows who were shining around the pretty teacher. It was *their* vacation, for which they had been working all their lives, living thriftily and soberly for all their increasing ease and prosperity. Now they had their chance to enjoy themselves, and they were taking it, both of them together. For the first time, she was really glad that none of the children were along.

Some of the dates were ready boxed "to send back home to the folks in the East." Mrs. Ferguson was elated because Fred seemed just as much taken by the idea as she was.

"Think we might get some of these, Annie? Might send a box to Ella and Ben, in return for that nice breakfast."

She assented happily. Too often, when she and the girls were taken by this or that on their earlier brief excursions, dad had wanted to drive along, saying cautiously they didn't want to be in too much of a hurry, they might see something better by and by—and it had ended in their going home empty-handed! Their lives *could* change—they still could change. Something

602

might yet be in store for them. The stuff looked pretty nice, dad was saying—maybe they might get a box to send to Carl's folks too. The boys would enjoy it. Better for them than candy. She let him determine the size of the boxes, since he was doing the buying. But when dad *did* do things, he did them right. She would have liked to send back something to the Vieles and the Morgans. But she couldn't ask dad to get so much. He picked out a nice box for Ben and Ella, and a larger one for Carl and Lillian. Then he himself suggested, looking a trifle shamefaced at the way he was blowing himself for the stuff, that it might be nice to send a little something to Reverend and Mrs. Lowrie—and maybe to Essie Bartlett and her mother. Mrs. Ferguson felt a sense of smothered impatience that it must always be the same ones, dad's own folks, and the church people, *his* friends; but she was ashamed to make any protest—dad was so good, he always thought of the people he looked after, and of course they *were* the ones who needed it. She could pick up some little presents for Mrs. Viele and Mrs. Morgan later on. And if dad hadn't been intent all these years on looking after and providing for his own, he and she could never have taken this trip together!

"I suppose it's too far to send a box to Margaret," she did suggest, somewhat wistfully.

Dad said it was. "And anyway, she can get plenty of things in New York," he added dryly.

Mrs. Ferguson silently agreed.

But this was only a faint, transient shadow on the fresh beauty of the morning. The gifts had canceled the memory of that small aging group standing shivering under the darkening sky. Now they were really free for their own enjoyment! Everywhere along the way there was something to take her eye. She would have liked to sample all the fruits she saw, and to lay in great supplies of possible presents. The golden globes of oranges piled in pyramids on the open stands were simply too much for both of them. Fred had to admit that these people out here knew how to make a show of what they had!

"Well, I don't know, we had a good breakfast, but these oranges kind of make my mouth water," he said.

He stopped again and bought a big sack of them. Might as well have some, the things were so cheap—they could give Jesse and Dorothy what were left. He did wonder how they could sell them so cheap. Must be kind of hard on the folks who had to do the producing. Mrs. Ferguson shrugged impatiently—she didn't want to think about that. Anyway, this seemed like too good a chance to lose.

"Don't spoil your dinner," she warned Fred.

"Oh, oranges won't spoil my dinner. They're mostly all juice."

He put the skins carefully in a piece of newspaper, not wanting to litter up the roads—some people were so careless, and as a respectable town father he didn't believe in that kind of business, even if they were a long ways from home.

They drove into a medium-sized town for lunch. Dinner they would have when they got to Dorothy's. But that was a long while from now. They both admitted that they were hungry. It pleased and amazed them to find that the sun was almost *too* hot at noon. It made them wonder what kind of weather they were having back home—Mrs. Ferguson exultant because this was so lovely—it bore out her desire to come to California.

"Well, they might be having pretty nice weather back there too," Fred said loyally.

"Yes, but it was getting cold even when we left."

They drove through the bright new business section. Mr. Ferguson liked the ordinary restaurants and Mrs. Ferguson had a weakness for tearooms. But this noon they found a place that suited them both. "Home Cooking" was what attracted dad. It was a frame house, of gray shingles, what they recognized now as a California type. There was a beautiful great palm tree in the yard, which was enough to give the place a pleasingly exotic air. The rooms inside seemed to them a little chilly; but the woman—a plump, flushed woman, in a bright pink bungalow apron, with somewhat dubious mahogany-colored hair—obligingly lighted a small gas fire.

"Folks from away seem to notice the cold more," she said.

She was smiling and friendly, seemed nice in spite of her hair; and she sociably let them in on the details of the meal.

"Excuse me for being kind of slow, but I hurt my foot yesterday," she confided. "I don't know how I come to do it, but as I was coming downstairs, it just sort of turned over. Guess I'm kind of heavy on my feet."

It made them feel a trifle uncomfortable to have her waiting on them. But she seemed to get around all right, Mr. Ferguson noticed. They were both of them too hungry to want to be very sympathetic. She brought them fancy pink napkins and green-tinted glasses of water.

"Now what can I give you folks? I have Swiss steak, pork chops——"

"I believe I'll have the Swiss steak."

"The Swiss steak is lovely," she said approvingly.

"Well, I believe I'll have that too."

While they were eating, the woman sat down in the other room, just beyond the open doorway, ready for conversation.

"You folks from out of the state?" she asked.

They said they were.

"Well," she assured them, "you'll enjoy it this winter."

There weren't quite so many people through this year, she confided, when she came to get their plates. Times weren't so good. "I guess we don't feel it here like they do some places," she said brightly. "We don't have the cold weather to contend with, anyway." She hobbled out to the kitchen and back, making no attempt to conceal her infirmity—far from it; she was martyred but cheerful, and evidently quite proud. She came from back East, too, she told them. But she had been out here fourteen years, so she called herself a Californian.

"It's a wonderful place," Mrs. Ferguson said.

"Oh, it sure is."

She thanked them effusively when they paid the bill, and begged them to stop in again. You couldn't say folks out here weren't cordial, Mr. Ferguson noted—anyway, when they had something to sell! Had they enjoyed their meal? They assured her that it was very nice.

"Well, most everybody likes my meals. I have lots of folks comes regular, all the time."

Yes, and you couldn't accuse them of hiding many of their lights under bushels! But Mrs. Ferguson didn't want to hear even this much censure by this time. She did have a fleeting wonder as to what that woman did to her hair. But it was no use speaking about that to dad. *He* would never notice. And since it seemed to reflect a little bit on California, the woman being now a citizen, she didn't want to speak of it anyway.

She had one moment of sorrowful reflection as they got into the car and she saw the oranges. Once it would have been Howard and Jennie they would have thought of first of all, when they were buying those presents. It would have been nice to send Howard some of the dates anyway—but she wouldn't have dared suggest that to Fred. To him, it would have meant "countenancing" that woman.

"I believe I'll swing in somewhere, Annie. I don't quite like the feel of that back tire."

Mrs. Ferguson assented. If she *had* been afraid on those mountain roads, she could at least trust dad always to see that the car was in good shape.

They turned into the yard of a service station across the way.

"Guess you'll have to get out. This is going to take a little fixing."

She assented again. She didn't mind waiting out here in this sunshine. There was a place for the lady to sit down, the oil station man said politely, nodding toward a bench. She thanked him smilingly, and came back to it, after a trip to a clean, bright restroom. Everything was nice out here, she thought. Some of the restrooms she'd seen on this trip—! She felt flattered in her status of tourist. As she sat resting, she saw that some old fellow had come up and was talking to dad.

"From Ioway, are you?" the old fellow said. "What part?"

Mr. Ferguson told him.

"Don't know as I'm familiar with that section. I come from Ioway myself. Abbotsford, down in Scott County. But I been out here four years now, guess I rate as a native Californian."

Mrs. Ferguson sat and listened while the two men talked. Dad was always stiff with strangers at first.

"Belmond! Say, I did use to know a fellow there, come to think of it! Relative of my wife. Ran a grocery store. Allen, was his name. Jim Allen. Don't believe he's living now. Ever know him?"

Allen! Why, of course they knew him. Mrs. Ferguson was amused. She knew Fred hadn't thought so much of Jim Allen, but it was exciting to run across a man who knew anyone at home. He began to loosen up and get friendly at once.

"How's the son doing with the business?"

"Well, not quite so well as the old man did," Mr. Ferguson admitted. He didn't like to say that Gardner had run it pretty well into the ground, or cast any kind of reflection on his own town.

"Well, yep, that's often the way," the old fellow was saying wisely. "These young folks ain't brought up to work the way their folks did. Well, it's our fault. That's what I always tell m'wife when she don't like the way the children act. It's our fault, I tell her, we was the ones that raised them." Mr. Ferguson soberly assented—to Mrs. Ferguson's indignation. Yet she secretly agreed too—it hurt her when she thought of Margaret —of Bun . . . . "The way my son's going," she heard this old codger proclaim, "*he* won't be able to retire and take it easy when the time comes—he's taking it too easy all along!"

And Fred assented again—as if Carl didn't work as hard as you could ask *any*-one to do! and Bunny too, learning photography in that place in Chicago, and getting almost nothing for it—certainly he was *work*-ing hard enough.

"Well, I'll tell you, though," the old fellow confided, getting down to business now, "with these chain stores and all, store-keeping's not the business it used to be. *I* wouldn't stay in it. No, sir, not these days. I'd go into the *gar*-age business if I was to start again. That's what the folks are after now! All on the go—the whole country's on the go. They'll buy gasoline if they can't buy bread and butter."

And what did he think *he* was doing, out here in California? And how had he got here? Mrs. Ferguson uneasily agreed with part of what he was saying, but she was indignant, defending her children.

"How's times back there?" the old fellow was asking now.

Fred answered cautiously, they were pretty fair.

"You'll stay here," the old fellow told him.

Of course Fred wouldn't agree to that.

"Sure! Why, your wife won't let you go back!" Fred shook his head, and Mrs. Ferguson laughed. Now she was beginning to think the old fellow a character. She felt herself siding with *him*. "After you've been here one winter, you'll never go back to shoveling snow."

And now he began to spread himself and expatiate on the awful climate back there in the East. "Hot? Why, the summer's hotter than anything I've experienced in the four years I been here." That irritated the Fergusons, while it made them uneasily respectful. His voice had taken on a proud, boastful note they were beginning to recognize. "Why, let me tell you, just two miles from where we were living, just two miles as the crow *flies*, I see a cyclone that ripped a fellow's barn right off its foundations and then set it down hind side to! That's a fact. And say, did you ever get caught in a blizzard?" It seemed he'd been closer than they ever had to a great blizzard too. Cyclones in the summer, blizzards in the winter—life at home was one running to cover, to hear him talk! The Fergusons laughed, both shaking their heads now, Fred somewhat nettled, as the old codger went on with his stories. "Earthquakes! Oh, yes, we have an occasional earthquake—not so many as the folks there try to make out we do. But an earthquake just lasts a minute and then it's all over—the Lord just gives us a little shake, to let us know He owns the earth."

Fred put in dryly that he didn't think some of this land out here was so much to own!

But the old fellow didn't hear that. It was evident that *he* was the one who was doing the talking—the quips and the tall tales were *his* special property. Mrs. Ferguson, although she sympathized, began to feel sorry for his wife. "Course, it can do some damage," he admitted, with a confidential, off-the-record air, "but we don't have 'em here like they do up there in northern Californy. I wouldn't live *there* for anything you was to offer me!"

But when he had said his worst, he let down, and conceded that Belmond was a pretty nice town. (Mrs. Ferguson began to think that his wife might not have such a hard time after all.) Abbotsford was too. Sure, he never went back on Abbotsford. Couldn't go back on the place where he'd made his money! All at once there was something pathetic about the old man, for all his big talk. They remembered how fast he had come hobbling over the moment he saw their car.

"Well, you know, you like to hear about the old place," he told them. "I tell you, the climate may be the worst on God's earth" (which Fred by no means was admitting!) "but you can't find any nicer folks than you can find right back there. No, sir, not anywhere. Well, when we get 'em all out here"— he perked up again—"then we'll have *every*-thing!"

The Fergusons had to laugh; and they returned his good-byes heartily. They watched him go hobbling off, solitary and chipper, down the street.

The car was ready now. They climbed into it and drove away. For almost three weeks, it had been their chief home. Soon they could put it away for a while. Now Mrs. Ferguson began to feel tired. She wondered if she hadn't taken a little cold, after all, sitting out on that bench. She couldn't look any more at the groves, the palm trees, the flowers. They didn't want to stop to eat anywhere before they reached Dorothy's, and it took them longer than they had supposed it would. She seemed to have had enough of oranges!

But as they finally drew near the city, both of them brightened up again. On the whole, it could scarcely have been a lovelier day. There was almost a reluctance in taking up ties again, in leaving this golden freedom, which they had shared. Evening brought a different kind of beauty. There was a strange limitless breath from the sea. At last they saw before them the misty fairy lights of San Diego—it was as if they were driving down into an enchanted land, where their lovely and fortunate daughter dwelt, and was waiting to welcome them.

609

They cruised around for some time among the unfamiliar
streets, Mrs. Ferguson sitting tense and staring out at the houses,
able to think of nothing now but her closeness to Dorothy.
Suddenly she told Fred to stop.

"Look! Isn't that Jesse?"

A tall young man was standing near a parked car. Now he
came toward them, waving. It *was* Jesse. They saw with excited
pleasure how handsome he looked in his light overcoat and his
light felt hat. Mr. Ferguson drew up to the curbing. Now they
saw Jesse's dark eyes and the flash of his white teeth.

"Hello, there!"

He shook hands with Mr. Ferguson, hugged and kissed his
mother-in-law; and he kept his arm around her, with a light
flattering tenderness, as they all three stood together beside
the car.

"Well, did you come out here to make sure we knew where
to stop?"

"I came out to hail you. How are you?"

They told him, fine.

"It was sort of hard to find the place at this time of day,"
Mr. Ferguson admitted. "That's the house, is it?"

"Well, that's it," Jesse said laughing but slightly embarrassed.
"But as a matter of fact—oh, say, there's Petey in the car. Poor
little mutt, he's been waiting all day to come and meet you.
Here, Pete—"

Jesse opened the door of the big car parked farther down
the curbing, and helped out the little fellow, now almost in
tears.

"Here they are—here's grandma and grandpa."

They crowded around the child, who lifted his little arms in
a bewildered, half-frightened way. "Well, *Pe*-ter!" Of course
he didn't know them. All day he had been looking for them;
but now when he saw them, he realized all at once that they
were strangers. He turned back, clutching a fold of his father's
overcoat around him. He would know them soon, Mrs. Ferguson said compassionately. She wouldn't let Jesse make him

come to them. But she kept looking down at him, and smiling, as they stood there, trying to make out this little face that she had only seen when it was a real baby face. Both Dorothy's children had been born at home. The child's bright eyes were clouded at first. Then they began to grow interested; even a little flirtatious. He began to swing in and out of the fold of the overcoat daringly.

"It won't be long before he knows us."

Mr. Ferguson said, turning toward the car to get out their suitcases, "Well, maybe we better go inside."

That slight embarrassment came over Jesse's laughing face again. They realized all at once that there was something strange —the car here, Jesse in his hat and overcoat, and Dorothy not running out to meet them.

"Nope. Not that way." He grinned.

"Why! Didn't you say this was the place?"

"It's the place all right. But we don't live here."

"Don't *live* here!"

They stared at him in astonishment. At first, they could scarcely take in what he was telling them. It was the house, sure enough, but for the time being it was rented. Well, they had struck a good chance—and things weren't so hot right now . . . "Guess you know that, dad, if you've got any stocks." Jesse was a little vague in his explanations. But the upshot of it seemed to be that he and Dorothy had seen the chance to make a little money out of the place—these people from the East had seen it, and it was just what they wanted—and so Jesse and Dorothy were living for the present in, "Well, a little joint that was for rent.

"You know, everybody does that around here. Everything's for rent. So we're just being cagey for a while."

Jesse laughed easily, turning off their bewilderment. It wasn't until they were in their own car, following Jesse's as he had instructed them, that the Fergusons seemed to get back their wits and wonder just what it was all about. But Mr. Ferguson was fully occupied in keeping up with Jesse, who drove too fast like all these young fellows; and Mrs. Ferguson was still in too excited and confused a state really to consider what it meant—although she *did* wonder why Jesse and Dorothy hadn't written them.

They drove up and down hills, and swung around corners, at a much faster clip than Mr. Ferguson liked, especially in a place with which he wasn't familiar. It began to seem as if Jesse was taking them out to nowhere. But at last he stopped in front of some sort of little place—they scarcely noticed what it did look like in their excitement. Now Dorothy *was* running out to meet them. Her mother, fumbling with the door of the car in her haste, had her own beloved child again. And Rosemary—

"Well, I should say we *do* see her! *She* knows grandma, doesn't she?"

Laughing and talking at once, after the greetings, they all went into the house.

It was some time before they calmed down enough to look around them and take much account of the place. After all, it was almost four years since they had seen Dorothy—almost that long since she had last come home to stay with them, the summer that Peter was born. Rosemary wasn't much more than a baby when they had seen her last. And Peter was *just* a baby. Mrs. Ferguson had enough to do in noting with pleasure that Rosemary's hair was still light, although her eyes were brown —that Peter was fair like Dorothy, that he looked like Carl at the same age—that Dorothy . . . but wasn't she thin? Oh, that was what the girls strove for these days, Jesse said laughing. It was fine, it suited him! When they were first married, he used to have to bring Dorothy a box of candy every week. Now she wouldn't look at the stuff!

"Here, old lady," he chided, putting his arm around her, "what are you weeping for?"

"Well, I'm just glad to *see* the folks," Dorothy said.

She let Jesse wipe her eyes with his handkerchief, to the children's wonder, and got back her smiling composure. But underneath it, she was still fluttered and excited, her mother could see. Now they must take off their wraps, and be shown where they could wash. A whole array of Dorothy's pretty towels was ready for them in the bathroom. The queer little coop was crowded with brushes, lotions, contraptions. But there was no time now for really looking at the place.

"I know you're just starved, mother," Dorothy said, with a touch of breathlessness. "Dad, are you starved? We have everything ready."

The little breakfast nook, too, where it seemed they were to eat, was crowded with dishes. The candles softly glowing above the beautiful bowl of roses gave the place such a festive air that at first Mrs. Ferguson was dazzled and scarcely noticed how small it was. But the children—

"Oh, they're going to have their own little table."

When the four adults had squeezed into the two painted settles, they felt—Mr. and Mrs. Ferguson, at least—as if they were trying to eat in a doll's house. The somber elderly colored woman who served them made things still more complicated. Was this all the dining room they had? Visitors were going to make things pretty crowded! Dorothy's face was flushed, her mother thought. She was carrying it off well, following Jesse's lead of acting as if the whole thing were a good joke. But it wasn't a joke to her. Mrs. Ferguson could see that well enough, and felt anxious. Dad, she could tell, was worrying too, and trying to make things out. There was an undercurrent of anxiety all through the meal, which had been better planned than cooked, and which the colored woman served dubiously. Why, the Fergusons had supposed that Dorothy and Jesse had everything they wanted! Dorothy's marvelous good fortune was still one of Belmond's favorite topics. But dinner, of course, wasn't the time to ask about it. And Jesse didn't seem to be worried at all.

Dorothy laughed. "I hope you like my dishes, mother!"

"Are these yours?" Mrs. Ferguson looked at them for the first time.

"Yes? Aren't they lovely? No, they're what we get with our handsome house."

"Somewhat augmented by Woolworth additions," Jesse observed.

Their own dishes, Dorothy explained, had to be left in the house. Oh, yes, that was customary. The people wanted to rent the place just as it stood; and if she and Jesse were going to get the price they asked for it—well, they had to agree. They were lucky enough to find people who wanted to pay such a price at this time! "I did snitch a few—a few little things," Jesse finished hastily, with a sidelong glance at Dorothy which she sedately refused to meet. He remembered now, with an inward chuckle, that "the folks" were strict Prohibitionists. It amused him, and somehow he rather liked them the better for it; he liked to tell at parties that Dorothy's parents were Bone Drys; although it seemed incredible, almost legendary, actually to find people like that.

"But aren't you afraid to have other people use your lovely dishes?" Mrs. Ferguson was asking.

"Oh . . ." Dorothy shrugged her shoulders.

"Oh, they won't break as many as we did," Jesse said easily. "You ought to see them, mother. They're an old couple from the East, as sedate as two old ducks, come from Boston. I believe they think they're really braving the wilds, coming out here. Always have gone to Europe before on their vacations. Never been west of the Hudson before. That's the kind. No, the point is, the furniture's really getting a rest, without the kids there!"

"I don't break furniture, daddy," Rosemary said, from the little table.

"Don't you? Well, I meant Peter!"

"No! No!" Peter cried.

The grown people laughed, and the grandmother sided with the children.

Well, Jesse made light of it, but there was *some*-thing behind it. The dinner was really very nicely planned. A little wine would have helped it out, Jesse thought somewhat ruefully. Mother, he surmised, would have taken it all right—yes, and enjoyed it; but dad—hardly. Well, "the folks" were all right, just the same, and he was glad to see them. His father-in-law's slow, provincial caution always amused Jesse. He rather liked its old-fashioned quality. Dad was a big man in his own town— Jesse appreciated that. Dorothy was using her own filet doilies, and her own pretty napkins.

"You see we kept out the coffee set," Jesse hastily told the folks; but Dorothy wouldn't let him catch her eye.

It was that lovely little after-dinner coffee service that one of Jesse's aunts (almost a stranger to her nephew, but dutifully honoring the occasion) had sent the children for a wedding present—Mrs. Ferguson recognized it. Aunt Ella, she remembered, had thought it was funny, saying, "Don't these things look old? Funny his aunt would send an old set,"—not realizing that the faded purple and gold was the very thing that made the cups so charming. Dad, of course, would have liked a bigger cup. He hadn't thought much, either, she could tell, of the avocado salad—he had never grown to like salads, or "those sauces" as he persisted in calling the dressing. However, he was doing manfully and making no complaint, although the poor man didn't have room to move his arms.

They all talked about the trip, about the children, about people and conditions at home. So dad was now a man of leisure! Well, this was the place for him to come. Dad didn't quite like that. He was careful to call the trip "a vacation." Dorothy seemed more like herself now. Her mother was getting used to the new way of combing her hair, swept severely off the forehead, as all the girls were wearing it now. It looked very *chic*, Mrs. Ferguson admitted. Still, she missed the soft waves about the face. Perhaps this hairdress was partly what made Dorothy look thin. She seemed to be radiant-eyed and glowing. But she had all she could do, looking after the children, and managing the colored woman who had been brought in for the occasion—their own maid, Jesse had said, laughing at the solemnity of this helper, went with the house. "This one looks as if she's about to shed tears all over the dishes." "Well, Jesse, maybe she has trouble or something at home." "Well, let her keep it there, then—we haven't got room for it," Jesse said. The frozen dessert, ordered from a catering place, was very fine. Still, it was a relief to have the dinner over.

"We'll drive around by daylight and see our late palatial residence," Jesse promised the folks.

Jesse would have liked a little evening's entertainment. But the folks were tired, Dorothy said, and they admitted it. The children were upset, too, with the excitement. Peter hadn't got used to his grandparents yet. Tomorrow they could have a good time. Tonight it would be better for them to go to bed.

The Fergusons were even more tired than they had acknowledged. But going to bed wasn't such a simple matter, either. It seemed that there were only two bedrooms, and one of those was really a sun porch. The children had that. So what *they* had must be Jesse's and Dorothy's room!

"But where are *you* going to sleep?"

"Now, mama, don't say anything," Dorothy pleaded, fearful that mother was going to think there wasn't room for her and dad.

"Look here, mother," Jesse proclaimed.

He took hold of an odd-looking handle on the wall and partly drew out a wall bed, with a flourish, pushing it in again.

"There?" Mrs. Ferguson marveled.

"There. It's a California bed," Jesse said laughing. "People sleep around anywhere out here."

"But I don't like to take your room."

"Forget it, mother. We're just picnicking, anyway."

Mr. and Mrs. Ferguson had to take the bedroom. Dorothy would have felt dreadful otherwise. She had fixed this nicely for them, with flowers, and her beautiful down coverlet. Those people must have let her keep out a few things anyway.

But the bedroom itself wasn't any too comfortable for Mr. and Mrs. Ferguson used to the quiet of their roomy house. This little house seemed to be made of paper. They could hear the children out on the porch. Peter was restless. Overexcited, poor little fellow. Mrs. Ferguson said "Sh!" to Fred, not wanting Jesse and Dorothy to overhear them. The bathroom was scarcely large enough for so many towels.

All in all, it was pretty much of a come-down after that lovely Spanish house of which they had so proudly showed everyone at home the pictures. The Fergusons couldn't help feeling that, although they didn't like to say much. Surely, if the children had to move, they could have found something better than this! The place wasn't much more than a tourist cabin.

616

"Oh well, when they're here by themselves they have room enough."

The bed was pretty fair, however—and the bedding was lovely. If only those two children were comfortable in there in that funny bed! Jesse had insisted that it was as good as any other. But their things were all in here, of course. It couldn't be very comfortable for them, this way.

"S'pose those kids are going to keep it up like that all night?"

"Oh, they'll calm down after a while. They're just excited. Sh!" Mrs. Ferguson warned as an after-thought.

She was more uneasy and wakeful, though, than dad. She supposed there wasn't really any cause for worry. Jesse, in fact, acted as if the whole thing was a lark. They hadn't found out much except that he had had some losses in the stock market. Mrs. Ferguson was ashamed to acknowledge part of the sources of her disquietude. But she had always counted upon Dorothy as the fortunate one, who had "everything she wanted." And now she didn't want to take up the old maternal anxiety again, which she had thought to put away, as futile, after Bun had disappointed her so. She didn't *want* to worry about Dorothy. That was one reason why she had come out here! This "vacation" at least—if that was what it was—must be all sunshine. But she could see that Dorothy was chagrined too. Treacherous sympathy for her child struggled with her own desire for this season of undisturbed pleasure. Hadn't they served their time? She turned restlessly.

"Aren't you going to sleep, mama?"

She hadn't meant to say it so soon, but she did. "Fred, I just wonder if we ought to stay here."

He was silent for a while. She thought he might have dropped to sleep, and perhaps not heard her after all. But he had just been mulling the situation over.

"Well, why didn't they tell us they'd moved?"

"Oh . . ."

Dorothy had been afraid they wouldn't come out, then. She knew that was the reason.

He was thinking it over some more. She waited in distress.

617

Now she looked back to the lost freedom of this day as a golden memory.

"Well—do you mean, we should go on to Louie's?"

She didn't want to say what she did mean. Of course they couldn't leave Dorothy after just this tiny visit. Fred had counted on staying here. Dorothy and Jesse had asked them so often. And they had thought there was plenty of room. She didn't like to suggest any extra expense. But she counted stealthily on dad's desire for comfort, which had been growing with the years. He told her finally:

"Well, better go to sleep now. We'll see about it in the morning."

That amounted to a promise from dad!—so she did go to sleep.

This morning, it was dad who didn't wake up. That was almost unheard of; but the driving had tired him out. Mrs. Ferguson, although she had slept fitfully, was uneasily wakeful from the time it began to be light, listening for sounds in the other room. She couldn't let Dorothy do everything, with those children to attend to, as well. Mrs. Ferguson thought with considerable chagrin of how proudly she had always told the other ladies about the servants Dorothy had—her cook, and the nursemaid for the children, and the man who looked after the grounds. That would make it harder for the poor child now, being used to help. Jesse might talk about picnicking; but she doubted if this was a picnic for Dorothy!

It was none too early, at that, when she heard them stirring. Dad would never be able to stand it, on other mornings, if they were as late as this. She suspected they would be. As soon as she heard Jesse go to the bathroom, Mrs. Ferguson went softly into the living room. She was tired, frayed, and secretly much irritated to find work awaiting her when she had expected such a beautiful rest. "I expect at Dorothy's you'll be treated like a queen!" Mrs. Viele had said. But she was concerned, really concerned for her child; and long training would not permit her to refrain from offering to help, in fact from insisting, no matter how she felt.

618

"Let me do that." Dorothy was hastily making up the wall bed. The living room was strewn wildly with clothes.

"Oh, mother! You didn't have to get up so soon."

"Well, I was awake," Mrs. Ferguson said evasively.

"Did the kids make an awful fuss?"

"Oh, they didn't bother us for long," Mrs. Ferguson lied brightly.

"They were so excited."

"Yes, I know they were excited. They always are when someone comes. You don't know how you children used to be whenever Aunt Louie came to see us."

"Were we awful?" Dorothy asked, laughing.

"Oh, no, not *aw*-ful. You never were awful."

"I was afraid dad would be up before now. We're sort of late risers."

"Well, he slept this morning—for some reason."

She couldn't help a touch of dryness in her voice.

The wall bed went up quite nicely, although it was rather heavy to handle. Jesse might have done this for Dorothy, Mrs. Ferguson couldn't help thinking. Jesse had a beautiful disposition, but she could see that he had never been used to exerting himself, or going outside his own inclinations. She perceived already, shrewdly—and with a sigh—that it was Dorothy who did the adapting. Mrs. Ferguson sighed again impatiently at having to give up—it seemed—the cherished notion of her younger daughter as a petted household queen. After all, she had only seen Dorothy and Jesse together on occasions when Dorothy naturally held the center—at the time of the wedding, and when Rosemary and Peter were born. Mrs. Ferguson hurriedly put the room into some kind of order so that Dorothy could go out to start the breakfast. Already the two women had entered into an unspoken conspiracy to get things going smoothly before the tempers of their menfolk could be ruffled.

"Oh, what lovely juice!"

Dorothy told her how cheap fruit was in the markets. She said what a grand electric refrigerator they had in the other house. "It's just too *bad* you can't be there!" she burst out.

619

"Oh, well . . ." her mother said consolingly. "It's you we came to see, not the house."

"I know it, darling. But—"

Now Mrs. Ferguson *was* ashamed to admit that there could be any disappointment.

The children were awake. Jesse did look after them, it seemed. Mrs. Ferguson was mollified when she heard his voice. Dorothy, however, had half her attention on the other room. She had refused to let her mother do anything more about the breakfast than to set the table; but now, when she hastily turned down the gas flame under the bacon to rush into the other room, Mrs. Ferguson turned it up again and finished things herself. She couldn't help looking anxiously at the clock, knowing that Rosemary went to school—and thinking how dad used to worry about their all being on time in the mornings. Well, there were advantages, too, in having the kind of husband who took things on himself. She had a fleeting remembrance of how poor Mrs. Christianson used to look upon *her* as the wife who had everything she could ask for. "My, if all the husbands treated their wives like Mr. Ferguson does you—!" Rosemary came in now, shining and fresh; and her grandmother had to stop and give the child a hug and kiss, saying she hadn't really seen her last night. Little Peter followed, shy but subtly mischievous. In the morning, she saw with triumph what beautiful children they were, the kind of children Dorothy *would* have —more robustly handsome than Carl's boys, she might have thought, if it hadn't been disloyal. Jesse, handsome, big and smiling, stood now in the doorway.

"Well, mother, is this where I find you? Come here, you didn't come out to California to fry bacon. Come on, kids, let's take grandmother out and show her the poinsettias."

"Oh, Jesse—" Dorothy had come back into the room. "I'm afraid there isn't time."

"Sure there is."

"Well, look at the clock!"

"Oh, I'll have all morning to look at things," Mrs. Ferguson said hastily—flattered, in spite of herself, by the clasp of his large, well-tended, sun-browned hand.

But she was on Dorothy's side. She knew too well what it meant to get breakfast for company and get children off to school at the same time. Dad had got up pretty good-natured after his long sleep, she saw with relief—she didn't know how it would be after this big trip. *She* could be out of sorts, but she could hide it better than dad. He greeted the children with unaccustomed joviality and helped them to squeeze into the breakfast nook. There wasn't time to put up the little table this morning. It worried Mrs. Ferguson that Dorothy wouldn't sit down with them and made *her* do it. Already she was assuming her old protective maternal rôle. But she knew how it was—and Dorothy could really have a better breakfast when the rest had gone and left her in peace, and she didn't have to look after them all. Jesse didn't quite like that: to have his wife standing and serving them as if she were the maid. He could be a trifle lordly at times. Well, Mrs. Ferguson thought, *she* didn't like it, either. It was much too reminiscent of Grandma Ferguson severely refusing, according to her code, to be seated when she had invited the folks all to dinner, and waiting assiduously on the menfolks but on the women very grudgingly. Not that soft little Dorothy was in the least like Grandma Ferguson!

Mrs. Ferguson didn't quite like a number of things. That Rosemary had so little time for her breakfast, for instance. Surely they might have got up a little earlier! Well, perhaps they did sometimes. Anyway, she mustn't allow herself to say anything, even if she did see that Dorothy had her difficulties. But she couldn't keep herself from half-wearily planning ways to help.

Jesse gulped his coffee and put down his napkin.

"Well, friends, I'll have to leave you. I'm a business man."

"Yes! Tell them *what* business," Dorothy said, delicately jeering.

"He's got some land business, hasn't he?" Mr. Ferguson said. He had never rightly known exactly what it was that Jesse "did"; although, of course, it didn't so much matter, since Jesse had money.

"Yes, dad, but I regret to state that the real estate business is not at present exactly flourishing in the land of sunshine. I've had to turn to my native talents for the nonce and set up a little competition for Ely Culbertson."

The folks didn't just know who Ely Culbertson was. Their education in bridge was not extensive. Jesse had to tell them. Jesse was giving bridge lessons, it seemed, along with a friend of his, or an acquaintance, to the grandes dames of San Diego. The acquaintance having formerly built a block of swank little shoppes, on spec, and most of these shoppes being now on the rocks, these two had set up shoppe for themselves—trying to get a little use out of the building. The Fergusons were not exactly shocked; the old taboo against card-playing was long ago lifted; still, it didn't seem like a *business,* to dad. Folks seemed to get into all kinds out here. They had noticed, as they drove along, a lot of funny signs on the houses. They were not yet used to Jesse's lordly young plutocratic way of treating life as a game in which he was sure to get the best breaks eventually. It was out of their experience; and somehow it seemed to put their own caution in the wrong. Before they could think of what to say, Jesse had left the table and gone into the other room.

He came back now, with his light overcoat over his arm. They didn't seem to have cut down on their clothes, either Jesse or Dorothy—Mrs. Ferguson had noticed that. Jesse looked too big for this little house. He hadn't grown a day older since the time of his marriage, so far as they could see. His hair was shining black. No one could resist that attractive smile. With his smooth, handsome, sun-tanned skin, he looked like a splendid young play boy who had nothing harder to do than keep up his tennis and lie out on the beach—he might have posed for a magazine advertisement; not at all like the father of a household, Mrs. Ferguson couldn't help thinking. And when he spoke, he did seem to make the whole thing sound like a kind of easy, adventurous stunt, which it was provincial to take too seriously.

"Well, mother and dad, you just loll about this morning, while I'm instructing the dames how to snatch the prizes from each other. Then we can take a drive this afternoon, maybe go out and have dinner and see a show tonight."

622

"You mustn't do too much for us," Mr. Ferguson said uneasily.

"Oh, we want to go ourselves! You're our excuse."

He caught Dorothy and gave her a kiss. She called breathlessly after him—"Jesse—Rosemary!"

"Oh, come on, Rosie. Almost forgot you. Come on and hop in."

They heard the noise of the engine outside. The car was gone.

Well, no doubt there wasn't any need to worry. It *was* just a temporary thing. After all, Jesse would inherit when his grandfather died. So perhaps he didn't need to get into any regular business. It was not a way of living that the Fergusons understood; but away from home, they could accept it more easily. Somehow, Jesse's mere presence was flattering. Helter-skelter as things seemed to be, there was really more pleasure in being here than at Carl's. Mrs. Ferguson thought that surreptitiously. Lillian often made her secretly impatient. But she couldn't hold her complaints against Jesse.

The whole household seemed to be lower-keyed when he was gone. If she had come out with her real feelings, Mrs. Ferguson would have admitted that she missed him. The situation became a little more realistic without him, however.

Now there was the question of what to do with dad while she helped Dorothy. He never knew how to occupy himself away from home. He didn't care much about the radio. Too much of this dance music, he said. But he was being more amenable than she had expected.

He said, "Oh, I'll just look around. Maybe Peter and I'll take a little walk around the place."

Well, that disposed of Peter too. The little fellow seemed to have accepted his grandfather. How splendid he looked in his little sun suit, husky and blond, with his strong bare legs and the straps over his fine square shoulders. When the children were so healthy, why worry?

The whole house seemed full of leisure when they had got the menfolks out of it. Now at last there would be the chance for a good talk with Dorothy. Mrs. Ferguson felt anxious for it, but slightly nervous.

"Mother, you don't have to help with these dishes."

"Why, do you think I'm going to let you do them all alone?" Mrs. Ferguson asked indignantly. "I guess I know what it means to entertain company, with children."

"*You're* not company."

Dorothy all at once hugged her mother in her old little-girl way, hung upon her, finally pushed her over to a chair and sat down in her lap.

"Big baby," Mrs. Ferguson said laughing.

A pang shot through her. Her real baby was lost.

Dorothy was heavy to hold, thin as she was. But her mother wanted her. She hugged her closely, straining for consolation, thinking emotionally that this was the one child whom she understood. She pushed back Dorothy's waved, brown-gold hair, taking her old pleasure in its softness. Now that she was keeping house and doing her own work, like the rest of them, Dorothy seemed to have descended to her old familiar status. She was no longer the silken smiling lady of leisure whose visits had been proud events in Belmond. Her mother missed the old splendor. But she felt that she and Dorothy were comrades now. She studied Dorothy's face anxiously, holding back the loosened waves of hair. It *was* thin. Tiny lines were etched about the lips. Of course this western air was dry. The skin was fair, but the old roselike bloom was gone. It made the mother indignant for a moment, thinking of Jesse's handsome smoothness. She divined that there was a little strain for Dorothy in keeping up with Jesse's requirements. He wouldn't know that she couldn't work and play at the same time. And Dorothy was too much like herself: Dorothy would feel that she *must* be what her husband expected and desired; otherwise—even if that was contrary to her own way—she had failed. Dorothy closed her eyes luxuriously under her mother's stroking hand. But she did not let go of her restraint. She wouldn't permit even a suggestion that her married life wasn't perfection. And Mrs. Ferguson had to approve that, although she longed to be closer to her child. It was her own code—the code of all women, she somewhat complacently supposed; unless they *weren't* what she thought of as womanly.

Peter had come in and was staring at them.

"You didn't know mama sat in grandma's lap, did you? Well, she's one of my babies, just as you're hers."

The little scamp looked mischievous, and tried to get into Dorothy's lap. He made his grandmother think of Forrest, just such another rascal. And yet this one's brand of mischief was subtly different. They were all different from each other. She felt the endless fresh interest of children . . . a complacency, a pang because it seemed Margaret was going to miss that— foolish girl! she thought with a rather confused indignation. And Bunny—who could tell about that girl, and what *she* might want? But it was too much, when Peter climbed on— they all had to get up, spilling him.

"Now let's go and do those dishes."

There was an intimate pleasure in working with Dorothy. Mrs. Ferguson longed to tell her about Bun and Charlotte, and her fears for Margaret, to get the solace of her understanding and sympathy. If Carl was closest to his mother's heart (or Bunny—who could say?), Dorothy was like a part of her own self.

"Isn't it too much for you to have us here? If we had known you were living in this little house—"

"That's why I didn't tell you."

"I know it was." Mrs. Ferguson sighed.

"Now, Mama Ferguson, you aren't going away! Jesse thought—" Dorothy looked confused—"maybe if it was too tight quarters here for you and dad, you might take a little place nearby. There are all kinds of them." Her voice was anxiously pleading.

"Well, I don't know," Mrs. Ferguson said vaguely. But then, Dorothy understood that she would have to ask dad first. "Oh, it isn't for myself—*I* wouldn't mind it." Which wasn't strictly true—but at the moment she thought it was. "You're the ones it's really hard on."

"No, it isn't," Dorothy lied valiantly.

At any rate, there was no use talking about it now. Dad would be the one to decide—although she might do the suggesting. They chattered about a lot of small things while they were washing the dishes, and then they went into the living room.

The place didn't look so bad when they had put it to rights—if it hadn't been for the glory of the other house.

"Oh, mother, I want you to see our house! It makes me mad we're not living there—I mean, while *you're* here. Everything is so sweet."

"I want to see it. Do you like the renters?"

"Oh, yes." Dorothy laughed. "They've taken possession, though! Except when anything's the least bit wrong. Then they're quick enough to suggest that the place is ours! 'I thought perhaps you'd like to know, Mrs. Woodward, that the enamel in the breakfast room has sev-er-al scratches. They were made before we took the house. No doubt you'll want to see to them before they get worse,' " she mimicked. Her mother made a face. "Couldn't dad have rented your place this winter?"

"*Our* house? Oh, dad would never have done that."

Although she hadn't meant it to sound like a criticism of Jesse—

They heard the toilet running. Dorothy jumped up. "Oh, that awful thing!" Dad must have left it. She hurried into the bathroom to fix it; and then came back laughing. She plumped down in her mother's lap again.

"What are *you* laughing about?"

"Oh, I was just thinking about our other bathroom—it would be a new experience for Aunt Ella."

She giggled, and leaned childishly against her mother's shoulder, playing with a little tendril of silver-brown hair. Her mother had to laugh too. Aunt Ella was well-known throughout the family as a connoisseur of toilets. It was a very ancient joke with Margaret and Dorothy. What particular pleasure Aunt Ella found, no mortal could say. But well did they remember, even out on the farm in the old days, how they had gone prancing and whimpering in childish haste, while Aunt Ella sat placidly ensconced reading old yellowed newspapers she wouldn't look at anywhere else, and Grandma said bitterly, "You might as well give up, when *she's* in there, I can tell you that." On all their drives, Aunt Ella kept an eye out; and

626

whenever they stopped at a service station, she was off, saying, "Well, I'll try this one"—and returning with heavily whispered detailed reports, in a state of disgust or of great complacency, as the case might be. In any department store, the restroom was her first goal. Dorothy giggled.

"You naughty girl." Her mother shook her a little. "You were both naughty girls."

Mrs. Ferguson sighed—Margaret had got so far away from them.

Dorothy slid off her mother's lap and sat on the floor, resting her head against those familiar comforting knees.

She asked dreamily, "How did Meg look when she was at home? She's simply spiffy in the picture she sent us."

"Oh, she looked—very nice."

"I think she's got terribly good-looking, mother. I don't know. Sort of stunning. She's found her style."

"She *looks* fine. She was a little . . . Dorothy, did you know anything about it?"

"What? That man?"

"Oh, you *did* know!"

But how much she knew, her mother couldn't ascertain. Dorothy was always able to keep her own counsel. It hurt dreadfully to think that Margaret might have let her sister into the secret, and not her own mother. But that was the way with the girls! There had always been a bond of alliance between them, different as they were. She would never find out from Dorothy! It made her feel, with a lonely pain, the gulf that separated the generations. She saw now that Dorothy might even defend Bun's choice, and she shrank from revealing her own feelings. She was thrown back on dad, after all.

"I don't think there's anything to worry about, mother," Dorothy said consolingly, almost as if she were talking to a child. "You know Margaret always did go her own way."

"But do you suppose she still . . ."

Dorothy shrugged her shoulders. "*Quién sabe.*" She didn't want to talk about it.

Fortunately Peter came in again. The children were always a

safe topic. Rosemary ate her lunch at school, Dorothy explained, and Jesse brought her back in the afternoon.

"Does he always have to take her both ways?"

"Oh, yes. It's all right. I'm really glad of it. It gets him up in the mornings. Jesse does hate to get up."

"Yes, and dad gets up *too* early."

They both laughed.

Dorothy said, "Oh, the men are awful duds." She burrowed her head into her mother's lap.

"Of course you know, mother, we're just living like this for the time being," she added, looking up, and forestalling the possibility of criticism. "We aren't hard up like this *all* the time."

"Oh, no, of course not," her mother said quickly.

"Jesse wanted me to have someone in to help while you were here. I suppose we *would* have more fun. But I think that's silly, if we're saving money," Dorothy said with severe good sense. "We ought to be able to do it. *You* used to. I can remember when you used to entertain the folks from Nebraska, that whole big bunch."

"People don't work as hard as they used to do."

"Oh, mama—you just mean the people you know!"

"Well—maybe. . . ." Her mother assented.

But she didn't quite like that. It made her feel old.

"I think we *ought* to work . . . well, something . . ." Dorothy's voice shook a little. She sat up. "I just mean—oh well, nothing, I guess." She slumped against her mother's knee. Her eyes darkened.

Her mother sighed uneasily. It was hard to give up her old dream of the fortunate child! She didn't really *want* to hear anything more. It was as dad said—they must work it out for themselves. She felt a slight resentment against Dorothy for not being contented with good fortune. Well, she and dad had had enough work! She thought again of yesterday, seeing it all in a golden light. Her own trouble had always been that dad was *too* industrious—and now, it seemed, Dorothy was going to suffer from the opposite—! Did there always have to be something? She looked with a sudden sharp curiosity at

628

Dorothy's face, perceiving the determination that lay under that softness . . . Dorothy, her own child, was a Ferguson, after all. A fleeting thought touched her with pain, that she might have missed some point of likeness with Margaret, who had seemed so different, so alien, because she had Grandma's black hair . . .

But she had seen her girl again. She was *with* her. She could understand the troubles of Dorothy, the married one. The actual, tangible sunshine came in through the windows. Life worked itself out—some way—and maybe there was no getting around it. If dad was just willing to take a place here, she could see enough of Dorothy's household and no more.

Mrs. Ferguson was awake again before dad was. Dad was getting to be quite a late sleeper. They all carefully encouraged him in that—Mrs. Ferguson trying to close her ears when he said, well, there was no use in getting up, nothing to do around here. But taking this apartment was his own choice! He was the one. Dad had declared for a place with a furnace. He had regarded the little gas heaters with a profound contempt, saying often— she telling him "Sh!" for fear Dorothy would hear—"might as well have stayed at home if we're going to be *this* cold." She felt secretly triumphant, that he had come to be so tied to familiar comforts—she could have given up those things far more easily, if only she had fresh interests, places to go and see, touches of real luxury. But she remembered, with resentment that had never quite died out, the stern frugality of Fred's folks, and the restrictions it had put upon their early married life. This place was a long way from Dorothy's, and she had thought she must protest about that. Actually, she was relieved. And why shouldn't they have the comforts they wanted, and spend their money upon themselves?—if they couldn't have their children anyway. She felt a horror at her own secret selfishness, along with a strained triumph. Something active and maternally anxious seemed to have died out of her when she had lost Bun to that girl—she had felt the blow at the time, recognized it, but only now was she realizing the actual results.

She didn't want to get up before dad, even if she was awake.

629

She wouldn't interfere in any way with this fine new laziness that he was developing. He would never admit himself to be "retired"; would only say cautiously, well, he had "pulled out of the bank," would let "a younger man have charge"; and that he and mama were enjoying a little vacation. What his real plans were, she didn't know, and dared not ask. News from home worried him at times—"Conditions," as he phrased it. Mrs. Lowrie had had another sick spell; this one and that one had dropped out; a bank at Hanging Rock had failed. He "didn't like the looks," dad sometimes said. But she would close her eyes, would not believe that existence was not working out in the ordained way to which they had always looked forward. And this winter sunshine was on her side, bore her out.

It was not really late, of course, when they did get up. They were earlier than most of the people in the house. Mrs. Ferguson went out to the kitchen, while Fred went out to the near-by drug store for the Los Angeles paper. Sometimes he got to talking there. The girl at the drug store had shocked Mrs. Ferguson once by saying, "Oh, I do enjoy talking to your husband, I think he's the nicest old man!" Silly little thing!—no doubt every man over thirty was "old" to her, with her mat of overly golden curls, and her real eyebrows shaved off and others painted on, à la Hollywood. And dad was silly too, enjoying talking to that girl! But Mrs. Ferguson wouldn't say a word if he was late—she was only too glad to have his set, industrious routine broken. Every deviation from it was to be adroitly and preciously guarded.

Their kitchen was rather dark. The front room got the sunshine. There was no real dining room in this apartment. Mrs. Ferguson had persuaded Fred to let her set the table in the living room instead of in the kitchen nook, it was so much pleasanter. That seemed to him rather a frivolous way of doing; but he was getting very indulgent. "You fix things the way you want to, Annie, you're the one." It was more like play, eating in here. She set the little gate-legged table with the bright Mexican cloth she had bought one day when she was shopping with Dorothy. The dishes were all good enough in this place, but they were perfectly ordinary. Mrs. Ferguson secretly made pretty little additions to them from time to time, trusting Fred not to take notice. Well, he had told her that this time belonged to her. She was justified in doing as she pleased.

He was back on time. He was getting to be a great devotee of the paper, read it from cover to cover. His wife was amused to see that he didn't even miss the movie items. The fashion notes were about all that he passed up. Sometimes he would say, "Here, Annie, here's a show you might like to see—Rosemary would enjoy it." He had always considered the movies a waste of time at home, and put them with the things that were undermining the churches. Jesse joked, and said that dad was developing leisure tastes, and losing his morale. Dorothy was too tender to make fun of him. She smiled, but she kissed the top of her father's head, softly rubbing her cheek against the thin hair. Perhaps she knew too much about leisure tastes by now! She seemed to be more anxious for her dad to have a good time than her mother. Mrs. Ferguson resented that a little. Jesse and Dorothy both seemed to trust her to enjoy herself— or maybe they didn't think she had worked, and was in such need of enjoyment; but they were always thinking up things for dad. The boys would have been tender of *her* . . . only both the boys were lost to her. Yes, Carl too. Since that unfortunate time—of which none of them directly spoke—Carl had taken the reins of his life in his own hands. His smile, gentle and affectionate, admitted a secret distance from his mother, which she must help him to maintain.

The place was pleasant at this hour. They liked having their breakfast to themselves. They had suffered more than they would have admitted from the cramped quarters at Dorothy's. Poor child!—so anxious to make everything nice for them, and knowing all the time that they were uncomfortable. Mrs. Ferguson had been taken with those little Spanish-style apartments in the court that Jesse had shown them. But of course she hadn't expected Fred to like those. He had accepted this apartment with relief—it was more like home, not so "crazy." It was one of the two upper apartments in a large shingled frame house with palm trees and a border of enormous geraniums on the lawn. It stood on a nice wide street, one of the older streets,

631

that looked as if middlewesterners had settled there. It had their own atmosphere—too much of it for Mrs. Ferguson's taste! The rooms were large, with good ordinary furnishings, nothing attractive but "all in good shape"—that was what men noticed in a place, workable and adequate equipment, not charm. "Now, Annie," Fred had said with satisfaction, "we've got everything we need here." He didn't want her to spend her time on housework, she was to take it easy. But she couldn't help making little purchases, putting on new cushion covers, getting the place to seem more homelike. She couldn't stand something just adequate and no more.

They sat long at their meal. Dad was finishing the paper. Mrs. Ferguson tried to get a glimpse of the shopping items as he read. But she didn't really like to go downtown alone—and of course she wouldn't have dad hanging around waiting for her; there was nothing he hated worse than that. It disappointed her that she and Dorothy could so seldom go shopping together. She had looked forward to long happy days. It was a job taking Peter; and Dorothy couldn't often get away. Jesse wanted her to get help; but as she said (with a touch of indignation) what was the use being hard up, if they still had everything they pleased! In a way, Dorothy actually relished their situation!—again like Grandma Ferguson, who had liked to feel that she had grim, hard tasks on hand. But if she counted on its changing Jesse in any essential way (as her mother surmised that she did) she would be disappointed. And surely the grandfather would leave them money. Why couldn't Dorothy take things as they came? Mrs. Ferguson had tacitly put aside any real shopping until she was with Louie. She was getting more and more secretly anxious to be with Louie. They enjoyed their nice breakfast, with the orange juice, and the muffins. Fred had said they would get some of their meals at a place nearby; but when she saw with what relief he returned to her cooking, she couldn't hold him to that. Secretly she resented cooking a single meal. Wasn't this her vacation? Fred liked to make excursions to the markets, to pick out the meat as he did at home, to select the fruit and vegetables, smoothing the pears carefully with his hand, satisfying himself that each one he paid his money for was the best possible value. And she couldn't interfere, for he had to have something to do. Much of her time was occupied in subtle attempts to keep him contented and occupied. Her own activities—although this was *her* vacation—had to be slipped around the edges.

They heard the bell.

"Is that ours?"

Before they could get up, they heard feet running up the stairs. Jesse appeared, handsome, and fresh as the morning, in the doorway.

"Hello, there, folks! Well, you're getting to be great dawdlers. I thought I'd find you through breakfast and dad out sprinkling the lawn."

"Oh, we're not so much earlier than you are."

Jesse agreed cheerfully when they asked him to sit down with them. "Mother, you know I never refuse any of your cooking." He ate the muffins that were left with unabashed appetite. Mrs. Ferguson thought again how young he was. She couldn't resist his big, healthy, handsome presence. Even the clothes he wore—the thick rough suit of English tweed— gave her a feeling of elation. She felt still more impatient with Dorothy—why couldn't she be satisfied, and take things as they came, when she had a husband as attractive as this!

"Well, mother, I've come to lure your husband from you."

Dad looked dismayed.

Mrs. Ferguson was instantly on Jesse's side—and dad knew it. She tried not to show it in her face.

"Aren't you going to the office?" Mr. Ferguson asked. That was what he had elected to call Jesse's "shoppe."

"No office today. Only three dames coming and Mark can handle them. I only take the good-looking ones."

Jesse grinned. His mother-in-law smiled forgivingly. Dad made no comment.

No, Jesse said, he had to take a drive—go out and see some of his unproductive property; and he'd thought maybe dad would give him the pleasure and consolation of his company.

"Where's that?" Mr. Ferguson asked.

633

"Oh, a sort of dude ranch I own shares in, out in the desert," Jesse answered carelessly.

They hadn't known Jesse owned such property. He had all kinds of irons in the fire—all of them white elephants in the present beautiful state of affairs, as he said cheerfully. At the same time, he laughed at the business prospects of southern California—surely not the way to regard his own community, Mr. Ferguson thought. He told about the grafts, but wherever he himself thought there was a chance, he said with good-natured cynicism, why not? As well I as another. Sure, it's all a graft. It wasn't a way of doing business that they understood; but Jesse came of a moneyed family, so they were half respectful.

"Isn't that a pretty long drive?" Mr. Ferguson asked cautiously.

"Oh, no, only about a hundred miles."

Mrs. Ferguson kept discreetly silent, knowing that Jesse's "about" might mean a hundred and fifty. Jesse never set minimums.

"Why shouldn't you go, dad?"

There was no reason why; and so, to her pleasure, she saw him forced to consent. Jesse said he would enjoy seeing the ranch. There weren't many dudes, worse luck, but it was swell country. Dad said he didn't think much of the desert.

"Oh, Fred, you know you liked that place where we stopped!"

Mrs. Ferguson would have enjoyed going far more; but she perceived that Jesse was sidestepping the idea of asking her. Now he came out with the reason. Dot's bridge club met this afternoon, he said, and he thought maybe mother would keep the children—if she could stand the little rascals.

"Oh, of course," she said at once.

"Yes, mama'd be glad to do that," dad asserted, with relief.

Maybe she would and maybe she wouldn't! It didn't exactly please her, if they had known it, this readiness of the menfolks to think she enjoyed nothing better than doing things for them all!

But anyway, she wanted Fred to go. Jesse said, stopping and

giving her hand a squeeze, he was going to run off with mother one of these days! He'd thought she wouldn't enjoy this long drive (oh, wouldn't she!—a lot more than dad would) but some time he was going to make off with her, and they wouldn't tell any of them where they were going, either. She understood the cajolery. But still she was flattered by his touch, and his good looks.

"Well, Annie, what'll you do this morning, before the children come?"

Oh, she'd get along.

Maybe she could go over and see those people from Dike, he suggested.

She didn't reply—but she didn't intend to do anything of the kind.

From the front window, she watched the two drive off together, with very mixed feelings. It gave her a little thrill, the nonchalant ease with which her son-in-law handled the low-slung car. Even Carl didn't have that light hand on the wheel.

Mrs. Ferguson let the dishes stand. She settled down in the big chair to read the Woman's Page at her leisure.

But she didn't want recipes. She was sick of cooking! She had a feeling of forlornness. Not that she had wanted Fred to stay. No, there was a sweet, secretive, rare sensation in having this whole morning to herself. Fred never enjoyed things much if she wasn't with him. But she wanted to do things without *him,* sometimes—it gave her a sense of freedom and expansion, a hidden relief. She was always aware of his inclinations when she was with him—while he was so often innocent of hers. It made her angry to think of the easy way in which Jesse had turned the children over to her. No doubt his inviting dad to go off was partly a sop. Of course, she wanted Dorothy to have a good time. Her feeling horrified her. She remembered when she was a child, a tender-hearted little girl loving her dolls and all living things. How dreadful it had seemed to her to see the cat, their old three-colored cat, slap away the kittens when she had "got through with them." She used to scold the cat, spank her (very gently), try to make

635

her return to her offspring. "Why, kitty, your *own* kittens!" And now, was *she* like that? Were people all just animals, subject in spite of themselves to nature? It was against all her beliefs about herself. No, it wasn't quite like that. Sitting here alone in the quiet room, she felt it, deep within herself, as a kind of strangled striking back against a deep, subtle hurt her children had given her—yes, all her children.

Those people from Dike! She didn't intend to be saddled with them. Well, she thought rebelliously, she had always tried to be nice to her neighbors. She had never let herself act superior to Mrs. Dunn, although—oh, dear! And now she ought to have a little time for herself. She hardened herself against the thought of the old couple's pathos. The pathos itself was an irritation—to her, the soft-hearted! But this was where she had come to have a good time. There was a callousness even in this empty golden sunshine; and with that she allied herself. She had so little time left . . . that was what she felt now, like a sudden step into cold shadow . . . except for this winter sunshine, in which the roses bloomed, which she could believe lengthened the time endlessly. Thought for others belonged at home, along with responsibility. Those people from Dike did, too, and that was one reason why she avoided them. They were like Mrs. Rist, Essie Bartlett, all the old couples in the church. She had faithfully filled her rôle there, as Mrs. Ferguson, but these had never been her own kind of people. The old couple lived a few streets away, in a dreary little frame bungalow with a drooping banana tree in front. They had come up to the Fergusons when the car was parked one day, because they had seen the Iowa license. And of course, that was enough for dad! They were out here all by themselves. The old man had chronic bronchitis. Their children had got together to enable them to spend the winter in California. And now here they were, and roses were blooming, and they didn't know what to do with themselves. Dike! that they talked about. She had never seen it, but she felt she knew just how the place looked—the scrubby little town, with only the main street paved; even the bleak house where those people lived, beside a row of evergreens. They had no car, and dad thought he must take them places. "Maybe those people from Dike would like to go along," he was always suggesting uneasily. They had come to be dreadfully typical figures, to Mrs. Ferguson—with their sad, vacant presence, the old lady in her cotton stockings, the old man with his mournful cough. Lately they had joined, they called it "united with," an evangelistic sect, and they were always trying to get her and dad to attend one of the meetings. They talked solemnly about the second coming of Christ, sadly and patiently, with an empty hope, looking for that to free them from all their troubles, to prove that after all they *were* better than happier people. Although they were what dad called "good people," Mrs. Ferguson always felt embarrassed, even shocked, at such references. Religion oughtn't to come into everyday conversation. The old couple counted on the Fergusons as their link with home.

"No, I won't get tied up in that again!"

She rose rebelliously. The light in the bedroom was somewhat dim. She saw herself in the mirror, in her trim housedress, wearing the pretty old-blue sweater that Lillian had knitted for her. Her looks were not entirely gone. Beside the old lady from Dike, she was a pretty, fashionable young lady! She thought of the elated excitement of their departure from Belmond—the neighbors, the good-byes, herself in her new hat and with Mrs. Morgan's flowers pinned to her fur collar. Perhaps this was the perfect time, at last, that she had seen shining ahead of her all the years—no matter how they had been driven to embark upon it. She had never really stopped believing in such a time. What she wanted was something for herself—before it was too late—just herself, in relation to no one else, in no other capacity. Oh, for this little while, she didn't want to know it, if other people had troubles! She knew that she had had a pleasant life, but had she ever really taken time to *enjoy* herself? She felt as if she were—not renewing her youth—but returning to an old phase of herself, where she had left off when she was married. If this holiday should turn out to be a disappointment, then in some subtle way it would infuse all her personal life with disappointment . . . the life that still hiddenly existed apart from her children.

She trembled at her own hardness. It made her feel as if she had been a fraud all her days. In some ways, she had! To offset it, she went to get the tea-rose sweater that she was knitting for Rosemary.

There was a knock at the door. Oh dear, if it was that old lady—! She wouldn't be able to help acting cordial and pleased. She could only be hard when she was alone. Then she recognized a cough outside the door, and called gladly, "Come in!"

"Well, so she's a widow lady this morning!"

"Yes, I'm a widow."

"I saw that man of yours go off!"

"I haven't even washed my dishes—" Mrs. Ferguson began.

"Oh, now, dearie, don't you go apologizing for that. Not to *me*. I'm not one of these snoopy neighbors. I guess you know that by this time. I never wash my dishes until I feel like it, anyway."

Only too well did Mrs. Ferguson believe that! She had once caught a sight of the kitchen next door.

This was their neighbor, Miss Marcella Potter. She had the other apartment upstairs. She was a large, somewhat masculine-looking woman, and unplaceable as far as they could see. The Fergusons couldn't just make out what her business was, except that she had a remote connection with some real estate office, and sometimes spoke with great enthusiasm of avocado lands. She often referred to Portland, Maine, but she seemed to be evasive when they asked, with natural curiosity, whether that was where she "came from." She said largely, "Oh, my dear, I couldn't begin to tell you where all *I've* lived." Once, it seemed, she had been a nurse; and at one time, a sort of preacher. Her apartment, into which Mrs. Ferguson had only once been invited, was as heterogeneous as her experience. Antiques were mingled with ordinary overstuffed chairs, draperies of the nineties, ancient sentimental pictures that had been relegated to other folks' attics for years, framed poems of Edgar Guest, a German soldier's helmet, some valuable English Wedgwood, and all of it cluttered and dusty and jammed together in such a way as made Mrs. Ferguson gasp. But she must have some money from somewhere, Mr. Ferguson had shrewdly surmised. The men laughed at Miss Potter, Jesse especially. She *was* a funny mixture. She had a heavy face, and quite a mustache, but her hair was waved and done in elaborate coils; and she wore heavy silk dresses, of expensive goods, although in the general style of 1912, and rings and bracelets that looked both valuable and old. Nevertheless, Mrs. Ferguson enjoyed her, and defended her against Jesse and dad. Dad said he hadn't seen mama take to a person so much in years. Miss Potter seemed to have taken mama under her wing, so that once dad said slyly, "Well, mama, that lady seems to be sweet on you—if she was a man, I'd have to be getting jealous." Mrs. Ferguson scoffed at him. But all the same, she found flattery and comfort in Miss Potter's attentions. And it was interesting to talk to Miss Potter, she declared. She knew a lot of nice recipes—yes, she did; but you could never tell when, in the midst of shrewd sensible talk, she was coming out with some highflown notion that took your breath away—if you could believe it. And it seemed that Miss Potter did.

"Well, what's my little lady going to do with herself, when she's all deserted?"

"Oh—nothing much. I'm going to keep the children when my daughter goes to her bridge club this afternoon."

"That's good," Miss Potter approved, sitting down and stretching her legs. Miss Potter was a firm believer in children and large families, she often said. ("Why don't she get some of her own, then?" Fred had once suggested.) "Well, she's a dear little mother, isn't she—you can tell that to look at her. She doesn't often go and leave them, doesn't gad around like all these women do now, as if they weren't mothers!"

"Oh, Dorothy's a very good mother. I like to have her get out."

"I wish she'd let me take her to my doctor," Miss Potter suggested firmly, with a gleam of the eye. "He'd put some flesh on her in no time. I've known him to build people up as much as twenty pounds in two weeks! He has his own method, dearie—it goes back to the ancient tribes. Oh, these little mothers, it's hard on them." She sighed voluptuously. "You ought to go to him too, little lady."

"I?" Mrs. Ferguson laughed, flustered. "Oh, there isn't anything the matter with me."

Miss Potter shook her head wisely, and sucked in her lips.

Mrs. Ferguson tried to laugh again. She knew that Miss Potter might be said to have her peculiarities; but all the same, she was flattered by these admiring attentions. It was a new thing to find someone who wouldn't let her do anything on her side, but wanted to do things for *her*. When she had gone with a plate of cookies to Miss Potter's door, in duteous exchange for gifts of dates, health candies, and vegetized breads, Miss Potter had pushed her straight out into the hall exclaiming, "Oh now, my dear little lady, you aren't going to cook anything for me—you're here to rest and recover your strength, and I'm just going to see that you *do* it!" Dad might grumble uneasily, "What kind of an invalid does she think you are?" But all the same, there was something flattering in such treatment. As a "dear little mother," Miss Potter thought that she was entitled to soothing and building up for the rest of her days. Miss Potter was horrified at the notion that they should ever go back to Belmond. "Why, it would be the death of you!" Miss Potter treated her as if she were a fragile thing, almost too tender to be about in the world—at corners, took her arm and swept her across the street, landing her safe but breathless. "There! I'm not going to have *you* run over."

Now Miss Potter pitied her richly for being alone; and Mrs. Ferguson, although she had the grace to be ashamed, knowing well that poor dad hadn't wanted to go, still couldn't help reveling in this attitude and responding.

"If hubby's out enjoying himself," Miss Potter now said— and there was severity in her tone, "why shouldn't we go on a little toot of our own? I can't have this little ladykins getting lonesome!"

The children—Mrs. Ferguson said weakly; but Miss Potter declared that they would be back in plenty of time. Oh, she wouldn't keep the *little ones* waiting! "No, my dear, I never forget the children." Miss Potter left her to get ready, to put on her best things in some kind of confused but happy expectation.

"Oh, here's her ladyship ally ally ready!" Miss Potter herself had appeared in a velvet picture hat weighted with feathers. *There* . . . she adjusted her charge's coat and buttoned it for her. "Why, she's just too pretty for words in that little *shappeau*. I don't see how hubby can let you out of his sight!"

Mrs. Ferguson tried to laugh. She felt guilty for letting Miss Potter talk as if dad were a careless gadabout. But all the same she liked it. She had the feeling that it was coming to her. She knew she didn't deserve pity on just these lines, but perhaps she was a little tired of being told that she had a good husband. Ella thought, too good! As for the being pretty and all, it was nonsense—but people *did* use to say such things about her. There was that young principal at the Teachers' Institute—and there had been others. Fred seemed to have forgotten such things, that once they had been her due; and the children had never imagined them! Unless Carl . . . and that she had to deny herself, tremblingly fearful for her son's good and happiness. She didn't want the praise of some other man. She had sense enough to know herself too old for such business. And besides—she was unable to imagine anyone besides dad. But she didn't see how it could hurt anybody if she let Miss Potter give her a little admiration!

Miss Potter's car was waiting—a good, but somewhat battered sedan. Miss Potter made the arrangements with elaborate care for her little lady's comfort, making Mrs. Ferguson feel fragile and small.

"There—let's fix that cushion—that's right. Now, all comfy, sweetness?"

Oh, yes, Mrs. Ferguson said, she was fine.

If any of the others had seen her, she would have felt foolish. But there weren't any of them around. She looked out happily as they drove along, feeling more at ease with someone else driving than with dad. The gold of the winter sunshine exhilarated her. She could never get over the romantic delight of the exotic trees and flowers. She loved to drive past all the nice houses and imagine what they were like inside.

641

"Now, we're going to have just as much fun on *our* drive as that hubby of yours is having," Miss Potter said piously.

Mrs. Ferguson blushed.

She caught her breath at the hills. After all, she wasn't so sure with a woman driving. She had a boundless distrust for as well as a boundless alliance with her own sex. But Miss Potter, breathing a little heavily, handled the car with reckless assurance. Miss Potter pointed out the beauties of the city, dilating upon them in true Californian style. When they exclaimed over the charms of a Spanish house set back in bowers of greenery, "That's the kind of place *you* ought to have," Miss Potter declared. "I can just see you in a place like that." She was going to show her little lady the glories of the land, and then she would never lose her. And it was true—Mrs. Ferguson felt the settled sanctities of the house at home fading in the sunshine.

"And now we're going to see the greatest sight on God's earth," Miss Potter said solemnly. "Do you know what it is?"

Mrs. Ferguson wasn't sure.

"The ocean, my dear."

"Oh—oh, yes."

They stopped the car at a point near the beach. It was not crowded at this time of year. A lonely man sat out on the sand. The gulls clustered at a place near the rocks. Mrs. Ferguson looked uneasily at them. They were like chickens and pigeons combined, she thought. It frightened her to think of their making their home on the waters. She felt that she ought to be thinking great thoughts instead of nervously taking refuge in details. Miss Potter would expect it of her. She watched the long breaking of the waves.

"Do you know what that power is?" Miss Potter demanded solemnly. "It's the power of God. Every one of those waves is the beating of His great heart."

Mrs. Ferguson said nothing. This kind of talk always made her feel embarrassed. It was different with the prayers in church —prayers belonged there, were an established part of "the service." Yet she *did* need something. Yes, she, however fortunate, was faintly embittered, lost, and alone. She looked out over the silvery expanse. Its immensity frightened her, making her quickly draw back her gaze. She could see no reassuring land. All the waste of water seemed to come out of emptiness. Beyond there was . . . nothing but China. She had a moment of believing that fearful things, *the worst,* might have reality—something with which her love for her children, and Fred's love for her, and their standing in their own community, were not able to cope. Of course, she nervously admitted this was beautiful. But it held some challenge that she couldn't meet. She wanted sheltered places. When her children were born, somehow she had lost that kind of courage—except for *them.* She didn't know how to explain.

Miss Potter took her hand protectingly.

She said in her deepest tones, "I want you to drink in God's power. Take it back with you to your little home. When those dear children come this afternoon, they will feel that grandma has a new strength to give them. That's why I brought you to this holy ground."

Well, perhaps it was true. Oh, yes, she *did* need something. There was a mysterious shining in the silver emptiness. All the same, she was glad when they drove back among houses again.

Miss Potter insisted on taking her to luncheon and picking out the foods most suited to her bone structure. "That's very important, my dear. We have to think of the material man as well as the spiritual. Be all-rounded beings. Don't we?" Mrs. Ferguson didn't like all of the foods; but still, it was fun eating new things. And maybe there was something in what Miss Potter said about the bone structure. Who could tell? Doctors didn't know everything.

She got home just in time to take off her things before Dorothy and the children came. She felt strangely elated with her excursion, as she hurriedly put away in the cooler the gifts of health-building fruits with which Miss Potter had showered her. She was half ashamed, half laughing; took off the pink camellia flower Miss Potter had pinned to her dress, telling her it was like her "own dainty self"; yet she felt a sense of renewed girlhood—a pleasant soothing of something long unsatisfied. She had already half decided that she wouldn't tell the others. As she took off her new hat in the bedroom, and loosened her hair, she gave her head a little toss. "Well, I don't care!" A subtle smile curved her lips. Something remained from her glimpse of the ocean—disturbing, or illuminating—she didn't know . . .

Dorothy was distressed because Jesse had asked her to keep the children.

"Why, my child, you know I *like* to do it. Of course you're going to go."

She *did* feel a mysterious strength—whether it was the ocean, or what. Now she really looked forward freshly to the afternoon with the children. But she intended to have a good time with them—she wouldn't pay too much attention to Dorothy's careful modern regulations.

Dorothy was looking curiously at her. "Mother, you look great," she said suddenly. "I believe vacation agrees with you."

Vacation—yes, they were very anxious for her to have a vacation! "Oh, I've been outdoors a little while," Mrs. Ferguson said vaguely.

Dorothy was wearing a smart little costume, with her hair waved and brushed glossily back, a dash of geranium-colored lipstick on her soft mouth. But her mother thought this mode didn't agree with her so well as the more girlish styles. Dorothy wasn't exactly meant for it. She noted again the slight strain in Dorothy's thin face. But she wouldn't listen when Dorothy tried to suggest that she would rather stay here than go to the bridge club. She knew that Jesse liked to have Dorothy go to things, and she wouldn't abet her daughter in her relaxation. And she herself felt impatient at the idea of her pretty child turning into too much of a homebody. That wasn't the way people did things out here! But she felt all too much wary compassion for Dorothy—she knew too well what being wife and mother meant, to have her own concerns sunk beneath those of others, submerged but still uneasily alive, as she herself might have testified—the delicately shaded fibs, the valiant lies that kept things smooth, and other people happy . . . she felt as if she had just risen out of that into possession of herself again. Oh, she approved Dorothy, disapproved Margaret, but all the same she could have told Dorothy some things!

She didn't lose that renewed feeling all day. She seemed to manage the children easily. They recognized some kind of seasoned maternal authority in her. After all, she wasn't wholly dependent on her family's consideration! When she and Jesse took that excursion, if they ever did, she might show him that his mother-in-law wasn't such a poor companion. Dad wouldn't be along, holding her back. That subtle smile lurked in her lips. They would laugh about today—the health-food restaurant and all. Well, she wouldn't tell them. She could say, if necessary, that she "took a little ride." Of course, there wasn't anything to keep from them. It was just that they didn't need to know.

4

The Fergusons were in Pasadena now, at Louie's and Henry's. They were up in their beautiful bedroom, getting ready for dinner. Their suitcases were where the maid had neatly and discreetly placed them, convenient, but not too much in sight. The maid had offered to unpack for them, but Mrs. Ferguson had refused, with a quick deprecating smile, knowing that Fred wouldn't like it. They would do it later themselves. Anyway, she felt, now she had seen the house, that her things, although nice enough, were not quite equal to what Mrs. Sands' sister should have. She couldn't seem to get down to the business of dressing. At first she had simply walked softly about the room, looking at the lacy bedspread, the pastel cushions, the charming ornaments here and there, drawing aside the curtains to look out at the little Spanish balcony—until Fred got uneasy and said, "Annie, you ought to get ready." How lovely everything was! She couldn't get over it. And they could stay here as long as they pleased, without feeling they were making trouble, since Louie had plenty of help. She sat down at the princess dressing table between the tall candlesticks of thick creamy ware. Every movement was a delight, with such beautiful things surrounding her. She had not truly known until this moment—or not admitted—the desire for luxury that had always been part of her. If she had been staying with strangers, she might have been oppressed and shy. But with Louie, her own dear sister, she could let out her delight and revel in her surroundings.

She warned Fred, "We'll have to put on our best things tonight, dad."

"Well, it won't take *me* long to choose," he answered dryly.

Mrs. Ferguson was in a state of soft excitement. Her face looked flushed and youthful in this becoming light. She was happy in calling attention to the lovely things, even if all she could get from Fred was a cautious, "Yes, pretty nice, all right." She felt an elated sense of possession since all this belonged to Louie. She was with *her* people. *She* had relatives too. A thrust of impatience went through her at the thought of Ella. How had she ever stood Ella and her flat comments all these years? . . . although a sort of sad remembrance sank down into her when she thought of Ben, and the little group standing out in front of the house telling them good-bye. But now she had the proud feeling of coming into her own.

She put on her black-and-white georgette. At home, it looked very nice. Here it was ordinary. Her only jewelry was the string of artificial pearls, and of course her wedding and engagement rings.

"Oh, I wish I had something nicer!"

"What's the matter with this? You look nice enough for anybody."

"Oh, Fred, but Louie—!"

Still, she felt like a different person—a different person, and yet never so much herself. She answered happily when the maid knocked at the door.

"Are you ready, Fred?"

"You're the one. I didn't have much getting ready to do."

Oh, if Fred was going to be dry and sarcastic about the place—! He had never wanted to acknowledge that she had a family just as much as he did. His family had always been "the folks." Still, there was Henry. Fred respected his business success.

646

She would never forget her first sight of the house looming before them in the misty twilight, when she had realized that this was where they were going to stay! She felt lapped in noiseless comfort. The little place in San Diego she now regarded with a shudder—those people from Dike—with a pang of stifled remorse at the thought of Dorothy courageously meeting the conditions of her new home. But the children could get along without her, no matter what Jesse said. Jesse would have liked "the folks" to stay as a convenient anchor for himself and Dorothy! Mrs. Ferguson had felt that clearly through all his flattering cajoleries. And she didn't *want* to be thought of like that. She had had enough of it.

She went down the stairs into the great living room. Louie's place in Kansas City had been lovely. It had always been an excitement to think of visiting Aunt Louie. But it was nothing like this! Here, in this new house, they all seemed to have entered a different plane of existence. Tonight the place had a Christmas air, from the bright fire of logs in the fireplace, in spite of the flowers blooming outside. The front window, huge and theatrical, looked out upon misty twilight, its heavy curtains only partly drawn.

Louie came to meet them now. Mrs. Ferguson was proud that this was her sister. How well she fitted the place, giving its newness an air of soft dignity—her fine ample figure in the long-sleeved lace gown of delicate color, with the elegant soft simplicity that was her note. This was little Louie Luers, who had been born in Woodside, Ohio! Annie thought of her in fat buttoned shoes, with blond bangs unevenly cut. Louie, the child of the gentle, simple father and mother from "the old country"—and she had become this beautiful woman! Louie put her arm lovingly around Annie and kissed her again. An aroma of delicate fragrance, expensive, and subtly personal, breathed from her lacy clothes. Annie noticed the dull gleam of the pearl earrings that set off the light-brown waves of her hair, now grained with wavy streaks of silver.

"Oh, Louie, I think this is the most beautiful house I've ever seen!"

647

"Oh, do you, Annie?" Louie was gentle and deprecating. "There are so many Spanish houses—still, we like it."

They moved to the window together and looked off at the distant airy glitter of lights.

"You look so young, Louie!"

"I?" Louie was deprecating again. She gave a little laugh and a shrug. "Oh dear, Annie, I'm afraid you won't think so by daylight!"

"Yes, I will," her sister asserted indignantly.

Mrs. Ferguson sighed, she scarcely knew why. How Margaret would enjoy this, she couldn't help thinking with triumph. If Margaret had been willing to stay with them, *she* might have been enjoying this too. Mrs. Ferguson thrust back her old pain and confusion at the remembrance of her exiled daughter.

Henry, small and dry, was still the host. His riches conferred authority upon him. Almost aggressively insignificant as he looked, the others listened to him with respect.

"Dinner is served, Mrs. Sands."

"Thank you, Joan."

They moved into the candlelighted dining room.

Annie's state of soft excitement was lifted almost to ecstasy by the roses, the delicate glitter of crystal and silver on heavy lace. She felt more than ever as if she had stepped into a story in which she had always dreamed of taking part. With a small motion of dignity, she let Henry seat her. If she had been visiting anyone else, she would have gathered all the details to write to Mrs. Viele; but she couldn't with Louie, her own sister, it would have sounded like boasting. Still, she might work them in. It was all like a play. Even the maid had a touch of theatricality. The golden shade of her hair seemed marvelous by candlelight, swept back and falling fluffily about her neck. Only a glimpse of her heavy ankles spoiled the vision at times. But everything was almost too beautiful to be true!

"She looks like Greta Garbo," Annie said to Louie, when the maid left the room.

"Oh, they all do, more or less!" Louie said. She laughed.

"I'm sure her real name isn't Joan. She calls it Jo-*ann*. I don't doubt she has dreams of the movies."

"She really looks pretty enough."

"Oh, Annie! You won't think so tomorrow. And the time that girl spends on herself—it's all she does when she's off duty. Well, thank heaven, the cook at least is no Garbo. She's really a treasure."

She certainly was. The food was delicious. Annie looked once or twice at Fred to be sure he wasn't leaving the wonderful mushroom soup because of the whipped cream. But he was eating valiantly, and without comment. At home, when she and the girls had tried using candles at dinner, he had always observed, "Well, are we back to candles again?" Mrs. Ferguson sighed luxuriously, as she broke her dainty bread stick. Now she would have Fred off her mind. He would have Henry. She could give herself up to sheer enjoyment of Louie and luxury.

The dark red roses and the green candles gave the table a festival air.

"We've put off our Christmas to celebrate with you," Louie explained. "Oh, Annie, we did so hope you could be here!"

Annie explained eagerly—Dorothy wouldn't hear of their going, the children would have been disappointed. Louie agreed, with her soft consoling acquiescence, her sympathy that seemed almost to breathe a fragrance. She asked after the children lovingly.

"Oh, they're all right. Rosemary is so pretty."

Annie felt that she couldn't stop to explain now. Louie thought the children were still living in their own house. She didn't want to spoil the festivity of this meal. But she looked forward voluptuously to a long talk with Louie in which she could unburden herself of all her accumulated anxieties, finding someone at last with whom she could be completely at home. Tears almost came to her eyes, as she felt the happiness of this reunion, that seemed not to have a jarring note.

She felt the past drop away from her. Here they were, all four of them, who had been young people together, having reached the leisure and ease and prosperity which was the certain reward of their time of life, and tonight enjoying it.

"Annie, you aren't eating anything!"

"Yes, I am. I'm almost too happy to eat. It's so good to see both of you again."

She had put in the "both" politely. But Henry now said with unexpected gallantry, "Better still for us!"

The wonderful meal was over. Annie couldn't have told just what there was,—the meal was a dream of delicately flavored delicious things, the tinkle of ice as the "glamorous" maid poured the water into the crystal goblets, the mint-steeped drink into the tall glasses, the placing and removal of the lovely dishes. Louie said they would have their coffee in the living room. Annie gave a quick glance at Fred. She was so afraid he was going to say that they didn't drink coffee at night. But he said nothing. She gave another luxurious sigh. She felt rebelliously that she didn't care whether she slept tonight or not. The meal was perfect, and she was going to enjoy every bit of it.

The sense of festivity remained as they seated themselves in the beautiful living room, she and Louie together on the wide low couch. Annie didn't care what the coffee might do to her, when she could drink it from these exquisite rose and gilt cups.

"Louie, you have all different dishes!" she exclaimed.

Yes, they had started new out here, Louie said. They had kept only a few of their old things. They might as well—the things were scarcely worth moving (think of being able to say that!); and although at another time she might have been shocked at the easy abandonment of all those nice furnishings, Annie now happily agreed. She felt rebelliously that *she* didn't care whether she ever saw anything at home again. *She* wanted to start new. If her lovely daughter (who had married the handsome prince) hadn't quite been able to hold her part as heroine of the fairy tale, Louie could almost take over the rôle.

Henry offered Fred cigars. Of course dad refused! "No, I guess not, Henry." Mrs. Ferguson felt a slight sense of impatience. In spite of the traditional feeling against the evils of tobacco, which she had always supposed she shared, now she realized the pleasant manly elegance of the blue twist of fragrant smoke rising from Henry's excellent cigar. But of course she couldn't hope to change dad! It was marvelous enough that he had eaten the whipped cream, and not carefully pushed aside the dressing on his salad to find the bare unadorned pieces of fruit underneath. Now the night beyond the great window had become a startling darkness that held a dramatic suggestion of mountains and sea—but they were secure, in this lovely room.

The whole evening was a sort of dream. It was New Year's Eve. There seemed a beautiful omen in that. What should they do? Louie asked. She had thought they would wait and see what Annie and Fred felt like doing.

"I hope you haven't refused any invitations because of us!"

"Why, Annie Luers, where would I want to go, when you were coming?"

They both laughed at the familiar name.

There were dozens of things going on tonight. But Louie had thought perhaps they wouldn't care for the noisier places. Fred said hastily that they wouldn't. Annie was well aware that he would rather have stayed right here, but this time she wasn't going to help him out. They couldn't get an admission out of him of what he would prefer. "Whatever you folks have planned." And they didn't know what a concession *that* was! Louie said finally, well, they might drive through the Mile of Christmas Trees. "That's a terribly folksy suggestion! Still, I *have* heard it's rather pretty." Annie thought it would be wonderful. Then they could just come back here, and talk, and perhaps hear some good music on the radio.

"But maybe you're too tired to go out."

Annie hurriedly disclaimed that. In spite of the long drive, with so many cars on the road because it was holiday time, she felt as if she could do anything. Louie might call the Mile of Christmas Trees folksy; but it was something that her friends at home would want to hear about.

She went happily to put on her fur coat. They might as well be dressed warmly, Henry had warned. It was colder than it looked at night. Oh, not really cold, Louie scoffed gently. "I don't believe Henry would be warm anywhere!"

Henry made no comment. But Annie put on her fur coat anyway. It was so much the nicest one she had. The flowers Miss Potter had given her on leaving—an odd assortment— were all wilted. She unpinned them and put them into the enameled wastebasket, making a queer little face. Now that strange companionship was so far away it seemed as if it had never been. She remembered, with a kind of wonder, half flattered and half embarrassed, Miss Potter's grief at seeing her go, tears dripping from her jowls as she went out with them to the car. She had made Fred angry with her warnings about taking care of the little lady. "Does she think I'm going to upset you?" he had wanted to know. "I guess I've taken care of you a good many more years than she has, and nothing's happened to you yet!" He had actually been jealous at the end! The subtle smile curved Annie's lips as she smoothed the fur where the flowers had been pinned. Still, she was glad to have that companionship over. It had become—well, just a little *too*—

At that, she was ready before the others. Jo-ann had come softly in, with a discreet but haughty air, and the stiff rich curtains were drawn. It was the start of the New Year. People were beginning to speak of change and trouble and suffering; but Annie, in the comfort of Louie's house, would not believe it. The curtains shut out everything unhappy from the warm spacious quiet of this lovely room. This night *was* like the beginning of a fairy tale. What she had first felt in the golden air was coming true.

The drive seemed to her the most fairylike of all. At times, she felt herself wanting to share all this with the children. But she checked herself. Why shouldn't she have something of her own? She and Fred were not *only* parents. Often Fred used to tell her that. Now *she* was the one. Fred was worrying still over the incomprehensibleness of Jesse's wide and handsome but seemingly "unsolid" business transactions. He wondered how Bun was "making out" in the city back there. Annie didn't want to be reminded of these things! Now she and Fred were with their own contemporaries. And certainly there was nothing relegated about Louie! The children were dear,

652

but they were Dorothy's. She wouldn't feel responsible for them. She would only enjoy them. We can have some fun too, was what she thought.

They had scarcely heard the big, dark, gleaming car roll up the driveway. Annie felt still more luxuriously lapped and sheltered in the softly upholstered interior.

"You don't do the driving, Henry?" she heard Fred ask.

"No, I let Percy take care of that."

Percy, Louie explained in a murmur, was their man of all work—making a little face at Annie to express her amusement at the name. They could see that he was colored. "All our servants have such imposing names—except cook, bless her heart, she's just plain Bessie.

"Well, we really need a chauffeur," Louie explained further. "Henry can't take me everywhere I go."

Annie hastily and sympathetically agreed.

She was impressed by the way in which her sister spoke of "servants," as if they were a special class. Not at all the way in which she thought of Mrs. Entwhistle—or of dear Mrs. Christianson! But she thought that Louie had the right.

The car went purring out and down the curving driveway between the dark exotic shrubs and trees.

"I want you to see this in the morning, Annie. This whole slope is a bank of color."

Annie said warmly, she *wanted* to see it.

"Who takes care of this?" Fred wanted to know.

"A gardener," Henry explained. "Have to have one, you know. Hard to keep things growing out here."

"Why, Henry Sands! Where is it *ea*-sier?"

Fred was noncommittal. If Henry didn't drive the car, or look after the place, what *did* he do? Well, no doubt he could afford to do nothing.

They were still moving in a fairy tale. Annie had no idea of where or in what direction they were going, up and down hills, and along curving roads. When they reached the long avenue of heavily branching deodars (Louie laughed at the title "Mile of Christmas Trees," but *she* thought it was lovely), then she did truly believe that she had entered her fairy

653

land. The cars were lined up blocks away, but they need have no fear with Percy's careful, smooth, assiduous handling of the almost noiseless gears. They slid between two other cars, one a little old Model T Ford rattling along like a mechanical insect out of some well-forgotten age, and the other a battered family sedan. Annie felt that *they* were a favored, almost royal party. She didn't quite believe in it, but she loved it. Even Fred was impressed by this evidence of civic activity. He gave it his highest praise. He said, "It's certainly pretty nice." Annie heard the two men. Let them talk about "conditions" and "the market," and figure out just how the lights were put up. The women sat happily together. Louie had to make no such effort to be interested in all Henry's concerns as Dorothy in Jesse's. She was with Louie, her own beloved sister—Louie in her soft moleskin coat, even that giving out some faint fragrance. Annie held Louie's warm gloved hand. All sad things faded out under the holiday glitter of the lights—and why need any of them ever worry or work hard again?

The holiday was extended, indefinitely it seemed. One pleasant event followed another.

On New Year's Day, there was the famous Tournament of Roses. Fred had been dreading that, for he hated getting into a crowd. But with Louie and Henry, all was made easy—as they might have known! Henry had engaged fine seats long ahead of time, so that there need be no hurry in getting there, no long waits; and then they had Percy to find a place to park—*that* was off their hands. The morning had started with a flat, chill, strange-smelling fog from the sea. Fred, of course, was uneasy. He was afraid that it might rain. He wanted to know if they had covering downtown there, in case. Louie said with smiling confidence, "Oh, it never rains on New Year's!" "The Chamber of Commerce won't let it," Henry put in dryly. Both the women contended that the fog was nothing, the sun would shine. "You'll see!" Everything out here, even the weather—Mr. Ferguson thought—sided with the women. By the time they took their seats in the grandstand, the sun *was* shining.

"You'll find us, Percy?"

"Yes, Mistuh Sands."

They felt the comfort of leaving the car to Percy, the delight of having the best seats reserved for them. The Fergusons were used to having things good, but not the very best, not the top-notch—not what Fred was still apt to speak of as "tony." Well, they *were* tony today. There were rich-looking elderly people in the grandstand—people needn't be young to have a good time, Mrs. Ferguson thought defiantly. That had been, still was to a great extent, the code of Belmond. She was excited by the crowd. *She* liked it, liked to be where things were going on. And with such seats, even Fred couldn't mind it. Even he must enjoy the beautiful floats.

"Margaret would like this," she exclaimed sentimentally.

"Oh, she'd find something to turn up her nose at," Fred said.

Mrs. Ferguson watched everything eagerly, gathering details to report to Mrs. Viele and the other ladies at home. If Mrs. Morgan could see *these* flowers! The precious gloxinia plant was far surpassed by these moving masses of exotic bloom. In fact, it was beginning to seem as if she could never bear to return again. Why should she?—when the children were all gone. She felt happy in the midst of this crowd. There was a joy in seeing people without ties. Doubtless there were many from home. But here in this grandstand, there was little fear of seeing any of those sad, reminding figures like the old couple from Dike. Fred got somewhat restive toward the end. Henry was polite but uninterested. But then, you never could tell about Henry. After all these years, Annie felt that she didn't know him any better than at first. She wondered if even Louie did. Annie drank in every bit of the spectacle—eager for color, for show, trying to satisfy all the tastes that she hadn't admitted in herself for years; that were the opposite of Fred's. Fred made fun of the blond beauties who sat swaying in thrones above the flowers. He said he should think those girls would be pretty cold in their bathing suits, must think they were in a picture show. But Annie stood up for them, too, for their beauty golden and empty like the sunshine, in its synthetic perfection.

"They don't look real."

"They look better than real!" she said triumphantly.

It was amazing whom they did run into! Of course they had known she was living out here, had meant to pay their respects to her, to call some day in state. They had walked down the street when the parade was over, to the place where Percy was to meet them—and there, in front of one of the hotels, was an old lady beckoning to them. It was old Mrs. Spencer! Wonderful that she should recognize them after all these years. Fred was inclined to be embarrassed, since he had had what almost amounted to a disagreement with Richard. But if the old lady knew of that, she gave no sign. It was years since she had left Belmond; years now since old Mr. Spencer had died. But here she was, tiny, withered, but quite regally dressed in purple, and still evidently very much alive!

Annie was proud to have such a sister as Louie to introduce to Mrs. Spencer. She saw an instant approval of the moleskin coat and the violets in those small, sharp, aged eyes. She was not at all sorry to be able to make a showing in front of one of the Spencers! The old lady had always been nice enough to them. She had sent Dorothy quite a lovely wedding present. But it had been rather in a gracious, grand lady way. In the old Spencers' time, Fred hadn't been much more than their clerk. They had looked upon him as the Fergusons themselves now looked upon Ray Seeley. However, the old lady seemed shrewdly and willingly to have accepted the changed status. She certainly couldn't expect to patronize Louie!

And now they were going to have the afternoon with her.

"You'll enjoy it, won't you?" Annie said anxiously to Louie.

She had feared that Louie might not be interested in such an old lady. But if Louie did feel that way, she didn't show it. The two sisters had a gala feeling starting out together. It was almost as they used to feel when they were young girls setting off for a party. They pretended to be remorseful about leaving the men; but they weren't. Fred had consented to go out with Henry to the golf links. He was proud that old Mrs. Spencer should have invited Annie. However he might regard Richard, he still kept much of the awed respect of other days for the old Spencers. Fred never seemed to think of anywhere he wanted to go by himself; and Henry couldn't live without his golf. In fact, that was why Henry submitted to living in California, Louie said with a little shrug—because he could play golf all the year round. *That* was what Henry did, Fred had discovered—he played golf. At home, Fred would never join the golfing crowd, Richard Spencer, Dr. Redmond and the others—they were too tony for him, he thought, and he didn't like golfing anyway, it was another thing that kept people from the churches. But it was different when Henry played—must be, since Henry was an able man, and his own brother-in-law, and since the game seemed to fill up the empty places of Henry's existence. For the two women, there was more than they could get in, all the time!

It was too warm today for their fur wraps. Louie wore a soft woolen ensemble; and Annie was having the chance to wear the new outfit she had bought in Los Angeles. It was black and white—she had worn that combination often enough—but it was the style that seemed to change her altogether. The price had terrified her. She couldn't tell Fred of spending anything like that simply for something to wear. But Louie was on her side. Louie had been determined that she must have that suit and no other. Louie had offered to make up the price herself. "Yes, Annie—now you must let me. I get tired of buying things only for myself." That vacant, dimmed look came over her lovely face, which Annie had noticed before. "If I can't do something for my own sister, for whom can I?" Annie had to agree. She wouldn't tell Fred, of course—it worried him, he thought they were accepting too much already. Dad wasn't used to doing less than his share. *He* was used to being the provider. But why shouldn't I take a present from my own sister? Annie had thought. And then she had to get a smart hat and shoes to match. She had left the shop elated. She felt the enjoyment of going into stores with Louie—the instant respect shown by the clerks. She herself

657

always entered the stores in Geneva a little deprecating and uncertain—although not at home, where they knew her, and knew that Fred was well-fixed. But then, there wasn't anything much to buy at home! Of course, when she brought back her new purchases, Fred had to take her down a little. Not that he had any idea of the price! He wasn't going to commit himself, but he wouldn't say either that he liked the suit. Finally he came out with what was the trouble. It was a nice enough suit, he said, but she didn't look so much like herself in it. "Now, maybe you haven't known," Louie told him, "how Annie can look!" Annie stanched her disappointment with Louie's approval. She was going to wear the suit even if Fred didn't like it! But she had given up the idea of getting earrings. She didn't know why she shouldn't have some—but she just never had worn them. Maybe the thought of Grandma's sharp tongue was still in her mind; even now, she couldn't quite get away from it. Nevertheless, she felt smart and gay starting out, carrying the lovely bouquet of roses for old Mrs. Spencer that the gardener had cut for them. She felt much gayer than if Fred had been along.

She never could get over her gratification at their smooth arrival—at stepping out of the handsome limousine, noting the respectful glances turned toward them from passers-by. She stood aside happily while Louie made her arrangements with Percy. Already she had got out of the way of wanting Fred to drive her anywhere. It was all so much easier with Percy.

Old Mrs. Spencer was awaiting them in the lobby of the hotel. They saw her, sunk into a big soft chair, valiantly arrayed in her purple gown and hat, and with great pearl earrings fastened upon her withered ears.

She looked them over and greeted them with satisfaction. She still had the Spencer eye for appearances! But Annie felt that she was ready to stand the scrutiny.

"I thought I'd be here," she told them, "and not make you come to my bungalow. Later, I must give you a little tea there."

In fact, she was *very* welcoming. She held Louie's hand, and she actually kissed Annie! Yes, it was plain that they had passed her tests. The kiss signified final acceptance and approbation. She professed herself delighted with the roses. She made the bell-boy take them to her bungalow, giving him many instructions, all very definite, to which he replied with a seemingly respectful, "Yes, Mrs. Spencer, we'll see to that." Louie couldn't help smiling; not, however, disapprovingly. The old lady gave a slight grunt of satisfaction. She rose, grasping both their arms. They were to have a little theater party. There was a new bill at the movie theater across the street; and she told them that she never missed a change of program.

"I'm a great lover of the movies," she announced with firmness.

Both the guests declared that they were delighted to go. It was only a step. Perhaps they would walk over. "Oh, no, my dear—not worth while calling your car. Besides, this is my exercise. I'm so pleased to be able to go without Sarah—my maid. That's what it means to be old! I have to take her with me. *And* of course pay for her seat! Has to have just as good a one as I do." Louie raised her eyebrows slightly at Annie. This was going too far even for Louie. But they were affected, in spite of themselves, by the old lady's air of authority. They piloted her over the crossing. They could see how dreadfully old she was when they walked with her. Louie, with that gracious, sympathetic way which her sister so admired, took Mrs. Spencer's arm and carefully held her back waiting for the change of traffic—the old lady herself, it seemed, would have charged straight into the midst. Truly, she could scarcely lift her feet. At any moment it seemed as if those great earrings might come rattling down upon the pavement—as if there weren't enough of her any more to hold her adornments together. But she was chipper and determined, and she wouldn't lose a moment of her pleasure.

"Marlene Dietrich!" she said. "Beautiful creature! I never miss *her.*"

Old Mrs. Spencer to be so fond of the movies! Annie had always associated her with the cool high-ceilinged rooms of the Spencer house, and with things like the old Shakespeare Club. She had been somewhat in awe of Mrs. Spencer's "culture." And this foreign actress, who was reported to be a "siren," and whom Mrs. Stark had once declared the kind who ruined the ideals of our young people! But then, Mrs. Stark—she was altogether *too* . . . Annie felt a strange flicker of unholy interest. Mrs. Spencer insisted on getting tickets at the window, opening her lustrous beaded bag with her tremulous fingers, and minutely counting out the change. Louie took her arm again as they went into the theater.

The show had not yet started. They stepped into the hushed darkness before the matinée. The theater was full of old ladies, coming in groups or by twos, the less decrepit helping along the feeble ones. Annie and Louie piloted their old lady. They exchanged glances of affectionate amusement, feeling delightfully young, since they had the use of all their limbs and faculties. Louie helped Mrs. Spencer into an upholstered seat, helped her off with her purple wrap, and then laid it around her shoulders. "Thank you, my dear," the old lady panted—but with firmness still in her tone. "Now I believe I'll let you take my hat off too. I'll enjoy the picture much better when I'm comfortable." Louie gently lifted the rich little purple hat from the thin yellow-silvery waves, that parted, showing the dry old scalp, and freed the veil softly from the great earrings.

"That's nice. That's very deft." The old lady commended. She patted Louie's hand. "*Much* better than Sarah could do."

Louie and Annie exchanged another smiling glance.

Well, they didn't mind, they felt so young, they *could* do things for the old lady.

Both of them were amazed at Mrs. Spencer's command of movie lore. They had feared she would get tired; but not at all, it was evident that she wasn't going to miss an item on the bill. "Oh, I'm a great lover of the movies!" she warned them again.

Even so, when she thought of the stately old frame house in Belmond, with the long windows and the cupola, it was difficult for Annie to associate Mrs. Spencer with the picture they were seeing now. Mrs. Stark would have been horrified! Mrs. Stark was particularly indignant against the unwholesome influence of "foreign actresses." The Woman's Club, she believed, should take it upon itself to censor the pictures that came to town. Annie had never considered whether she really believed that or not. Maybe at home, she wouldn't have patronized such a picture, that certainly didn't hold up the right ideals. But it seemed that the old lady took an epicurean pleasure in the overripe luscious beauty of this subtly decadent European flower. She surveyed the clinging "love scenes" with satisfaction, fixing her sharp little eyes upon the opulent slow movements of the lovely figure on the screen.

"I like the way this man makes love to her," Mrs. Spencer whispered complacently. "I couldn't bear that last one. A perfect stick!"

The two guests were amused but somewhat embarrassed by their hostess's frequent comments in most authoritative tones.

The picture, certainly, laid too much emphasis on sex. That was what Mrs. Ferguson told herself. Was Margaret, was her own daughter, an initiate of scenes like this? But she, too, watched it all with a hidden wistful interest, half charmed, half alienated. The exotic flower-face of the star shone strangely luminous through the tawdry working-out of the mechanized story. Mrs. Ferguson noted all the details, the butterfly sweep of the brows, the deep-set evasive eyes, the hollow cheeks with their Old World beauty—the suggestion the actress carried of something old, passive, too tired to hold its burden of finished aristocracy, letting it slip, with a lovely contempt, into tawdriness . . . The lovely face held a spell of fatalism, against which the bland American brightness of the ladies rebelled. Yet they found themselves fascinated, and a little frightened.

"Well, my dear, whatever you may think of her morals in the play," Mrs. Spencer said with satisfaction, "she's a beautiful creature!"

Now there was the business of getting the old lady out of the theater. The sisters supported her on each side as they went slowly across the street in front of the panting cars. No, she wouldn't hear of their leaving. Not until she had entertained them in her bungalow. In fact, it seemed to Annie that she was clutching at them.

Sarah, a middle-aged, patient-looking woman, had every-

661

thing ready for them. Mrs. Spencer had finally to acknowledge that with a grunt. She dismissed Sarah then; but Annie and Louie noticed that Sarah didn't take it very seriously—she didn't go far. She had a stolid seasoned look of humoring her mistress. It was fearful to see Mrs. Spencer lift the silver teapot with her trembling little hands. But she wouldn't let Louie take her place. They could see how she still enjoyed the authoritative rôle of hostess.

"Well, now," she said, turning to Annie, when the business of pouring was over. (Sarah, by the way, had appeared again to pass the cakes.) "I suppose you're expecting me to ask you all about Belmond. I'm not going to do it. All my friends are gone. I'm not interested in the others. So why ask?"

Annie couldn't help feeling a little shock, although Louie gave a soft spurt of laughter. Mrs. Spencer said that Fred had done exactly right in leaving the bank. There was no use in people working forever. "My husband worked too long. He couldn't enjoy his leisure when he took it. But I do, my dear," she said firmly. "Every bit of it. I suppose you wonder, too, why I stay alone out here. Well, why shouldn't I? What would be the gain in coming back to look after Richard? Ethel manages him anyway. And very proper. I admire her for doing it. If he isn't good by this time, he never will be. I've done all *I* can about it."

With that, the old lady seemed to have dismissed Belmond, where she had dwelt as a highly important citizen for so many years. Annie felt a guilty half-sympathy, a shock. Mrs. Spencer wanted to know where Louie lived. In fact, she inquired minutely. She nodded her head with satisfaction at the address.

"I had a house too," she said. "But after my husband died, I sold it. I didn't want the responsibility. The only desire I have is to enjoy the few years left to me. I suppose they're few! They're longer now than anyone gave me credit for. No, I don't want a house. Here, I live as easily as I could anywhere. They know me. They give me good service. I suppose, on the whole, I might as well make up my mind to put up with Sarah. Too much trouble to look for anyone else. When

I want to buy clothes—I still like clothes—I can step just a few doors down the street. And I can go to see my movies. I can't miss them!"

Louie agreed, with her fragrant sympathy. But Annie couldn't help that shocked, guilty feeling. It was as if things only dimly formed in her mind were now sharply visible. The living room of the small expensive bungalow had a clear-cut modern brightness. The tea things were exquisite upon the little table. Piles of bright-colored movie magazines stacked the shelves. Why not? Mrs. Spencer complacently demanded, sharply noting the glance. She had read the classics, she said, and she couldn't abide this modern stuff. All full of horrors and diseases, poor people, people she wouldn't have cared to know. She wanted to have youth about her! It was as if she were warming her little old body determinedly with pictures of golden hair and luscious, painted lips. Oh, yes, she kept up with them all, she said, nodding—Ann Harding, Greta Garbo, Joan Crawford—she knew all of them, all of these heroines of the day, deplored divorces, was pleased with rumors of romances. And this was old Mrs. Spencer!—the Mrs. Spencer they used to know: who had put on a sheer white apron with knitted lace to pour coffee from a silver coffeepot at the Congregational church supper—who had brought with her a breath of New England decorum whenever she stepped into the bank, so that the men shook their cuffs into place surreptitiously, and cleared their throats. It was always as if the sharpness and purity of New Hampshire snows had hung about her . . . and there was still a last, frosty glitter out here in the bland sunshine. But the sharp steeple of the white church had dwindled until it couldn't be seen. Annie Ferguson felt as if she didn't know the world any more.

"Now, my dear, I see I've shocked you." Mrs. Spencer was as firmly complacent as before. "But let me tell you. My old life has gone from me. Why reside in memories of it? That's what I tried to tell my husband. But he wasn't able to take it in. When I came out here, I put the past behind me. I believe in doing things thoroughly. I'm too old to make new friends. But the movies take the place. People are disappointing when

663

you come to know them. I can take these as I see them. These young people may do wild things, but they're beautiful, and young. They do what I didn't do in my day."

Annie listened in mingled disagreement and sympathy. The old lady sat in her comfortable chair like a frail little derelict of another age—of an afternoon, when the dust was golden, when the old Spencer surrey went slowly and decorously down the residence street, the fringe shaking, the shining horses placidly trotting. Now the old woman was like a frail white shell left on a distant sunny beach, all affections, experience, feelings washed out of her by time and change, nothing left of her but her dauntless resolution. Annie felt a slight shudder in this heated air.

They drank their tea, and ate their delicious little sandwiches and cakes. Annie did try to slip in some mild praise for Sarah. Even when they had finished, it seemed that Mrs. Spencer didn't want to let them go. Even if she didn't care for people! At last she allowed them to slip on their coats and gather up their gloves and bags. But she held Annie's hand for a final word.

"Stay here, my dear," she said earnestly. "Don't let yourself get old until you must. You'll do for other people, and even so you'll have no one but yourself left in the end." The old lady nodded her head, an earring ominously rattling. "You'll find that out. Then get all the pleasure that you can. I deny myself nothing."

Annie withdrew her hand, half shocked, half pleased. The air had a hothouse warmth in the bungalow. It seemed as if the great rich roses were already too fully open.

Annie and Louie drove back in the late afternoon, through the flat, salt-smelling sea fog again. It blotted the avenues, turned the palms and graceful pepper trees to ghosts, pushed in waves against the lights of the car, thick but meaningless— like a spirit out of the emptiness beyond. Annie felt far from home. She was frightened at this moment by the distance, the dreamy unreality that had come over old attachments that seemed to be slipping away from her. Old simple truths were dissolved. Was *she* going back on them? she, one

664

of the mothers? She felt again the passivity of the actress, the subtle emanation from something too old and fatal for her to understand. It seemed as if all behind her was settling, tottering—and before her was emptiness. The face of the star seemed to float luminous somewhere, with the butterfly sweep of the brows above the enigmatic eyes. All this chain of bright new cities had become unreal in the fog from the sea. And the land beneath them was old, was cruel, and strange—old, older than the Old World their ancestors had left behind, before the time of man. There was no beginning and no ending.

This was a cloudy day. Mist softened and darkened the brightness. The gas furnace kept the large house evenly heated; but Louie, shuddering a little at the cloudy chill beyond the space of the big bright window, had declared they must have a log fire to make the place more cheerful. Fred was sitting by the fireplace reading, glad, no doubt, that the weather was at last so bad that the two women couldn't urge him to go out to the links with Henry. But Annie felt restless and queer. She couldn't settle down to read. After a while, she went upstairs to find her sister. She knocked on Louie's door.
"Oh, come in, Annie!"
Annie had only a few times stepped into this bedroom. Its spaciousness made their own seem small. It was all in light, delicate colors, pale but warm. Now, in this setting of misty, darkened air, it seemed to hold a kind of feminine enchantment. Louie was doing her nails. Her paraphernalia was spread out around her. The glitter of bottles and jars made the large modern dressing table seem like the secret, shining, magic center of the house—an altar, almost. Annie went toward it with a wistful reverence.
"Oh, you do have such lovely things!"
She had to think of the meager equipment of her own dresser at home—the flowered china manicure set given her (by Louie herself) years ago, and still set out in state, although she used little articles from the ten-cent store. Except for that, and a bottle of toilet water, she had no extras. Unless she counted the lotions bought from Lily Weyant, because she had felt she

665

must give Lily some help, and which were of such poor quality she had stuck them away and never used them.

She sat down in a little low, chintz-covered chair. Louie was half turned toward her, sheathed in her pastel satin negligee, holding up her soft, finely cared for, middle-aged hand toward the light. Annie had the somewhat excited feeling of having penetrated the secrecy of a hidden rite. She was not sure whether she ought to be here. She felt again, with a voluptuous realization—almost as if she were listening to music—how lovely Louie was. Yes, still, in her middle-age. The fading of her face made it all the more interesting, with the loosened fragrance of a rose just before the petals fall, holding about it the poetry and fragrance of a long afternoon of summer sunlight now slowly drawing to a close.

Annie drew back from the glimpse of herself in the glass, moving her chair self-consciously. It made her seem aged and commonplace. She felt like a fraud in this lovely room—she had worked too much, there were too many anxieties behind her. And there was something still unsatisfied in her heart, beneath all the pleasure. On this cloudy morning, while she was watching the leaping of the fire, she had felt unresolved troubles and fears suddenly alive.

"I haven't had any letter from Margaret," she said.

"Oh well, she probably has so much to do."

Annie watched Louie reach out for a small jar of paste and dab her finger deftly into it. Loneliness came over her. She moved restlessly. She felt that she had never been able to talk about Margaret to anyone who would understand, that she had been saving it all up for Louie. She couldn't betray her child to the neighbors; and of course, with any of Fred's folks she must be on the defensive. Now she was with Louie, now she was with her own. She heard herself confiding all her pain and fears. The words crowded to her mind—"Some man—I know she was with some man—" But when it came to speaking them, she could do it only haltingly, and not in the luxurious detail that she had imagined. Louie's face was turned slightly aside. Her brows were puckered; and Annie felt in her something polished and blandly unresponsive, something that she

666

had met before when she had tried to talk about their uncertainty over Jesse's financial state. Louie would say only, "Oh well, it's just temporary—probably this little experience will be all the better for them." And now she felt with disappointment that Louie refused to take in the meaning of Margaret's escapade. The pearl-mounted nail buffer that Louie was manipulating was like some delicate weapon holding her away.

Louie had to say *some*-thing.

"Oh well, Annie, it may not be what you think. I'm sure it isn't. Young people act differently nowadays. We mustn't think too much about that."

"But, Louie, she made this trip with him—I know she did."

"But still it may have been just a pleasure jaunt, a little unconventional, but without anything more to it."

"Do you think so?"

"Why, yes, I don't see why not."

Annie was silent. She tried dubiously to look at the trip in that way. She didn't know how to meet Louie's bland, determined consolation, and tried feebly to gather her forces for assertion. Louie seemed to feel that she was not quite living up to the sympathy expected of her. She put down her nail buffer.

"Didn't you tell me about this man who sent flowers?"

"Yes, but *he* wasn't the one!"

"Now, Annie, he might have been. I think very likely he was."

Annie was forced to be silent again. She remembered Margaret's dark face—the sound of muffled crying, when she had stood outside her child's door, feeling too obscurely guilty, fearful and uncertain to go in to her.

All her fears for her children rose in her like the mounting of a dammed-up flood, that had been gathering through the years. She wanted to tell Louie—she wanted to speak to someone to whom she could at last admit the bitter truths and the painful intuitions which all this time had lain underneath her bright, covering repetitions . . . "Carl and Lillian—getting along nicely—oh, yes, much better"—when all the time, she had the dark knowledge, never given words, even with Fred, of what Lillian had done. She wanted to speak out her bewildered perception of Carl as defeated under his apparent success. To speak, and to have what she said comprehended, *acknowledged* —that was what she asked. Their trouble with Margaret—the feeling that they themselves might have helped to drive her away, the old guilty crying sense that this was the child they had never known . . . to say all that, at last—and to hear arguments persuasive enough to dispel it. It seemed as if she must have someone with whom she needn't keep it up, to whom she could admit failures, and then to have that person assert, "Yes, but, Annie, you did the best you could."

But now it seemed as if all the space of the large, uncrowded room was between her and Louie, and it couldn't be crossed. The worst of it was, that she recognized Louie's attitude! It was just the way she herself had acted, more times than one, when Essie Bartlett, for example, had tried to talk to her. For she hadn't wanted to feel the desperateness of Essie's situation, had tried to ease it and shove away realization with false cheer, not letting it spoil her content in her own better fortune. Not, of course, that *her* life could be compared to Essie Bartlett's! But it humbled her, the way Louie met her confidences, making her feel inferior. She saw herself as a dreary small town woman worrying tediously over her children. She still was careful not to catch any sight of herself in the glass.

No, it wasn't that. It was more that Louie was afraid of giving a response. Louie wanted to smooth the surface so that she need not open her heart to trouble. And all at once, Annie felt her greatest sorrow—Bunny's marriage—banked up in her, with no relief. She could taste the bitterness on her lips. She could imagine herself telling all about it to Louie and Louie meeting every point with that sympathetic sweetness which Annie now saw as masking in silk her disinclination to understand. Wasn't it the same way that she had wanted to meet trouble herself? "Oh, but, Louie, that girl is three years older!" "Yes, but, Annie, that doesn't really mean anything." "I know, if she were his kind—!" "Now, Annie, they may be more congenial than you think. Those marriages are often the happiest sort." It would be useless to try to make Louie understand about Charlotte—how her very existence threatened all the

668

sunny peace of a settled life. And it was *she,* their antithesis, whom Bunny, their youngest, had chosen to love! The pain, fear, threat of that knowledge was alive again . . . but in a dull aftermath, since nothing could be done about it. It was there, no matter how far she ran away from it. But even to hint at the fear that it gave her was ridiculous and out of place in this lovely room.

Louie gave a little shiver. "This is a horrid day," she said deprecatingly.

She reached over for another of the thick, shining jars, took a dab of fragrant cream and spread it over her hands, then studied them thoughtfully. Annie watched her, wanting in some way to feel close again.

"That smells nice," she offered.

"Try it," Louie said encouragingly, handing her the jar.

Annie spread the rich paste listlessly over the backs of her own hands. But it was too late in the day to achieve the perfection of beauty that had formed part of her girlhood dream. And her pleasure in Louie's things had turned into a faint resentment.

"It feels nice," she murmured. "But my hands have seen too much work."

The glitter of the jars and bottles tired and disturbed her. She looked surreptitiously at Louie's face. There was something empty, almost querulous, in its softness. In that moment, she made a subtle revision of her pride in her sister's beauty, her modesty in regard to herself. Annie had always been accustomed to sorrow over the fact that Louie had no children. But now she could see that Louie had changed. It was as if she had crossed over an invisible boundary line— she had turned her back on her old longing, she would no longer acknowledge it. Perhaps, indeed, she did not feel it. If she *had* wanted children, she had fortified herself against the lack by comfort and ease and beauty. For so long, there had been no one but herself on whom to expend her efforts, that now at last—by a substitution, half merciful, half blighting— herself had come to be all in all to her. Louie was too deeply and softly embedded in the ease and luxury which she used to regard so deprecatingly. It was no longer possible to reach her.

Louie moved uneasily, and gave a little laugh. "I think the weather has affected us both. It just doesn't seem right when we don't have sunshine. I was wondering—wouldn't you like to drive down to Los Angeles and go to a matinée this afternoon?"

"Yes, that would be nice," Annie said carefully, but somewhat distantly.

Louie reached over and gave her sister's hand a little squeeze. "You don't know what a comfort it is to have you here to run around with me! I suppose Henry will have to have his golf, rain or shine!"

Annie returned the squeeze faintly, but said nothing. There was something that made her unhappy. It sounded in Louie's voice. She felt that Louie had no real respect for Henry, although she would never say so in words—no, she, too, must still keep up the pretense of perfect happiness according to the ancient feminine code! Annie moved uneasily again. Reluctantly she felt that she understood, and was ashamed to understand, the disappointment and dry failure of this marriage. She seemed at this moment to be looking straight down into it . . . aware of the gifts and the freedom from responsibility that Henry tacitly piled upon Louie—of a cautious defeat in the shifting of his glance—of the price that had been paid for this enchanted life, in which Louie's beauty still softly bloomed. Once the determination to admit nothing wrong might have been loyalty—but now it had overshadowed everything else, until Louie's gentleness and silence had become mere fear of trouble and desire for smoothness. Oh, but, Louie, to *me*—to each other! I would love you so much better— But it was impossible actually to say those words. Annie felt a disappointment that rose like a sob. And already she had penetrated too far. She had come too close to this shining altar. She had seen what her position as the fortunate one, the Lady Bountiful, meant to Louie, and how Louie couldn't risk endangering it by any impulse of confidence or intimacy. Louie sat at her altar alone. Her shining peach-tinted robe was a symbol of the immaculate good fortune by which her beauty was surrounded and it must not suffer a touch.

Annie said, somewhat nervously, but smiling, "I believe I'll go outside for a little while."

"It's chilly," Louie murmured.

"Oh, I won't take cold."

"Put on my cape, then, Annie. It's in the closet downstairs. I always like to slip it on in weather like this."

"All right. Thank you, dear."

Annie put on her own coat instead. The soft, too soft, enfoldment of the woolly cape seemed to her unreal.

But the garden, all the place, was unreal too. The blooming things were strange in the sea fog. The colors of the flowers were dimmed. She felt an alien sadness in the tall eucalyptus trees with their dark blots of foliage against the gray sky. Again the land seemed old—and this moment was like an interlude. She could not find its meaning in the stealthy fog. For the first time, she had a faint, painful thrill of homesickness. Yet all her anxieties lay back there still unresolved. She shivered, thinking of old Mrs. Spencer. Again she saw that image of the white shell, lying empty and cold in the sea mist. The stealthy distance grew between her and her only sister. Solitude drew in upon her from out of this ghostly mist. She thought, with a shudder, of the long, slow, empty sound of the ocean. The coast, to have come to the coast—she felt a meaning in that now—something hidden in the very heart of the fairy story.

She turned back and went into the house, almost with a sense of flight from ghosts. Fred was still reading beside the fire of eucalyptus logs—or, if not reading, solacing his idleness with the pictures in the *Geographic*. His glasses were pushed down upon his nose—there was something oddly comforting in that homely touch. He looked up over the glasses.

"Hello, mama. Well. That you?"

The days went on until they were almost losing track of time. More and more, Fred was aware that the others were conniving to wean him away from thoughts of home and to persuade him that the holiday need never end.

"You'll stay," Henry predicted, with a dry twinkle in his eye. And Louie added complacently, "Everyone does, you know." Louie simply couldn't understand why they should ever think of returning to Belmond.

Even Annie was on their side, Fred saw, and joined in the conniving. She wouldn't come right out with it. But when they were alone, and he talked about Belmond, Fred could see that she was indifferent. She gave a little movement of impatience when he spoke about the church. When he mentioned Essie Bartlett and her mother, wondering whether their fuel was holding out, she didn't answer and turned away. She wouldn't even show any interest in how their own house was getting along. What had happened to Annie since they came out here? Of course he wanted her to enjoy herself—this was mama's chance; but sometimes he felt with dismay as if he didn't know her any more. Once she broke out, almost with bitterness, that they had done everything *they* could in Belmond, and it wasn't as if the children needed them any more.

"Well, what do you want to do, Annie?"

But she wouldn't give a direct answer to that.

Fred couldn't answer clearly himself. He didn't know just what he had intended when he came away, he didn't know what he intended now. He seemed to be waiting for something to turn him one way or the other. He would stroll around the highly developed landscaping of Henry's grounds, asking the gardener the names of the strange plants, and watching him run the water from intricate systems of irrigation. It was clever. But when he thought of finding a place out here for themselves and putting all this care into keeping a lawn green and queer plants flourishing, it seemed to him a puttering sort of life. Nature here didn't seem to do anything; it was all like hothouse gardening; Annie might enjoy the great roses and geraniums and lilies, but he couldn't interest himself in things that seemed to be mostly for show. Of course, it *was* pretty fine to go right out into your own yard and pick an orange off the tree. It still seemed marvelous to him to pick oranges, while to pick an apple was natural and commonplace. Not that he liked oranges better. No, there was nothing that could come up to a good apple.

"What would you do back there?" they demanded. He didn't want to go back into the bank.

No, he knew he didn't. But just the same . . .

It hurt Fred to think that Annie could adjust herself so easily. In fact, she was blooming in the freedom from care. She never seemed to have enough of gadding and jaunting. Sometimes he thought she was trying to put the children out of her mind; and then again it hurt him because she *could*. But it worked upon him. Whether he would admit it in words or not, what mama wanted "went a long way." He didn't say so to any of the others, for that would be conceding too much, but he kept his eye out for a modest place "with garden maintenance" where he and Annie might try it out for a while. After all, he told himself, he had finished his work. He wanted mama to be happy. He saw some streets that appealed to him, not so showy, with an older look, like that place where they had stayed in San Diego. He talked to the neighbors, where one of these houses was for rent, and discovered that they were ex-Nebraskans and Presbyterians, and were just about like folks from home. He even broached the subject cautiously to Annie.

"Well, mama, would you like to look at a few houses? I saw one place that seems pretty nice."

But Annie didn't take to the place. She didn't seem to care much for the neighbors. What *did* she want, then? he asked her. He couldn't get her to say. When it came to *her* making a decision, she seemed fluttered—she wouldn't answer, and turned her face away from him.

When bad news came from home, Louie and Henry thought this clinched it. Now they wouldn't consider going back.

The first real shock was the news of the failure of the other bank. And not only had the bank failed, and closed its doors, but Mr. Hoagland had vanished. Yes, H. L. Hoagland! who, since the death of old Mr. Spencer, had been recognized as the town's first citizen.

673

Henry didn't see why that need affect *them*. They had nothing to do with it. Fred was lucky to be out of there, Henry said. He'd better withdraw completely. Fred hadn't any good arguments against that—or any arguments that would seem valid to Henry. He wouldn't admit that he was worried about his own funds, for that would seem like a reflection upon his own bank; and although he was "no longer connected," he must uphold the honor of the institution. He couldn't acknowledge that he didn't wholly trust Richard. He had never done that, even to Annie. But he was made to realize, as never before, the difference in the way that he and his brother-in-law looked at finance. Fred was humble, and felt he couldn't say much, for Henry, in the common phrase, had "done better" than he had. Fred had been proud all these years of claiming relationship with a man who had made as much money as Henry. But now it gave Fred a secret shock to see how coldly Henry viewed these things. Henry did his business in cold figures; that was the way all the big fellows managed it; and maybe he just couldn't understand how it felt to be bound up with a place and the people there. Although Henry didn't say as much in words, Fred had the feeling that he didn't condemn H. L. Hoagland for getting away while the getting was good. He raised his eyebrows and slightly shrugged his thin little shoulders. If people lost, that was their own lookout. They shouldn't have trusted the fellow so much. And anyway, Fred wasn't involved.

But the next piece of news struck even closer. The church was gone. Mrs. Lowrie, who had seemed better when the Fergusons left, had suddenly taken a turn for the worse and died; Mr. Lowrie, unable to face his loss and carry on a dwindling cause, had resigned; he had gone to Montana to live with his son; and the church, hastily summoning a meeting, had voted "not to continue." The other element had won. They were going in with the Congregationalists.

At first Fred was so upset that he couldn't take in anything more than the fact itself. The church was gone. Now, when he looked back toward home, he faced a painful blank.

The others all tried to persuade him that it would have

turned out the same if he had been there. He couldn't have carried the whole thing forever on his own shoulders. And maybe they were right. He wasn't sure himself that he hadn't been expecting this all along. He couldn't say just how much the canny pre-knowledge might have had to do with his coming away. He couldn't expect to live forever; and after he was gone, who would there have been to take his place? Still they had taken such advantage of his absence! He could never get over that. Resentment, loss, a stony relief that the worst had come to pass without him—Mr. Ferguson didn't know what he *did* feel. One thing grew more and more sure—Belmond would never be the same to him again. Sometimes he felt in dazed bewilderment that he *had* no home. His day there was over. He was out of the bank, the church was gone, and there were none of his children to carry on his work. Then what had he been working for all these years? Perhaps the best thing he could do now was to stay and live out his days in the sunshine. He went again and looked at that house, trying, as he examined the pipes and the heating arrangements, to crush down his pain at the idea of putting his money and efforts into some other place than the one he had so long called home. It might be a great relief to attend a church, like that big flourishing one the people from Nebraska so proudly referred to, where he needn't feel that the responsibility rested with him. It even seemed to him that Louie regarded the news from home as providential! And maybe, for all he knew, Annie in her heart did also.

"Oh, you'll stay," everyone said with complacent triumph.

For a time Fred seemed to be adrift. He mutely accompanied the others on their excursions, viewing the wonders of California; taking a feeble hand once or twice with Henry at golf. He sat in the park at Los Angeles, while Louie and Annie did their shopping, and got into conversation with other old fellows who were sunning themselves.

But everywhere he heard the same thing: "You'll stay." He heard it at the great Iowa winter picnic, the one gathering which he really wanted to attend; although he didn't know

675

whether it gave him more pride or more disgruntlement to find so many of his fellow countrymen away from home.

Fred and Annie went by themselves. The others had encouraged them, saying the picnic was "a great spectacle"; but such a gathering didn't appeal to Louie and Henry. Fred was glad to be driving his own car. To be taken everywhere—well, it was pretty fine for a little while, but it didn't suit him. He felt as if he were getting soft. He was glad to have Annie to himself again. These folks hadn't been driven here by chauffeurs!—and he would have felt queer arriving in such style.

Cars were lined up around the park as thick as they could stand, and for two blocks on either side. There was a special policeman. Yes, it was a big occasion. Again Fred felt a thrill of dubious pride in realizing that he was part of such a crowd as this. His thoughts were confused as he and Annie joined the others. The world that he had left behind was not the same—perhaps he would find the memory of it here, among these people who had come together to honor their old home.

Parties were still eating dinner, at tables or seated on the grass. It made Annie and Fred feel out of things. At home, they would have had their own group.

"Would have been nice if those folks from Dike could have been here," Fred remarked.

But somewhere in a crowd like this they would be sure to find familiar faces. The grounds were divided up into the different counties, just as the papers had described. The Fergusons found Bell County and went there at once. Some twenty or twenty-five people were grouped around the sign. The Fergusons waited for their chance to sign the register that lay on the wooden picnic table. Fred put down their names with some self-consciousness:

Mr. and Mrs. F. W. Ferguson, Belmond.

Surely there would be someone to recognize that signature! But although one or two of the names were certainly familiar, and people looked at them hopefully, suspiciously, or just blankly, the Fergusons could see no one whom they had ever known before.

676

It was too hot right out in the sun. Even Annie admitted that by taking off her silk jacket. She hadn't put on her new black-and-white suit for this occasion, to Fred's relief. If they did meet old friends, he wouldn't have wanted it to seem that he and Annie were trying now to be different than at home. They wandered off into the shade of a eucalyptus tree, where they tried to watch the crowd for someone they might know, without too apparent a hopefulness. Other people, it appeared, were doing the same. Louie and Henry had told them that they would find so many old acquaintances today that they would feel more at home here than in Belmond.

Well, they might have known almost any of these people! The middle-aged and elderly predominated. Except for that, it could well have been taken for some big gathering at home. It was pretty good, Fred thought, to see just ordinary folks again. Those fellows around the golf links were too high-toned for him. They talked about nothing but the market and their scores. He was hungry for some of the old local topics. He wanted to hear about crops and conditions. He and Annie caught bits of conversation around them. A man said in a bright, chatty tone to a woman: "You know Lulu died"; and she answered eagerly: "Oh, did *Lu*-lu die!" There were some queer characters, of course. Bound to be, among this many people. They saw one old man with a long beard, like a Bible character. "Must not have cut it since he left home," Fred observed. "Look at those!" Annie said, faintly scandalized. She nodded toward a rough-looking family clad all in dungaree pants. They were the kind whom she and Fred had noticed sometimes on their drives, living in one of those little shacks on a canyon edge, that looked ready to be swept away in the first flood. Annie thought *they* didn't look as if they had come from home. But they weren't so different from the others, Fred observed. They might have come out with less money, only a hundred dollars or so; but for the same reason, the reason all these people had come—because they wanted a softer life. They all seemed to have the same look, when you saw them in a crowd like this—a kind of rootless, drifting, meaningless look, against the alien background of palms and

677

gaudy tropical flowers. Well, Fred reflected, his life hadn't been soft. Maybe he would have liked to take his ease, like the rest of them. But it seemed as if he couldn't be easy thinking of the news from home. He couldn't take Mrs. Lowrie's death, for instance, in the way that those two folks seemed to be taking Lulu's. The eucalyptus in the shade had a bitter foreign scent.

"Well, mama, we might walk around again—see if we meet anyone."

They got up, and somewhat forlornly wandered through the great park. In such a crowd as this, they seemed to have lost their old identity. They, Mr. and Mrs. Fred Ferguson, so well established in Belmond, were only newcomers here, only ex-Iowans like the others. It didn't seem to Fred as if picking oranges from the tree and cutting roses in February could make up for that.

Well, there was one thing more that they could do. They could go over to the western county where Fred's brother Will had lived, and where they had occasionally visited, and study the list of names fastened to a eucalyptus tree. And here they *did* meet someone they had known. Fred was just turning around when he felt a hand on his shoulder.

"Wait a minute, wait a minute," a voice said.

He stared into round light eyes behind owlish spectacles—a face that could have been the face of half a dozen men.

"Now I've got it—your name's Ferguson! Am I right?"

Fred admitted that it was, and shook the proffered hand, dubiously at first, then heartily and in relief as the explanations followed.

"I knew you were a Ferguson the minute I saw you, even if your back was turned to me. Couldn't mistake *that!* But for a minute you had me up a tree. You looked so much like Will you gave me a turn—and I knew you couldn't be Will, since Will was dead. Fred. Sure. I place you now. Will's brother. Why, *I* met *you* when you came to Clarion. Lafferty—insurance—don't tell me you've forgotten that fishing trip!"

Fred hadn't forgotten it. And of course he remembered Lafferty now. Why, he was the fellow who had made the

678

coffee! The two men shook hands again, long and heartily. And Annie nodded. Yes, she remembered Mrs. Lafferty. All three were beaming.

"So you've left the old town—that's right, Belmond!— and come out here where all the good folks go." Mr. Lafferty clapped Fred on the shoulder again. "Oh, sooner or later— sooner or later. We get them all."

No doubt that *he* had become a Californian! But now he was insisting that they must find the missus. "She'll be tickled to death to see you folks." They must have a little reunion of their own. With a hand at the elbow of each, Mr. Lafferty was pushing them through the crowd.

"Ah, *here* she is!" he cried proudly.

Now the Fergusons *did* receive a shock. For this could never be Mrs. Lafferty!—this vision confronting them in an effulgence of pink and gold, this face smiling coyly out at them from the girlish shade of a wide pink hat, this golden hair. Mrs. Lafferty!—whom Annie remembered, a plump middle-aged matron like the others, at the meeting of the Aid Society. It had astounded them to see the magnificence to which familiar geraniums and calla lilies attained in the sunshine. But this was the most astounding blossoming of all! It *was* Mrs. Lafferty, though. She was extending a fat, bejeweled hand.

"Well," Fred said feebly, as he took it, "I guess this climate agrees with *you*."

But they had little time for astonishment or anything else. Mr. Lafferty was taking charge of them. He seemed to be constituting himself their host, and to be presenting to them all of Southern California. Already, like everyone else, he had made up his mind that they must stay. Go back to Belmond? He laughed at the idea. They would laugh themselves, when they had been out here a little longer. Why, there was no place in the world that had the destiny of Southern California! Grapes, oranges, melons—he named the products. What was a little corn compared to all those? He made them feel humbly that corn was a back number. Mrs. Lafferty smiled, with coral-tinted lips, above the shining expanse of her bosom. The Fergusons were dazzled.

Now Mr. Lafferty was suggesting that they go over to hear the program. Listen to some fine entertainment. Join in the singing of the grand old song. He knew some of the speakers personally, they were men who counted out here. If Fred would like to meet them afterwards, Lafferty could arrange.

"Oh, no, I guess not," Fred said diffidently. He still had a great respect for "speakers." But he thought they would like to hear the program. "Wouldn't we, Annie? Since these folks are kind enough to show us around." Even if corn was just a rustic product, it would be pretty good to hear the old song again.

Already the music was playing, and they started in the direction of the sound. It made the Fergusons feel that they had some part in the gathering. Mrs. Lafferty tucked her hand brightly into the curve of Annie's arm. But Annie noticed that she was panting a little. Her plump ankles bent inward as she tilted along on her shining high heels. Annie gave a surreptitious glance down at her own matronly oxfords. At first she had been dazed by Mrs. Lafferty's transformation. But now she was recovering her equanimity. The flat, middle-western intonation of the voice that issued from those coral lips had not changed; and the golden hue of eternal youth hadn't quite reached around to the back of Mrs. Lafferty's head. Annie's eye was sharp enough to take note of the tell-tale ends under the pink shade of the hat. She tried to hide her embarrassment, since the Laffertys were being so kind.

The speaker's stand was at the edge of the grounds. The crowd was a little disappointing. There couldn't be more than a hundred or so. But Fred supposed they were late in gathering, just as they were at all picnics.

"You want to listen to this fellow," Mr. Lafferty warned. "He's slated for governor some day. Oh, I tell you, it's the good old stock that's making California what it is." He slapped Fred's arm jovially.

Fred prepared to listen with respect. The speaker, a round-bodied man with a rosy public face and half-bald head, was launched on the story of "the little red schoolhouse on the country crossroads" where he had got his start. There was emotion in his voice. Fred felt a nostalgia for his own boyhood. He thought of the old Buck Creek schoolhouse where Annie had taught. He could almost smell the milky corn and the warm summer dust. But he was disturbed when the speaker made a quick transition. "Those happy days, when we milked the cows and shoveled snow, are fine to remember, aren't they, folks?—At a distance—from beneath the sunny skies of California!" Everyone laughed.

In fact, the longer he listened, the more disturbed Fred grew. These fellows scarcely mentioned Iowa at all, except to tell how lucky they were to get away from bad weather. Every speaker was just the same. "Privileged to enjoy the blessings of this wonderful climate!" That wasn't what Fred had come to hear today. His local patriotism was outraged. He felt homesick and sore. This old fellow who was introduced as "ninety years young," up there cavorting on the platform, telling how he had found his youth beneath the sunny skies— when all his antics only served to show off to everyone how decrepit he was! All of them started from the little red schoolhouse, but from there they seemed to reach the same point in the end: the "problems of the day" in California. Everything was perfect, of course, that they all must say, no one could doubt the great destiny. But there were unpatriotic, un-American elements coming in. There was more need than ever for having the right men in office.

Fred turned to Mr. Lafferty and said, "Why, these sound like political speeches."

Mr. Lafferty laughed easily. "Oh, sure. The Iowa vote is important," he explained; taking it for granted that Fred understood these little matters. "And we got too good a place, we can't let these radicals get hold out here."

Fred didn't answer. Well, maybe that was true, he thought. He himself was afraid of "radicals," although he was vague as to the meaning of the term. But he didn't like the notion of having to hear one thing when he had come to hear another. He didn't care to be made a fool of in that way. He gave a sideways glance at Mr. Lafferty. These fellows wouldn't get *his* vote, he thought privately, even if he were to stay.

But now the song leader was being introduced. Sleek, breezy, plump, with wavy hair, he stepped easily in front of the microphone.

"Ladies and gentlemen, good afternoon. I suppose you're all from Iowa or you wouldn't be here today. All *from* there." The crowd laughed. "Well, it's fine, isn't it, to get together like this once in a while, just to celebrate? Now, everybody knows Iowa as 'the state where the tall corn grows'—they don't grow our oranges and lemons and figs and dates, and all the fine things we're privileged to enjoy—but they *do* grow corn. So we ought all to be ready to join in a little burst of song. You know how the song begins.

> We're from I-o-way, I-o-way—

Iowa, of course, *we* all know the correct pronunciation is, but the song calls for Ioway, poetic license I suppose, so we've all got to sing it as written. Now, folks, as we come to the line 'where the tall corn grows,' I want you all to raise the right hand—see?—just to indicate how high that old corn can get. Pretty high, you bet you. Higher than some of our heads. Will you do that? Fine!"

This was something like. Fred cleared his throat. He wasn't much of a singer, but what he lacked in voice he was prepared to make up in patriotism. He had read of the singing of this song by thousands, joining their voices, so the papers said, in praise of their native state. It was something he had always wanted to hear.

But this was another thing that didn't turn out according to the papers! If these folks had ever known the song, they seemed to have forgotten it. It was like a difficult hymn in church, one with too many turns and high notes. The leader sang cheerily, waving time, but only a few embarrassed voices joined. A few hands were timidly raised—but as for those thousands!

Fred could hardly keep from showing his disappointment to Mr. Lafferty. But he was getting a little wary even of the Laffertys. Their cordiality was almost too shining. Fred felt tired. He wanted to get away. At last he said that he thought they ought to be going home.

The Laffertys insisted on going with them to the gate. Mrs. Lafferty's smile was fixed now. She went forward with short stubby steps. Her panting was interspersed with tiny moans. Mr. Lafferty took Fred's hand when they came to say good-bye.

"Well, folks, we'd certainly like to see more of you. Old friends are the best. Isn't that so? Say, I'll never forget that fishing trip!

"I think I could help you," he added confidentially, drawing Fred a little aside, "when you decide on that house you want to build. Why not come over and have dinner with us some time? And first, I tell you—" he squeezed Fred's arm—"I'd like to drive you around to look at some sites. Oh, sure you're going to stay! They all do. Folks like you are just what we need."

The Fergusons got away at last. They did not look at each other. They had driven several blocks before Fred spoke.

"Well, mama, I guess I better get you home before summer begins, or else maybe *you'll* be blossoming out with golden hair, like this lady."

It was almost the only comment on the occasion that he made—except to say dryly, when Louie and Henry questioned him, yes, there had been lots of people there, maybe half as many as the papers said!

But Annie knew that she had lost her case. If, indeed, it had been a case! Her feelings were as mixed as Fred's. When Fred had suggested that they take a house, she hadn't been able to answer. Tears had glistened for a moment in her eyes. She couldn't after all these years assert her will directly above Fred's. If it *was* her will. When she thought of staying here, she felt a painful, secret triumph against her children—if they didn't want to come home, maybe they would find that home was no longer there! But the old loyalties wouldn't let her admit that her home wasn't the same to her as ever, or that any other place could be better in the end.

No, sir, when summer came they were going. Fred was sure of that now. He had really been sure of it all along. If mama had insisted . . . well, no, he wouldn't have stayed even then. And he knew that mama wouldn't insist when she understood his feelings. The news from home had been slowly sinking into him, and all the sunshine couldn't blot it out. He couldn't help feeling that this was no time to be sitting around and looking at roses. He remembered the day he had left the bank, that feeling of storm in the summer air. He couldn't be easy any longer in the sunshine. He felt as if he ought to be there to join with the others—ought to be there to look after things. Maybe, as the others said, his work was accomplished. But he couldn't be satisfied until he had seen for himself. It had appeared to be the destiny of all good Americans to go on toward some final rosy sunset. Fred supposed that he, like the others, had been working with that goal in mind. But now that he had reached the goal, he found that he couldn't accept it. He couldn't be like Mr. Hoagland. He didn't want to escape his share. He couldn't forget that little group of aging people left behind and standing out under the darkening sky; or their own house locked and empty in the midst of the snow. If a storm *was* coming, that was where he wanted to be. Belmond was his own stamping ground; and it was there that his sunset lay, in the somber glow that followed the long working day of the prairie.

5

"Well, mama, we've crossed over the line!"

Fred said that with scarcely concealed satisfaction. Mrs. Ferguson sat up, straightened her hat and smoothed down her skirt. At first she had an impulse to protest at being back, and then a feeling she hadn't expected swept over her. She let down the window a little more, and the warm morning smells of earth and clover came in to her. They seemed new—fresh-minted and new—and yet carried a sense of familiarity too deep to be described. She felt as if she had awakened from a dream into the freshness of reality.

Both of them were looking around them now with the emotion and excitement of return. How green everything was! And

684

how good everything smelled! The ground smelled good, and the green, green grass. Even the strong rank smell of the pigsties had an odor of fertility. They drove between fields of alsike clover and a scent of honey and strawberries came warm from the pink clover heads thickly crowded. It seemed as if this air—no longer dry, rarefied and golden—held and intensified all the teeming summertime odors.

"Well, there's no soil quite like this," Fred said. "I didn't see anything to beat it."

He had a feeling of exaltation as they drove along—up and down, gently up and down, on the great smooth billows of the rolling country. Talk about the ocean! The land was just as big. The rich earth that spread on every side was rounded by the sweep of the globe. And yet it was all close, familiar, it was home. Always, at the end of the road, he could see the tall trees on either side, with one side overhanging. Nothing was waste, all was put to use, made into a compact pattern of farms. He looked out at the scattered clusters of house, barn, grove and silo, some of them hazy they were so far away. There was a short detour that took them along a narrow country road and across a little rattling bridge over a sluggish prairie stream with a dark sparkle in its muddy water. But it was almost all on paving now. Fred noted that with pride. The whitish miles of asphalt glaring in the sun gave a modern, all-connected look to the towns and farms. Why leave a country like this, he thought, such a good country, and just when they were getting things fixed the way they wanted them?

The fields they were passing now were crumbly and moist with fertility. He was proud to see the fat, black-and-white hogs out in the wet barnyards. Coming into a town, they rode through green caverns of shade. There was a sense of teeming thickness in the close-built streets under the heavy trees. The leaves were so dense that a blackness lay at the heart of the foliage. Then they came out into open sunlight again. Wild roses were in bloom along the roadsides, fresh in their morning stain of pink, but some of them, a few of them, bleached white already with the heat. It gave the feeling of having

685

come into the warm, unconscious, breathing interior of the mighty continent.

They stopped at a restaurant at noon. They had struck a dreadful bed last night, in some little burg; and for breakfast, at the only café, they had drunk pale coffee out of thick white cups. This time they had a good dinner. No fancy fixings, but what Fred called real food—real chicken and noodle soup and fresh strawberry shortcake. The fellow at the filling station had recommended this place. A widow woman ran it, and she knew how to make coffee. Cooking-school teachers might palaver about fruit juices, Fred announced, all they were a mind to; but he would give all the juice ever squeezed out for a good home-fried chicken. He wiped his lips with heartfelt satisfaction.

But as they drove on, and it grew later, their first exaltation of homecoming sank into weariness. The view was misty at the end of the road; trees stood mournful against the orange sunset; the scattered farms had a lonely look; and they felt the underlying sober sadness in these great stretches of brooding fecundity.

It was almost dark when they drove into Belmond. Both felt tired and secretly dispirited. The town looked small and local under the heaviness of the trees. The air was hot and thick. The frame houses seemed to have settled close to the ground. Now they had returned to their old responsibilities and there was no more getting away from them. They drove down the small Main Street. How drearily small it looked! There was the closed bank. Fred turned his eyes away uneasily from the sad, evening stare of the windows. He didn't want to pass his own old place of business on the corner. There weren't many people on the streets. The Fergusons felt unwelcomed, as if the place had closed against them in their absence, and they didn't know it any more. And yet they knew it too well!

"Shall we go home or shall we drop in to Ella's?"

Fred knew that Annie would have preferred to go home. She didn't feel like visiting tonight. But nothing would be ready in the house. They hadn't written exactly when they would arrive. They drove past the place, undecided. How strange to see it there in the twilight, closed against them too! —the shades down, even the lawn with an air of vacancy.

"Might get out and see how it looks," Fred suggested doubtfully.

There was a homesickness in his tone. They both got out of the car, stiff and tired, and stood on their own cement walk.

But the place seemed strange to them. They had always thought of their house as pretty good-sized. Now, after Louie's and Henry's great white house in Pasadena, their own was small and commonplace. They tried the door to the screened porch. But it was hooked and dusty. The key was over at the Morgans', and they didn't feel like going after it. Besides, there were no lights next door, the Morgans must not be at home.

"Well, I guess we better go over to Ella's for tonight."

But there seemed to be no lights at Ella's, either. Annie sat waiting in the car while Fred got out to see if there was anybody at home. Why couldn't they have stayed somewhere along the road, reached home in the morning? Fred wouldn't hear to that, of course, as long as he was near any of his folks. But *her* folks . . . Annie thought of her own sister, feeling the helpless, misty sense of distance that had grown between them. She turned her eyes away from the outline of the narrow frame house where Ella and Ben were living out the bleak end of their fruitless marriage. Fred knocked on the closed front door.

"They're not home!" someone called out from the porch next door.

She came out on the lawn now—Ella's neighbor, Annie couldn't think of her name.

"The folks went to Geneva yesterday," the neighbor said, staring, yet pleased to give information. "They took Mister to the hospital there."

Annie waited, her heart beating thickly, until Fred came soberly back to the car.

"The folks have gone to Geneva—"

"Yes, I heard."

"She don't seem to know just what the matter is, except

687

that Ben had a bad spell of some kind. They think maybe they'll have to operate."

The Fergusons considered the situation nervously, wondering what it might mean for them. But they couldn't seem to take it in tonight. They had got back too recently, and were half strangers still. Fred climbed into the car again.

"Well—" he said heavily. "Guess there's nothing we can do about it tonight."

And now what were they to do? Fred couldn't help a hurt feeling because none of their friends or relatives were around to welcome them. The Lowries, too, were gone. This little while away, and already the small tight group that had stood out in front of this very house telling them good-bye, had been scattered and broken. Of course there were other places—any of their neighbors . . . But it didn't seem right to come down on the neighbors without warning. Annie couldn't bear the thought of their own empty house.

"Well, shall we go to the hotel?"

It seemed foolish in Belmond, right at home here, where any number of folks would have been glad to take them in. As if they hadn't had enough of hotels on their trip! But mama was out of spirits, Fred could see, and if that was what she preferred . . . He wished himself that they had stayed somewhere else and reached here by daylight. Everything looked different then. This was pretty bad news to meet them at the outset. It didn't seem like much of a homecoming. Fred had an uneasy feeling of guilt and responsibility. He knew that he was the one who had wanted to come back.

They drove around to the Belmond House. It was a familiar enough place to Fred. He had eaten here every Thursday with the Rotary. But for him and mama to be staying at the hotel made them seem like strangers in their own town. They entered the close, leather-smelling, local interior of the elderly brick building.

The thin young clerk looked up at them, his face shiny in the heat. At first it seemed as if he *did* take them for strangers. Then he saw who they were, and they had the satisfaction of at least a little welcome.

"Well! I didn't know you at first. You folks been away a good while, haven't you? Going to stay with us tonight?"

"Yes, we didn't feel like opening up the place," Mr. Ferguson explained.

"Well, glad to have you with us."

The old fellow who used to work here seemed to be gone. Fred thought he would ask about him in the morning. He was too tired for any inquiries tonight. A young fellow Fred couldn't remember having seen before took their bags. They followed him up the wide stairway with the worn rubber matting. The door of their room stuck in the heat. The young fellow put down their bags and pushed with his shoulder. He opened the window, took a nonchalant look at the rack of towels, accepted Fred's tip, and was gone. The old man would have been more concerned about their comfort.

They had asked for a cool room, and it seemed pretty hot in here. But Fred didn't like to make any complaint. "Give you the coolest we've got, Mr. Ferguson," the clerk had promised. Fred wouldn't acknowledge anything amiss with their accommodations in Belmond. He disregarded Annie's tremulous look. It hurt him that she didn't seem more pleased to be back. He realized that he couldn't always tell about Annie. He couldn't be sure that he knew her mind. When they were out there, she had shown a side that he had never seen before. Both of them were feeling somewhat disconsolate, here in this hotel room, with the smell of varnish, the air coming faintly in through the screen, the grinding noise of cars outside. But no matter how gloomy things might look tonight, Fred knew that he was stubbornly glad to have got back.

Thank goodness, the bed was pretty comfortable! Fred let Annie have the side toward the window. They would find it a whole lot cooler, he told her, when they were in their own house again.

As things turned out, Annie fell asleep sooner than he did. He himself felt oppressed by the still heat, the brooding heaviness. The future weighed upon him. He asked himself what he was going to do now. He was out of the bank . . . the church . . . all to which he had given his life. . . . And yet

689

he couldn't get rid of the old sense of responsibility. He could feel the whole great fertile country, burdened with its wealth of farms and towns, surrounding him in the night, and seeming to raise a silent question. He remembered the desolate look of the house, with the grass shaggy along the sidewalks. None of his children were there, and he had built the house for them. What would become of it when he and Annie were gone?

The concerns of the family lay heavy upon him. Just by going away he hadn't got rid of them. He might turn his back upon them, but still they existed. Louie and Henry could take their ease; they thought of nobody beyond themselves. But he and Annie couldn't be like that. There was no use to worry about Ben until they had some further news. Still, whatever was going to happen, Fred knew that he would be the one, Ella would look to him. The children were gone, but they were on his mind. Margaret—he didn't understand her, what she was after, what was going to become of her. He and mama had had to give in, and let her go her own way, whatever it was, but that didn't absolve them of responsibility. He could understand Bunny even less. It hurt and bewildered him that the boy seemed to have gone back on all the old ideas. Just the same, Bunny was their youngest. Whether they liked the girl whom he had married or not, they had to regard her as Bunny's wife, and do their duty by her as best they could. Lillian . . . he had never spoken of this to mama, knowing how much she cared for Carl; but he knew things hadn't been right between Carl and Lillian. If Carl had failed her, then it seemed as if *he* ought to do something to make it up to her. Her own father had gone back on her too. Fred had never forgiven Howard. Dorothy they had always regarded as the one who was provided for. But now that he had seen how things were going with her and Jesse, Fred couldn't even be sure of that.

He turned uneasily, but cautiously, not wanting to disturb Annie.

He was aware of a sense of change pervading everything, although it wasn't a thing he could touch or locate. He couldn't

690

say how or when it had happened, but the old simple surety seemed to be gone—the old bright, simple faith in the way things had started and were likely to continue. The church of his fathers was empty. Even his town, in which he had placed his trust, never doubting that it must follow a steady growth to a fine destiny, seemed instead to have come to a standstill. There was something beyond him, something that he hadn't taken into account, some force that he was only blindly aware of working stealthily and bringing a right-about-face. His own children were allied with that force. He had given them all their start, but none of them had yet taken his place. It was he who was still back of it all. They still depended upon him. He felt a heavy solitude. He wasn't sure of anything. Only that he was here again—back home—and that no matter what changes there might be, the old demands were still upon him.

There had been rain some time before morning. What a relief that was! Now the air that came through their window was bright, clean-washed and fresh. Now mama had no excuse for bringing up California. The Fergusons began to feel a genuine excitement in getting home. They were just saying, what should they do, get breakfast here, or what?—when the clerk called them and told them they had a visitor downstairs.

Mr. Ferguson went down. It was Mr. Viele!

"Well, well, well! Here's the stranger returned!"

The two men shook hands heartily, while the young clerk smiled, and one or two traveling men turned to look at them in sympathy. Fred almost forgot, in the pleasure of the meeting, that it was Mr. Viele, and not one of his own church members, who had come to welcome him. The familiar clock, advertising the jewelry store, was ticking above the desk; the boy was sweeping; and the big shabby room with its doors standing open had the summery aspect that Fred knew well.

"Just got in last night, did you?"

"How did you find out about it?"

"Oh, Ada Rist telephoned Mamie this morning."

Someone had seen them stop at the folks' last night, and the news had got around that they were back.

"Say, if we'd known you didn't have a place to stay! Why, we've got all kinds of room, you know, would have been tickled to death to have you."

"Oh, that's all right, Melvin," Fred answered, ashamed that he had thought no one welcomed them. "We wouldn't have wanted to trouble you."

"Wouldn't have been any trouble at all. What do you think your neighbors are for?"

At any rate, he had orders to bring them right along, to accept no excuses. Mrs. Ferguson had come downstairs, wearing a fresh new summer costume, smiling and pleased at Mr. Viele's hearty approbation. "They must have treated *you* well in California!" he exclaimed. But had they had their breakfast yet? The Fergusons looked slightly embarrassed, were forced to admit that they had not. That was fine, then! Just what he was hoping.

"Verne, I'm going to steal your best customers."

The clerk allowed this, smiling. Mr. Ferguson paid the bill, lying nobly—since this was Belmond—and declaring that they had had a fine night. Oh, yes, a little hot, but the rain had fixed that. The dark thought of change seemed only a dream as Mr. Viele ushered them both out of the hotel into the busy summer-morning noises. He led the way, and they followed him in their own car, dusty from travel—driving along the street that still glistened from the rain, looking out at the fresh lawns and flowers. There seemed to be an effulgent June-time warmth about the whole town. The air smelled of green grass and bridal wreath. Where had their dark thoughts flown? This was the same old place they knew. They were back in Belmond.

The Viele house stood trim and well-painted on its bright green lawn. Mrs. Viele, in a thin voile dress, was at the door to welcome them. The ready tears overflowed her eyes as she clasped Mrs. Ferguson. They stepped into the clean, fresh, homelike living room; breathing in, through the fragrance of a big bouquet of wet snowball blossoms, the crisp welcome smells of bacon and coffee.

692

Mrs. Viele was effusive with sympathy and self-reproach. "Oh, you poor folks! Getting here without a soul to meet you. And having to sleep in that hotel!"

Oh, it was all right, had a good bed, Mr. Ferguson assured her uneasily, not liking the hotel to be maligned.

But it was certainly nice to be here! With a long sigh of ease, Mr. Ferguson sat down in the living room to talk with Mr. Viele while Mrs. Viele was getting on the breakfast. Mrs. Ferguson took off her hat in the immaculate guest room, spending some little time with her hair at the mirror, and noting with some excitement how trim and modish this little cotton suit looked. It was nicer than any she could have got in Belmond. Her black-and-white costume she would save to wear to the club, when it met at Mrs. Hoagland's . . . forgetting that the Hoaglands were no longer here. She stopped to smell the snowballs on the living room table, burying her face a moment in the soft bloom, wondering how her own flowers were getting on, thinking with a sigh of Louie's.

"Well, folks, you can come now."

The breakfast, of course, was delicious. Mrs. Viele was a wonderful housekeeper. It was pleasant to eat again from the familiar flowered Haviland. Mrs. Ferguson laughed apologetically when Fred declared he had tasted nothing like this for months. "Why, Fred, you know we had lovely things at Louie's!" "Oh, yes, but we had to have that girl with those fixed-up eyebrows hanging around us all the time." The women both laughed, but with indulgence. Annie tried to explain about Louie's maid. "All the girls out there want to get into the movies. Well, you can't blame them. Think of the wonderful salaries they get." But the memory of Louie's sunroom was even now fading—with the great windows open, the great curtains drawn here and there against the light. . . . And she didn't know whether she was sorry or not.

The conversation seemed to consist mostly of broken sentences—the Fergusons starting to tell something about their travels, the Vieles breaking in with news of affairs at home. The failure of the other bank, of course, was the great topic. Some folks said one thing, some said another, but no one was really sure. No one knew what had become of Mr. Hoagland. "She" was with her family in Illinois. Bert was left here with the whole thing on his hands. There was talk of a trial. "Think of a man skipping out and leaving his own son to bear the brunt!" "Oh, well, they're in cahoots," Mr. Viele said wisely. Mr. Ferguson shook his head, reserving his judgment.

Still, it was both exciting and comforting to hear the news of home, even when it wasn't good news. None of the people at this table were directly involved. There was no doubt about it—the last slight constraint between the two families had faded now that the barrier of the church was gone. They would no longer belong to different denominations. They talked about it a little, Fred noncommittal, Mr. Viele heartily consoling. "Well, Fred, I know how you feel, but if you look at it in this way—it's pretty nice after all to think that we're all united. For my part," Mr. Viele said boldly, "I'd like to see even the Methodists join in!" He looked triumphantly around the table. And it did seem to be true, Fred couldn't think of good arguments against it—in this way, all who believed in the churches and the work they were doing could make a real stand against the forces that were trying to overwhelm them. It made them feel that the older people and their ideals weren't, after all, a thing of the past. Of course, Mr. Viele added hastily, that didn't include the Catholics. The Methodists were as far as he could go. In the midst of breakfast, Fred was called to the phone to answer the call he had put in to Carl. And even this was good news. Or, at any rate, it held bad news suspended. Ben was in the hospital for observation, and it hadn't been determined whether he was going to need an operation. Well, he would have Carl and Lillian to look after him. He wouldn't be left entirely to Ella, who was notoriously poor help in sickness!—although Annie, of course, wouldn't have dared say this in front of Fred. Now they could finish their breakfast secure in the knowledge that there was no present need for them to go to Geneva. The Vieles, prosperous and optimistic, saw everything in its most cheerful light.

After breakfast, the Fergusons suggested that they had better go over to the house. But Mrs. Viele wouldn't hear of it. Oh, no, they needed a rest. She hadn't begun to ask all the questions she wanted to about their vacation. It seemed as if she and Melvin had done all the talking so far! But they were *so* glad to have the Fergusons back. And besides—she squeezed Annie's hand and whispered mysteriously—they didn't want her to go over there yet. Well, she might as well tell them why. Ada Rist had planned to get everything in order for them; she was working there now; and she would be terribly disappointed if they came into the place when it was looking *this* way. Mrs. Ferguson consented in pleased surprise, ashamed of her disappointment last night. They had barely got into the living room when the telephone rang again. This time it was Mrs. Dunn, who had heard that they were back, and was coming over to see them.

Now they were really getting their welcome. Their status of returned travelers shed a glory over them, which, after all, there need be no hurry in giving up. Indeed, what hurry was there about anything? Mrs. Ferguson tried to think of some, on principle; they must get settled, get their things unpacked, in a few days at least they must be going over to Geneva. But she was glad to have this overruled by Mrs. Viele's fond sympathy, and to sit, with a pleasing touch of fashionable strangeness in her new dress, ready to be seen and welcomed, and enjoying the scents of grass and flowers.

Mrs. Dunn, heavy and perspiring, came panting into the room. So they were back, she told them—everybody'd about given them up; thought maybe they liked it so well out there they weren't ever going to leave. She greeted them with solemn significance, bringing with her the odors of sickrooms and funerals, at variance with the freshness of the Vieles' nice living room. It brought back the dark thought of change again, and made Mrs. Ferguson feel guilty and uneasy.

"Well," Mrs. Dunn said, as soon as she was seated, "I suppose you didn't think you was returning to this!"

But of course (thank heaven! Annie would have liked to say) she couldn't be quite as mournful as she would have liked here in front of the Vieles, who were Congregationalists.

695

Soon she was rocking in heavy comfort, and finding plenty of consolation in recounting all the sad facts to Mr. Ferguson, shaking her head, sighing at intervals, letting out a little surreptitious gleam of funereal interest in the excitement and trouble from her small, suspicious eyes—wanting to see most of all how they were going to take it! Annie kept her face warily composed. Mrs. Dunn made mournful digressions, describing Mrs. Lowrie's death, groaning and predicting the worst for Ben. "My, it seems as if we're just losing everybody!" she said with gloomy relish. But the church—careful as she thought she had to be—was the main theme of her lament. One thing she could do, Vieles or no Vieles, and that was unburden herself to the full about "that other element." Fred shifted uneasily in his chair, hating to hear the private affairs of his church given out, even to such good friends as these; feeling guilty too, his wife could see, at Mrs. Dunn's accusing reiterations of "if you folks ud been here," and "we couldn't do nothing without you folks." It made Annie indignant. As if Fred hadn't carried the load of that church long enough! and now must be saddled with the blame of its going to pieces!—and all the more so, because Annie knew that in her heart she was glad to be on the other side at last from Mrs. Dunn, comparing her with those people from Dike, finding comfort in the knowledge that at last she belonged with her own friends, "the ladies," the nice people.

One thing, though, did cause her an unwilling pang. That was when they asked about Essie Bartlett and her mother. Even the Vieles then, resolute in their attitude of looking on the bright side, had to give murmurs of sympathy. Mrs. Dunn was only too willing to expatiate.

"Well, you know, she's kind of dropped out—it's real too bad." And Mrs. Dunn, it was apparent, had no idea of doing that. She was finding consolation aplenty in forming part of "an element" in the new congregation! There would be a struggle, Mrs. Ferguson could see with a sigh, between the old element of the Congregationalists and the new element of the Presbyterians. Mrs. Dunn was continuing, gloomy satisfaction creeping through her voice, "I guess the young folks didn't want Essie. Well, they've been getting tired of her for a long time, even in our *own* church." Mr. Ferguson made an uneasy movement again. "She was the one most set on the churches not uniting. I don't believe she'll ever be reconciled. The new minister called on her—"

"He's *so* nice," Mrs. Viele murmured placatingly.

"—but he couldn't get her to go. Essie's been getting awful kind of funny," Mrs. Dunn said, shaking her head. "She won't hardly go out at all. She don't even seem to want to see people. But I guess she'll be pretty glad to see *you* folks."

Mrs. Ferguson made a movement too. The Vieles, at once, were warm with consolation. That was too bad! It *must* be hard on her. People got notional living so much alone. Still, Mr. Viele said, that wasn't the way to feel. They were sure that the attitude of the young people had been exaggerated. Everyone was glad to welcome the other members. And she wouldn't feel that way long, Mrs. Viele was certain. The ladies must all call on her. And now that she has *you* folks back—! Mrs. Ferguson murmured her sympathy. But she didn't dare steal a glance at Fred.

Anyway, it was evident that most of the members had accepted the change. Fred saw that with an inward feeling of blank incredulity. The Vieles had taken it for granted at once that he and Annie were with them, and he didn't know how to demur, since they were such good friends.

Of course, it was hard on the older members. Well, it was hard on Fred! But Mrs. Ferguson at last was able to confide that she was glad Fred had the whole thing off his shoulders. She was glad that this had happened—since it *had* to happen, and she believed even Fred had seen that—while they were away. Of course he wasn't going to take it any too easily. She didn't know . . . But all seemed friendly and possible, as the two women washed dishes together in the sunny kitchen. Mrs. Dunn, thank goodness, hadn't stayed very long. But it was long enough for Annie to be relieved to be out of her sight, away from those suspicious glances that seemed to penetrate her long, loyal pretense of really belonging with the Presbyterians. Mr. Viele had left for his office some time ago, after

Fred had said, "Well, Melvin, we don't want to keep you"; and Fred himself had now gone to town to have the car looked after. He thought there was something wrong with the brakes. The two women had the house all to themselves for the moment. They could drop the feminine veil of sweetness and smoothness and acquiescence and gossip to their hearts' content. Even Mrs. Viele, once you got her alone, could gossip. Nothing unkind, of course, but she could go into things. Mrs. Ferguson herself could tell about Louie's beautiful home, denying even to herself the sense of distance that had grown between her and her sister, believing in the wonderful time she had had there; and Mrs. Viele could break in with long, satisfying, intimate stories of old Mrs. Bird and her fragile health—"She'll be *so* glad to see you"; of Mrs. Brattle and Virginia; of the people who had lost money in the other bank; and of the historic downfall of the Hoaglands. Annie kept the secret of Dorothy's and Jesse's fall in fortune, making use of Jesse's easy version of the whole thing as a kind of lark. She wouldn't mention Bun. She had assumed her old rôle of the wholly fortunate wife and mother. But many things could be confided, never spoken of before, now that the two women felt themselves really united: how, although everyone was sorry for Mrs. Hoagland, still some thought it was a comedown that she had deserved; how Mrs. Stark, now that they had lost all their money, had quite stepped off her high horse; how everyone wished that Fred had stayed in the bank and just couldn't feel the same about Richard; how *no* woman, they should think, could be content to cut herself off from her family as Annie said old Mrs. Spencer had done; and how Annie's sympathy lay with Ben and not with Ella. When the sink was scrubbed shining white, and the soft white towels hung up to dry, the two women returned to the living room, glowing and intimate, appeased, and slightly ashamed of themselves.

A long pleasant day stretched ahead of them. Fred had telephoned that he wouldn't be through, and thought he had better get a bite downtown. Mr. Viele never came home at noon. They themselves could eat just what they pleased. But at last they began to feel that they had given Ada time enough, and that they couldn't wait any longer to go over to the house.

It did have a different look this morning. Mrs. Ferguson began to have a feeling of excitement, of emotional return, mingled with disappointment, alienation . . . she scarcely knew what, as she and Mrs. Viele approached the place. The doors were open, she could see that the curtains had been freshly put up. The two women went inside. There were sounds from somewhere in the house, but the living room was empty. All was in shining order. Great rose-and-white peonies bloomed in a flower basket near the piano, and on the table stood a vase of Mrs. Morgan's choicest roses. The big fern, glossy with freshness, was set in its old place near the window.

"We can tell who's been here!" Mrs. Viele archly exclaimed.

The sound of their voices had disturbed the workers. Mrs. Morgan, wearing a newspaper like a medieval peasant cap, accentuating her gauntness, looked over the banisters and then came hurrying downstairs.

"Well, for the love of Mike! Ada! She caught us!"

The call brought Ada in from the kitchen, flushed, eager, awkward and shyly happy. Now there was a great embracing. Mrs. Ferguson emerged from it smiling, flushed, with moist eyes. The women were all talking together.

"We thought we were going to get all through before you came over. Mamie, you let her steal a march on us."

"I just couldn't wait any longer!"

"Well, anyway, it looks better than it would have if you'd seen it last night."

"Better! I don't see how anything could look as nice."

Mrs. Morgan cried: "The trip must have done you good! Look at her little suit. Did you ever see anything so stylish? Just look at her, girls."

Mrs. Ferguson stood blushing and laughing, turning gayly around to show off her splendor, once again the center of her own small admiring group. She answered their questions happily. She could never admit to these ladies the small disappointments of her trip. And indeed it was already glowing in a rosy retrospect. Mrs. Viele took one arm, Mrs. Morgan the other, and she was led triumphantly on an inspection of the house. Ada, clumsy and happy, breathing heavily, trailed along behind the matrons.

"Do you see what these women have done!" Mrs. Ferguson marveled.

Fresh flowers in all the rooms, the curtains newly washed— and in the kitchen a whole set of supplies for the next day. Loren Morgan had seen early this morning about getting the electricity, water and gas turned on.

"Well, we thought we'd help you young folks get started keeping house," Mrs. Morgan explained, embarrassed by the thanks, laughing them off. "Have to do something to keep you here now we've got you again."

When they were through with the house they went outside. It didn't look as nice as it might, Mrs. Morgan said, worried. Loren had been cutting the grass since Mr. Graham took sick; but of course he had to do it nights and mornings, he couldn't take a minute from that old store.

"I was going to get after the grass around the trees myself— if I'd just known you were coming."

As if she hadn't done enough as it was! Explanations had to be gone into—how they had written to Ella, thinking she would pass the news along; and of course Ella hadn't been here to receive the letter. Ben's illness had to be talked about a little, with expressions of sympathy.

"I noticed," Mrs. Morgan said, "he seemed to be working awful slow, the last morning he was over here. I wondered then if there wasn't something the matter. My," she added, "you ought to have seen the place when *he* was taking care of it! I believe there wasn't a single day he didn't come over."

A low, dull pain with an edge of threatening sharpness was aroused at the words. But Annie put it hastily away from her. She was going to enjoy her homecoming, anyway, since she had had to come home. The flowers were blooming. They weren't like Louie's, of course, but still the whole place looked nicer than she had secretly expected. The porches were swept, no longer did the screened doors have that dusty, dispiriting

700

look. Ada had stayed away from work, and Mrs. Morgan had been over since seven o'clock this morning.

"Now!" Mrs. Viele said triumphantly. "You didn't have any neighbors like these in California!"

There were still a few things that they wanted to do. The Fergusons weren't to be allowed to move in before evening. Mrs. Ferguson accepted in happy gratitude.

She waited on the porch for Mrs. Viele, who was talking to the others inside. As soon as Mrs. Viele had finished, they would go over and see old Mrs. Bird. It was a comfort, Annie felt, that there was no longer anything to separate her from the other ladies. Fred had insisted that they should return; but still, he didn't have things *all* his own way. The rich grass glistened in the sun. She was aware, even here, of changes. The rented house next door was empty again. Mrs. Morgan didn't know where the people had gone. Across the street, in the old Gilbert house, she saw the faded tourist sign. But it seemed as if her own house still stood secure in the sunshine of the long afternoon. The busy sounds from within the house let her stay for a little while in the privilege of return. But she knew that the time was coming, was ahead of her, when she wouldn't be able to put off feeling included any longer. Everything that she saw, here at home, was significant with associations. Grandma's yellow rose bush was in bloom. The tree where the children had had their swing, beneath which Dorothy had stood to be married, cast its pleasant shade. The geraniums were blooming in the urn. Garden vegetables, which Ben had put in, were up and ready. Her great holiday was almost over.

Mr. Ferguson had taken the car to drive downtown. However, he thought that first he would stop a moment at Ben's and Ella's place and see if he could learn a little more from their neighbor. She was in the thick of her Friday cleaning, and he didn't talk to her very long; only long enough to say to himself, "Well, we'll have to go over there pretty soon." No matter what the folks had said this morning, he couldn't leave the whole thing to Carl. Ella was his own sister.

He felt a hurt, secretive desire to drive past the church. But he was afraid of being seen. Instead, he drove down the cross street, slowing a little when he came in view of the place. The building stood there just as always, with the manse next door. Only now, both of them were empty. The load of which he had often complained was off his shoulders at last. But the ache of it was still there. He wouldn't be seen looking, so he drove on past. The memory of the locked doors and the bleak windows stayed with him. Now he actually understood that the long years of work, loyalty, responsibility were over. And what had it all been for? Just leisure wasn't enough. The street blurred, and for a moment he was almost afraid to drive. The faith of his fathers was gone, which they had come to found in a new land, carry with them, make greater and stronger than ever before. And this had happened while he was away enjoying himself on the fruits of his own labor! Still, there was mama—she had claims too—for once in his life, as she had told him, he had to put her before the rest. He felt a numb sense of loss, rather than blame. Mrs. Dunn talked darkly about "the other element"; but something larger than any "element" had been at work. Even if he had carried the load a little longer, this same thing would have come to pass; and there was a faint relief that he had not been forced to face the very hour, which his canniness and foresight had long told him was approaching. He could remember years back when this church was built. Then his father had felt, triumphant, that he had done his work for succeeding generations. The church still stood, but the generations had stepped out beyond it. And Fred's own children had been among the first! He might have stopped them, he might have laid down the law . . . but he had done that once, and they had lost Margaret. He couldn't say how or why it had happened; the faith had just faded out; no good trying to revive what wasn't there. And now that the church was gone, he had a queer feeling that the faith had faded from his own heart. He didn't stop to analyze it exactly. But the feeling was there. The loss would deepen and spread, like the slow creeping of old age through his bones. Just sitting in the sunshine wouldn't have stopped it. His faith had been the church, which his father had left to him. It was the church that he had helped to build, the institution that he had tried to carry on. First the faith, then the institution to make it secure, then the faith diminishing and leaving the structure that was to hold it empty. It was the institution that had been left to him. That had been *his* place in this long sequence. Now that it was gone, what did he believe? Anything more than his own children?

He felt the false cheer of the talk this morning, brightly covering realities. In spite of all the arguments, the new congregation could never mean anything to him. He would always be a stranger there. He and his folks belonged to the other fold. But Annie didn't. He acknowledged now, in pained bewilderment, that she never had. He felt estranged—felt himself in a void. The intricate pattern of marriage held him enmeshed in invisible ties. For years, he had brought Annie with him. Now, at last, her day had come. She had drawn him away from the folks. He felt as if he had failed them, just as his children had failed him. Yet he was conscious of a strange new sympathy for the children, embedded deep in humility. He had made mistakes, even when he was doing his best. Now, at the end of his life founded on trust, he was coming into uncertainty.

But the old responsibilities, although broken and shattered at points, still weighed heavily on his heart. It didn't seem as if he could go to town right now. Instead, he turned, and drove into the fading side street where Essie Bartlett and her mother lived. He stopped in front of the low frame house.

Even before he had a chance to knock, Essie came to the door.

She cried, "Mr. *Fer*-guson!"

"Yes. We're back, you see."

He tried to summon a reassuring smile, as he stepped inside, embarrassed and more moved than he cared to be, by the hysterical joy of her greeting.

She tried to be arch and welcoming at first, fussing about to get him a chair. But he saw her haggard look, and the awful brilliance of her eyes. While she talked and exclaimed, he sat down heavily. The bleak poverty of the room struck him with a breath of cold that slowly enveloped him, tearing wider the hidden wound that the sight of the church had made. He noticed that the stove was still up. He would have to see about having it taken down. He could have done it himself easily enough. His time wasn't valuable now. But there would be someone who needed the job, small as it was—he would have to think who. Essie was asking about the trip, with a brave assumption of her old vicarious delight. How was Dear Daughter Dorothy? And the darling children! It was so beautiful to think they could have this time with Dorothy and her handsome husband in their lovely home. Fred could answer only in monosyllables. His holiday had turned bitter to him. He could scarcely bear to meet Essie's withered girlish animation. He wanted nervously to put off the subject of the church. He had expected Essie to refer to it at once, and yet she didn't. She seemed to be sitting amidst the emptiness of the ruins after the disaster had struck and passed. But all the while he could see her thin hands grasping and grasping at the arms of her chair. There was a smothered wildness that unnerved him in the ceaseless scrape of the rockers. She began to chatter bitterly, gayly, hysterically, in seemingly irrelevant snatches, after every hint of a pause; while Fred sat uncomfortably mute, in helpless, guilty sympathy.

At last they reached a glassy silence.

Fred roused himself then to the old question: "How is your mother?"

Essie summoned the old bright smile, as she answered valiantly: "The same." For how many years had she been saying that, while the old wrecked body sank by imperceptible stages further and further toward decay?

But wouldn't he come in and see mother? Now Essie put on her brightest company air, with which she always ushered visitors into the invalid's presence. Fred got up silently to go through with the inevitable rite. He stood in suffering masculine discomfort in the close air of the little bedroom. Its meager neatness was unchanged. The smell of medicines had sunk into the very carpet, thin and worn as it was, showing in dim patches the boards of the floor. It sickened Fred to hear the slow scrape of a branch against the window. Essie was trying with dreadful gayety to rouse her mother to recognize him, excited and buoyed up by his return. "Don't you see who's here, mother? Mr. Ferguson's come to see you. You haven't seen *him* for a long, *long* time!" Fred gave a step forward and put out his hand. But the old body was finally past response. Even a glance of the filmed eyes, a movement of the feeble fingers, was now too much. Essie shook her head. She whispered, with a bright whisper of apology, "She just lies there"; as she straightened the bedclothes, smoothed the pillow with scrupulous care. But the doctor had said she was no worse— might live a long while—no one could tell . . . Fred nodded mutely. The young folks had laughed at Essie and all her little ways. But she had done her best to keep her tragedy within seemly bounds, growing unseemly herself with the effort.

As they left the room, Essie suddenly burst into tears. Fred heard the sound, aghast. It was terrible in this muffled place. Then his sympathy and comprehension rose above his silent embarrassment. He took Essie in his arms. How seldom his canny reserve had allowed him to do that with his own children! Only with Annie—and that was different . . . The terrified clutch of Essie's hands told him that he was her one rock of dependence; and he could feel his own slowly abating strength gather itself to meet the need.

"Oh, I'm so afraid I'll go before she does!"

The frightened words came out, in cries and whispers, and he braced himself to meet their import.

"I'm so sick sometimes—getting worse—sometimes I can't stand it!"

Fred led her into the other room before he tried to answer. In spite of the shock he felt, it seemed to him that he had known this ever since he had stepped into the house. But he made no falsely soothing answer to silence her. His mind was already seeking ways and means. And mute anger was slowly mounting inside him at the blunt misunderstanding of Mrs. Dunn, the bland reassurances of the others, signifying to him at this moment "the world," as he shared with Essie her gnawing secret in the bleak silence of the little house. He felt that he was face to face with something more irrevocable than he had ever known. The old optimism and trust had come to the edge of an abyss. What lay there, in those awful mists? He didn't know. He never had known. He felt Essie trembling in his arms, waiting for what he would say, as her final authority. He sought refuge in his practicality—it was what had always been, still was, expected of him.

Had she been to the doctor? he asked her.

Essie whispered, no. Fred did not reply at once. He understood that she had been afraid of what the doctor might tell her.

"I don't care for myself, I have nothing to live for now that the church is gone, but I can't leave her to the care of others. Not after all these years. All I've done is take care of mama. Now if I should go first . . ."

Well, something must be said, beyond the hard mute grasp of the hand that seemed to be all people had for each other in extremity. Easy promises, such as other folks could give, even good people like the Vieles, were out of his power. He had never liked to make promises that he hadn't been reasonably sure he could keep. That was one reason he had broken with Richard. But he couldn't hold too sternly to facts and probabilities—he must give a little comfort. Essie whispered something now about "the bank." The bank was all right, he assured her stoutly, above his own freshly reawakened uncertainty. As long as they both lived, he would promise that she had enough to take care of her. He would see her through. That, at least, he could feel was the truth.

He urged her to see the doctor. It was the right thing, even if it was useless. "Maybe something can be done. You mustn't make up your mind to the worst before you know, Essie."

Essie shook her head in feeble terror. But Fred felt relief in the weakened clinging of her hands. She was looking to him, as all the rest of them had, even when they were going their own ways. The old sense of protectiveness was deeply stirred; but mingled with it, a cold breath of solitude—for

706

he felt that there was nothing in the world *he* could count upon, as this one poor woman counted upon him.

For a while the room had been blurred. But now its sparse furnishings began to grow sharp and clear. Mr. Ferguson's mind was still soberly searching for ways and means. There were other calls—there was his family, Ben—and who knew these days what was safe? But somehow it must be done. He felt that for once he had risen above practicality. In a way, in the void of their shattered loyalty, he and Essie were closer together than any two people in the world. Annie was the one he loved. And he loved his home. But it was here, in this little house, that he was king. It came to him, with proud humility, with a deep wry solace—that he had this fruit at least of what he mutely believed a lifelong effort to do the best he knew how. For the first time, he was able to see an awful grandeur in irrevocability.

"Now, Essie, don't you worry. You're going to leave things to me." He said that in his old way, as he had said it so many times before, must say it still. He led Essie to a chair. "I want to talk things over with my wife." Essie nodded mutely, humbly accepting that. "She'll know better than I do—she'll be over to see you soon. Can you get along until then?" He felt guilty about worrying Annie with this so soon after he had brought her home, but it couldn't be helped. He began to be aware that he needed a woman's aid. He felt proudly that, fine and delicate as she was, Annie had never failed to rise to a call. Essie's hands lay exhausted and trembling, but quiet now in her lap.

Fred cleared his throat, calling upon practicality again. "First of all, I'm going to send someone over to take down that stove. You don't want that standing in here now. It's just in the way." He frowned at the stove. It helped him to be able to work up a little indignation about the thing.

At last he got away, and climbed heavily into his car. Now there was Essie to be looked after—and Ella and Ben . . . For a moment, it seemed too much. His strength seemed to creak and strain, too old and worn for the load he had tried to drop. But he would have to take care of things the best he could. He felt that this responsibility—now that the church was gone—was closest to his heart. Yes, in a way, the claim of poor Essie and her mother was deeper than that of his own children. He had given them the best start he could. What they did with it was their own affair.

The solemn light of grandeur slowly faded, leaving him with the ways and means of his task. And now it seemed as if the brightness of the morning welcome had faded, too, from the streets. He noticed for the first time that the frame houses had lost their newness. Even the town was getting elderly. After those bright new glaring towns in the West it looked settled, established, fixed in its ways. He had always thought of it as a young town, with all its future before it. But now it seemed that that "future" had become the present, was even here and there beginning to be the past. So long as Fred Ferguson could remember, trust in the future of the town had been as much a part of his life as his daily bread. The feeling wasn't gone, exactly. But now that he had done some traveling, Belmond was no longer a place apart. Well, anyway, it was where he belonged; it was still, to him, the best place on earth. Even if it never became any bigger, he could still say that it was a pretty good little town in which to live.

He hadn't exactly meant to stop at the bank, but it seemed as if he had to see for himself how things were getting along. In a way he couldn't have explained, it was a surprise to see it still standing there, just as he had left it. It was strange to be going into that familiar place and to feel that he was no longer a part of it. His footsteps seemed to have a hollow sound as he crossed the hard white floor. He was a little doubtful as to how they would meet him; was conscious of having broken his ties. In spite of himself, that gave him a guilty feeling.

"Well, F. W.—didn't know you were back!"

Richard had come out to shake hands, as spruce and jaunty as ever. His hair was slicked glossily back, and he wore a pink rosebud in his buttonhole.

"Yes, we got back."

"Well—how was the trip?"

As they stood and talked, some of the first embarrassment wore off. Nevertheless, the meeting between the two men was full of discomfort. Richard was carrying it off, but he wouldn't quite let his eyes meet Fred's. Ray came up now with a shy but quite evidently heartfelt greeting. Fred had to speak to all the staff. The girls smiled at him, told him they had missed him. Richard asked if there was anything they could do for him; and when he said yes, if they'd take his check, the others all laughed and made a joke of his being a stranger.

Customers came in then, and he had to stand aside. He cleared his throat as he put his bills neatly in his folder. He hated to leave without asking how they were getting along; and yet he didn't know that he had the right any longer. So far as anyone could tell, business was going on much as before. Still, he didn't know—there was something different. If H. L. Hoagland couldn't be trusted, who could? The bright new modern splendor of the building had an air of being prematurely faded. There was a false note somewhere in the jaunty cheer. Ray looked thin and worn. His back was bent as if he carried a secret burden. Fred had always thought of Ray as a young fellow; but he saw now that Ray was middle-aged. Even Richard was getting older. His shining hair was streaked with gray, and his teeth were bad. It gave Fred a curious feeling to be looking on while the others worked, and to be standing here idle himself. What had he intended to do?—he had supposed, get into something, some new enterprise. But now he doubted if he had the heart for that. He had given too much of his life to the bank. And besides, what new enterprises *were* there? No, he couldn't say that he was sorry now to be out of it. He had felt it due to his own family to get out when he hadn't liked the way things were going. What he saw, what he could feel in the air, only confirmed his decision. But he thought of Essie's poor little funds—Fannie Allison's . . . he felt as if he had betrayed them. And he couldn't tell them to withdraw, either— that would have been treachery to the bank and to business. Some of his own funds were left here, against his secret judgment, and he would have to let them stay. Life wasn't so simple as he had thought. All was in flux, all in doubt, and allegiances

709

were divided. A right here made a wrong there. He wondered against all reason if maybe he shouldn't have stuck to his post.

"Well, Richard, I guess I'll have to be getting on."

"Well, good-bye, F. W. Glad you stopped in."

The others were busy. They didn't see him go. That was all right. He had stepped out of his own accord. He didn't want any fuss made about him. But it was a pretty queer feeling to be out of it after all these years. Retirement wasn't what he had pictured. Should he have stayed out there after all? Now, as on the day when he had broken his connection, he felt as if he were walking in emptiness.

Still he hadn't taken his car to the garage—the thing that supposedly he had come to town to do. The clock outside the jeweler's told him that it was almost noon. He thought he would assuage his guilt by stopping in and asking Hy if he couldn't look after the car a little later.

But there was a change here too. His sense of welcome met another check. Hy wasn't in the garage any more. He had sold out the business and gone down to Florida. To this young fellow, the name Fred Ferguson meant no more than any other. The car would have to wait its turn. He might get it around five this afternoon—they might not be able to touch it before tomorrow. It was a small thing. Fred couldn't expect the fellow to make time for him. But Hy had always done his work, knew what a good customer he was, and would have got the job in somehow.

Fred thought he would telephone Annie. He didn't feel like going back this noon. He shrank just now from explaining what he had been about all morning. The two women would have enough to talk about together, he thought dryly, even somewhat bitterly. Annie had always preferred Mrs. Viele and the other ladies in the club to those in their own church (unless maybe it was poor Jennie). It was for his sake that she had confined herself to them. Well, now she and those others could be as close as they chose. He wouldn't interfere. After all, Annie had always stuck by him. She, too, was lonely, with the children gone, and he wanted her to be contented. Well, he would attend services at the other church, but that was all they could expect of him.

"But what will you do, Fred?" Annie asked.

"Oh, I'll get a bite down here." He said vaguely that he had a lot of things to see to.

The dinner wasn't much to brag of; and he didn't know the folks who ran the restaurant. But if he had gone to the hotel, he might have run into Richard and some of the other business men. He didn't belong with them now. He didn't want to come among them as an outsider.

His heart was still sore over Essie's plight; sore, and yet strangely solaced by the thought of her loyalty. The little circle wasn't yet all dispersed. There he still counted for something. Otherwise, nothing was quite the same. He had stepped out of his old place and now it wasn't there any more. It wasn't there—and his faith in it was gone.

A blind instinct led him to seek out his childhood home. He didn't care to leave his car with that fellow. Tomorrow he would take it to the other garage. "If he don't care any more than that about my trade, he needn't have it." He couldn't rest now until he had seen how the farm was getting along.

Fred drove out along the familiar road, where he knew every foot of the way. The country looked as nice as when they had been driving yesterday, but now he regarded it more soberly. He couldn't look at it as scenery, not when he had his interests tied up in it.

He turned into his own driveway. He still thought of the place as his own, although it was a good while now since any of the family had lived here. He would have to be looking after things now that Ben was laid up. Well, in a way that was what he had always done. Yes, he saw that he would have plenty, even without the bank and the church. Yet there was a sadness, a sense of diminution, in this narrowing of range. Expansion, for him, was over. For a moment, it seemed again as if it might have been better to have stayed out there. As long as he was here, he would be necessary. But if they had

had to get along without him, maybe they could. Still . . .
did he want them to be able to get along without him?

He got out of the car stiffly. There seemed to be no one
about. The long-closed windows of the old rock house stared
blankly. The white frame house, that had been getting steadily
more seedy since it had been left to renters, stood in the silence
of the early afternoon.

Fred wandered around at first somewhat disconsolate. He
tried the gate of the old fence of fancy-twisted wire that
enclosed the rock house, and that his mother had made Grandpa
put up to protect her flowers from Ella's chickens, against
which she had cherished a deeply satisfying grudge. The gate
was loose on its hinges. The white paint was almost worn away.
In frowning pain, Fred looked at the house now empty. It had
been a big job to get those stones hauled from the quarry
more than fourteen miles away. But mother had wanted a
stone house. She had wanted it to be like the old homes in
Scotland, about which *her* mother had told her. That had
been her idea of grandeur and establishment. Both the folks
had been proud of it. It was the finest house in Buck Town-
ship in its day. And it was just as good now as the year it
was built. It needed only a few repairs, and it would still be
better than most houses. Fred started to go toward it; but he
didn't want to open the door on that stale emptiness. Anyway,
he didn't have the key. He stood and studied the place. It
wasn't right, to his thrifty sense, that such a house should be
standing empty. Father had thought he was building for the
future when he had put up this house. He had never dreamed
that none of his children would choose to live here. Well, Fred
thought, it was much the same with his own house. It gave him
another idea of his own children. He felt the loosening of
another secret grievance into the slow, forced pain of tolerance. Anyway, the folks had had the satisfaction of living
here during their own lifetime. Maybe that was as much as
you could expect.

But the frame house looked strangely deserted, too, in spite
of the litter of household articles on the back porch. It spoke
to him as strongly of Ben and Ella as the rock house did of

712

his folks. Ella stormed and stewed because the renters didn't keep it up as she had done. But Fred, although he hadn't come out and disagreed with her, felt a little differently about that. After all, good tenants as they were—as tenants went—they were only here at the owners' will. They couldn't be expected to put the same into the place.

For the first time, in this silence of country sunshine, Fred actually realized that Ben might go. In spite of his impatience with and criticism of his brother-in-law, that gave him a pang. He thought of their young days together, the days when he and Ben had both been young fellows taking out their girls. The boys used to tease Ella about her beau and his slow ways, ask her when they were going to get around to getting married, suggest methods of hurrying Ben to the point. Well!—it might have been better if they had just let things rest, when he thought of how the marriage had turned out. When the two had finally got together, they had never hitched. Fred had always taken the part of his sister, on principle, since she was one of his own folks; and it had been a slight cause of dissension between him and Annie because he had known that her sympathies were with Ben. Now it seemed as if he could look back and see the injustice in the criticism. Annie had been after intangible and he after tangible things. But now Annie's viewpoint seemed at last to be fused with his own. Ben's faults and lacks seemed no longer important. Fred thought of how kindly he had always been. He had meant well. Folks didn't know what they were doing when they made fun of that old phrase! Maybe it could be applied to them all in the end. Not that Ben's life had been exactly a failure. But it seemed as if he had deserved more than he had got. Fred could feel only a painful wonder that Ben's life, after the young days, was going out in empty loneliness.

Fred heard a cry, and saw Vina crossing the yard. She came up hurrying and breathless.

"Oh, Mr. Ferguson! Why, I didn't know you was back."

She had been out in the garden, she told him. Her hands were too dirty for her to shake with him. Some kind of bugs were getting into the vegetables. They had gnawed all the

radishes. She had wanted Rolfe to get after them, but he didn't
have time. One of the horses had hurt his leg and Rolfe had
been doctoring it. Fred listened impatiently to the long recital. Renters were always behind. But he was a little ashamed,
knowing that since the garden and the horses belonged to
Vina and Rolfe, they had to wait until the rest of the work
was done.

"I'll go in and get this dirt off," Vina said breathlessly at
last.

"Oh, don't bother, Vina. Not on my account. Here—we can
shake like this."

He took hold of her wrist and shook it heartily, while her
soiled hand dangled. She gave a pleased, breathless little laugh.
Fred knew that she liked him. She and Rolfe had always preferred to deal with him. He wasn't soft—no one had ever
accused him of that—but he did have the reputation of being
fair. And Ella wasn't always so easy to get along with—Fred
admitted that to himself, although he wouldn't have done so
to anybody else. Not even Annie.

Now Vina was talking on breathlessly. "My, but I was surprised when I looked over here and saw it was you! We were
beginning to wonder if you was ever coming home."

"Oh, yes, we had to come back. Couldn't let you have things
all to yourself."

"Well, I don't know as we want to." But she gave a little
self-conscious laugh.

She asked him then if he had been over to see Mr. Graham.

No, they hadn't yet. But they had talked this morning to
Carl. Yes, he seemed to be getting on fairly well. Fred was
cautious of making any admissions concerning his own family
even with a person he knew so well, and who was so interested
as Vina. There was the self-consciousness between them of
owners and renters. Fred felt as if he mustn't let down too
much. But it touched him when Vina said with naïve sincerity:

"My, I hope it ain't going to be as bad as they thought!"
Tears misted her faded eyes. She looked around for something
with which to wipe them, and finding nothing—embarrassed
at using her sleeve before Mr. Ferguson—stared straight ahead

714

and sniffed. After a moment, she put up her hand and brushed her eyes, leaving a streak of dirt across her cheek.

Any display of feeling made Fred awkward. Besides, he was tired out after the session with Essie this morning. He made no reply. But a dull pain sank deeper into him. Somehow, the sight of Vina's tears made him see Ben in a different light. He understood how, to her, Ben had seemed better than Ella. Maybe even than himself. That hurt Fred. He thought he had always been pretty good to Rolfe and Vina. But he had stood on the other side.

"We sure do think a lot of Mr. Graham," Vina said softly, after a while.

Fred made no answer again. But looking off across the land, it was almost as if he could see Ben's slow, patient figure— hear his friendly, companionable talk to the horses in the evening, after he brought them in sweating from the field. And he could hear Ben's mild, half-humorous replies to Ella, for which they had always been inclined to despise him. It seemed sad now that in the long grinding strain of the years the mildness had slowly declined into a feeble bitterness. Yes, there were other values than he himself had been taught to acknowledge. Fred had always taken the Ferguson stand of activity, work, getting ahead. They might all have been kinder to Ben. Except Annie—she had always been good. But then, Annie wasn't a Ferguson. Fred used to dislike it because Ben took the part of the children. It had made Ben seem kind of childish himself. But maybe, Fred thought, if I had been closer to them, they wouldn't have got so far away. Now he could see that Ben himself had been only a tenant—the place had belonged to Ella and her folks. Was that what had lain at the bottom of the whole trouble, after all? And Ben, in some ways, had been more of a natural farmer than any of them. At least, he had the faculty of getting things to grow. Now, looking around, Fred saw that the place was as much Ben's as Ella's. Only it was pretty late to admit that now.

"Well," he said uncomfortably, "we'll have to be going over there to Geneva, I guess, pretty soon."

He asked Vina where Rolfe was.

She blinked her eyes to clear the tears. She said that he was out cultivating. Should she call him?

"Oh no, don't do that," Fred answered mildly. "I just came out a minute to see how things were getting on."

At that, a worried, half-secretive look came into her face. She launched at once into her troubles, her talk interspersed with little allusions to Ella, to which Fred listened uncomfortably.

"Oh, they aren't so good. Rolfe told Mrs. Graham, what can we do when hogs ain't bringing in more than they do? Rolfe can't get any more for things than they'll give him. My—I guess it ain't any too easy for us!"

It was a long, wandering recital. Fred had always been inclined to discount impatiently the grumblings of folks on the farm. That had been a prime tenet in town. "Oh, the farmers are always grumbling." And there was no real reason for it, town folks said, when they had the best land on earth. But Fred wasn't a business man any more. He couldn't help a feeling of fellowship as he listened to Vina's recital, as she stood with troubled eyes, speaking out of her simplicity. Fred had liked to think of the farm as a haven of quiet certainty; he had never paid much attention to the grumbling. Renters always thought they were getting the poor end of the deal, that things were against them. That was why they were renters. So Fred had always declared. But now it seemed to him as if he and Vina stood together in the grip of a long slow movement of change which neither of them could comprehend. Fred felt a sense of helplessness. Vina seemed to be appealing to him as if *he* could do something about it. He was the owner. He was the one in charge. Now that Ben was sick, the farm would, to all intents and purposes, or the care of it, return to Fred. He listened half incredulously to Vina's account of changes. A lot of farms were lost to their owners. The insurance company had got Ed Davison's. That was bad news—that hit Fred: for Ed's father had taken up that place when his own father had taken this. Fred felt his town faith at war with his country faith. It was the latter which was slowly rising and taking possession of him. He saw the land again as when

716

he had come into it yesterday morning. That feeling had not died away. He could see that Vina looked to him, even though there was a slight hostility somewhere in her manner. She said excitedly that some of the farmers were getting mad. Fred heard that with resentment and dismay. Yet when it came down to Ed Davison, his old boyhood friend and neighbor, it was pretty close. He couldn't think of Ed as a stranger. His sober, distressed sympathy was at war with his business man's policy of never admitting that things weren't going right ahead. He tried to tell Vina that things weren't so bad. That seemed to be required of him since he was the one in authority.

He said at last, "Well, I guess I'll wander around a little bit."

"Would you like to go into the other house?"

"No, I guess I'll let that go for today."

Vina's talk was a strange mixture. A feeling of disgruntlement, which Fred saw now had always been there at the bottom, ran through her respect for him. Yes, the disgruntlement was there, although she admitted, "Well, I guess we're better fixed than some." It made Fred feel lonely again, as if the old foundations were gone. But that didn't absolve him from the care of the farm. Vina and Rolfe might not be here at all if it hadn't been for his folks who had built up the place. They owed their living to that. Fred thought of all the little favors, all the little jokes: Vina making butter for him, anxiously picking out the best chickens when Annie was going to entertain; leaving bouquets of her best flowers when she came in with the eggs. Yet disgruntlement had lain at the bottom of it all, and now the times were bringing it out. And he himself —he was in it too; for while he always had done, always would do, the best he was able for Rolfe and Vina, still he knew guiltily that the interests of the farm came first.

He wanted to get off by himself. He had heard enough about people's misfortunes. It seemed as if folks were due to have peace, not more trouble than ever, after a lifetime of work.

Vina anxiously watched him go. She was afraid he would discover something to find fault with. But Mr. Ferguson had no desire to find fault. He felt too heavy-hearted for that.

He went out toward the field, thinking he might call to
Rolfe. But then he thought better of it. He had talked to
enough people today. He had his own troubles, too, although
others might not think so, seeing only his prosperity. He began
to feel the healing of the country stillness. It seemed as if he
never had quite known what the place meant to him. It was
the heart of his feeling of return.

As he walked about, in spite of his anxiety, that feeling
grew. Rolfe had the twenty in sweet clover. The soil needed
replenishing. The clover wasn't in bloom yet, but it was
getting rich and green. There were small green apples in the
orchard where the grass was long. Rolfe didn't have much time
for the orchard. It looked rather neglected, but Fred wouldn't
say anything about that. He knew from the waning of his own
strength that a man could not do more than his powers allowed. He hated to see anything amiss. It hurt his thrift and
his sense of ownership. But he felt humbly that after all this
place didn't belong to Rolfe. He wouldn't feel toward it quite
as if it had been his own. Fred looked soberly across the road
at the Davison place. It wasn't right to think of others there.
"Others" were here, on their own place—but he didn't consider that. He came to the edge of the cornfield. Rolfe was far
away. He wouldn't disturb him at his work. "He's busier now
than I am." He caught the smell of the hot rich earth overturned by the cultivator. He looked down the rows of young
green corn. Old feelings long buried stirred. There was no
smell on earth so good to him as this, now that he had been
away and come back. He felt that he almost envied Rolfe.
Now, after all these years, was he going to turn around and
wish that he had stayed a farmer?

As he walked back toward the house, he wondered what
was to be done with this place when Ella was gone? There
were no children of hers to inherit it. His brothers, too, had
gone away. Their sons had gone into this business and that.
None of them into farming. And he didn't see any of his own
children managing the place. As things stood now, it was more
likely to become an encumbrance than anything else. Perhaps he ought to urge Ella to sell it while she could. But then

there were Rolfe and Vina to be thought of. There were so many things to be thought of, all opposing each other, but all working in together. And he was the one who had to think of them all. Young fellows like Bun looked all toward the future, and could say just how things ought to be. But things were just as real in the here and now, and had to be dealt with according to the present facts. Suffering and injustice were suffering and injustice, no matter to whom and when they happened.

Some of Bun's notions had stuck in his mind, crazy as he had proclaimed them to be. They came back to him now. He thought furtively, as he considered ways and means—well, maybe the boy wasn't so far wrong. He would never have confessed such heresy; but he felt that he would almost rather see this piece of land go back to the government than coldly sell it. And maybe land so good oughtn't to belong to any one man, particularly if the man wasn't going to live there. He felt ashamed, as if Rolfe were doing *his* work—only that wasn't true. The folks were gone, anyway. Maybe they had done their own share in bringing the place to bear. Then his mind shifted half angrily. Bun ought to come out here and see what *he* could do, instead of talking about Russia. Let that girl of his live the life of a farmer's wife. They might find out a few things, both of them. Yet Fred couldn't feel real resentment against Bunny. He had a queer, respectful humility toward his youngest, who had had the best that they could give him. He himself had striven and worked to raise his children above the country life, as he had thought, and Annie had thought; but now he wondered. And what was going to become of the farm?

He walked along, noticing many things that weren't quite what they should be. He felt an old tree trunk with his hand. He touched the stones of the old house. That belonged to him. It was a shame to see it just standing here empty. For the first time, Fred felt there might be a sentimental value in fixing up the old place. It had belonged to the folks. He couldn't see it go to pieces before his eyes. Maybe some of them would be glad of it sometime.

719

The rich smell of the country surrounded him. It wasn't like those desert places, not wild. He remembered with scorn the big talk of those fellows at the picnic. He never could have gone back on the old place the way those fellows had done. The smell of the cultivated earth held peace. There ought to be peace and plenty for everyone. Wasn't that what had been meant at the start? He was in the grove now. His foot struck against something, he bent down to see what it was. An old pewter spoon buried in the ground! That dated back to their childhood when they had played out here. Ella had buried this spoon, when the boys wouldn't let her playhouse alone. She'd always been one to hold tight to her own! Well . . . Ella hadn't made much of her home, though, when she'd got it. Maybe she'd held too tight. And then again, maybe she wasn't to blame. She and Ben didn't hitch, weren't meant for each other. That made his own heart warm toward Annie, through all their differences. She had softened his sternness, had made life sweet and rich for him. When he thought of the meager lives so many people led, it seemed as if he and Annie had almost too much. But Ella—he defended her mutely, although he knew what Vina thought of her, and with reason. He saw the heavy black-eyed girl fiercely putting her playhouse in order, although she could never get the look to it that Grandma gave to whatever she touched. Ella just missed out somehow—she didn't quite have it in her. She felt it, too, although the others thought she didn't. Fred put down the spoon, shoved the dirt over it with his toe. He guessed Vina was luckier than Ella, after all. She and Rolfe had their children, and they stood together. The ground smelled good where he had disturbed it. He felt the rich growth all around him. There was almost a song of growth in the summer air.

Well, anyway, it was good land. His father hadn't made any mistake about that. It was good land, and they had owned it for a while, worked it, and received its benefits. This belief in the goodness of his native soil lay underneath the tottering structure of business faith, religious faith, everything. Whatever folks might do with it, the land was here. That was good. If folks treated it right, it would never let them starve.

The Fergusons had dinner with the Morgans. Then at last they went over to their own house.

Mrs. Ferguson waited while Mr. Ferguson opened the front door. This was a soft, balmy June evening, very different from the one before. Mrs. Morgan had put on her porch light for them. It lighted up the evergreens along the driveway and shone part way across the lawn. The place still had an air of loneliness, they had been away so long; but here in the soft evening, so pure and yet dense with fragrance, everything held a peculiar intimacy. Annie felt a wonder that she should actually be here. But Louie's place—all its exotic features, the great slope of the grounds beyond the spectacular frame of the window, with the flowers, the drooping sprays of the pepper trees, the ragged tall grace of the eucalyptus—had retreated into a dream. Only this was real.

"Well, Annie, you can go on in. I'll put away the car."

Mrs. Ferguson went into the house. It seemed different to her, entering it alone. It had a ceremonious air. This afternoon, she had still been a fêted guest. Now came the moment she had secretly dreaded: when she must come back, and take things up where she had left them, only with the prospect of less instead of more ahead of her.

But once here, the familiar objects made their mute appeal. She went into the living room, switching on the central light. She thought with gratitude again of all that those women had done! The welcome that she had received everywhere had opened her heart again. Now she couldn't believe in her own secret turning away. This was where she lived. The great bouquet of peonies warmly perfumed the silent air. The deadness that had lain over the place was gone. Now, on return, all was living again, in a shimmering texture of contentment and pain. Her small rebellion—smothered, only partly acknowledged even to herself—was over. Again she would have to make the best of everything.

She saw the pictures of the children, waiting for her. On the piano stood the family group taken a year or so ago of Carl, Lillian and the boys—showing, although Carl was smiling, that they had been through things, that her oldest was already middle-aged. On the wall hung the framed photograph of Dorothy in her wedding dress. There was no good photograph of Margaret. The silly child had always fought against having one taken, from some queer, perverse notion that she didn't like her own looks. When she was last at home, Margaret had been disgusted to find this old picture of herself, when she was a junior in high school, that her mother had dug out and set up among the others. It didn't do her justice. The mother looked with a mixture of compassion and bafflement at the dark little face with the big, alien eyes. Still, after Margaret was gone, she had put the picture back, for she couldn't bear to feel that she was leaving out any of her children. The dark eyes seemed to be looking straight beyond her with a fierce, unfathomable reproach, which she was never going to be able wholly to comprehend or to answer. The face, intense and reserved, was foreign among the others. But the graduation photograph of Bunny, youthfully solemn, brushed and thin, wasn't like him, either. It held none of his oblique, smiling charm. Familiar and beloved as that face was, it was unfamiliar too. The mother gave it a quick, beseeching glance, which she felt was only half returned. Now all her children were gone, matured and set in their own ways, and there was nothing any longer that she or dad could do about it. They had come to the place where they must accept what was. The ideal household which she had always dreamed that her own would become some day had vanished, even from the dream . . . unless for an hour it had existed, unrecognized, fragrant with roses, bright with tears, on Dorothy's wedding day . . . All the same, there was a richness in having these faces all around her, unsatisfactory as the pictures were. She thought with a faint, incredulous shudder of old Mrs. Spencer in her bungalow; of that one special view of the petulant emptiness of Louie's face. It seemed to her that she had escaped—although from just what, she didn't know. How could she have tried to deceive herself? She had made herself into a wife and mother, bent and shaped herself to that rôle; and she could never go back to what she had been before. Tenderness was in the marrow of her bones; and now, at this return, it was achingly

722

alive again. She felt her love trying painfully to encompass even Charlotte, although it stopped, in bewilderment and fear. She would be here, at any rate, when the children wanted to come home. "The folks" would be here.

However, she didn't want to have dad catch her looking at these pictures. She turned out the light.

Mr. Viele had brought over their suitcases. They were neatly piled in the hall. When she went upstairs, she found more evidence of her neighbors' care. Those women had hung fresh towels in the bathroom and set out a beautiful fresh cake of soap! They all said Belmond was more like itself now that the Fergusons were back.

Her bedroom was in spotless order. On the dresser stood a bouquet. Ada had set it there. She recognized the old-fashioned mixture of flowers all squeezed into the blue glass vase with its scalloped edge. After all, the newness of homecoming had not yet faded. It would linger for a long while, spreading its brightness over familiar things. Now she thought of many things to which she could look forward: a visit with old Mrs. Bird, in the white house she had always loved; her first club meeting, when she would appear as a returned traveler . . . even if there had been changes, if other things not so pleasant lay ahead of her. But strangely enough, her greatest comfort lay in the thought of Ada Rist. To Ada, she could talk of the children as much as she pleased. Ada would never tire of hearing. And in long, intimate conversations with Ada, in the sleepy leisure of Sunday afternoons—showing pictures, reading bits from letters, before the hungry, happy shine of Ada's eyes—the illusion of the ideal household could shimmer for a while. She had come back to find the complete response she had longed for in this lonely, aging girl, who had never had much life of her own, and who looked upon "the Ferguson children" as figures of romance in a bright fairy tale.

Her holiday, her one great time "just for herself," had been and was over. She couldn't say it hadn't been satisfactory. Most people, her neighbors, envied her. But how brief it seemed now when she looked back upon it and thought, This is all I'm going to have. The one moonlit night, the one golden day, when she and Fred and been together again, in renewal of their early days . . . and then the queer little personal consolation of Miss Potter's worship. . . . She thought of the vision of the old sinking world far beyond the pale flower-image of the actress's face, and of the silver emptiness of the Pacific Ocean; and she was glad to be at home again with dad, now when night was coming.

Mr. Ferguson drove the car into the cemented coolness of the garage. He looked it over, carefully tested all the tires, and then locked it with a feeling of relief and satisfaction. It had taken them safely on their long journey and it wasn't much the worse. Now it was back where it belonged. He brought the garage doors together and pressed down the foot-bolt. He snapped shut the Yale lock.

He went through the warm semi-darkness of the back yard, where the apple tree was standing, and let himself in at the back door. There hadn't been time for him to see to the house before, but he would have to take a look at it before he could go to sleep.

He turned on the cellar light and went down the steep, somewhat rough wooden stairway, where he was met by the same old smell of cement. He tapped the body of the furnace, hearing the hollow sound. All seemed to be as he had left it, except for a vague mousy odor. That could be looked after tomorrow. He wondered if he could afford to put in an oil furnace, with all the other things he had to do. Mama and he, if they were going to stay here, might as well have things as comfortable as they could.

He climbed the stairs again and went back into the kitchen. The painted doors of the cupboard stuck. He pulled one open, and took out a glass, carefully choosing one of the old jelly glasses that were always saved for kitchen use. He got himself a drink of water before he went upstairs. The water was warm at first, and he didn't want to stop to let it run. But it had the familiar taste, no other suited him so well. He drank slowly, and then put the jelly glass in the sink.

There was no need for looking around much in the other

rooms. Mama would see to them. He didn't notice details, but he felt the familiar atmosphere around him.

He hadn't said anything to mama about Essie yet. That could wait until tomorrow. It gave him a guilty feeling that he had brought Annie back to so much trouble. They would both have to pitch right in again. Fred had always thought of himself as a worker, and scorned slacker men. If a man was willing to work, so he had always said, he and his need never want. But now it had begun to seem to him that, as things went, he and Annie had been let off pretty easy. What had happened to Essie might have happened to anyone. *He* might have died, as John Bartlett had died, before he had been given time to make provision. And if he had happened to have gone into the other bank, the provision wouldn't have counted for much, anyway. It no longer seemed to him just and inevitable that some should have and others not. He and mama ought to be willing to help out where they could.

At dinner, Fred had been quiet, admitting in answer to questions that he guessed he was tired. The memory of Essie troubled him now in the midst of his own peace and comfort. It seemed to him that he hadn't given her the consolation he might. Essie, like him, had held to the church. Yet what comfort had he been able to muster, when they had stared together at the abyss? He thought of her life of starved devotion—he wasn't willing to admit that this could be the end. Yet the only assurance he seemed able to give her was that she could count on his support until she died. He felt heavily upon him the support of others which had helped to shape and make up his life. Maybe Bunny was right, and the world was changing—Bunny had had all the advantages, there must be something in what he said—but he himself still had to think about ways and means if he wasn't to let down those who had been taught to look to him. He felt proud of his part, and disdained the others—yet he felt hurt, humbled, defrauded somewhere. Was that all he was for? And he wondered sometimes if the great day he had been building for his children—that they had been building, the folks—had turned out to be their own day, after all.

725

He looked to see that mama had locked the front door, and carefully hooked the screen. Then he took the suitcases they would need, and went upstairs.

"Well, everything seems to be in pretty good shape," he said.

It was a little warmer in their room than downstairs, but still it was comfortable. Now that the trip was over, he began to look back upon it with pleasure and satisfaction. He would never have taken it, except for mama. If it hadn't been for her, he would have stuck just like the rest of his family.

He was ready for bed, at that, before Annie was.

"Aren't you coming, mama?"

"Yes, just as soon as I've . . ." He didn't hear the rest.

He waited uneasily, not able to sleep until she came.

"Well, this is the best bed I've had for a long while," he declared, with a sigh of satisfaction, when she got in with him at last.

Now that they were at home again, he felt that he had got Annie back. At least he had been able to give her this trip. Even if some things had happened while he was away, that he might have prevented, he was glad they had gone when they did. Mama's claims came first. He believed he had made Annie happier than Henry had made Louie, even if he hadn't been able to give her quite so much. They had their home to come back to—some folks, when it came to the end, didn't even have that much. Folks as good as *they* were. That made him humble tonight. As things went in this world, he and Annie had no cause to complain.

And yet things had changed. The era of his effort had passed. It was left for him to wind up his affairs the best he knew how. New undertakings had to be left now to the young folks, and there was no telling what *they* would do. He realized that he was seeing their own lives in a certain completion. It had been a pretty good day for them. He had always trusted implicitly that his children were destined to do better; but now he was hoping they would do as well. Simplicities were shifting into complexities, and in the darkening

726

twilight that he and Annie faced, along with the others that were left, he couldn't see what was beyond. He reached over and felt for Annie's hand, and drew her up to him. "Well, mama . . ."